the
liar's
girl

Previous Work by Catherine Ryan Howard

DISTRESS SIGNALS
Short-listed for the CWA John Creasey (New Blood) Dagger

"Readers of Paula Hawkins, Tana French, and Ruth Ware will love this exceptionally well-crafted thriller."
—*Library Journal* (starred review)

"Although Howard meanders a bit through the streets and shops and pubs of Cork and Dublin, she picks up the pace when it most matters—and tosses a lovely curveball at the end, too."
—*Kirkus Reviews*

"*The Liar's Girl* is an addictive page-turner that... ladles out the suspense like spoonfuls of sugar, building to a heady rush of tension—and a heart-breaking final twist in the tale."
—Jo Furniss,
author of the bestselling *All the Little Children*

"*The Liar's Girl* is a haunting thriller about one woman's attempt to escape a horrific past... and her inability to fully do so. I found myself continually surprised and even shocked by the twists and turns in the plot. This is a fast-moving, crackling good novel."
—David Bell,
author of *Bring Her Home*

the
liar's
girl

CATHERINE RYAN HOWARD

BLACK STONE
PUBLISHING

Copyright © 2018 by Catherine Ryan Howard

Published in 2019 by Blackstone Publishing

Cover and book design by Kathryn Galloway English

Printed in the United States of America

Originally published in hardcover by Blackstone Publishing in 2018

First paperback edition: 2019

ISBN 978-1-9825-4644-1

Fiction / Mystery & Detective

1 3 5 7 9 10 8 6 4 2

CIP data for this book is available
from the Library of Congress

Blackstone Publishing
31 Mistletoe Rd.
Ashland, OR 97520

www.BlackstonePublishing.com

To Dad, for publicity services rendered

It's 4:17 a.m. on Saturday morning when Jen comes to on a battered couch in a house somewhere in Rathmines, one of those red-brick terraces that's been divided into flats, let out to students, and left to rot.

He watches as her face betrays her confusion, but she's quick to cover it up. How much does she remember? Perhaps the gang leaving the club on Harcourt Street, one behind the other. Pushing their way through the sweaty, drunken crowds, hands gripping the backs of dresses and tugging on the tails of shirts. Maybe she remembers her friend Michelle clutching some guy's arm at the end of it, calling out to her. Saying they were moving on to some guy's party, that they could walk there.

"*Whose* party?" he'd heard her ask.

"Jack's!" came the shouted answer.

It was unclear whether or not Jen knew Jack, but she followed them anyway.

Now, she's sitting—slumped—on a sofa in a dark room filled with faces she probably doesn't recognize.

The thin straps of her shimmery black dress stand out against her pale, freckled skin and the makeup around her eyes is smudged and messy. Her lids look heavy. Her head lolls slightly to one side.

Someone swears loudly and flicks a switch, filling the room with harsh, burning light.

Jen squints, then lifts her head until her eyes reach a single bare, dusty bulb that hangs from the ceiling. Back down to the floor in front of her. A guy is crawling around on all fours, searching for something. She frowns at him.

This place is disgusting. The carpet is old and stained. There are broken bits of chips, hairs, and cigarette ash nestled deep in its pile. It hasn't been laid. Instead, the floor is covered with large, loose sections of carpet, ragged and frayed at the edges, with patches of dusty bare floor showing in between. The couch faces a fireplace that's been blocked off with chipboard, while an area of green paint on the otherwise magnolia chimney breast marks where a mantelpiece once stood. Mismatched chairs—white patio, folding camping accessory, ripped beanbag—are arranged in front of it. Three guys sit in them, passing around a joint.

Another, smaller couch is to Jen's left. That's where he sits.

The air is thick with smoke and the only window has no curtains or blinds. The bare glass is dripping with tributaries of condensation.

He can't wait to leave.

Jen is growing uncomfortable. Her brow is furrowed. He watches as she clasps her hands between her thighs and hunches her shoulders. She shifts her weight on the couch. Her gaze fixes on each of the three smokers in turn, studying their faces. Does she know any of them? She turns her head to take in the rest of the room—

And stops.

She's seen them.

To the right of the fireplace, too big to fit fully into the depression between the chimney breast and the room's side wall, stands an American-style fridge/ freezer, gone yellow-white and stuck haphazardly with a collection of garish magnets.

Jen blinks at it.

A fridge in a living room can't be that unusual to her. As any student looking for an affordable place to rent in Dublin quickly discovers, fridges free-standing in the middle of living rooms adjacent to tiny kitchens are, apparently, all the rage. But if Jen can find a clearing in the fog in her head, she'll realize there's something *very* familiar about this one.

She's distracted by the boy sitting next to her. Looks to be her age, nineteen or twenty. He nudges her, asks if she'd like another drink. She doesn't respond. A moment later he nudges her again and this time she turns toward him.

The boy nods toward the can of beer she's holding in her right hand, mouths, *Another one?*

Jen seems surprised to find the beer can there. Tilting it lazily, she says something that sounds like, "I haven't finished this one yet."

The boy gets up. He's wearing scuffed suede shoes with frayed laces, jeans, and a blue and white striped shirt, unbuttoned, with a T-shirt underneath. Only a thin slice of the T-shirt is visible, but it seems the design on it is a famous movie poster. Black, yellow, red. After he leaves, Jen relaxes into the space he's vacated, sinking down until she can rest the back of her head against a cushion. She closes her eyes—

Opens them up again, suddenly. Pushes palms down flat on the couch, scrambling into an upright position. Stares at the fridge.

This is it.

Her mouth falls open slightly and then the can in her hand drops to the floor, falls over and rolls underneath the couch. Its contents spill out, spread out, making a *glug-glug-glug* sound as they do. She makes no move to pick it up. She doesn't seem to realize it's fallen.

Unsteadily, Jen gets to her feet, pausing for a second to catch her balance on towering heels. She takes a step, two, three forward, until she's within touching distance of the fridge door. There, she stops and shakes her head, as if she can't believe what she's seeing.

And who could blame her?

Those are *her* magnets.

The ones her airline pilot mother has been bringing home for her since she was a little girl. A pink Eiffel Tower. A relief of the Grand Canyon. The Sydney Opera House. The Colosseum in Rome. A Hollywood Boulevard star with her name on it.

The magnets that should be clinging to the microwave back in her apartment in Halls, in the kitchen she shares with Michelle. That were there when she left it earlier this evening.

Jen mumbles something incoherent and then she's moving, stumbling back from the fridge, turning toward the door, hurrying out of the room, leaving behind her coat and bag, which had been underneath her on the couch all this time.

No one pays any attention to her odd departure. The party-goers are all too drunk or too stoned or both, and it is too dark, too late, too early. If anyone notices, they don't care enough to be interested. He wonders how guilty they'll feel about this when, in the days to come, they are forced to admit to the Gardaí what little they know.

He counts to ten as slowly as he can stand to before he rises from his seat, collects Jen's coat and bag, and follows her out of the house.

She'll be headed home. A thirty-minute walk because she'll never flag down a taxi around here. On deserted, dark streets because this is the quietest hour, that strange one after most of the pub and club patrons have fallen asleep in their beds but before the city's early-risers have woken up in theirs. And her journey will take her alongside the Grand Canal, where the black water can look level with the street and where there isn't always a barrier to prevent you from falling in and where the street lights can be few and far between.

He can't let her go by herself. And he won't, because he's a gentleman. A gentleman who doesn't let young girls walk home alone from parties when they've been drinking enough to forget their coat, bag, and—he lifts the flap on the little velvet envelope, checks inside—keys, college ID, and phone too.

And he wants to make sure Jen knows that.

Mr. Nice Guy, he calls himself.

He hopes she will too.

will, now

The words floated up out of the background noise, slowly rearranging the molecules of Will's attention, pulling on it, demanding it, until all trace of sleep had been banished and he was sitting up in bed, awake and alert.

Gardaí are appealing for witnesses after the body of St. John's College student Jennifer Madden, nineteen, was recovered from the Grand Canal early yesterday morning—

It was coming from a radio. Tuned to a local station, it sounded like; a national one would probably have reminded listeners that the Grand Canal was in Dublin. The rest of the news bulletin had been drowned out by the shrill ring of a telephone.

As per the rules, the door to Will's room was propped open. He leaned forward now until he could see through the doorway and out into the corridor. The nurses' station was directly opposite. Alek was standing there, holding his laminated ID to his chest with one hand as he reached across the counter to pick up the phone with the other.

In the moment between the silencing of the phone's ring and Alek's voice saying, "Unit Three," Will caught another snippet—*head injury*—and by then he was up, standing, trying to decide what to do.

Wondering if there was anything he *could* do.

Unsure whether he should do anything at all.

He decided to speak to Alek. They were friends, or at least what qualified as friends in here. Friend*ly*. Will waited until the nurse had finished on the phone before he crossed the corridor.

"My main man," Alek said when he saw him. "They said you were sleeping in there." Alek was Polish but losing more and more of his accent with each passing year. Five so far, he'd been working here. The last four in Unit Three. "You feeling okay?"

"I was just reading," Will said. "Must have dozed off."

"Anything good?"

Will shrugged. "Can't have been, can it?"

Alek picked a clipboard up off the counter and started scanning the schedule attached to it. "Shouldn't you be in with Dr. Carter right now?"

The news bulletin had moved on to the weather. Rain and wind were forecast. In keeping with tradition, the disembodied voice joked, *tomorrow's St. Patrick's Day parade would be a soggy one.*

Will hadn't realized that was tomorrow. It was hard to keep a hold of what day of the week it was, let alone dates and months.

"That got moved to three," he said. "I think because she has a court thing …?"

Alek looked up from the clipboard. Patients shouldn't know anything about what the staff did outside of the high-security unit but Will had just revealed to Alek that he did.

If Alek was going to reprimand Will for it, now would be the time.

But Alek let the moment—and the breach—pass.

He treated Will differently than the others. They all did. That's how Will knew his counselor had a court appearance in the first place. She'd let it slip at the end of their last session when she was advising him of the schedule change, less careful with him than with her other patients. He appreciated this differential treatment and never took it for granted. He felt like he'd earned it over the last ten years. He'd never caused them any trouble. He'd always done whatever he was told.

And now he was going to have to take advantage.

Will checked the corridor. No one else was around. Mornings were for counseling and group sessions; Will wouldn't be here either if it wasn't for Dr. Carter's trip to court.

It was pure chance he'd heard the bulletin.

"Ah, Alek," Will started. "The radio—"

"Oh, shit." Alek dropped the clipboard onto the counter and moved in behind it, reaching up for the little transistor radio sitting on the top shelf. The radio clicked off. "Sorry. That isn't what woke you up, is it?"

"No, no," Will said. "It's fine. I was just going to ask you—were you listening to the news just now?" Alek raised an eyebrow, suspicious. "I thought I heard something there about the, ah, about the canal?"

A beat passed.

Alek picked up his clipboard again. "I wouldn't worry about it, man."

"Do you know what happened?"

"Why do you want to know?"

"I was just wondering …" Will paused, swallowed hard for effect. "Was it about me?"

"About *you*?" Alek shook his head. "No. What made you think that?"

"We're coming up on ten years, aren't we? I thought maybe it was something to do with that."

"It's not."

"No?"

"No."

"Are you sure?"

Alek looked at him for a long moment, as if trying to decide something. Then he sighed and said, "That was Blue FM. They do their news at ten to." He met Will's eyes. "It's almost one. I'll put on a different channel."

"Thanks," Will said. "I really—"

"Don't thank me, because I didn't do this." He reached up and switched the radio back on, moving the dial until he found a station promising a lunchtime news bulletin after the break. Then he took a seat behind the counter and pushed a leaflet about the benefits of mindfulness toward Will. "Pretend you're reading that, at least."

It was the top story.

The leaflet's text blurred in front of Will's eyes as he banked each detail. Jennifer Madden. A St. John's College student. A first-year, going by her age. Found in the Grand Canal near Charlemont Luas station yesterday, having last been seen at a house party in Rathmines on Saturday night. Gardaí are treating her death as suspicious. Believed to have suffered a head injury before going into the water. Anyone with information should call the incident room at Harcourt Terrace.

And thanks to the weather report, Will could add another detail: this had happened a few days before St. Patrick's Day.

Warm relief flooded his veins.

Finally, after all these years, it was happening.

And just in the nick of time, too.

"Alek," he said, leaning over the counter, "I need to speak to the Gardaí. Right now."

alison, now

They came to my door the morning after Sal's dinner party.

I was still suffering. It'd been a St. Patrick's Day one, held in my honor, me being the sole Irish member of our group. Sal and I had drifted into a motley crew of ex-pats who'd bound themselves to an arrangement to get together once every couple of months, taking it in turns to be Chief Organizer. There was a core group of six or seven who could be relied upon to show up, and then several more who occasionally surprised us. We called ourselves "The EUs" because while we could claim nationalities in nine different countries, they were all within a train ride or Ryanair flight of our adopted home. One of Sal's goals in life was to infiltrate Breda's American ex-pat community and convince at least some of them to join our gang.

I'd arrived early to help Sal and Dirk set up, but was forbidden from doing anything except sitting on their sofa holding a champagne flute of something

Instagram had apparently claimed was called a Black Velvet. It looked a bit like bubbly Guinness. I don't actually *like* Guinness, but I kept that tidbit to myself. Instead, I watched as Sal, looking like a 1950s housewife in her belted green dress, bright red lipstick, and neat blonde bun, unloaded a bag of garish decorations onto her dining table: gold confetti, rainbow-colored novelty straws and serviettes with cartoon leprechauns on them.

"Classy," I remarked.

"They are compared to what else was on offer," Sal said. "You can thank your lucky charms I didn't get any hats."

"You know 'lucky charms' is more of an American thing, right? A breakfast cereal? We don't actually say that."

"Is a rant about 'Patty's Day' coming next?"

"No, I'll wait until everyone else gets here for that. They all need to hear it."

Sal rolled her eyes. "Something to look forward to, then."

"I still can't believe you're throwing a dinner party," I said. "Even if it is one with novelty straws and leprechauns. You're such a grown-up."

"Don't remind me." Sal paused to appraise her table. It was set for twelve, an impressive showing for The EUs. "We own white goods, Ali. *White goods*. And then there's this bloody thing." She held up her left hand, wiggling her ring finger. The platinum band glinted under the ceiling lights. "I'm still not used to it."

They'd only been married a month. Dismissive of tradition, Sal had had her wedding here, forcing her family to travel over from London. The skin on her forearms was still lightly browned from their honeymoon in the Maldives, and I hadn't yet worked my way through all the luxury toiletries she'd swiped for me from the bathroom of the five-star resort they'd stayed in. My bridesmaid dress was still at the dry cleaner's.

The doorbell went then and Sal hurried out of the room to answer it. I wondered where Dirk was, then realized he must be the one making all the clattering sounds coming from the kitchen.

I took a tentative sip of my drink and discovered it was, literally, bubbly Guinness. Guinness topped with champagne. A crime against both substances. I was grimacing at the sour aftertaste when the door to the living room opened and an attractive man I'd never seen before walked in, closely followed by Sal, smiling demonically and making suggestive faces at me behind his back.

"*This*," she announced, "is Stephen."

I knew what was coming before she said it: Stephen was Irish too. He had that look about him. Not the red-headed, freckled one we're famous for, but the more typical reality: pale skin, blue eyes, black hair. Sal had found another one of us and she seemed *very* excited about it. As she explained that he was a colleague of Dirk's, that he'd just moved here a fortnight ago, that he didn't really know anyone yet but we'd snared him for our group now and did I mind sharing my Guest of Honor spot with him for the evening, I realized why: she thought she'd found him *for me*.

Groaning inwardly, I stood up to shake his hand and exchange hellos.

"Drink?" Sal asked him. "What'll you have?"

Stephen looked to my glass, then to me, and I shook my head as much as I could before Sal would see.

"How about a beer?" he said.

A South Dublin accent. Our age, as far as I could tell. Thirtyish. And if he worked with Dirk at the software company, that meant he likely had a college degree …

I knew where this was going.

I had to concentrate on keeping a pleasant expression on my face.

"You won't have one of those?" Sal pointed at my glass. "It's a Black Velvet. They're delicious."

"I, ah, I don't drink Guinness," Stephen said. "That's why I had to leave Ireland, actually. They found that out."

I forced a laugh. Sal's smile faltered, because although neither Stephen nor I knew this yet, her main was Guinness stew.

They settled on a Heineken and Sal left to fetch it, leaving Stephen and I to have the standard So, You've Just Met a Fellow Irish Person Abroad talk. He confirmed my suspicion that he was from South Dublin, told me he'd spent the last three years in Abu Dhabi and that, this time around, he was trying to avoid repeating what he'd done out there: so assimilated himself within the Irish ex-pat gang that he'd ended up playing GAA every weekend and only ever drinking in an Irish pub that could've been called Six Degrees of Stephen's School Friends. I told him I was from Cork, that I'd been in the Netherlands nearly ten years, that I worked in Ops Management for a travel company, and that Sal and I had met in the laundry room of our student accommodation in Den Hague. We'd recognized the confused look on each other's faces as a shared inability to process the instructions posted above the machines, and been friends ever since.

"Don't tell anyone," Stephen said, "but the guys at work were saying 'den hag' for three days before I realized that meant the Hague."

I smiled. "Don't worry about it. When I first got here, I thought Albert Heijn was a politician." Stephen raised his eyebrows. "It's a chain of supermarkets," I explained. "The supermarket I was going to, on a regular basis, for at least a month before I put two and two together. Dutch sounds nothing like it looks, half the time. To us, anyway. That's the problem."

"Do you speak it?"

"A little. *Very* little. Nowhere near as much as I should. Everyone speaks English here, so you get lazy. And Suncamp is a British company. It's all English at work."

"Did you go to college here then or …?"

"I went here." I took another sip of my drink, forgetting that it tasted like something they make you drink in a hospital before they scan your intestines. He hadn't spoken by the time I'd forced a swallow, so I asked, "Where did you go?" even though I had already guessed the answer and I didn't want to hear it said out loud, didn't want to hear those three bloody words—

"St. John's College."

All I could do in response was make a *hmm* noise.

"I could walk there from my parents' house," Stephen said, "and both of them went there, so I really didn't have a choice."

I fixed my eyes on my glass. "What did you study?"

"Biomedical science." He paused. "Class of 2009."

I did the sums: he'd have been in his third year back then. But I didn't need to do them. That tone he'd used, an odd mix of pride and solemnness. The dramatic pause. The fact alone that he'd felt the need to tell me when he'd graduated.

It all added up to: *Yes, I was there then. I was there when it happened.*

"Do you get back home much?" he asked me.

"Sorry," I said, standing up, "but while I have the chance, I'm going to find a potted plant to dump the rest of this concoction in. Back in a sec."

And that was it. The swift and sudden end of Sal's dream that Stephen could be the man for me coming before she'd even returned with his drink.

I'd never be able to tell her why.

Not the *real* reason, anyway.

For the rest of the evening (through three courses, goody-bags consisting of packets of Tayto and Dairy Milk bars, and an hour's worth of *Father Ted* YouTube clips because trying to describe it to our mainland-Europe diners wasn't getting us anywhere), I concentrated on enjoying myself, thankful that Sal's never-ending hostess duties prevented her from grabbing me for a sidebar.

She did it via WhatsApp the next morning instead.

> What happened with Stephen? I brought
> him for you and you barely spoke to
> him! Since I know you're going to give
> me some I'm-concentrating-on-my-
> career BS now and I'M going to have to
> give YOU the Cat Lady talk again, I've
> just saved us both the bother and given
> him your number. He was STARING at
> you all night (not in a serial killer way).
> In other news, am DYING. May actually
> already be dead. Haven't even gone
> into the kitchen yet. Too afraid. Sent D
> out for caffeine and grease. Was good,
> though, right? Send proof of life. X

I read it at my kitchen table, nursing my second cup of black coffee while my stomach gurgled and ached, protesting at last night's abuse.

So Sal had given Stephen my number. How in absolutely no way surprising. When it came to such stunts, the girl had priors. I wasn't annoyed, but I feared Sal would be soon. Because if Stephen did call or text, I'd just deploy my usual, terminally single strategy: say I was busy until next week, cancel *those* plans last minute and then repeat as required until he got annoyed and gave up. It wasn't a great plan, but it beat having to tell him—or Sal—the truth further down the line.

I typed a quick reply, assuring Sal that I was indeed alive, thanking her for the party and promising I'd call her later. I didn't mention Stephen at all.

I'd just pressed SEND when I heard the knock on the door.

I thought it was the postman with a parcel. Or that there was a new guy delivering my neighbor's groceries, and he'd accidentally come to the wrong house. But huddled on my doorstep, heads dipped beneath the gutter's narrow overhang in a futile attempt to shield themselves from that morning's heavy rain, were two men about to introduce themselves as members of An Garda Síochána.

The younger one wasn't much older than me. Tall, with a thick quiff of reddish-brown hair and a beard to match. Bright green eyes. Not unattractive. He pulled a small leather wallet from an inside pocket and flipped it open, revealing a gold Garda shield and an ID.

Garda Detective Michael Malone.

The other one I recognized, even though I'd only spent a few hours with him, one afternoon almost ten years ago. The sparse tufts of gray hair left on the sides of his head had been made thinner still by the rain, and patches of bald, pink scalp were shining through. He was turned away, eyes on something further down the road, hands stuck in his pockets.

Garda Detective Jerry Shaw.

"Alison Smith?" Malone asked.

"What's wrong?" I said. "Is it …? Are my parents—"

"Everyone's fine. Everything's okay." He glanced down the hall behind me. "Can we come in? There's something we need to talk to you about. Should only take a few minutes." He flashed a smile, but if he was going for reassurance he fell way short of the mark.

Two Irish detectives. Here at my door in Breda.

And one of them was Detective Jerry Shaw.

This could really only be about one thing, but I asked the question anyway.

"What's this about?"

Shaw finally turned toward me. Our eyes met.

"Will," he said.

alison, now

I led them down the hall, into the kitchen, suddenly conscious of my loose gray sweatpants and misshapen old T-shirt, the dregs of last night's makeup smudged around my eyes. I'd hit my bed around four, just about managing to kick my shoes off before I fell asleep. Turns out that after you've had five of them, Black Velvets don't taste so bad after all.

While my back was turned to the detectives, I licked a finger and swiped underneath my eyes as discreetly as I could. I tucked my hair behind my ears and ran my tongue over my teeth. I hadn't even brushed them yet.

I glanced down at my sweatshirt. No discernible stains. Good.

I pointed them to my kitchen table. My cup and phone were still sitting there, marking my spot. The detectives took the two seats across from it.

The pot of coffee I'd brewed half an hour before was still half-full. I offered some and both men gratefully accepted a cup. While I watched Shaw spoon a genuinely alarming amount of sugar into his, Malone started telling me about how they were both exhausted because they'd caught the dawn flight out of Dublin and then driven here from Schiphol in a hired car.

"Has he been released?" I asked. I'd interrupted a complaint about the lack of signage on local roads, but I just couldn't wait any longer.

Shaw said, "No."

This was the first word he'd spoken since he'd come inside.

My shoulders dropped. I'd been tense with this possibility ever since I'd pulled back the front door.

"He's still in the CPH," Malone said. "The Central Psychiatric Hospital. Although he *is* scheduled to be moved to Clover Hill next month."

"The holiday's finally over," Shaw said.

"Clover Hill is a prison," Malone explained. "It'll be a big change for him."

"Sorry if this is a stupid question," I said, "but shouldn't he be in prison *already*? Why is he in a hospital?"

"A psychiatric hospital," Malone corrected. "It's still secure, but he can receive treatment. At some point—very early on in his incarceration, I think—it was decided that his needs would be better served there."

"He was getting treatment? What for?"

Shaw snorted. "For being a serial killer, love."

Malone said to me, "Will was very young when he entered the system, and he was a … Well, let's just say he was very much a unique prisoner. The Prison Service decided that the CPH was the best home for him. Until now, at least."

"Why are you here?"

The two detectives exchanged a glance. Then Malone asked me if I kept up with the news at home.

"No," I said. "To be honest, I couldn't even tell you who's Taoiseach."

"Well," Shaw said, "you're not missing anything there, love, let me tell you."

"What about your parents?" Malone pressed. "Might they mention things to you?"

"If you mean deaths in the parish and the year on next-door's car, then yeah. As for actual news, no." I looked from one to detective to the other. "Why don't you just tell me what's happened because obviously something has?"

"We found a body," Shaw said. "In the Grand Canal. Nineteen-year-old girl. A student at St. John's."

His tone was so matter-of-fact that it took me a second to put the words together and process what he'd actually said. Malone turned to glare at his colleague but all he got in response was Shaw picking up his coffee and taking a grotesquely noisy slurp.

"What happened?" I asked. My mouth was suddenly bone dry. "What happened to her?"

"We're still trying to—" Malone started.

"Stunned," Shaw said, "it seems like. By a blow to the head. Probably went into the water unconscious then. Cause of death was drowning."

A cold brick of dread settled in my stomach.

Malone leaned forward. "We got a report last Saturday morning. A pair of joggers were passing under the Luas tracks at Charlemont when they spotted something in the water. It was the body of

Jennifer Madden, nineteen. A student at St. John's since September. She'd last been seen at a party in Rathmines the night before."

The weekend before St. Patrick's Day, then.

I said, "Could it just be a coincidence?"

Malone shook his head. "Doesn't look like it, no. Jennifer … She, ah, isn't the first. She's the second. Louise Farrington was found in January, by Baggot Street Bridge. It looked like a tragic accident, at the time. But now with this second case … Well, the dates fit."

"Why did you think the first one was an accident?"

Malone went to answer but Shaw cut in. "Because that's what it looked like."

"What's important," Malone said, shifting his weight, "is that we don't think that anymore."

"Someone's copying him," I said.

They both nodded. Shaw said, "Seems that way."

I placed my palms flat on the table in front of me and willed the walls to slow and still.

Then I asked the detectives if they had any idea who.

"We're following a number of leads," Malone said. "One of them is the reason we're here."

I honestly had no clue what was coming next. I hadn't lived in Ireland in nearly ten years. I hadn't been in Dublin since the weekend of Will's arrest. I wasn't in touch with anyone from home except for my parents.

How had any lead led back to me?

"It seems," Malone said, "that Will heard a news report about Jennifer the day after her body was found. According to a nurse on staff at the CPH at the time, Will became upset, and asked if he could make a call to the Gardaí. He said he needed to speak with us. We"—

Malone indicated himself and Shaw—"went out there yesterday. To the CPH."

"You've talked to him?" My mind was racing. *How was he? How does he look? What did he say? Is he sorry? Did he tell you* why? I had to concentrate in order to pluck a single coherent thought from the noise. "But he can't know anything. He's been inside, all this time. Unless … You don't think …? You don't think he was working with someone back then, do you? That there were two of them? And this is the other guy, back at it now? Is that a possibility?"

"Why would you ask us that?" Shaw was watching me closely. "Do *you* think that's a possibility?"

I met his eyes. "I think I learned ten years ago that anything is possible."

"But," Malone said, "specifically."

I looked to him. "I can't say I remember anything that made me think that, no. But then I didn't think that my boyfriend was a serial killer either." I stopped to take a breath, to steady my voice. "What did Will say?"

I hadn't said his name in so long the sound felt like a foreign object in my mouth, one with sharp edges that pressed painfully against the soft skin of my throat.

"Well," Malone said, "that's just it. When we met with him, Will told us he did have information that could potentially assist us, but that he wouldn't tell it to us."

"That's ridiculous." I looked from one man to the other. "Why would he bother telling you he knows something and then refuse to say what it is when you get there? That doesn't make any sense."

"What I meant was," Malone said, "he wouldn't tell *us*."

Shaw leaned back in his chair, folded his arms across his chest and mumbled something under his breath.

I thought I heard *waste of time*.

"Admittedly," Malone said, "it's unlikely that Will would have any valuable information. But that doesn't change the fact that he does have a relevant role here, even if it's one he hasn't actively participated in. Our working theory is that this is a copycat. If that's the case, by this time next week, we'll have another dead college student on our hands. A third innocent victim, unless we catch this guy. And if we don't do everything we can possibly can, if we don't explore every last lead, however small or unlikely, then we will have that girl's death not just on our hands but on our consciences, too."

He'd lost me.

I said, "I think I've missed a step ...?"

"We can't force you to do this," Malone said. "So we're here to ask."

"Ask me w—" I stopped, realizing.

No. No way. Absolutely not.

And then I said those words out loud.

"How about you have a think about it?" Malone said.

"I don't need to."

"If it's the press you're worried about, that won't be an issue."

In my mind's eye, I saw a flash of a tabloid newspaper's front page, one side taken up with a picture of me in cut-off shorts and a bikini top, taken on a girls' holiday to Tenerife the summer before I'd started college. The other side was all headline. SERIAL KILLER'S KILLER GIRL.

They got the photo from my Facebook page, which I'd only signed up for a couple of weeks before Will's arrest. This was before the press copped on to the fact that people's social media profiles were treasure troves of personal information just waiting to be mined, so it was far more likely that a friend I was connected with on the site had screenshot the photos and sold them.

"We'll take steps to ensure that your involvement in this will be kept top secret," Malone was saying. "We'll get you in and out before anyone even knows you're in Dublin."

"No," I said again.

"Well," Shaw said, hoisting himself up out of his chair, "thanks for the coffee." He looked at Malone with an expression that said he'd known all along it was going to go this way.

"Why don't you take the day?" Malone said, standing up too. "Like I said, we can't force you to do this. But we don't know what he might say. It might be important. It might give us the break we need." He took a business card from a pocket, placed it on the table. "We need to know no later than four this afternoon, Alison, so you can fly back with us tonight. If you say yes, you'll be meeting with Will at the CPH first thing tomorrow morning. All the necessary arrangements are already in place."

alison, then

"Liz?" I whispered. "Are you awake?"

The light was faint and blue-gray. Morning, then, but very early, still. The room was chilly—we'd turned the dial on the thermostat all the way to the snowflake symbol before we'd gone to bed—but the reddened skin on my back and arms still burned hot, every contact with the sheet like the rough scratch of sandpaper. Various items of summer clothing and accessories were taking shape in the shadows, messy little mounds on the tiled floor. I could see the neon strings of bikini tops, the tie-dyed print of cover-ups we'd bought from a beach stall, straw hats, damp towels, plastic flip-flops. Empty or half-drunk plastic water bottles of various sizes stood like an audience on top of the scratched chest of mahogany drawers stood against the opposite wall. Outside, the resort was uncharacteristically silent but for the clicking call of the cicadas.

In the other single bed, Liz began to stir.

"I don't feel well," I said into the semi-darkness.

Her first response was something indecipherable, her voice thick with sleep. But then she rolled over to face me. "What time is it?" She swiped at her hair, pushing wayward strands of it out of her eyes. "Ali?" Liz raised herself up onto her elbows. "What's wrong?"

I was sitting up on the edge of my bed, arms wrapped around my stomach, hunched over, wincing as a sharp pain bisected my abdomen from hip to hip. It'd started a couple of hours ago, just brief stabs at first, but after a couple of trips to the bathroom that I could only describe as traumatic, it was now worse and near constant. I'd also broken out in a cold, clammy sweat.

I felt awful.

"I think I might have food poisoning," I said miserably.

"What? Why?" Liz sat up, swinging her spindly legs onto the floor. "Have you been sick?"

"No, but I think I'm going to be."

"And have you been—"

"Yeah." I made a face. "Twice."

"Oh boy."

"I think it was the burgers. I was the only one who had a chicken one, wasn't I? But"—I inhaled sharply as an especially painful pinch gripped some part of my insides—"those Sambuca shots probably didn't help. And then there was the ice. Do they make that with tap water? Are you supposed to drink the tap water here?"

"We're in Tenerife," Liz said, "not Calcutta."

Our third day in Playa de las Americas was dawning. *Only* our third day and here I was, doubled over with stomach pain. Presumably still asleep elsewhere in the apartment were another two girls from our class, and elsewhere in the resort were the remaining eight members of the group. So far we'd spent our time sunbathing, drinking, and overspending, and then sleeping those activities off until we were ready to go again. The quintessential post–Leaving Cert holiday.

I'd actually been dreaming that I'd accidentally burned through my entire fortnight's budget in just the first couple of days, and thought the panic of this is what had woken me up in the middle of the night. Then I'd felt the shooting pain, the sudden movement in my gut, and realized I had real problems.

"Warning," Liz said, standing up. "I'm turning on the light."

There was a *click,* followed by a blinding glare. When my eyes adjusted, I saw that Liz was bent over, rummaging in her suitcase. It was lying open on the floor where she'd left it on the first day. Her wavy blonde hair was a tangled mess, her eyes still rimmed with the thick eyeliner, and the T-shirt her drunk self had pulled on to sleep in was inside-out, the label and seams clearly visible. She found a small box of something—tablets— and straightened up, bringing the box close to her face to read the label.

"These are the job," she said, throwing it to me. She selected one of the water bottles and passed it to me. "Take two of them."

"What are they?"

"Imodium. They keep things in and they keep things down."

I swallowed the tablets with a swig of water.

Liz left the room, returning half a minute later with the large plastic dish that had been sitting in the sink, clean towels, and a bottle of sports drink, ice-cold from the fridge. She set them all down within my easy reach. Then she wet a facecloth in the bathroom and wiped my forehead and cheeks with it, tying my hair back from my face with an elastic band she'd had in hers.

"God," she said, "you look awful."

I smiled weakly. "Thanks."

"Any time." She patted my shoulder, then jerked her hand away. "Jesus, the heat off that!"

"Sunburn," I said. "Unrelated."

"Unless you have heat stroke."

"Does that make you ...?"

"I don't know. Maybe. Do you want me to put on some more after-sun?"

"No, no. It's okay."

While I sat perched on the edge of my bed, clenched and tense, Liz worked around me to straighten my pillows and smooth out the crumpled sheets. When she was done I lay back down, drew my knees up to my chest to help with the pain, and closed my eyes.

I spent the rest of the day like that.

And then three more days after that the very same way.

The pain did dull to mere discomfort, but I was hot and sweaty and sick, and too much of all those things to lift my head up off the pillow. I faded in and out of sleep. I couldn't eat and only drank because Liz would appear every couple of hours with a bottle with a straw stuck in it, forcing me to take a few sips. Had this happened to me at home, in my own room with my mother nearby, it would've been horrible but tolerable. Here, hundreds of miles away, on a thin mattress on a hard, uncomfortable bed in a bare-bones holiday apartment, it was nightmarish.

On the second evening Liz went to reception and arranged for a visit from a local doctor, who took my temperature, wrote me a prescription, and told Liz to start feeding me bananas. That's what she said, anyway. I didn't understand much of what he'd muttered in Spanish to me, but I got the feeling he was bemused more than anything. I guess he saw plenty of eighteen-year-old Irish girls away from home for the first time whose bodies quickly balked at their bad decisions.

I pleaded with Liz to leave me to suffer alone, but she refused to go further than the resort's swimming pool without me, and she only went there for short periods while I was asleep. Instead, she brought me magazines, played cards with me, and made sure I was drinking my water and eating my bananas. She had housekeeping bring fresh sheets and she dragged the TV in from the living room, although we couldn't find anything on it in English except BBC News.

The other girls wandered in and out, wrinkling their noses while they made the sounds of sympathy, but they didn't let my sickness get in the way of their holidaying. I was vaguely mad at them for doing that and angry at Liz for not doing it at all.

"I'm ruining your holiday," I said to her. We'd been living for this fortnight for nearly nine months and now, thanks to me, she was spending it in the apartment. "You should go out with them. Go out tonight. I'll be fine. Really."

"Are you serious?" She rolled her eyes. "If I was sick and you left me by myself, I'd bloody murder you. We'll both go out when you're feeling better."

"But we don't know when that'll be. You could miss this entire holiday."

"Eat your bananas."

The Plague, as we started calling it, lasted nearly four nights and days. I'd spent my first forty-eight hours in Tenerife sunburnt and hungover, so that was pretty much the entire first week chalked down to a loss. The second one was great, and I flew back to Cork with a tan, fabulous memories, and plenty of group photos I didn't feel comfortable showing my parents, but I still felt bad that I'd reduced Liz's holiday by half.

I didn't even mention I'd been sick until I was safely home. My mother's open mouth and eyes grew bigger and bigger while I gave her all the ghastly details. She wasn't at all impressed that I hadn't called to tell her while it was happening, and she was convinced that it was alcohol, not food, that had caused the problem, even though I pointed out that I didn't think that was medically possible.

"Well," she said, "aren't you lucky you had Liz? She sounds like a right little Florence Nightingale." Then she muttered, almost to herself, "I didn't know the girl had it in her."

*****

The summer that starts with the Leaving Cert exam and ends with the publication of their results—which alone will determine our college places—is the most glorious one of all for Irish teenagers. The worst is over; school's out forever. College and adult life await. It's the only one filled with possibility and adventure, but not yet sullied by reality. Anything could happen yet.

But there's a price to pay: it rushes by. One minute it was all stretched out ahead of us, the next it was a Wednesday in the middle of August and the college place offers were coming out.

I was already awake when my phone began to chirp at 5:55 a.m. I'd barely slept, and whenever I had I'd dreamed of disappointment.

I reached for my laptop, fully charged and waiting for me beside the bed. I booted it up, navigated to the CAO homepage and entered my log-in details. By then it was 5:56 a.m.

The laptop's fan buzzed and whirred, as if protesting at being woken up at this ungodly hour on a summer's morning. The clunky machine was years old, on its last legs. I'd been dropping hints to Mam and Dad for months, cursing the thing every time it couldn't handle new software or it failed to save my work. I hit REFRESH now because leaving it idle was the quickest way to get it to freeze up and I just couldn't deal with that this morning on top of everything else.

5:57 a.m.

I felt sick to my stomach, a hangover without the headache. What if I didn't get in? I could barely remember now what I'd put down as my second choice, symptomatic of my refusal to accept that I'd ever have to do it. If I didn't get in, I'd repeat. That was the only option. Do the Leaving Cert all over again, try again next year.

Please God, though, don't let me have to do that.

5:58 a.m.

The house was silent. I'd warned Mam and Dad not to get up, promising I'd wake them when the results were posted. There was just no point in us all getting up for six, especially if it was bad news.

The truth was, I wanted to find out by myself. I wanted to *be* by myself with it, just for a minute, whether it was good or bad.

5:59 a.m.

I wondered where Liz was checking hers. Probably sitting in bed with her computer, like me. Only, knowing Liz, once she saw them, she'd roll over and go back to sleep. She hadn't even bothered going into school the week before to get her exam results. She'd just checked them online and then headed for the pub, cool as a cucumber, bemused at me when I said she was missing out on a rite of passage, on that moment of opening the envelope, on seeing the grades slide out.

"I just don't need all the amateur dramatics," she'd said. "The day my brother got his there was a full-on *performance* going on outside the school gates. I just can't be arsed with that."

I thought the real reason might be that she didn't want to *have* to perform if things didn't go well for her.

I'd gone in.

6:00 a.m.

Time. Heart thundering in my chest, I hit REFRESH again.

First round offer: English Literature, St. John's College Dublin (SJC0492).

I leapt out of bed so fast I nearly sent the laptop crashing onto the floor. I ran out of my room and across the hall into Mam and Dad's room, ready to burst out, "I got in!" at the top of my lungs—but their bed was empty. I went back out into the hall, saw the bathroom door standing open, the light off.

Where were they?

I heard it then: muffled voices a floor below me. They were up already.

I raced downstairs and into the kitchen with a flourish, pushing the door open so fast that it swung back and hit off the wall with a clatter. They were at the table, both still in their pajamas. Dad was sitting down and Mam was standing over him, about to fill his mug with coffee from the machine. They looked up at the noise, then at me with raised eyebrows.

I indulged myself with a dramatic pause before yelling, "*I'm going to St. John's!*"

She squealed. He started clapping.

"Brilliant," Mam said. "I knew you'd do it."

Dad got up and patted me on the back. "Well done, well done."

"What are you guys doing up, though?" I felt breathless with adrenalin. "I told you there was no point in us all being up at this hour."

"I had to." My father pushed his glasses up his nose. "I wanted to know sooner rather than later whether or not I have to remortgage the house. Is it too late to change your mind and go to UCC, do you think?"

This had been his running joke all summer. All year, as a matter of fact. If I went to University College Cork, I could live at home. St. John's meant campus accommodation fees, to the tune of nearly six thousand euro per academic year.

A bottle of Buck's Fizz and three champagne flutes appeared.

"Mam," I said, "it's six in the morning."

"It's only fizzy orange juice, love. You'll be out tonight drinking shots of God knows what."

"Paint stripper," my father said.

"I'm sure you can manage a glass of this."

I rolled my eyes and took a sip.

"We got you a little present." My father moved back the dining chair next to his and lifted a huge box up onto the table. It wasn't wrapped, but there was a red ribbon tied around it.

All I had to see was the Apple logo and I gasped. The drink nearly flew out of my hand. My mother saw this happening and took it from me.

"*What?*" I pulled the box toward me. "No way. No *way.*"

"She seems more excited about this than St. John's," my mother said wryly.

"Look after it," Dad said to me. "And use it for *studying.*"

"I will, I will. Thanks, Dad."

"Your mother did the bow."

She rolled her eyes. "*And* I made sure he got the right one, more importantly."

My phone beeped with a text message.

"Liz," I said, looking at the screen. The message just said, *call me.*

"Oh—Liz." My mother was pouring a glass for my father now. "How did she get on, I wonder?"

"I'm about to find out."

I took my phone out the back door and into the garden, stepping carefully onto the patio in my bare feet. The sky was clear—it was going to be a gorgeous day— but the garden was in cold shadow, the sun still hidden behind the house.

I selected Liz from my speed-dial list and put the phone to my ear. It only rang once before I heard her voice saying tonelessly, "I didn't get in."

"*What?*"

"Don't make me say it a second time."

I didn't understand. We had a plan: Liz and I, together at St. John's. I was going to do English literature and she was going to do English and French. We were going to share an apartment on campus. We were going to have the time of our lives living in Dublin. We'd been talking about it for years, planning every detail for months.

A week ago, we'd celebrated us both getting enough Leaving Cert points, at least based on what we could guesstimate from last year's threshold for entry. I had a few more than Liz, but then the course I was hoping to get demanded a few more. For all our stress and anxiety, neither of us truly believed we wouldn't end up with what we wanted when the college offers came through today: a place in St. John's.

"You mean you didn't get your first choice?" I said. Both of us had put down more than one course at St. John's, just in case.

"No," Liz said. "I got like, choice number five."

"Which was what?"

She sighed. "Bloody business at CIT."

"You put down a course in *Cork*?"

"I didn't think I'd have to worry about getting it," she snapped. "God. This is *such* bullshit."

The cold cement beneath my feet was making the rest of me shiver. "The points must've gone up," I said.

"Oh, you think?"

I forgave the snappiness, considering.

"You didn't accept it, did you, Liz? You should wait for the second round."

"Why?" she said. "I'm not going to get it then either."

"You never know."

"Yeah, I do."

"So, what? You're going to stay here for the next four years?"

"Rub it in, why don't you?"

"I'm just asking what your plan is."

"My plan right now is to go back to sleep."

I knew from the tone of Liz's voice that she was in one of her moods and there was no point trying to talk her out of it. She'd decide when and where she'd get over this, and I'd just have to wait for it to happen.

"Okay," I said. "Well, I'll call you later. And I'll see you tonight anyway."

"I'm not going tonight."

I rolled my eyes. "*Liz …*"

We were supposed to be going a party at this girl's house, Sharon. Her parents were away in France for a fortnight so she'd the run of the place, and the house was out in the middle of nowhere, on some back road past Ballygarvan, so there'd be no next-door neighbors to worry about disturbing. She'd invited half the class to it. A CAO Offers Day Party.

The thing was, Sharon was really Liz's friend. They played hockey together. I didn't know Sharon well enough to go along by myself, so Liz flaking out on tonight's plans left me out of them as well.

"Go back to sleep for a while," I said. "I'll call over in a few hours. You might feel different then—"

"I won't."

I was about to repeat that I was sure she'd get something at St. John's in the second round, and that to ignore this first offer, that we'd be laughing about this next week when—

Beep-beep-beep.

She'd hung up on me.

It was only when I turned to go back inside that I realized she'd never asked me how I'd got on.

*****

Liz was mostly MIA for the next week. We talked on the phone a couple of times and on Sunday night I did manage to coax her out to go pick up some McDonald's, but she was sullen and snippy for the whole hour and I was relieved when she dropped me back home.

It was only then the subject of what course I'd got came up, and the conversation was brief. She said, "So you got English lit, then?" and I said, "Yeah," and then she started talking about something else.

The following morning, two girls from our class came into the cafe where I had a summer job helping out in the mornings. We talked about where everyone was headed—one of them was going to Galway, the other had found out months ago that she'd secured a place to do something somewhere in the UK—and what we were wearing to our Debs ball, which was coming up.

"How come you didn't go to Sharon's party?" one of them asked me.

"Oh …" I didn't want to say it was because of Liz, because that would be inadvertently revealing that she'd failed to get the college course she wanted *and* that I wouldn't go places without her in tow. "Something came up at the last minute. How was it?"

One of them, Fiona, started laughing. "Brendan Richards drank some *insane* amount of vodka and went berserk. Didn't Liz tell you?"

I raised my eyebrows. "Liz?"

"Yeah. She had, like, a front-row seat for the projectile vomiting. I think some of it even went on her shoes."

So Liz had gone to Sharon's party. Without me. Without even *telling* me.

She wasn't avoiding the world because she hadn't gotten into St. John's. She was avoiding me because I had.

To make matters worse, there was bad news waiting for me at home.

"This letter came this morning," my mother said, handing me something official with a St. John's College logo stamped on it. "They're saying you never confirmed your campus accommodation offer and now, if you still want it, you're going to have to go on the waitlist and hope something comes up."

I scanned the letter. "What do they mean, never confirmed?"

Mam frowned. "It says something about an online portal."

"I got a message from them, yeah, but I'm sure I clicked 'confirm.'"

The doorbell went.

"You get that," my mother said. "Give me the letter. I'll call them and find out what's going on."

It was Liz at the door.

I'd spent the whole afternoon alternating between being mad at her for going to Sharon's party without me, and trying to dredge up some sympathy for her because I could imagine how disappointed she must be about not getting to go to St. John's, and I understood how the last thing she needed on the day she found that out was to be around someone who was celebrating the fact that she was getting to go.

But the first words out of her mouth were, "Ali, I'm so sorry. I've been a right bitch, I know. I know." And then she swung a pink gift bag out from behind her back. "This is me making up for it."

She handed it over.

It had a handwritten note tied to the handle that said, "College Starter Pack." Peeking inside, I saw a pair of fluffy socks, a shower cap, a box of Berocca, a box of star-shaped fairy lights, and a framed photo of Liz and me, taken at her birthday party last year.

"What's this?" I said.

"Oh, wait." She reached in and pulled out the photograph. "You won't be needing this"—her face broke into a wide smile—"because *I'll be there in person*!"

I looked at her blankly, not understanding.

"I got into St. John's! I got an offer in the second round. Came through this morning. You were right."

"I … Oh, my God. That's great!"

We hugged, which was awkward with me holding the gift bag.

"Sorry for being such a bitch," Liz said. "I've been living for us moving to Dublin. College just wouldn't be the same without you."

I was still wondering how she managed to get over this for the duration of Sharon's party, but Liz's moods could change so fast, I didn't want to initiate a change back right now.

It was just a party. No big deal. Think of what I'd done to her on holiday. What she'd done for me.

I could hardly hold this small infraction against her.

And anyway, now we both had something to celebrate, we could do it together.

"Not to put a damper on things," I said, "but I just got a letter from them saying I've been waitlisted for campus accommodation. Some issue with my online portal or something."

"Well, I'm definitely on the waitlist for it. All second-round-place people are." Her eyes widened. "Maybe we can just find a place to move in to together? Someplace off campus. Wouldn't that be amazing?"

"And expensive," I said. "This is Dublin we're talking about."

"But there'd be two of us, and think of how much we'd each be paying to stay in Halls anyway."

"Yeah," I said. "I don't know." In all my college-days daydreams, I'd lived on campus. I wasn't sure I was ready for independent living in a capital city. One massive life change at a time, please. "I'm still holding out hope that we'll both end up in Halls …"

"Oh, me too," Liz said. "Me too. But we should

probably look at other options, just in case. Go up to
Dublin for a weekend, view some places. I mean, it can't
hurt, right? What are you doing Saturday?"

alison, now

When my alarm woke me the next morning, my eyes opened to black.

My own bedroom at home in Breda had a skylight with no blind, ensuring I always woke up to daylight or, if it was still dark outside, at least the amber glow of streetlights. I knew I wasn't at home then, but for a second I had no idea where I was. Then I remembered: a two-hour drive north in Malone and Shaw's rental car followed by a bumpy flight from Schiphol, the plane descending into the curve of Dublin Bay just before midnight, the coastline separated from the black sea by tributaries of city lights. Garda uniforms at Passport Control. An assault of Irish accents echoing off the walls in an over-lit Arrivals Hall. Malone steering me past the reception desk at some nondescript chain hotel, my room key in his hand, arrangements already made.

All the while asking myself why I would agree to return to Dublin.

Every so often, with a little shock, realizing that I already had.

I was armed and ready to blame Detective Malone. He'd guilted me into it, made me feel like I'd have those girls' blood on *my* hands too if I didn't fly back here and talk to Will.

And coming here was the right thing to do. Wasn't it?

I'd tossed and turned for most of the night wondering whether it was.

I hit the silencer on the alarm now, wishing there was a similar button for my brain. It was 8:15 a.m. I rolled over to face the room's floor-to-ceiling windows. Slivers of gray light were pushing through the gaps in the black-out curtains.

Sal had sent me a message late last night. She was wondering if I wanted to come over and watch a movie tonight. Normally, I used Sundays for boring stuff like laundry and oven-cleaning, and Sal used them to drag Dirk around various home décor stores against his will. I thought I was safe. But of course *this* Sunday, of all Sundays, she wanted to meet up. Murphy's Law. I didn't know how to explain why I was suddenly in Dublin, so instead I replied saying I had cramps and that me and a box of codeine tablets were going to spend the day in bed together.

I felt awful about lying to her, especially when a night spent on her couch talking and laughing our way through a movie until we'd both lost track of the plot sounded like just what I needed right now.

I showered, then pulled on the clothes I thought most suitable for the occasion: black jeans, a white T-shirt, my black leather jacket, and a huge, woolly scarf. Plain and dark. Layers, an armor of sorts. I applied the same light makeup I did every day and opted for glasses over contacts. Didn't bother with jewelry or perfume, or much hairstyling. The last time I'd been to the hairdressers I'd gone sun-kissed blonde and had it chopped clear off my shoulders; it had just grown back to the point where I could pull it into a ponytail. I did that, looked in the mirror, then took it down again.

Trying to ignore the undercurrents running beneath every step.

What will he think when he sees me? What do I want him to think?

Why do I care?

Just before I left the room, I pulled the curtains back. It had been dark and raining when they'd dropped me off, so I had no idea where in the city I was. I'd avoided looking out the car's windows, uninterested in whatever was out there. I'd long been inoculated against nostalgia for my brief Dublin life.

Now, the sun was shining and the street outside quiet. Three cars queued at a set of traffic lights. The footpath in front of the hotel, slick with rain and sodden leaves, was deserted but for a handful of pedestrians. Joggers and tourists, it looked like. Across the street, a line of towering trees, their bristlelike branches bare. And beyond them, the blue of the sky reflected in its mirror-still waters, was the canal.

The canal.

Five minutes later instead of, "Good morning," I greeted Malone with, "I have a canal view."

We'd met in the lobby, as arranged. He was dressed

casually in jeans, Converse, and a navy-blue rain jacket so similar to the one he'd been wearing yesterday I thought they must be standard Garda issue. His hair was wet. One white earbud was tucked in his left ear, the other one dangling casually from the matching white cord, the cord disappearing inside his jacket. He was holding a takeaway cup of what smelled like coffee with what might have been *Mike* scrawled on the side, which he promptly handed to me.

He looked at me. "You have a what?"

"My room," I said. "It overlooks the canal."

"Everything around here does. We needed you near the station, and this was the closest place that had a room on a few hours' notice on a Saturday night." A pause. "That's all."

His unmarked car was parked by the valet stand. The air was warmer than I'd been expecting, and I immediately began to feel clammy and uncomfortable. Once inside the car, I lost the scarf, folding it in my lap.

For the first five minutes of the drive, I silently drank my coffee and let the noise of a local radio station fill the car while the Dublin suburbs flew past outside. Georgian terraces lining busy thoroughfares gave way to red-brick mansions on quieter, leafy streets, which then gave way to newly built three-bed semis and apartment blocks. Nothing more than three or four stories high; in most places, the trees reached above the rooftops. We passed a strip of shopfronts where tacky, plastic signage competed for attention, and what looked like a restaurant with a large number of chrome tables and chairs outside. I admired their optimism.

The rain may have stopped, but the sky promised it'd be back again soon.

I recognized nothing from before, but still I felt the pull of the past. From the green of the street signs, the *as Gaeilge* translation in italics beneath the English names. The license plates on the other cars—every one had a code representing an Irish county, and guessing them had kept me amused in the back seat on many a long drive as a child. Even the voices on the radio, all those Irish accents …

My chest tightened and the sensation brought back one particular memory with a cold, sharp shock: what it was like to have a panic attack. It'd been years, but there was no mistaking the early warning signs. I knew that if I didn't get control, dizziness, shaking hands, and shallow breaths would come next. I inhaled as deeply as I could, held it in while I counted to five. Imagined my pulse slowing. Let the breath out. Did it again.

By the fifth time I started to feel a little better, like I was edging my way back into my body.

I felt Malone looking at me. "Are you all right?"

"Yep," I said. "Fine."

"Are you sure?"

I looked at him. "If I said no, would you turn the car around?"

"Yes."

A van overtook us on the right side, blaring its horn, clearly unaware that this was a stealth Garda car.

I asked if Will knew that I was coming.

"We haven't told him, no." Malone had two hands on the steering wheel. No rings, digital watch. "But we were only there Friday. By now he'll know he has a visitor coming, so he'll probably put two and two together."

"Won't he just think it's his mother, or something?"

"Not on a Sunday, no. There's no visiting hours on Sundays. And, ah, I don't think his parents visit very much, actually."

I'd only met Will's parents once. It hadn't gone well. They'd both struck me as cold, unpleasant people. The opposite of Will.

Or at least, Will as I knew him at the time.

I mean, *thought* I knew him.

Malone asked me what had changed my mind.

"It's the right thing to do, isn't it?" I turned to look out the passenger window. "Will I be alone with him in there?"

"No. There'll be a member of CPH staff in the room with you, and a Garda right outside."

"Is it, like, through glass or …?"

"There'll be no barrier. We've commandeered some kind of meeting room, I'm told. Lots of tables and chairs. You'll sit at one opposite him. The staff member will be on the other side of the room, close enough for you to feel safe but far away enough to permit a private conversation. Well, as private as Will gets to have. Semi-private, I suppose you'd say."

"But don't you need to hear what he says?"

"All that's happening here, Alison, is you are visiting a patient. We can't use the facility's visitors' room because we're trying to keep this quiet, and we've had to get special permission from the hospital director to do this on a Sunday, but other than that, it's just a normal visit."

"Can anyone visit him, then?"

"All visitors have to be approved by the hospital director, just like in prison."

I saw a sign for the Central Psychiatric Hospital. We must be close.

I felt like I was hurtling toward something at full speed but had no idea how to pull on the brakes now.

"Why did he ask for this? I mean, why me? Why not just tell you guys what he knows?"

"I think he just wants to see you," Malone said. "Whatever he knows—if he knows anything—it's a bargaining chip. Leverage. So he says, yeah, I'll give the information to you, but I'm only going to tell it to Alison."

"What if he doesn't know anything?"

"At least we checked."

"But *why* would he want to see me?"

"We're about to find out."

The car slowed, then turned left into a large driveway that sloped uphill. We were facing two towering concrete pillars, between which hung a foreboding set of metal gates. Chain-link fencing filled the spaces between the railings, spiky razor wire curled across its top. Imposing gray walls stretched into the sky and away from the gates on either side. A sign with red lettering warned that ALL VISITORS MUST REPORT TO RECEPTION.

As Malone nudged the nose of the car forward, the metal gates began to shudder, then slowly retract. We moved through them and up the driveway, until we reached a nondescript, three-story concrete block. The only clue as to what was housed inside were the metal grates fixed over every window and the heavy, gun-metal gray gate blocking access to the front door.

All I could think was, *Will lives in there. He's not allowed to leave. This is the extent of his world.*

I remembered the spring of youth and limitless potential I'd seen—*thought* I'd seen—in him back in our St. John's College days, the bright, happy future I'd imagined for us, the one I thought we'd spend together.

How did we end up here?

I'd had ten years to think about it and I still didn't know. Probably because I mostly tried *not* to think about it.

Malone parked as close as he could and cut the engine. "You ready?"

No. "Yes."

We got out and started toward the entrance.

The tightness in my chest came back. I felt strange, as if at any moment everything in my field of vision might start to warp and slide away, as if it wasn't real, as if I wasn't. It all seemed far away, like I was seeing reality through a pair of binoculars.

Why am I doing this?

A buzzing noise, a clang of metal against metal. It was dark, then bright with florescent light. Yellow floor tiles, curling up at the edges. Hospital smells, rushing into my senses: bleach, stale air, antiseptic.

Because you might manage to save a life this time, instead of being responsible for the taking of five because you were too stupid, too naïve, too in love to see that the boy in your bed was a murderous psychopath.

We descended stairs into a long corridor whose pockmarked walls were the color of melted butter. Came to a security guard on a folding chair outside a thick, heavy door. A *click* and a *beep*. Another metallic clang. Down another corridor. Around a corner.

Malone said, "Here we are."

Up ahead, a uniformed Garda stood sentry outside a large door. It had been painted magnolia, but a long time ago. There were more chips missing than there was paint, and the bottom inch or so had been scuffed clean revealing dull steel. A small window of reinforced glass was set into the door at chest-level.

Standing beside the uniform was Shaw.

"You're late," he said to Malone. To me, "I thought you might be having second thoughts."

Fizzy stress was flooding my veins. All of a sudden this was too real, too fast, too *happening*.

I hadn't thought it through. I saw that now. I'd come here on a whim. It hadn't seemed real; I'd just been going through the motions.

But now Will was on the other side of that door.

And I couldn't go in there.

I was too scared to.

"Listen to me, love." Shaw stepped closer and clamped a rough hand on my shoulder. I could feel his breath on my cheek. "He looks the same. He acts the same. He will sound the same. Don't be expecting a forked tongue or red eyes. Don't expect a monster, even though that's what he is. He'll seem normal, because that's what these bastards do. They *pretend*." His fingers had started to pinch. "So when you're in there, keep that in mind. Keep in mind what he did." Shaw dipped his head to whisper something in my ear, so quietly no one else in that corridor could've heard it. "Remember what he did to Liz."

As if I had the pleasure of ever forgetting.

Shaw stepped away, but kept his eyes on mine.

Malone nodded at the uniform who moved to unlock the door.

"Wait," I said to him. "I'm going in *now*? Don't you need to talk me through this first? What am I supposed to do? What am I supposed to say?"

The magnolia door was opening outward, slowly revealing what lay beyond.

"All you need do is go in there," Malone said, "sit down, and listen to him. In ten minutes' time, Garda O'Neill here will knock on the door."

A sizeable room, like a classroom or meeting room, with three rows of desks, all facing the back wall. Windowless, lit by harsh fluorescents, one of which was blinking on and off. A yellowing poster about teamwork hung from the far wall.

Stop. Wait. Wait just a second.

The walls were the same sickly yellow as the corridors.

Hang on. Please. I'm not ready for this.

O'Neill stepped back and—

Wait—

Will.

Sitting at the table in the far-right corner, facing the door. A small figure, hunched over, looking lost in the big room.

I stepped inside.

A man in medical scrubs was standing off to my right, leaning against the wall with his arms folded. He nodded at me, just once, and then he looked to Will.

Then I did too.

Will's hair was darker than I remembered, more brown than blond now, and dull. It was still in the same style, though: short on the sides, longer on top, coarse and unruly when left to its own devices, as it was now. His skin seemed so pale it was practically translucent, like a vampire's. I could see the blue-green of veins running beneath it. He'd filled out. You could see it in his shoulders, down the arms. He'd lost all his sharp angles, swallowed them up with muscle and strength. And his face …

His face. Both so familiar and completely foreign. Older, obviously. Bearded now. But still him.

Still so open and so kind and so *Will*.

The old Will. The fake one.

I met his eyes.

He looked at me blankly for a second, then his mouth fell open.

I took another step forward.

I couldn't believe I was doing this. I couldn't believe that was him, *right there*, in this room, with me. That I could feel his presence. That we were in the same room, just feet away from each other, after all these years.

That I'd *agreed* to this.

I wanted to see him. I wanted to see how he was. Curiosity, call it. But standing in that room, feet away from him, I realized that I hadn't thought much beyond that.

I didn't know what would come next. I didn't know what to do *now*.

And then came the voice.

The one I hadn't been able to recall but which now brought everything straight back, all of it, the past a wave whose approach I'd been ignoring since last night, building strength all the while, coming now to crash down on me and knock me off my feet.

"Oh, Ali, thank God," Will said. His voice cracked on *thank*, and his eyes were wet with tears. "Thank God you came."

alison, now

My heart was hammering so hard in my chest I feared my sternum wouldn't be strong enough to contain it.

I was a keeper of secrets. There was no one in my life who knew all of me. Everyone at arm's length, at least. I'd designed it that way. I liked it. But now here I was, sitting across from the first and last person who'd been allowed to know everything, who'd seen things I hadn't even shared, hadn't even known about myself, and the thought of it all being there in his head, ready for recall, was excruciating.

His presence was a laceration and I was already bleeding out.

"I can't believe you're here, Ali," Will said. "This doesn't feel real."

That makes two of us.

I didn't know what to do or where to look. I dropped into the free chair and tried to fix my gaze on a shoulder of his white T-shirt, but soon wandered onto the collar of it, and then further again onto his bare skin. The knot of dark hair in the depression at the base of his neck.

A memory of me, pressing my fingers against it.

"Ali, it's okay. It's me. It's just me."

I moved my eyes to the tabletop. His hand resting on it, palm down. Pale skin, short square nails, tributaries of bright blue veins. I'd held that hand. Watched it touch me, tenderly. Felt it inside of me.

Before and after it had smashed five skulls onto the cold, hard ground. Lifted young, broken bodies into freezing black water. Pushed them under and down, down, down.

"Ali, please. Look at—"

"We don't have very long." I instantly regretted my choice of pronoun; the intimacy of it left a streak of hot pain hanging in midair between us. To compound this, I'd sounded small and weak. It was that that made me finally look at him, as if I could compensate for the timidity of my voice with the focus of my gaze.

The man sitting in front of me was Will, but he wasn't the boy I'd loved. No. That boy had died the day Will confessed, if he'd ever existed. The problem was that the man sitting in front of me looked and acted and sounded just like that boy's ghost.

And I could remember exactly how it felt to be his arms. Safe. Warm. Wanted.

The memory was like an open wound.

"Your voice," Will said. "I'd forgotten it." He smiled sadly. "Voices are hard to remember, aren't they? How are you?"

I didn't answer. Where to begin?

"You live abroad, right?" he went on. "They wouldn't tell me where ..." Will nodded, once, like he understood why I wouldn't tell him where either. "Are you …? Are you married? Do you have kids?"

I opened my mouth to say *no*, then stopped. Because I didn't want him to know that that was the answer. And then because I was angry at him, suddenly furious, hot with rage. Because he was the reason the answer was no.

Did he really think I'd escaped all this intact? That I could love him and he could kill people and then I could just go on and live a normal life? That I could have those things now, no harm done? Didn't he realize what he'd *done*?

Pressure was building at my temples.

"The Gardaí," I said evenly. "You told them you know something about the new cases. That's why I'm here."

"Ali, I'm … I *am* sorry. Really. For all of this."

A beat of silence passed.

"Why did you do it?"

The question had been on my mind for the last ten years, and on my lips since I'd walked into this room. I hadn't planned to ask him it but now I realized that, on some subconscious level, the opportunity to ask was why I'd come to Dublin. Not to do the right thing, but to find out why Will had chosen, all those years ago, to do the wrong one.

Five times.

And, after each time, he'd come home and tell me he loved me. Convince me that he did. That he *could*.

The liar.

But Will acted like he hadn't heard. "Who told you?"

"Told me what?"

"That I was … That I'd been charged."

It was uncomfortably warm. I could feel trickles of

moisture clinging to my temples and sitting under my eyes. I slid a finger up under my glasses to wipe them away.

"I don't want to talk about back then," I said.

"You're the one who just asked me why I did it."

"And you haven't answered me."

"This is part of it."

"What is?"

"Who told you I'd been charged?"

I sighed, frustrated. "What can that possibly have to do with—"

"It's why it had to be you," Will said softly. "Why this had to be."

The room started to feel as if all the air had leaked out of it, like there'd been a finite amount and now we were nearing the danger point. I imagined an alarm sounding, imagined me having to rush out, to run away, and leave him here.

"Shaw," I said. "Shaw told me."

"And what did you think? Did you believe him? Did you think I could have done that?"

"What has this got to do with—"

"Ali, *please*."

I looked back at the man in scrubs, the nurse. He was leaning against the wall with his arms folded, watching us. He couldn't have been more than ten feet away and, in this silent space, was surely privy to everything Will was saying.

I turned back to Will. "You told the Gardaí you had information."

"I do. And I'm getting to it. Just … Please. Tell me, Ali. Did you believe them? Did you think I was guilty?"

I really didn't want to go back to that weekend,

but I also wanted to leave this room. I needed to know what he knew.

So now, I pulled open the door to it, just a crack.

I thought it was my fault for not knowing. That Liz was dead because of me. That you couldn't possibly have been capable of love, so everything with us had been a lie.

And I thought that I couldn't possibly have not *known, and I couldn't imagine you killing Liz, and I believed our love, so the Gardaí were as wrong as they could be.*

"I don't remember," I said, shutting it again. "It was a long time ago."

Will waved his hand, indicating the room. "You're telling *me*?"

"I don't see how this matters. I'm here because you told the Gardaí—"

"I *know* what I told the Gardaí!"

The rise in Will's voice instantly drew the attention of the nurse. I saw movement in my peripheral vision and when I turned, he'd taken a step toward us and was wearing a look of intense concern on his face.

"It's all right, Alek," Will said, holding up a hand. "I'm sorry. I'm fine. Everything's fine."

The nurse—Alek—frowned. "You sure?"

"Yes. Sorry."

Alek lingered for a moment before stepping back again.

Will looked back to me, pleadingly.

I didn't know where he was going with this, but I didn't want to go with him. I also wanted out of that room. Him being in here, with me, right in front of me—it was pulling on that damn door, rattling it in its frame, threatening to yank it off its hinges.

"I suppose," I said, "I thought there must be something to it. They only charge people with crimes when there's enough evidence to convict them. And you told them you did it. You'd confessed."

That had always been the worst bit, the deepest cut, because there was no getting around it. It couldn't be explained away. My imagination had worked overtime to come up with innocent scenarios that accounted for almost everything else, but there was nothing to reconcile the fact that Will had told the Gardaí that he'd killed those five girls.

A memory, slipping around the door: Shaw perched on an armchair in my parents' front room, shaking his head and saying, "You don't want to know what he told us he did to them. What they must have gone through …" while my mother's pale face glared at him furiously and my father grimaced like he was experiencing chest pain.

"So you believed them?" Will asked.

"I believed *you*."

"But you must have heard I'd been arrested before you heard I'd confessed?"

"I don't know," I lied. "I don't remember."

"You know me, Ali."

"Yeah, well." I folded my arms. "I *thought* I did."

"It didn't make any sense to you, did it? What they said I did. It didn't then and it still doesn't now. Am I right?"

I didn't respond. I was afraid to. Because he *was* right.

But then, when would something like this ever make sense?

"It didn't make any sense," Will said, lowering his voice to just above a whisper, "because *it wasn't me*."

The silence that came after that seemed to pulse and throb. Or maybe that was just the pain inside my head, turning up the dial now as the seconds ticked by.

"It wasn't me," Will said again. "I'm not the Canal Killer."

I looked at him for a long moment. Then I said, "When did you change your mind?" I hadn't planned for it to come out in such a sarcastic tone, but I wasn't sorry when it did.

"I didn't change my mind," Will said, "I always—"

"You confessed."

"Yes, but they made—"

"And you pleaded guilty."

"I was advised to by my solicitor."

"And in ten years, Will, you've never once said this before."

"How would *you* know?"

I hadn't spoken to him since he'd been arrested. At first, I'd been desperate to, and it was a hysterical desperation. Screaming and wailing at my parents, sobbing for hours in my room. I remember feeling like I wouldn't be able to take another breath unless I got to see him, until I could touch him and tell him that everything was going to be okay.

But then he'd confessed.

"So you don't actually know anything," I said. "I see." I moved to go.

"No, no, wait, Ali. *Wait.*" There was something new in his voice. Panic? Movement in my peripheral vision again: Alek coming toward us. "I *do* know something, Ali. I do. I … I know who killed those girls. The recent ones. It's …" Will swallowed hard.

"It's the same guy who killed the girls back then."

I stood up then, the chair legs screeching against the floor tiles.

"It wasn't me," Will continued, talking faster now. "It really wasn't. It was *him*. And now he's back. I think he went away after they arrested me, went somewhere else, laid low until he was sure I'd got the blame. But now he's back in Dublin and back at it and I'd actually be glad about that, in a way, if it wasn't for the fact that the first thing that the Gardaí say is not, hey, maybe this is the real killer and that's why we couldn't get all the facts to fit back then but, hey, here's a copycat at work and I bet Will Hurley *gave him the idea*."

Alek reached us.

"I think that's enough for now," he said to me. He jerked his chin toward the door, indicating that I should leave.

Behind me, I heard the handle of the door turn.

"You have to help me prove this," Will said. "You're the only one I can ask. Ali, I need your help. I need … I need *you*."

No one but Will had ever said those words to me and I'd forgotten the effect they could have.

Intoxicating, like a spell.

For a moment, I felt frozen in place.

"I didn't want to do this to you," he went on. "If there was any other way … But I don't know what else I can do. If I say I'm sorry, they say what I've done is finally sinking in. If I say I'm not, they say I'm a cold-blooded killer who can't feel remorse. I just don't know what—" His voice cracked. "I didn't know what else to do."

"Will," Alek said, "come on, now. That's enough."

"Time's up," a new, loud, authoritative voice said: Garda O'Neill's, from behind me.

I was shaking, my blood hot with adrenaline, and when I turned around to face him, I nearly fell into the poor guy with relief. He motioned for me to move toward the door and I gladly obeyed.

"I didn't want this," Will said, calling at me over O'Neill's shoulder now. "I didn't want to bring you here. But you're all I've got. You know me, Ali. You're the only person who ever really did. And despite what you say, I know the truth. I know that you didn't believe it. I know you didn't because *I've seen proof.*"

My cheeks began to burn.

"Let's get him out of here," I heard O'Neill say, presumably to Alek.

I stumbled out of the room, pulling at my jacket, shuffling desperately out of it. Everything was sticking to me. The hair at the back of my neck was damp. I went straight to the far side of the corridor and leaned my forehead against the wall there for a second. The bare cement was mercifully cool.

I closed my eyes.

A hand on my arm: Malone, gently turning me around, slowly leading me away.

I let him bring me a few feet down the hall before I reeled on him.

"What *is* this?" I said. "Why did you bring me here?" Malone looked confused and I remembered then: they weren't listening. "He said he's innocent. That the"—I made air quotes—"*real killer* is the one who's out there killing those girls now. He's … He's—" I stopped to take a deep breath, to calm down. "He doesn't know anything. This was all just a game. But you guys, you took him at his word and brought me here, brought me back into all this, and for what? *Why?*"

Malone looked down the hall. I did too. Will was being led out of the room where we'd had our meeting, flanked by an angry-looking O'Neill and an annoyed-looking Shaw. Alek followed behind, smiling at me apologetically before following the rest of them around the corner and out of sight.

Malone looked back at me. "The thing is, Alison …" He bit his lip. "When Will says he's innocent, I think he might be telling the truth."

Sundays, they're for fishing.

This one is cold with painfully bright sun. He rises early, does his exercises and drives to three different newsagents so he can buy a copy of every Sunday paper without drawing attention to himself. He leaves his coat in his car at the first one, pulls on a woolen hat before entering the second and wears his coat going into the last. Everywhere has security cameras these days.

He parks then at a blustery Sandymount Strand, facing the sea, the gray cement of the Poolbeg chimneys an anomaly against the expanse of blue sky. Only runners and dog-walkers are on the seafront path this early in the morning, and his is one of just six vehicles in the car park.

Sitting in the driver's seat, he scans each page of each newspaper until the tips of his right thumb and forefinger are black with ink.

Jennifer has slipped from the front pages but there is no shortage of coverage inside. A few of the glossy magazine supplements have longer features reminding everyone what happened ten years ago, drawing comparisons, asking what the connection could be. For Jennifer, they have photos credited to Instagram accounts, condolences shared on Facebook, and a screenshot of her final, inane tweet (*Getting ready is the best bit about going out. It's all downhill from here!*), granted an undeserving resonance now by her dying less than ten hours later. The writers all ask the same question—why?—even though the answer is right there, all over their pages. There is, however, some talk of a curfew being imposed on St. John's students. That's something.

Just before ten o'clock, he leaves the car at the beach and starts the walk to the coffee shop to see Amy. It will take about twenty minutes, he thinks. She'll be there by then.

At Pembroke Road a young girl dressed all in black—a work uniform, he thinks—crosses to his side of the road and falls into step a few feet behind him. She's talking loudly on the phone. He stops, pulls his own phone from a pocket and frowns at the screen, letting her overtake him. It's just as he suspected: white buds are fixed in her ears, the cord threaded through her fingers, one short stretch held close to her mouth with her right index and middle fingers. That's why she's talking so loudly—because she doesn't realize she is. And she looks like she's talking to herself too, but she either doesn't know that or doesn't care.

He doesn't get this, this epidemic. There are hundreds, maybe thousands of people, walking around the streets of Dublin doing exactly the same thing. It drives him crazy. Just this past week he'd been passing a restaurant when a woman walked out its door and said, "Well, *hello*!" and he'd stopped and turned toward her, thinking she was addressing him, thinking she was someone he knew from work, maybe. He saw the little white buds just in time.

And they all talk so *loudly*, these earbud people. You can hear everything they say from several steps behind. Don't they realize the information they're giving away to anyone who cares to collect it? Don't they read the papers? Don't they see what's going on?

Really, he should do something. Draw this girl's attention to the risks she's taking, to the potential danger she's putting herself in.

But he has to go see Amy.

The coffee shop is just off Upper Baggot Street and huge, a big open space filled with overstuffed armchairs and communal tables. It's supposed to have a rustic, recycled look to it, but in reality everything is brand new, carefully arranged by the chain's corporate-America overlords.

He hates the place.

She's sitting at one of the communal tables, facing him. He's not sure it's her at first, it's been so long since he's seen her. He takes his coffee to the condiments stand, slowly selects a brown sugar while watching her out of the corner of his eye.

It's her all right. Definitely.

He chooses a seat on the opposite side of the table, but not directly across from her. There are plenty of empty seats elsewhere in the cafe; it would look suspicious to be any closer. He can't see any cameras but no doubt there's some sort of video-feed security system in here too.

This can't be a memorable encounter, at least not for anyone but him.

As he sits down, she glances up at him. But that's all. Her attention is reserved for her phone. She's holding it in her right hand, swiping at the screen with her thumb, while taking frequent sips from the cereal-bowl-sized coffee mug in her left. All he can see in it is frothy milk. Two hefty texts with the grubby, off-white page-ends of secondhand books sit on the table in front of her, a St. John's College academic diary sitting on top of them.

He takes his own phone out and starts swiping at it.

He lets a minute pass.

Then he says, "Sorry—is the Wi-Fi working for you?"

She looks up at him, frowning slightly, while she absorbs the surprise of the interruption. For a moment he worries she'll recognize him, remember him from their brief encounter several months before.

It's okay if she does. He can just leave her be. It's not yet too late.

But she doesn't.

She says, "Um … yeah?" and twists her wrist, angling the screen of her phone at him. A square photograph. The familiar banner text across the top. "It's working fine for me."

He smiles. "I bet I'm doing it wrong."

He goes back to his phone. Waits until he senses her having gone back to hers.

Opens up Instagram. Selects SEARCH, selects PLACES. The first option in the menu is NEAR CURRENT LOCATION. He scrolls, but the coffee shop is not listed.

St. John's, however, is. They are less than a block from the main campus entrance. He taps that. Thumbnails of pictures taken on campus fill his phone's screen.

"Ah," he says to Amy. "Working now."

She smiles at him briefly.

He scrolls down, past POPULAR to MOST RECENT. There she is, right at the top: a picture of her coffee and her textbooks above a caption complaining that the college library is too cold and doesn't allow hot drinks. Her username is some nonsense involving a word he can't make sense of and a string of numbers that seem random. She's even entered her name as "Aims B', which explains why he failed to find her on the app just by searching.

No matter now.

He should wait until he gets home—and he will, to really study them—but he can't resist scrolling quickly through her pictures, conducting an initial scan, careful to keep any view of his phone's screen away from her.

Book covers. They'll tell him what classes she's likely taking, and he can use the St. John's class schedule, available online if you know where to look, to find out when and where those classes will be.

Selfies taken in her bedroom show the view from her window. They'll help him pinpoint which campus accommodation block she's in, maybe even what floor she lives on.

Regular postings from repeat locations—a fast-food restaurant, a local park, the dressing room of a high-street clothing store—will fill in the blanks for him about the rest of her daily routine.

There's plenty here to add to her file, plenty to add

to what he's already gleaned from her Facebook page. That's how he found out she was coming here. A friend posted about how horrible the college library was, and Amy commented underneath: *That's why I go to the Starbucks. Warm, wi-fi AND caffeine. Really quiet early on Sunday mornings. (Most peeps in bed hungover?!) You should try it!*

But this, this account, these photos—it is much more valuable. The information they don't realize they're sharing always is.

Sundays, they're for fishing.

It's not even eleven o'clock and he's already caught all that he needs.

alison, now

I opened my eyes expecting to see the hotel entrance, but Malone had parked the car on a suburban street. My neck ached from resting my head against the vertical strap of the seatbelt, my jacket was crumpled in a heap on my lap and the thin material of my T-shirt felt cold and clingy against my back. All I wanted to do was wash the morning off me with a hot shower, crawl back into my hotel bed, and sleep for as long as my body would let me.

Sleep and forget.

"Where are we?" I asked Malone.

In front of us was a complex of seventies-era red-brick apartment blocks, mostly hidden behind leafy green trees. To my left, a row of kegs was stacked outside the entrance to a pub so quaint it could be on a "Greetings from Dublin" postcard. Emerald-green tiles clad the exterior and stained-glass windows protected the patrons' privacy, preventing passersby from peering inside. It looked like the kind of place that refused to show sports or play music. The kind of place that inspired the Irish pub back in Breda, which enthusiastically advertised the fact that it did both.

"A good place for breakfast," he said, opening the driver's door. He was out of the car before I could tell him I wasn't hungry, that I didn't have the energy to be. I grabbed my jacket and got out too, getting a whiff of stale beer as I did.

As I followed him across the street, I felt a vibration in my jeans pocket: my phone was ringing. Sal, no doubt. I let it go to voicemail and hoped she'd assume I was deep in a codeine-soaked slumber. I should text her soon, though, or she might get worried and call around.

We'd parked outside a café, a tidy storefront with a green awning stretched out over two sets of chrome table and chairs. The ashtrays on them were filled with rainwater, black cigarette butts floating inside. A few buzz words *du jour* were stenciled on the café's windows: FRESH, NOURISH, CLEAN. Inside, only three tables were occupied, all by lone diners. It was uncomfortably quiet. There were no sounds other than our shoes on the floor, the chipping of cutlery against china, and, deep in the background, the smooth patter of talk radio turned down low.

The hostess greeted us with a wide smile, and I realized we must look like a couple. I briefly fantasized about telling her the truth: that Malone was a Garda detective and I was a serial killer's ex-girlfriend brought here under false pretences to meet with him for the first time in ten years.

Best not, though.

We took the furthest table from the other diners and the door. Malone ordered full Irish breakfasts, overriding my request for no food at all. Two unappetizing plates of greasy fried things appeared in front of us minutes later along with a large glass beaker, the kind they used to have in the science lab at school. This one, mercifully, was filled with filter coffee. I quickly downed a cup's worth, imagining that I could feel the caffeine bubbling in my bloodstream. I cut up the various pig parts on my plate and moved them around until it looked like there was a little bit less of them than before, just to be polite.

Then I leaned back in my seat and said: "What's going on here? Really?"

Malone wiped at his mouth with the back of his hand. "We're the same age. I was a first-year in college back then too. NUI Galway. I went there before I applied to Templemore. I remember sitting with my mother watching the press conference about Will's arrest on RTÉ, and her turning to my father and saying, 'It really couldn't be any worse, could it?' But"—Malone put his elbows on the table, leaned forward—"it could be, Alison. It could be a *lot* worse. We could have got the wrong guy."

"But you didn't."

"How do you know?"

"I don't have to," I said, "because it isn't up to me to decide. Will was arrested because there was evidence that pointed to him, then he confessed, then he pleaded guilty. And a judge had to rubber-stamp the lot, right?" This was the argument I'd always clung to. That it didn't matter what I thought, because I wasn't trained in the law or crime detection. I was therefore absolved of all responsibility when it came to determining his guilt. All I had to do was accept the verdict of the ones who *were* responsible for such decisions and as nonsensical as it had once seemed to me, I didn't see that I had any choice but to do exactly that. "I don't see why—or how—him suddenly changing his mind ten years later changes anything."

"The new cases," Malone said. "I can't talk to you very much about them, because they're open. But you know we've had two and we're due a third any day. Now, there's things we can do to try to prevent another one happening. We're talking to St. John's about a campus curfew, for example, and we'll have the canal crawling with plain-clothes officers every night this week—"

"A campus curfew didn't work so well last time."

"Yes. Well." Malone cleared his throat. "Even if we stop him, we still need to catch him. As of right now, we've nothing to go on. No witnesses to any of his crimes, no physical evidence that we can match to anyone in our database, no motive that we can establish beyond he just wants to do this. It seems he's stalking them in the run-up to the attacks, yeah, but we don't know why. Why these girls in particular. We've nothing yet that might help us determine who he's out there following right now. We've got analysts building models of these girls' last days, looking for patterns, connections, but we have mountains of data to get through and we only established a connection between our two victims one week ago. And that kind of thing takes time. We don't have enough of it."

"I understand all that," I said. "I do. I get why you went to him. But Will was just wasting your time."

"The original Canal Killer case," Malone said, "the team on it, they worked around the clock. For months. They brought in help from other jurisdictions. Other countries, even. They consulted with the FBI. We're talking about a lot of man-hours, Alison. I've seen the files. The boxes take up half a warehouse. If Will is innocent, I can add all that legwork to my case. I can use it. If this is the same guy, I can look for him in there—because he *will* be in there. He has to be."

This sounded like wishful thinking to me.

"But Will *isn't* innocent," I said.

"Because he pleaded guilty, there was no trial. The evidence against him was never interrogated in open court. So …" Malone turned up his palms.

"But a judge has to sign off on it all, right? Or the DPP or whoever. You—or the Gardaí back then, Shaw—they had to prove their case against Will regardless. The evidence was good enough for that. And I don't know if I mentioned this, but *he confessed*."

"Plenty of people confess to things they didn't do," Malone said.

I made a face. "Even murder?"

"Sometimes, yes."

"And then they stick to that story for ten years or more?"

"No," Malone admitted. "That *is* unusual."

"Well, there you go."

I picked up my cup of coffee and drained it. Malone remained quiet, twisting his own cup between his fingers. It gave me the opportunity to study his face.

He looked tired, I realized. Exhausted, even. The team on this new guy, they were probably working around the clock too.

"Look," I said, "I get it. I do. You want to catch this guy. *I* want you to catch this guy. But this feels like ... this feels like clutching at straws. Sorry."

"Just imagine for a second," Malone said, "that Will *is* innocent." I couldn't—wouldn't—but I didn't have the energy to argue. "What's the evidence that suggests otherwise?" Malone pulled a sugar packet out of the cup in the center of the table, pushed his plate to one side and lay the packet down flat in front of him. He tapped it with a finger. "First of all, Will can be connected to all the victims. Both he and they were all students at St. John's and all living in campus accommodation. One of them, Lauren Murphy—the first one—even lived in the same block as him, on the same floor. And there was, ah, Liz Whelan, his last ..." I tried not to react to this and thankfully Malone pushed on, giving me no opportunity to. "Then we have the folder." He laid another sugar packet down. "Found in Will's locker in the lobby of the college library after his arrest. Filled with detailed information on each of the victims, to varying degrees. Not only was the locker secured with a padlock and assigned to Will, but they pulled five prints from its cover that matched those of Will's left hand." A third and a fourth sugar packet. "A key forensic find: a spot of dried blood under the desk in Will's room is a DNA match for Ciara O'Shea, his penultimate victim, although she was found last. Found while he was in Garda custody, in fact. And Liz's mobile phone records show that she called Will at 3:35 a.m. and that the call lasted for forty-three seconds. But Will says he never spoke to her."

"I thought you were arguing that he's innocent," I said.

"I'm about to."

"But all that makes it sound—"

"Open and shut, right?"

"Well, yeah."

"But, all evidence is open to interpretation," Malone said. "In isolation, what's the St. John's connection, really? Going by that logic every one of the school's six thousand and something students is a suspect too." He slid one sugar packet away to the side. "And Will knew Liz socially, so the phone call in itself doesn't prove anything. He might have had the phone in bed, rolled over and pressed the answer button by accident." Another sugar packet gone. He tapped one of the two left with a finger. "Now the folder, that's interesting. It was in Will's locker and his prints were on it. If we stop there, it's cut and dried. But consider this: the information inside had been typed on A4 pages, on a computer, so there was no handwriting for us to compare. And there were other prints on the cover—lots of them—that we couldn't identify. And if Will had been handling it a lot, and he would've had to in order to put it together, then why would there only be one handprint of his on the whole thing?" He pushed the one packet aside. "Now we're down to just one piece of evidence, the blood spot. Why would there be any blood in his room, when the murder took place in the canal? And why just one tiny spot of it? And why didn't the forensic team find it on their first search of the room? How come they didn't spot it until their second? There're enough questions there for reasonable doubt." He pushed the last packet aside.

Now there were none in front of him.

"Right," I said. "And remind me: Which sugar packet is him confessing to the crimes?"

Malone half-smiled. "Let's pretend for a second that Will is innocent. We'd have to explain how the blood got into his room and the folder into his locker, right? If Will had nothing to do with those girls' murders, who put them there if it wasn't Will himself?" Malone stopped, presumably expecting me to suggest an answer, but I didn't want to play this game. "The *real killer*," he continued. "The real killer would've had to put them there, presumably with the aim of framing Will. What would've needed to happen for *that* to happen?" Another pause for my benefit, another opportunity I didn't take to speak. "He had to have known him. Right? The killer knew Will. Which suggests that Will knew the killer."

I suddenly had an overwhelming desire to lie down. I was tempted to make a pillow out of my folded arms and lay my head down on the table, like we used to do in primary school during Quiet Time. Instead, I leaned on the table and rested my head on a hand.

I didn't want to hear any more of this.

"There was no trial," Malone was saying. "No one whose job it was to drill down into all this stuff and ask if it really pointed to Will's guilt. And he was only ever interviewed as the prime suspect. Never as a witness. They picked him up thinking they already had their man. It's textbook confirmation bias. Who knows what might have been missed? If we set his guilt aside, we might find he has information that can help us catch this guy. The real guy. The one who's out there now, following his next victim as we speak."

"Is this …?" I could feel color rushing to my cheeks at the mere thought of it, *at the anticipation* of the thought of it. "Are you telling me all this because of what … what I said to that newspaper?"

Malone frowned.

"Because that doesn't mean anything," I rushed on. "I was young and I was confused and I was upset—and I didn't know that before it'd go to print, he'd have bloody admitted he did it."

"I didn't—"

"What I mean is, don't take that as, like, evidence that I think he might be innocent. Because it's not. I didn't have all the information. I think he's guilty. I know he is."

"No," Malone said. "I know. I wasn't even … I hadn't even thought about—"

"Good."

My face grew hot in the silence that followed.

"Why do you want this so bad?" I asked Malone then. "It's almost like you *need* him to be innocent."

"And you don't need him to be guilty?"

"I don't need any of this. I don't even want to be here."

Our waitress materialized beside us and asked us if we were done. We let her take away the plates, and Malone asked for the bill. When she'd left us again, he said, "I knew Louise Farrington wasn't an accident."

"You … What?"

"The first new victim. Shaw and I caught the case. He thought she'd just had a slip and fall, drunk on the way home. She was caught on a CCTV camera walking along the canal alone, there were no witnesses, and the state pathologist said the injury to her forehead could be consistent with a fall. But something about it felt off to me. I didn't see how she could've fallen on the path and then ended up in the river by herself. It didn't match the physical evidence at the scene at all, the lack of it."

"I thought you weren't supposed to tell me—"

"But I didn't push it. I went with Shaw. And that's why we've already lost two months on this, why we didn't even know this guy was out there until last week. I won't make the same mistake again."

"And what does Shaw think?"

"Of what?"

"Of Will."

"That was his case too." Malone looked me straight in the eye. "We have to take that into consideration."

I wasn't sure what I was supposed to infer from this, only that I was supposed to infer something.

I didn't want to hear any more.

I put my hands back down on the table and he reached across and covered them with his. Such tenderness was, at best, a distant memory, and in the here and now, like an electric shock against my skin. I jerked my hand away like I'd been burned by him.

"I'm sorry," he said quickly.

I nodded toward the door. "Can we go?"

"Yes."

"Good."

"Are you going to leave now? Go home?"

"Why would I stay?"

"Look," Malone said, "Will didn't just want to meet with you. He said he'd only talk to you, period. But now

I need to talk to *him*. So if I'm going to do that, I'm going to need your help. And, you know, it might help both of us." He leaned forward, over the table, lowered his voice. "Don't you want to know for sure what happened back then, Alison? And *why* it did?"

alison, now

The hotel turned out to be just around the corner from the café, so close that the thirty-second journey there in Malone's car left me embarrassed. In fact, part of that red-brick apartment complex actually faced onto the canal.

He turned to me as we pulled up outside the main entrance, looking like he was ready to play another episode of *Malone Convinces Alison to Stay and Help*.

"I have your number," I said quickly, and got out of the car.

I was too tired to think, and grateful for it. I made my way to my room on autopilot. But when I got there, what I saw coldly snapped me back awake.

The door was open.

I stopped with my plastic keycard suspended in midair, ready to swipe, staring at the bright inch or so of daylight wedged between the edge of the door and the frame. The DO NOT DISTURB sign I'd left on the handle was still there; housekeeping shouldn't have been inside.

So why was it open? I doubted it had been my doing. I was sure when I'd left the room earlier, I'd pulled the door shut behind me and waited for the confirmation *click*.

I looked up and down the hall. There was no one in it but me.

I strained to listen, to see if I could detect any movement or noise coming from within the room.

Nothing.

I called out a "Hello?" but got no response.

When I pressed against the wood, once, gently, the door swung back, slowly revealing my unmade bed and my small suitcase sitting on top of it, the lid down but not zipped, the legs of a pair of sweat pants spilling out over the side.

Definitely not housekeeping, then.

I took a step forward, onto the threshold, called out "Hello?" again.

Still nothing.

I thought of something then: the electronic door lock.

Years ago I'd had to attend a Suncamp conference in London, which involved staying three nights in a soulless airport chain hotel that seemed to have been built at the end of the main runway, going by the jet engine roar outside. The real treat of the place was how every time I returned to my room and slid my keycard into the lock, the door refused to open for at least the first three or four attempts. Same thing was happening to my colleagues. I'd mentioned this to the front desk on check-out, and got a weary, "Yeah, it's the batteries," in response. Apparently there were batteries in these doors locks, that's how they worked, and these batteries lasted a certain length of time, and in this hotel they'd all been installed at the same time during a renovation a few years back, and were now all dying en masse. Was that what had happened here?

I slid my keycard through the lock. Nothing. No click, no indicator light glowing red or green. I didn't want to chance closing the door and repeating it from the outside in case I couldn't get back in, but I was willing to believe the lock was dead. Could that account for the door being open, though? If the battery died in the electronic part, did the actual door lock, the mechanical bit, just release?

I decided I was tired enough to decide that it did.

I went into the room, shutting the door behind me with a loud *bang*. I stopped first at the bathroom, throwing its door open, flicking on the lights. Back into the main room, pulling open the wardrobe doors, flipping back the top of the suitcase, appraising the arrangement of pillows and sheets on the bed. I unzipped the compartment on the underside of the lid of my case and slid my hand back and forth inside it until they met my passport. Everything seemed to be just as I'd left it, except for the door itself.

I thought I should ring the front desk about my dead door lock, but if I did they'd send someone up to fix it and that would delay my shower and sleep. I'd do it later. Afterward. Not now.

I closed the curtains, kicked off my shoes and wandered back into the bathroom. I looked at the bath, considering it, but I was so tired I was sure I'd fall asleep in there. Instead, I pulled off my clothes and got into the shower. I stayed in the spray until my fingertips started to prune and the skin on my chest was bright red from the heat. There was a luxurious toweling robe hanging on the back of the bathroom door. I wrapped it around myself as tight as it would go.

Thoughts of Will—memories, images of him from today, arguments for and against Malone's theory from the voice in my head—were just beneath the surface, all clamouring to burst through.

I pushed them down. I knew how to. I'd gotten good at it, over the years.

And if I didn't, I knew Liz would come next.

I filled the tiny kettle at the bathroom sink and then, back out in the main room, set it to boil. There were Barry's teabags in the little amenities tray. Even though I'd had at least one cup of Cork's own brew every day of my adolescence, I didn't think I'd tasted it once in the last ten years. I carried the cup back to the bed, setting it down on the nightstand before climbing under the covers, and then promptly fell asleep before I could take a single sip.

I dreamed I was back at St. John's, only with Sal instead of Liz. Will was coming to meet us, old Will, *my* Will, and I was so excited that I was finally getting to introduce Sal to him, to tell her about him, that when the ringing of a phone pulled me back to the surface, I felt disappointed.

I didn't know how long I'd been out, but I was groggy enough to know that it had been a while. Hours maybe. My hair was damp now more than wet, and the light in the room seemed different. I swapped out my cold, wet pillow for a dry one before I reached over to pick up the phone beside the bed, putting the receiver to my ear as I lay back down.

"Hello?"

Silence on the line.

"Hello?" I said again.

Beep-beep-beep.

Whoever it was had hung up. Wrong number, probably. A single incorrect digit would get you through to the wrong hotel room.

The LCD display on the phone was showing the time: 3:30 p.m. I'd been asleep for more than three hours. I went to the window and scanned the view I had of the street outside. Nothing much had changed from earlier, except for a clouded sky and slightly more traffic.

I looked across the water to scan the opposite bank.

That's when I saw him.

He was sitting on a bench by the water. The canal was between us, so his features were mostly indistinct to me. But he was definitely a *he*, wearing black tracksuit pants with a white stripe down the side and a bright red baseball cap. And, it seemed to me, he was looking up at my window.

Looking right at me.

The phone rang again.

I didn't say anything this time, just held the receiver at my ear and waited instead.

"Alison?" It was Malone.

"Oh," I said. "Hi."

"Were you sleeping?"

"No … Well, I was. I woke up before you called."

There was noise on the line. Wherever Malone was calling from, there were a lot of voices in the background.

"Everything okay?" he asked.

"Um"—I stifled a yawn—"yeah."

"Alison, there's been a development."

"What does that mean? Something's happened? What?"

"I'd rather tell you in person."

"Why?"

"And I need to show Will something."

I rolled my eyes. "You mean you need *me* to show Will something."

"Yes."

"What?"

Malone hesitated. "Really, I'd prefer not to talk about this over the phone. I can come to you?"

We arranged to meet at the hotel in an hour's time.

After I hung up, I went back to the window.

The man on the bench was gone.

alison, then

"What," Liz whispered from beside me, "the actual—"

My mother's head snapped toward us, and Liz fell silent, midsentence.

"I know it's small …" the estate agent said. His was wearing gold cufflinks in the shape of little keys and a pink pocket square, and his hair was so thick with gel that it looked to have hardened. "But look at it this way: you won't have far to travel to your first cup of coffee in the morning, will you?" He laughed heartily at his own joke.

"That's certainly true," my mother muttered. She glanced at the A4 page on which she'd printed a list of all the properties we'd booked appointments to view today. "And this one was …?"

"Only eight hundred a month."

The four of us were squeezed into a room smaller than my bedroom at home. But while my room had a bed, a wardrobe and a desk, this had a bed, a two-cupboard-wide kitchenette, a washing machine, a wardrobe, a dining table for two and, in the far corner, a tiny bathroom whose entire floor was also the shower tray and which had a plastic, accordion-style door because there just wasn't any room left for the arc of a normal door to swing out or in.

Everything looked grimy or damp, or both, and nothing matched. If I'd been told every item had been saved from a Dumpster, I wouldn't have blinked. The journey to the room hadn't been anything to write home about either. It was one of ten bedsits carved out of a three-story Georgian terrace house that seemed to be rotting from the outside in.

As a test, I put one hand on the cold, damp mattress of the single bed. I reached out and touched the buttons on the microwave with the other.

The crazy thing was it wasn't the worst property we'd seen today, nor was it the cheapest.

My mother pointed at us. "There's two of them, though."

The agent didn't miss a beat. "We can swap the bed for bunks."

Liz and I exchanged a glance.

We already knew what our lives were going to be like in Dublin; we'd spent the last year talking of little else. This place … They wouldn't fit into it. Looking around, I wasn't even sure I'd risk bringing my laptop in here. I wasn't even sure I'd risk sleeping in here myself. With each viewing our Dublin daydreams were increasingly just that: dreams. The reality was devastating. If I had to live in a place like this, I wasn't sure I even wanted to go to college here. I might just stay in Cork.

"Well," my mother said, "I think we've seen enough."

As we walked back down the stairs, carpeted in an ugly pattern of brown and orange, Liz whispered to me, "I bet we'll see this place again—on the news in a few years' time. Bodies under the patio. Mark my words."

My mother's phone rang and after she'd answered it and listened for a few moments, she turned to us with a smile. "Your father's novenas must have worked, Ali. A letter arrived this morning: you got a room in Halls. Thank *God* for that."

When Liz called home, she had one too.

At the time, it felt like the best news either of us had ever got in our lives.

*****

We traveled by convoy to Dublin, each set of parents having to take a car, because our stuff—suitcases full of clothes, boxes of books, packages of brand-new bed linen—wouldn't fit in one.

St. John's offered the option of moving in on either the Friday or the Saturday ahead of Freshers' Week, with an action-packed schedule of orientation and welcome activities planned just for Halls residents all day Sunday. Liz and I opted to travel up Friday. We planned to swiftly dispose of our parents and then spend Saturday exploring our new college and the city beyond it.

At that stage, Dublin to me consisted of O'Connell Street (the Spire), Grafton Street (shopping), and Temple Bar (tourists). I knew about Molly Malone and the Phoenix Park, and on a school trip once we'd visited Leinster House and seen the Book of Kells in Trinity College. I knew about Stephen's Green, but to me it was a shopping center, not a historic park. The first time I'd seen the canal was when Liz and I had come up on the train to attend the St. John's open day back in November. Before then, I hadn't even known there *was* a canal. I was yet to find out there were actually two of them: the Grand on the south side of the city, the Royal on the north.

"This is a nice area," my father said as we drove parallel to the water, down Mespil Road, toward the St. John's campus.

My mother didn't share the sentiment. "You'd better be careful," she said to me, "walking along here at night. Look, there's no barrier there. You could easily fall in."

"Fall in?" I rolled my eyes. "Mam, seriously."

"I am serious. I've seen you fall in our front door after a night out."

There were eight accommodation blocks for St. John's undergrads, modern glass and steel structures dotted together in manicured grounds toward the south end of the campus. Although Liz and I ended up in different ones, they were side by side. Block A and Block B.

We were greeted by student helpers in St. John's T-shirts who checked us off lists and bestowed upon us our electronic keys. We let our fathers carry our stuff up into our new rooms and our mothers make up our beds with new linen, something we probably wouldn't do in a few months' time after a single gender studies module convinced us we knew more about the world than our parents had learned from decades of living in it. My mother also insisted on stuffing three bags of groceries into the fridge while my father walked the whole apartment, flicking every switch and making me promise that I'd tell someone about the two dud light bulbs he discovered on his rounds. I posed for pictures (me in my new room, me in my new kitchen, me and Mam on my new couch), waited while Mam had a little cry about her only child going off to college (as if this, after eighteen years, was somehow coming as a complete surprise) and then I shooed them out as quickly as I could.

As the door shut behind them and the apartment fell completely quiet and still, I felt a tremor of anxiety.

I was all on my own now.

In college.

In *Dublin*.

Thank God Liz was just next door.

She came knocking not ten minutes later, having rushed her parents off as well.

"I think they're going to get some dinner together," she said. "On *campus*, my dad said." She rolled her eyes. "Let's hide in here until they're gone."

"You hungry?" I nodded at the fridge. "Mam stocked that before she left. Because, you know, they don't have any shops here at all and there isn't a subsidized cafeteria less than five minutes' walk away where we can eat three meals a day on the cheap."

Liz rolled her eyes again. "Let's see what we got."

I went into my room to unpack more stuff, leaving the door open so I could chat with Liz while I did.

"Any sign of your roommate yet?" I asked her.

"No. I hope it's someone normal, though. You know what I was thinking? We could ask one of them to swap."

"Is that allowed?" I didn't want to start rule-breaking before classes had even begun.

"Oh, they won't know," Liz said dismissively.

"Yeah. I suppose … Well, we'll see."

The truth was I was secretly glad Liz and I had ended up in separate apartments. I wasn't at first, because it jarred so much with the idea of us at St. John's that I had replayed over and over in my head. And I was glad now that in this sea of strangeness, on this cliff edge of adventure, a familiar face was just next door.

But in between, I'd found myself a *little* excited at the thought of there being some distance between us. Liz was my best friend, but she was also prettier, louder, and more popular. I wasn't quiet, but people seemed to think I was when she was around. I wasn't shy, but somehow I felt myself acting that way whenever I went to new places with her. So I thought it might be nice to have the chance to meet new people for myself, *by* myself. To not, for once, come as part of a package where I always seemed to be the bonus material, never the main feature.

"Ali?" Liz called from the kitchen. "Lunch is served. Well, late lunch. *Very* late lunch."

She'd found the crockery and cutlery that came supplied, and laid the table with it. From the food my mother had brought, she'd assembled delicious-looking ham and cheese baguettes. Also on offer were a bowl of chips, a tub of prepared mango chunks and cans of Coke.

Seeing the spread, I realized I was starving. We'd stopped for breakfast at motorway services that morning, but it was nearly four in the afternoon now.

We got out my new laptop, set it on the end of the

table and put in a *Lost* DVD to entertain us while we ate.

"What do you want to do tonight?" Liz asked. "In *Dublin*."

"We live here now," I said. "Can you believe it?"

"And there's nobody to tell us what time to be home."

"So what's the plan?"

Liz gave me a look like she was about to say something unpopular.

"What?" I asked. "Just say it."

"You know what I *really* want to do?"

"What?"

"Even though this is our first night of freedom, and all that?"

"Go on …"

"I want to go get some greasy takeaway, bring it back here, and watch more *Lost*."

I looked at her for a beat, then started laughing.

"That's exactly what I want to do, too," I admitted. "I'm bloody exhausted."

"It's been way too much excitement for one day."

"We can be Freshers tomorrow."

"And we will," Liz said. "We'll Fresher hard."

"But tonight, we veg."

"Veg and *Lost*."

"That could be a crime-fighting duo."

Liz yawned. "I'm so glad we're on the same page here."

"Let's maybe not tell anyone about this, though."

"I was going to suggest the same thing to you."

"If anyone asks, we went clubbing."

"And the sun was up by the time we got in."

So that's what we did. We spent our first night as students in the Big Smoke carrying greasy cartons of Chinese food back to my new apartment and watching *Lost* on a laptop while sat on my scratchy little couch.

With our whole lives ahead of us, our new lives, waiting for us. Postponed just until the following morning.

That night was like an airlock, a safe passage between the home I shared with my parents in Cork and apartment A3 in St. John's Halls.

I remember thinking, *This is it. This is what being happy feels like.*

And, *It's only going to get better from here.*

*****

I was awake with the dawn the next morning, energized by the novelty of waking up in a new place and terrified that my new roommate would choose to arrive at 8:00 a.m. on a Saturday and meet me for the first time just as I fell out of bed.

She actually arrived just after nine. Claire from Sligo who was going to be studying International Law, and after introductions I stayed out of the way while a guy who I guessed was her boyfriend helped her move her stuff in.

"He's going to Trinity," she explained after he'd left. "He's in his second year there. He's not back until next week so he's driving back up home now." She stuck her hands in her pockets, rocked on her heels. "I don't know, like, *anyone* here."

"Well, you know me now," I said. "And my friend Liz is in the block next door, so soon you'll know her too." I hadn't heard from Liz yet this morning. I thought about sending her a text but then, emboldened by the fact that I was here, meeting new people without her, I suggested to Claire that we go for a stroll around campus. Liz was probably still sleeping anyway. She wasn't a morning person.

"My mother filled the fridge before she left," I said, "but didn't leave any tea or coffee. Are you up for going to find a café somewhere?"

But there was nothing, seemingly, happening on campus at this hour on the Saturday before Freshers' Week. Aside from a few more early move-ins, the place felt like a ghost town. The coffee kiosk beside the library building was closed. We wandered out onto the expensive residences of Haddington Road, walked past its imposing church, in the direction of Baggot Street. I logged all the street names, labeling the map I was building in my head.

I spotted an adorable little coffee shop with a white picket fence resting uneasily on the paving slabs on the footpath outside.

"How about there?" I said to Claire.

She nodded. "Sure."

We'd only been in there five minutes when Liz sent a text, asking if I was up yet. I told her where I was and said she should come meet us.

The door to the café was behind Claire's back, so I saw Liz before she did. And I knew right away that she was pissed off. She didn't even look at me as she approached the table—she was looking to her left, out the windows of the café—and when she plopped down beside me, all I got was a cold, "Hey."

"Hey," I said. "Did you find us okay?" I didn't get a response to this. Liz just picked up the menu and started studying it intensely. "I didn't want to wake you," I added lamely.

I knew why she was mad. If I'd woken up and discovered that Liz was already off having coffee with her new roommate and had gone without asking me to join them, I'd have been upset too. The difference is I wouldn't have let her know that. I wouldn't have thrown a tantrum, or got odd with her. It wasn't in me. I couldn't do it. But Liz, she could put on a bad humor with the flick of a switch.

Claire probably didn't notice because Liz launched the full charm offensive on her. She asked her millions of questions and cooed over the pictures of her boyfriend that Claire had on her phone. They were soon laughing and joking like old pals and I could see the little sliver of advantage I'd had with Claire, the half-hour I'd been able to bank with her before Liz showed up, steadily diminishing.

I talked to Claire, Liz talked to Claire, and Claire talked to us—and I hoped we all did that enough for Claire not to notice that Liz barely acknowledged me at all. She didn't even speak directly to me until we were back on campus, and parting ways.

Liz had said she'd unpacking to do, and I'd lied and said I did as well.

Then she turned to me and said, "I don't think I'll be going out tonight."

We'd made plans to make the acquaintance of the campus bar, a place nicknamed the Haddy.

I knew what my next line in this scene was. We'd

rehearsed it plenty. I was supposed to try to coax her out, giving her an opportunity to decline again. Or maybe I was supposed to say, "Fine, I won't either," and commit myself to staying in with her, to keep her company, while she sulked.

But I couldn't bring myself to. So instead I told Liz to call me if she changed her mind.

When we got back upstairs, Claire asked me how well I knew Liz.

"Very well," I said. "We've known each other since the first day of primary school. So for like, what? Thirteen years now?"

"Are you two good friends, then?"

I nodded. "Best friends."

"Oh."

Claire was frowning, confused.

There was a defense of Liz on my tongue. *The way she was this morning? She's not always like that. That's not what she's really like.*

But then I thought, *Let Liz make her own first impressions.*

That night, Claire and I went to the Haddy. I left my phone at home.

*****

The next morning, Liz was all smiles again. She'd knocked on the door of our apartment early in the morning and had a cup of bad instant coffee with Claire and me. She didn't ask me how I'd spent the previous evening, and I didn't volunteer any information. It was as if yesterday had just disappeared into the past, swallowed up like a stone by

the sea, leaving the surface smooth and unbroken again.
She did have news, though: her roommate had arrived.
Liz had Claire and I captivated as she dramatically doled
out little drops of the story. She'd woken up this morning to discover a suitcase sitting in the living room even
though she hadn't heard anyone come in. Next thing the
door to the other bedroom opens and out walks this girl,
dressed head to toe in black and with piercings in her
cheeks. (Liz showed us exactly where, more than once.)
The girl picks up the suitcase, hauls it into her room and
closes the door again without saying as much as a word
to Liz.

"So I'm living with a *psycho*," she declared. "You two
might have to let me move in here."

I knew Liz was joking, but my laugh was to make
sure that Claire did too. A shadow of something had
crossed the girl's face at the suggestion.

St. John's Halls had an entertainment committee
made up of and voted for by student residents, and the
last responsibility of the outgoing one was to organize
the orientation program for incoming freshers. Most
everybody had arrived by now and a huge tent had been
set up on the lawn to house us all. We sat through some
boring presentations on things like health and safety
and budgeting for food, and then after that, outside, the
fun began. There were ice-breaking games, challenges,
quizzes, "speed-friending," and a five-a-side football
game. A barbeque was laid on for lunch. We were all
given stickers to write our names and courses on, and
encouraged to wander around striking up conversations
with anyone and everyone we could.

Normally, this would've been the kind of thing that

would've made me want to curl up in a corner in a ball of dread and shame. I considered myself sociable, but I wasn't exactly the stranger whisperer. Liz usually paved a path for me. But there was a leveling aspect to this day that somehow made things easier. After all, we were *all* new. We were *all* first-years. We were *all* wandering around, blinking in the light of this new world, away from friends and family, very excited but also a little unsure.

We started collecting people. We met Lauren, who had never met Claire but it turned out they shared a mutual friend they could bond over. She was studying art history and lived in the apartment next to Liz. We met Ray, an American who'd turned down the chance to go to Harvard for a chance to come to Dublin (we all thought he was bonkers, and told him so) and whose smooth, TV accent we couldn't get enough of. We met Daisy, a fellow English literature student who was dressed like she'd been in a teleportation experiment gone slightly wrong. All her clothes seemed to be patchworks of other bits of things, pieces of material jaggedly and inexpertly sewn together in some sort of Frankenstein's monster–style couture. She introduced herself by saying she did PR for Essence, which I think we were supposed to know was a club in town, and that she could get us on the guest list for tonight if we wanted.

Someone said, "Let's go," and one by one, the rest of us fell in. I felt like I was being swept away on a wave, but I wasn't entirely unhappy about it. We split to go back to our rooms and change, with a plan to reconvene under the arch at the entrance in an hour's time.

Liz came to our place to get ready. Claire produced a bottle of Smirnoff and made us all vodka and Cokes.

"I brought something for you," Liz said to me. She reached into the bag of clothes she'd brought with her and pulled out a gorgeous silk shirt. It was silver with a spray of green and purple flowers up one side and it wrapped around, tying with a large purple ribbon at one side.

It was absolutely gorgeous. I owned nothing like it. I'd been planning to head out in jeans and a plain black top.

"Oh, Liz," I said. "That's beautiful."

"It's a bit big on me," she said. "Do you want to try it? I'll probably just dump it in the charity shop otherwise."

A bit big on me.

I ignored the dig because there was no way I wasn't wearing this top, even though it was a little big on me too. ("No," Liz said, adjusting it for me. "It fits great.") I put on a white string vest to counteract the way it gaped a bit at the front, and pulled the ribbon as tight as I could to stop the extra material from bunching too much around my waist.

"That looks *amazing* on you," Liz declared when I was done. "You *have* to wear it out tonight."

I turned in front of the mirrored wardrobe door. "I will. I might never take this off."

It turned out, of course, that by "did PR for," Daisy meant *stood on the street and handed out leaflets*, and that by "get you on the guest list," she meant *pay twenty euro and win the bouncers' approval and, yeah, okay, we'll let you in*. But the club played good music, we saw plenty of faces from Halls and a good time was had by all.

Until just after midnight, when I felt someone tug

at the ribbon around my waist, and then the entire shirt start to loosen and fall.

Some drunken idiot behind me had untied the knot.

When I turned around to confront him, he reached out his hands and pulled me in, and suddenly his vile breath was all I could smell. I tried to wriggle out of his arms, but he just pulled me tighter. I was about to bring my knee up as hard as I could between his legs when I felt him move away, and then realized he'd already been *pulled* away, and now this other guy was standing between the two of us, squaring up to him, staring him down.

"What are you doing to my girlfriend?" he demanded.

I looked up at him—up, because he was at least a foot taller than me. He had unruly blond hair, left natural, messy with no gel, and his skin was tanned like he'd just come back from the beach. He was wearing a bright white T-shirt which only accentuated this, especially in the dim lighting of the club. I could smell him, the scent of some cologne or deodorant or something, musky and masculine, not the Lynx Africa the spotty boys at home liked to indiscriminately douse themselves in.

The drunk idiot was looking him up and down. "*Girlfriend?*"

This must have sounded like a challenge, because my defender reached out and took my hand.

"Yeah," he said. "Girlfriend. So you better apologize to her, and then you better piss off."

The drunk idiot hesitated for a second, then did as he was told.

"Thanks a lot," I said after he staggered away. "I was just about to knee him in the balls."

"Oh, no, were you?" The guy turned to look over his shoulder. "Should I go get him? I can hold him in place for you."

"Nah," I said. "It's all right."

"Is your shirt okay?"

I looked down at it. "It will be when I tie it up again." I looked back up at him. "Which I will do when you let go of my hand."

"You can't do it with one?"

"No."

"You're not even going to *try*?"

I smiled. "Can I have my hand back, please?"

He let it go.

"I'm Alison, by the way."

"I'm Will."

alison, now

Malone said he'd be an hour, but he took closer to three. He called to say he'd been held up at the station and would be a little bit late, and then again to say he'd be a lot later than that. I hadn't booked a return flight and neither Shaw nor Malone had said anything about one, although before we'd left the Netherlands they'd made vague promises about my being back in time for work on Monday morning. Earlier, I'd checked the Aer Lingus website and found one seat left on that evening's flight to Amsterdam, mine for just over half a month's rent. I wasn't sure I could book it and send the bill to An Garda Síochána, so I waited. By the time Malone called to say he was parked outside, the seat was sold.

I wondered if that had been his strategy all along and how much longer, realistically, I was going to stay here.

It wasn't the only strategic move I suspected him of. I hadn't actually agreed to go see Will again, but Malone was waiting for me in his car with the engine running. As soon as I sat in, he took off. When I asked what the development had been, what it was he needed Will to see, he said it was in the trunk and that I'd have to wait until we got to the CPH to see for myself.

"What about my flight?" I asked as we idled at a red light at Leeson Street bridge. "Do I book that or …?"

"We can do that for you. I'll get someone at the station to do it. When do you want to go back?"

"Well, I suppose now it'll have to be tomorrow."

"I'll take care of it."

"Does anyone know I'm here?" I asked.

"We've kept knowledge of your involvement to as small a group as we possibly can. We don't want the press getting wind of it." Malone glanced at me. "Why? Did something happen?"

I was thinking of the hotel-room door and the man in the red baseball cap looking up at my window. But what *had* happened, really? I'd called the front desk and told them about the lock, and the receptionist reacted in a way that made me think she heard this kind of thing all the time. The batteries would be replaced by the time I got back. Nothing had been moved or taken. No big deal. And as for the man in the red baseball cap, well … So what? Man Sitting On Public Bench Looking Around Shocker. And it might have only *seemed* like he was looking at my window. He was, really, too far away for me to be sure. Or maybe he'd just been looking at me because I'd been looking at him.

"My parents," I said. "I haven't told them I'm here. I wasn't going to, when I thought it'd just be for the night. Easier that way. But now I probably should."

"Do they still live in Cork?"

"Actually, no. They live in Bray now."

"*Bray?*" Malone laughed. Bray was a seaside town a little over half an hour's drive away, just over the county border in Wicklow. "You're going to have to call them, then. You'll never get away with that." The lights changed and we moved off. "Where in Bray? Are they near the seafront? I always think that'd be a nice place to live."

"I actually don't know. I've never been there."

"So they just moved there?"

My instinct was to answer yes. Yes, they just moved here and that's why I hadn't visited yet. If I was having this conversation with anyone else, I wouldn't even consider saying anything different. But Malone already knew the awful secret. He already knew who I was, who I'd loved, what I'd done. There was no point in lying to him. I didn't have to.

"I've never been back," I said. "To Ireland. This is the first time I've been here in ten years."

The freedom of this, the weight of my customary conversational caution lifted off my shoulders, made me feel momentarily lightheaded.

"How come?"

"My life is in the Netherlands," I said. "I've lived there since I was nineteen. It's my home now. I'm an only child and both my parents are one of two, so it's not like we've this huge extended family I'm duty bound to keep up with. And I see my parents, like, four or five times a year. They come visit me or we go on holidays together."

"But why don't you visit them here?"

"Because I don't want to be here."

Malone kept his eyes on the road. "Why not?"

Because of bad memories. Because of the constant threat of someone realizing who I am and asking me about him. Because every girl I went to school with, it seemed to me, had efficiently done all the things you're supposed to do by now—get coupled up, buy a house, add to the population—leaving me standing out like some unwanted, spinster thumb. Because you weren't allowed to *not want* those things, only to fail to get them. Because none of this existed in Breda, but my job did. Sal did. My lovely home did. Because there really was no good reason to come back here. Because being from someplace didn't mean you had to automatically like it.

Because *he* was here, physically and figuratively, and I didn't want to think about him.

But I didn't need to say all that, or even some of it, because mostly the reason I didn't like being here was because—

"I'm embarrassed," I said.

"Embarrassed? About what?"

"About falling for it."

"For …?"

For Will.

"For Will's lies," I said.

"Alison." Malone said my name so softly and sympathetically that I felt an abrupt unlocking, a loosening, and I turned toward the passenger window in case tears were coming next. No one ever said my name that way, because I never let anyone know that I needed to hear it. "You were nineteen. *Nineteen.* You have absolutely nothing to be embarrassed about. And embarrassment needs an audience. Who's in yours? Yeah, people remember Will, but that's about it. It's been ten years. I can tell you, most people don't even remember the victims' names. Unfortunately. Trust me, you really don't need to feel that way." A pause. "I wish you wouldn't."

We drove the rest of the way to the CPH in silence.

I'd been convinced that, in the fading light, the Central Psychiatric Hospital would transform into some sort of stereotypical horror-movie-style asylum, a *Psycho* house perched on the hill only with bars on the windows and tortured screams coming from somewhere inside. But the building where Will was looked no different than your average office block now, because its mostly dark windows and fading light made the grates fixed over the glass harder to see.

Will was meeting with his counselor, we were told. We'd have to wait a few minutes.

Malone and I sat side by side on gray plastic chairs in the lobby. He went to the vending machine and came back with two steaming plastic cups. Coffee for me, tea for him. We sipped them while we waited.

"Where's Shaw?" I asked. "He's not coming this time?"

"No."

"Does he know about this? Me being here, seeing Will again?"

"You're only doing what I asked you to, and I'm just doing my job."

I took that as a *no*. "Will you get into trouble for this?"

"Trouble?" Malone laughed softly. "No."

He had carried a large manila envelope in from the car with PLEASE DO NOT BEND stamped on it in red. When we sat down, he'd set the envelope on the empty chair on his other side.

"Is that the development?" I said, pointing.

Malone nodded. "We've got some CCTV images. Luckily. There aren't many cameras in that area. Mostly traffic ones, which point at the road. There's one mounted above an ATM machine near where Louise Farrington was found that we figured he'd have had to pass if he was on foot, but we found nothing on the night of her murder. Then one of the civilian analysts had an idea. She thought, okay, he avoided it the night of the murders, but he has to be familiar with the area in order to pull this off, so he must go there regularly. She started looking for regulars, but odd ones—like someone who only walks there alone very late at night, and tends to double back the way they came."

"And she found someone?"

"She found a few someones. But our prime candidate is a guy we see in the days after Louise Farrington was found, and both before and after Jennifer Madden was, walking alone along the canal late at night and, more often than not, doubling back the same way he came."

"Couldn't he just have been going to someone's house?" I asked.

"We're talking about him reappearing minutes later, like he's just walking up and down the banks of the canal."

A loud electronic buzzing noise cut through the

air, signaling that the door that led off the lobby was opening. A grumpy-looking security guard appeared and beckoned us with a finger.

"Go time," Malone said, standing up, collecting the manila envelope from the seat beside him.

We took the same route as we had the day before, descending into the harshly lit bowels of the hospital building. There was no way of knowing what time of the day it was outside. When we reached the room I could see Alek standing in there through the pane of glass in the door, but there was no uniformed Garda.

"I'll be doing the watching this time," Malone said when he saw the look on my face. "You ready?"

"No, not really. But then I wasn't ready yesterday either."

Malone put a hand on my arm and gave it a squeeze. This time, I managed not to bolt away. I could feel his touch, a buzzing heat source, through the sleeve of my jacket.

I couldn't remember the last time I'd felt something like that.

Actually, no. I could. There'd been that thing at Christmas, the dinner in Rotterdam with sales managers from the London office. One of them, Thomas, had said goodbye to me outside the restaurant by catching my right hand with his left and leaning in to kiss me on the cheek. Not the usual air-kiss, not a kissing sound made somewhere in the region of the other person's cheek, but an *actual* kiss, lips pressed against my skin, the bristles of his stubble rubbing against my cheek. But it was the hand, his fingers squeezing around mine, that really stunned me. Surprised me. Disassembled me.

I'd thought about it for weeks afterward. He probably didn't even think about it at the time.

I felt a sudden desire to throw myself into Malone, to bury my face in his chest, to let him hold me. To let him hold me together.

Because it was so utterly exhausting doing it all by myself.

So now I did pull away.

"The photos," I said.

Malone opened the envelope and slid out the contents: several A4-sized glossy photographs. I could only see the shot on top: a grainy image, dark, blown up to the point where, if you focused on any one section of it, you only saw squared pixels in shades of gray. If you looked at it for long enough, an image emerged: a figure in dark clothes walking along a stretch of footpath.

Wearing a baseball cap.

I swallowed. "That's him?"

"That's someone we need to talk to so we can eliminate him from our inquiries."

"Isn't that what you guys always say? Doesn't that actually mean *yes*?"

Malone smiled. "We just want to talk to him."

"And, what? You think Will might know him?"

"If he's the real killer and Will didn't do it, and the real killer framed Will, then yes." Malone sighed, acknowledging the astronomical odds of this. "Look, it can't hurt to ask."

But it could.

Every moment in that room would hurt.

"What about the general public?" I asked.

"We've released them to the press. They should already be on all the online news sites. We're too late for tomorrow morning's papers but we'll get them in there Tuesday."

"There's not much to go on, though," I said, looking at the photo. "Even if you knew this man, you'd have a hard time recognizing him from this."

"That's one of the traffic-cam shots." Malone shifted through the stack, pulling out one. "We got this from the ATM."

This shot was much better. It hadn't been enlarged as much as the others, so it was easier to collect an impression of the man's features without the intrusion of obvious pixels.

It was also in color.

He was also looking up, almost directly into the camera, with a hand on the peak of the cap as if adjusting it. He was pale and thin, with reddish hair, and he was wearing what looked like a gold ring on his left hand. Due to the angle of the camera, the shadow thrown by the peak of the cap covered half of his face but I thought maybe if you knew him, you could identify him.

The baseball cap was red.

I studied the photo, the face. I wasn't sure if I was imagining I was seeing something or making myself do it, but I felt a flicker of recognition. A faint one, but it was there.

I knew this man from somewhere. I'd met this man before.

And he was wearing a red baseball cap, just like the man I'd seen from my hotel-room window.

The door to the room opened with a *clang* and Alek stuck his head out.

"Let's get this show on the road, lads," he said. "Come on."

alison, now

Inside the room of buttery yellow walls, there was a marked change in Will's demeanor. His reaction to me was the exact opposite he'd had this morning. This time, he barely reacted to me at all.

He was slouched in his chair, his face slack, eyes glazed, arms folded. He looked like he'd just woken up, or *been* woken up. But he'd been meeting with his counselor, so I knew that couldn't be the case. I looked to Alek, who'd resumed his position against the far wall, but he was looking at his watch.

I pulled out the empty chair, sat down and fanned the photographs across the tabletop between us. With an index finger I spun the best photo around so that Will would see it the right way up.

"The Gardaí," I said, "they'd like you to take a look at these. Do you recognize this man at all?"

I said nothing about the fact that I thought I knew the man in the picture, because I didn't have the first clue from where. It was more of a feeling than a fact. But

I could picture his face, better than it appeared in these images, looking at me. Looking *down* at me. And … Smiling? I tried to visualize the background but there was no detail. Only gray, blurry blankness.

"This is important, Will," I said. Still, he didn't look at the photo. He was staring vacantly into the space over my left shoulder. "If you don't want to talk to me, just say so. I'll go."

I'd be happy to, because where I wanted to be right now was somewhere quiet, alone, so I could pick up my memories and shake them, see what might fall out. Who was the man in the picture? Where had we crossed paths? Had we ever, or was I just trying to convince myself that I saw something I knew in that image? All the answers felt just beyond my reach.

If I did know him from somewhere, it must be St. John's. Either at the college itself or during the time I was enrolled there. It was unlikely I had met him in the Netherlands. Here he was on CCTV in Dublin, after all. And I doubted very much that I knew him from my six years at an all-girls Catholic secondary school back in Cork. Plus, the camera had picked him up only a couple of blocks from campus.

St. John's, or something I did when I was there, had to be the link. Which linked this man on the CCTV— potentially, the same man who'd been sitting on that bench across the water—to Will, too.

You didn't even need Malone's cockamamie theory about the so-called real killer knowing Will. With the exception of lectures, I was nearly always with Will. Not because we did everything together but because we did almost nothing *except* be together. So if there was someone who looked familiar to me because we'd known each other or met somewhere during that time, wouldn't Will have known or met him too?

"You *didn't* believe it," Will said. "Not at first."

It took me a second to pick up the threads of his thoughts.

"Not at first," I said, "no. It was the day after, Will. I wasn't in my right mind. I was still trying to get my head around the fact that Liz was—" I stopped. I wouldn't discuss her with him. There was a line, and she was on the other side of it. "I didn't know which way was up."

He finally looked at me. "You knew enough to give an interview to a national paper about how it was all a huge mistake, how there was absolutely no way I could've done what they were accusing me of."

"And I was wrong to."

I'd been so stupid. But also, so completely convinced. And desperate to do something to help him, to alleviate the physical pain I thought I could feel in my chest at the thought of Will—*my* Will—being accused of something so horrific, so unimaginable, that I snuck out of the house to call the news desk of a broadsheet and gave their crime reporter an exclusive interview. GIRLFRIEND STANDS BY CANAL KILLER, the headline read—because by the time it went to press, Will had confessed to all five murders.

He'd actually been doing it while I was on the phone. He'd been talking to Shaw while I'd been telling a stranger about our love.

My body burned now with the shame of it.

"Is that why you thought I'd believe you now?" I asked. "Because I did back then, for a minute?"

"I hoped you would." He met my eyes. "I didn't do this, Ali. I wish I could … I don't know, find a way to make you feel what I feel or see into my mind or … I don't know. I don't know what to do to convince you. I can't seem to prove it to you, so words … telling you is all I have. I know that's not enough for anyone else, but I thought it might be for you. I hoped it would be. Hoped for ten long years, Ali. You *know* me. You say you knew me, past tense, but it's not in the past. Because I haven't changed. I haven't been *able* to change because I've been locked up in here, away from the world, waking up every morning in a punishment for something I didn't do that happened when I was nineteen years old. And I can't—" His voice broke. "I can't take this much longer. I *can't*."

His eyes had filled with tears and he looked away, embarrassed. In that moment, it was impossible not to feel sorry for him.

I had to remind myself that this was about more than feelings. It was also about cold, hard facts.

I asked *why now*.

He turned back to me. "What?"

"Why are you only saying this now? It's been ten years."

Will threw up his hands. "Because who'd believe me? I said I did it, they had—apparently—evidence to convict me, and I listened to my solicitor when he said I should do myself a favor and enter a guilty plea. Avoid a trial. He said there was no way in hell we were ever going to win it, and my parents …" He swallowed. "My parents agreed with him. It was like they couldn't get me locked away fast enough. I was such an *embarrassment* to them. And you were gone. So who could I even tell? The people in here? They hear it all the time. It was pointless. So I just … I just gave up. In more ways than one. The first few years here, I don't even remember them, to be honest." He glanced at Alek. Quieter now, he continued, "Then two things happened. The first was last year, when this new guy arrived on the unit. John. He was really … Well, he had a lot of problems. They ended up moving him into High Dependency, as far as I know. Anyway, he knew who I was. And it turned out that he was, like, obsessed with true crime and had read all this stuff on the internet about me and this case."

"I take it *you* don't have …?"

"What? Access to the internet?" Will snorted. "Ali, we don't even get to pick the TV channels around here."

"Right. Okay."

"So he tells me that there's this website that says I'm innocent and has all these, you know, documents and witness statements and stuff that apparently proves it. Or tries to. And he was able to tell me things that I never knew. For instance, you know that blood they found under my desk? Did you know they didn't find it on the first search? That it was during the second?"

"Under a desk," I said. "Easy to miss."

"Or easy to plant. There must have been thirty people in and out of that room in between those two searches. At least. Any one of them could have put it there. And the locker with the folder in it. There were loads of prints on that thing that weren't mine—but no fingerprints at all on the combination lock on the locker door. Don't you think that's weird? And apparently— get this—someone *sent a letter* to the *St. John's News* claiming to be the killer, talking about how girls should be more careful and not walk home alone and all this creepy stuff. Did you ever hear that? I'm not surprised. No one did. It was just dismissed. A crank, they said. But what if it wasn't? And not only that, but the student reporter who received it passed it onto the Gardaí, and they bloody went and *lost it*. Did you know that?"

The truth was, until yesterday, I'd done all I could to avoid knowing anything. Details were my enemy. They filled in the blanks, colored in my nightmares. And once you knew one, you could never forget it.

Like the shopping cart.

Hours after Will was charged, I'd flown to the Netherlands and taken refuge in my cousin's house in the Hague. My first few days there, the house was full of whispers. Ella and her husband whispered to each other in the hall while I sat in the living room; they whispered to each other in the kitchen before I came downstairs in the morning; they whispered to each other in bed while I lay awake, unable to sleep, in the room just next door.

And, sometimes, they forgot to whisper, sending shards of horror through the walls.

They think he was following them for weeks before he did it.

Knocked them out and then pushed them underwater so they drowned.

Her friend? Found tangled up in a rusted shopping cart.

They were obsessed with the details of the case, like everyone who'd bought those tabloid newspapers at home. I knew when they perched next to me on the sofa, patted my limbs and said that I could talk to them about anything, anytime, what they were really saying was,

Please, tell us more. Tell us everything. Leave nothing out.

"It was a joke," Will was saying now. "They made so many mistakes."

What he'd described sounded more like a few loose threads to me, and inconsequential ones at that. And were they even true? He'd heard about them secondhand, from someone who was receiving psychiatric treatment. And that person had read about them on the internet.

If any of this had even happened at all.

"What was the other thing?" I asked.

"The new cases. There really wasn't anything I could do to prove I wasn't the Canal Killer, but maybe out there somewhere, someone could prove that someone *else* was. Because he was still out there. But who'd bother when they thought he was me, and I'm locked up in here? Then, a few days ago, I hear a report about this girl Jennifer Madden on the radio. And everything's the same: St. John's, the canal, a head injury. And the weather report said something about the Patrick's Day parade, so I knew the timing fit as well. I didn't even know there'd been another girl before her until Shaw and that other guy told me that when they came here."

"Why would they tell you that?"

"I don't know." Will shrugged. "I asked if there'd been others, and they said yes. One other. I think they were trying to humor me, to get me to talk. But I said I'd only talk to you."

"Because you thought I'd believe you."

"Yeah. But I'd no way of contacting you."

"And then what? You get me here, I believe you—what then?"

"Then," Will said, "you help me."

"But *how*?"

"If I was out there, Ali, out of this place, I could look into these things. I could … I could *do* something. I can't do anything in here. They're not even letting me watch the news now, so I don't know what's going on with these new girls. But if you were … If you were on my side, maybe you could do those things for me. Maybe you would." He looked away again. "But it turns out, you think I did this. So none of it matters, does it?"

"What difference would it make, Will? Let's say I did find something. Let's say I find that letter. What happens then? It doesn't change the evidence against you, and it doesn't negate the fact that you confessed. You *confessed*. I can't …" I sighed, exasperated. "It's not going to change anything. You're not going to get out. So why even bother with this, dragging all this … all this *horror* back up?"

The silence that followed thrummed, like the air in a room where the TV is on mute.

"This horror," Will repeated softly. "This horror is your past, but it's my present." He leaned forward; instinctively, I sat back. "Ten years ago, they told me I'd committed five murders. They showed me what they said was evidence. They got me to say I did it. And no one—not my friends, not my family, not even *you*—put their hand up and said, 'Wait a second. Something's not right here. He can't have done this.' Everyone just accepted it. Everyone thought it was the truth. Which means there was something in me, something about me, that made people think I could have done this. And now, it's all so long ago, I'm starting to forget things. I'm on medication. It makes you foggy. And what I do remember isn't as clear as it once was. So sometimes, I think, *could* I have done this? Sometimes I wonder," his voice trembled, "*did* I?"

The last two words hung in the air between us.

"I just need to know, Ali. That out there is something real, something tangible, that proves I didn't do this. If it exists, I need to know about it. For me. It doesn't even matter whether or not the Gardaí give a shit. I don't think they will. But *I* need to know. Because the only thing worse than spending the next fifty years in here waiting to die would be spending the next fifty years in here waiting to die and wondering if maybe *I deserve it.*"

I met Will's eyes.

He held my gaze.

I didn't like what I saw in his face in that moment, what I felt pass between us, because it contradicted everything I thought I knew for sure, every conviction my adult life was built on.

And if this was a lie, just another performance, a manipulation …

Then why did it feel like the truth?

"You don't have to believe me," Will said. "You don't even have to help me. But there's a guy out there killing young women again and he's a few more to go. Forget about what that means for me. Think about what it means for *him*, out there. You could catch him. Stop him."

"You can too, right now." I slid the photograph across the table to him. "Do you know this man?"

Will said nothing, waiting.

"Fine," I said. "I'll look into that website for you. But I'm not promising anything. It might not even exist."

Which was exactly what I planned on telling him, should there come a time when I had to tell him anything.

Right now I was planning on never seeing him ever again.

"Thank you," Will said, relieved. "Thank you."

He picked up the closest print to him, the best one, studied it for what felt like an age. Then he set it aside and repeated the process with the photo underneath, and so on through the pile.

The seconds ticked by.

"He looks familiar," Will said, "but I can't remember from where." A pause. "Maybe St. John's?"

Without thinking, I said, "I think it is."

He raised an eyebrow. "What?"

Shit. "He, ah …" *Too late to take it back now.* "He looks familiar to me too."

Will looked at me for a long moment.

"But I don't know from where either," I added. "I just think if *I* think he looks familiar, and *you* think so too, then it has to be St. John's, right?"

Will looked down at the image again. "Could be someone we saw around," he said, "on nights out or something. I don't think he was in my class. Or yours. We'd remember him then, wouldn't we?"

"Well, it's been ten years."

A beat passed.

"Ali," Will said then, "do you still have the Brick?"

"The *Brick*?"

I'd lugged a digital camera around campus that first year, producing it at opportune moments with a (misplaced) smugness, like it was the first iPhone and I was Steve Jobs. It was a cumbersome thing, bigger than the kind that took film, and had interchangeable lenses. We'd nicknamed it the Brick. I hadn't thought of it in years.

"Cutting-edge technology, that was," Will said.

"For about five minutes. And long before I got it."

"Where *did* you get it?"

"My dad won it in a raffle at work and then gave it to me for Christmas. Problem was the raffle and that Christmas were, like, two years apart. He'd stuck it in a drawer and forgotten about it. By the time I was using it, it was practically obsolete—and three times the size of everyone else's."

"That's right," Will said. "Yeah, I remember now."

We both fell into our memories for a moment.

"I doubt it," I said. "It surely got thrown out."

"What about the photos you took with it?"

"What about them?"

"You must have had hundreds. And you had them in albums, with all the names and dates and stuff. Do you still have all those?" Will pointed at the pictures on the tabletop. "Ali, this guy—he could be in one of them."

Amy was supposed to work until nine, and then go straight from the café to meet her friends at a bar on Dawson Street. This is her usual Sunday-night routine. But now it's not even ten and she's come home, angry about something, stomping around and slamming things. She dumps a book bag onto the floor of her bedroom and something sparkly and black falls out of it, followed by one high heel: the clothes she'd brought with her to change into after work.

Her plans have changed, which means his have too.

He waits to see what she does next.

She spends some time in the kitchen. He's seen it: all the lights are on in there. Tonight, the remnants of a pizza delivery sit on the table amid numerous empty bottles, cans, and plastic cups.

The state of the kitchen, he can only assume, is what has apparently annoyed Amy even more. She comes back into the bedroom and starts picking through things on the floor—clothes, socks, the cables of various hairstyling instruments—while swearing under her breath.

While he holds his.

Amy plucks her phone charger from the detritus and shoves it into a wall socket. Connects her phone. Throws it on the bed to charge.

Thud.

Back out into the kitchen, switching the light off in the bedroom as she goes through the door.

It sounds like she's clearing things away while the kettle boils. Crockery clattering. A rush of water into the sink. The crinkling of a plastic refuse sack. Cupboard doors open and close.

Amy boils the kettle for a second time, and then there's the sound of tea-making: the tinkling of a small spoon stirring the contents of a cup. The microwave comes on, runs for half a minute or so. An odd, greasy smell fills the air. Dinner must be reheated pizza.

Click.

The light goes off in the kitchen.

Click.

Her bedroom burns with brightness again. The shade from her ceiling light is missing and that's what casts such a harsh light: the bare bulb.

Amy roots around in various places: among the cosmetics on the dressing table, in the drawer underneath it, in a toiletry bag that was upturned at the end of the bed.

Then she undresses.

She leaves the items where they fall, at her feet. She stands naked for a moment, turning this way and that, studying her body in a mirror he can't see. Then she takes the toweling robe that's hanging off the back of her door—it's purple and covered in orange make-up stains—and leaves the bedroom again.

Down the hall, the door to the shared bathroom opens and closes. For the next ten minutes or so, the shower runs.

It's too short a window for him. He can't risk it. But a shower—that's promising. She might be heading back out again, like he first thought.

But when Amy returns, she changes into what, for her, seems to constitute pajamas. A pair of shorts with a butterfly pattern on them and a T-shirt flecked with bleach stains. Then she turns off the light and crawls into bed.

It's so cheap and poorly constructed, it sags beneath Amy's weight—which isn't much—and the horizontal wooden slats shift and creak as she settles into a position.

It is completely dark, then it is dimly blue.

The light is from the phone, he realizes. Her phone. Amy has a new something. A message of some sort. But she makes no move to get up and see what it says, even though she has only just got into bed and has to still be awake.

Instead, she rolls over.

Soon, the room falls completely dark again.

Some time later, her breathing settles into a regular pattern.

Some time after that, she starts to lightly snore.

He waits another half an hour, just to be safe, before he crawls, slowly and stealthily, out from under her bed.

alison, now

The next morning I awoke with a start, as if disturbed by a noise. I sat up and surveyed the room, watching as the darkness relented, as forms took shape and slowly emerged from the black. There was nothing unexpected among them. Whatever woke me must have been in my dream.

I flopped back down and tried to go back to sleep.

Ding.

My phone was sitting on one of the bedside tables, its screen glowing.

Sal had sent me a string of texts. Some late last night, one just now. They were all along a similar theme: if I didn't call her soon, she was calling the police. Knowing Sal, she was only half joking.

I'd never told Sal about Will. Or Liz. When I first met her, it was much too soon. Too raw. I still hadn't made sense of it myself. Then, there never seemed to be a right time. Now, it felt like it was too late. I didn't know how she'd react to the news that I'd been keeping a secret from her as long as we'd known each other, and that I'd had to lie to her in order to do that.

Besides, I didn't *want* to tell her. I didn't want her to know. Sal had a husband now; I couldn't ask her to keep things from him. So telling Sal would be telling Dirk, potentially, and as much as I liked Dirk, I couldn't trust him to not tell someone else. It unnerved me even to imagine it, but I could: all this, in my other life. Whispers spreading like an infectious disease. Other members of the EUs Googling old news stories. Looking up at our next get-together to catch someone looking at me, and knowing by the way their face would start to color that they'd been sitting there thinking, *How could she have really not known? How could she?*

But I had to tell Sal something. I couldn't keep up the pretence of period pain for three days in a row. So I sent her a text saying something had come up, that everyone was all right but I'd had to travel to Dublin to see my parents on very short notice. I said she wasn't to worry and that I'd call her later today to explain all.

And I hoped that, by then, I'd have come up with something.

There was a thin gap between the curtains and for the next hour, I watched the sky brighten from a dull gray to a bright blue. Then I got up and pulled the curtains back for the full view.

This stretch of canal could be incredibly picturesque, especially on a cold spring morning that came with clear skies and a chilly sun, like this one. The water was almost level with the road. There was nothing between it and the paths on its banks except for some muddy grass, a negligible incline, and, here and there, clusters of thick, waist-high reeds. Over the tops of the trees I could see the boxy, boring office blocks that lined the canal on the opposite side.

The waters of the canal were so still the surface looked like glass. You could walk right in. *Fall* right in, if you were drunk and it was dark. There were some obstacles in other parts of it—you might meet a low wall or a sporadic stretch of iron railings—but here and for the most part, there were no barriers at all. When Liz and I had been searching for somewhere to live during those panicked few days before a room in Halls opened up, my mother had cited this as reason enough not to live anywhere near here. She was convinced she'd be getting a call from the guards to say I'd been pulled out of it in the early hours of a Sunday morning after drunkenly falling in.

But as it turned out it hadn't been me.

Or an accident.

I showered, dried my hair, and sent an email to Suncamp HR explaining that I had a family emergency and wouldn't be in today or, in all likelihood, tomorrow either. I promised to keep them updated. For a second I thought about what would go on in my absence, what wouldn't get done, the answers that would be delayed, but then I pushed those thoughts away. I couldn't even begin to worry about work now. In the scheme of things, it just didn't matter.

I rifled through my case looking for something clean, but nothing was. I couldn't face putting back on anything I'd worn yesterday, or the clothes I'd traveled in the day before. I settled for my pajama top, which, if you didn't study it too closely, might pass as a gray

T-shirt. I wondered if there was anything left of mine at my parents' house that I could fit into.

My parents.

At the thought of seeing them here, in Dublin, the cup of instant coffee I'd assembled from the amenities tray started to work its way back up my throat.

We didn't talk about Will, ever. In our family I'd gone to secondary school and done my Leaving Cert, and then gone to college in Den Haag. It was as if the year in between had been wiped from our collective memories. And as if the girl I'd been best friends with my first day at primary school, the girl who had featured in every obsessive phase (tap-dancing, Backstreet Boys, *The O.C.*) and every milestone, who spent more time at our house than anyone outside of our immediate family, had merely moved away somewhere. We didn't talk about her either.

But now I was here, back in Dublin, because the Gardaí had brought me back to talk to Will, and I'd be knocking on Mam and Dad's door in the hope that somewhere in their garage was a picture from ten years ago that, unbeknownst to me at the time, had captured a man who, maybe, was out there killing young women right now in exactly the same way Will had killed Liz and four other innocent girls.

The subject could hardly be avoided under such circumstances. We were good with the whole denial thing, but we weren't *that* good.

In the car on the drive back to my hotel last night, I'd given Malone the highlights of what Will had said. That he thought the CCTV man looked familiar and suspected he'd crossed paths with him during his St. John's days. I'd also told him about Will's idea of checking the photos and we'd arranged that Malone would collect me from the hotel at eleven this morning and drive me out to my parents' house.

I also told him that I thought *I'd* seen the man somewhere, and that just that morning, I'd seen a similar man wearing a red baseball cap sitting on the opposite bank of the canal, looking up at the hotel. I stressed that I couldn't make out much about him from that distance, and that I was aware more than one man in Dublin City was likely to own a red baseball cap.

But still. It felt like too much of a coincidence.

Malone said he'd check the area's security cameras to see if any of them had picked up this man, to see if we could determine if Bench Man and CCTV Man were one and the same.

I really didn't want them to be. It would make my open hotel-room door yesterday more than just a mechanical malfunction.

I went back to the window. The scene outside had changed dramatically in the last half hour. Earlier there'd been only a handful of people walking along the canal. Now there were herds of office workers hurrying past while cyclists carefully navigated the clogged cycle lane running parallel to the path. Nearly everyone was moving in the same direction: from my left to my right, i.e. from the nearest Luas station to the tech companies in Grand Canal Dock. There were so many of them that the scene had an unnaturalness to it, as if they were all extras on a movie set, following directions. Dublin rush hour presents *The Truman Show*.

But crowds were good. A person could go unseen in them.

And I desperately wanted to go outside and not be seen.

Since Saturday afternoon I'd spent my time in a car, a plane, another car, a psychiatric hospital, and holed up in this stuffy hotel room. I wasn't interested in strolling down memory lane, but I could do with a stroll in the fresh air. I believed Malone when he said that no one would recognize me or even remember who I was, that so much time had passed, people barely remembered the victims anymore, let alone the killer's college girlfriend. Plus, now there was no point worrying that someone who knew my parents would see me and tell them I was here—there was nowhere in Ireland you could go where that wasn't a fear—because I was going to be telling them that myself in a few hours' time.

So I went outside.

The instant I felt the sun on my face, I felt like I'd made the right decision.

There was a cluster of people, maybe four or five, right outside the hotel's entrance. I didn't turn to look at them, but they weren't talking to each other and I smelled smoke, so I presumed it was just the breakfast-time rush in the designated smoking area.

Instead, I turned right, toward St. John's, but with a plan to turn off into Baggot Street Upper. There were plenty of cafés there, it was only a couple of minutes' walk away and I'd be going in the same direction as the herd. If I spotted anyone who looked like the man in the red baseball cap, I could just duck in somewhere and call Malone. I figured that with so many people around, I'd be fine either way. I'd avoid going any further, any closer to St. John's.

Turns out, I didn't even have to go as far as the turn onto Baggot Street. There was a coffee shop before the corner. I ordered a large latte and took it to one of two tables just outside, grabbing one of the complimentary newspapers that had been piled on a counter inside out with me. I didn't plan to read it; it was going to be a prop more than anything. But just as I sat down, one of the headlines on the front page caught my eye: GARDAÍ ARRANGE CANAL—

I unfolded the paper, laid it flat on the table. GARDAÍ ARRANGE CANAL KILLER DATE. Underneath the headline was a picture of me.

Serial killer Will Hurley's former girlfriend, Alison Smith (29), leaves a hotel on Mespil Road yesterday, en route to a private meeting with him at the Central Psychiatric Hospital in Dundrum. Sources say this is related to the Garda investigation into the deaths of students Louise Farrington and Jennifer Madden earlier this year. For more, see page 2.

I quickly folded the paper up again and turned it over. My hands were shaking.

I hadn't noticed anyone outside the hotel yesterday morning. It had only taken seconds to walk from the door to Malone's car. But there must have been someone there, and with a camera. How did they know? How did they know I was there and where I was going? And where were those people now?

I felt dizzy and sick.

Someone had sat down at the other table. An older woman, wearing brightly colored Nikes under her skirt-suit. She'd got a paper too. She was reading it right now. Looking at that front page.

She looked up at the canal, then turned to look down the street.

Yes, that hotel right there. Yes, that very one.

Please don't look this way.

I looked exactly as I did in that picture. I was even wearing the same black leather jacket.

I had to go.

I took my coffee and stepped onto the street, turned in the direction of the hotel and—

A blonde woman was walking right toward me. Looking straight at me. Smiling.

"Alison," she said warmly, as if we knew each other. She turned and signaled at someone over her shoulder, and when I looked I saw a man with an expensive-looking camera hurrying to catch up with her. "Do you have a minute to chat?"

I put my head down, kept going. I had to get to the hotel.

"How is Will?" She'd stepped right in front of me, blocking my way. The path was busy with pedestrians and some of them were starting to turn and look. "What does he know that could help the Gardaí?"

I didn't know what to do now. I had my phone and I could call Malone, but what did I do until he got here?

I stepped around her, started forward again.

But then I saw, further up the street, what was outside the hotel: two men, chatting to each other with cameras slung over their shoulders and, just pulling into the car park, a satellite truck with a news station's logo stenciled on the side.

Plus as every second passed, someone else turned to look.

I don't, as a rule, run. My legs have no muscle memory of exactly how to and burn ferociously whenever I must, like when the train is leaving in thirty seconds and I'm still at the turnstiles. And running down a busy footpath filled with pedestrians *while holding a coffee* is the type of activity that draws the very kind of attention I was trying to avoid.

But what choice did I have?

I'm not saying it was the best idea. It wasn't an idea, not really. I didn't think about it at all. I just did it.

I turned in the opposite direction and ran.

alison, now

I'd never been to my parents' house in Bray, but I'd seen pictures. It was a neat, two-story terraced house tucked away on a quiet street a couple of blocks from the seafront, painted pale blue and almost completely obscured by the gnarled branches of an old oak tree in the front garden. My mother had explained that they spent most of their time in the conservatory-style extension to the rear, so the shadow of the tree across the front of the house didn't bother them and offered some privacy to boot.

Standing underneath the branches of that tree now, halfway up my parents' garden path, I felt sweaty and shivery. Back in the city center, I'd run for about a block before turning around to check that no one was following me. No one was. But I couldn't go back to the hotel, and I didn't want to have to wait on the street for Malone to come get me. So I kept going, all the way to the nearest DART station, where I'd boarded a southbound commuter train, put my head down and put my

parents' address into Google Maps. I'd only looked up
once, in response to the group of German tourists in
the seats opposite the aisle to me murmuring "Ah!" as
the full sweep of Killiney bay suddenly came into view
below us, almost a rival for the French Riviera in sunny
weather like this.

Almost.

"Jesus *Christ!*"

The front door to the house had opened and my
mother was coming toward me now, hurrying down the
uneven concrete slabs that formed the path, one hand
holding a mobile phone to her ear and the other waving
at me frantically. The cashmere cardigan she was wearing
floated like a cape behind her. "She's here, Jackie. At
the gate! No, *now*." To me. "Alison, what in the name
of …?" Back into the phone: "I don't know, I'll find out.
Yeah … Yeah … Look, I'll call you back, okay? I'll call
you back." To me again, "What in the name of God are
you *doing* here? What's going on? How did you get here?
Why didn't you *call us*?"

I was regretting this already.

"Hi, Mam," I said.

The phone slipped into a pocket, she grabbed both
my hands with hers. "Jackie just rang to say she saw
you on the front of one of the papers and then she says
to me, 'No, you don't understand, she's *here*, she's in
Dublin,' and I said—"

"Mam," I said, "take a breath. Please."

"I just want to know what's going *on*, Alison. Why
didn't you tell us you were coming to Dublin? Where
did they get that picture of you? Did you know you were
going to be on it?"

"Let's go inside." The street seemed deserted, but this could be a valley of squinting windows. "Come on."

As my mother walked ahead of me, muttering the names of Catholic saints under her breath, I had a moment to take her in. She looked well, wearing a neat, tailored pair of wool trousers and a silk shirt with a bright pattern. The thin cardigan she was wearing over it looked expensive, designed more for style than for warmth. Her mousy-brown hair was no longer streaked gray but highlighted with flattering white-blonde tones, and she was wearing costume jewelry. A new habit, as far as I knew.

"You're all dressed up," I said.

"Hardly." My mother made a scoffing noise. "I was just going to Dun Laoghaire for a look around the shops. Before Jackie called and nearly gave me a *stroke*."

"And then you immediately ran outside like a crazy person?"

At the threshold, my mother turned around to make a face at me. "Don't be silly. I was looking out the window and I saw you coming in the gate."

Inside the house, I was a bit taken aback. Pristine checkered tiles in the hall, a glimpse of a cozy living room that looked like a page torn from a Laura Ashley catalog, through a door into the sudden space and bright light of a mammoth extension that seemed to stretch out as far as the entire footprint of the original house and then half as much again. A radio was playing traditional Irish music at low volume somewhere in the house.

Our family home in Cork had been poky and dark, a mishmash of furniture my parents had bought on impulse during sales. Previously, my mother's idea of decoration had been the matching cushions that came free with the couch they'd picked in some hangar-sized furniture store off a motorway roundabout.

"It's lovely," I said. "Did you do this all by yourself?"

"Yes, yes," she said dismissively, waving a hand. "What's going *on*?" My mother was finally a bit calmer now and, I think, really seeing me for the first time since I'd arrived. "Your hair," she said, peering at it. "Did you change it?"

"No, I just didn't do it this morning." I hastily tucked a few strands behind my ears.

"Here, give me your jacket."

It was off before I realized I was wearing my pajama top underneath.

"I had to pack quickly," I explained when I saw her frowning at it. "I didn't bring enough tops. Actually, are there any of my old clothes here? I could do with grabbing something."

"Where's all your stuff? Your suitcase?"

"Back at the hotel."

"The *hotel*? But surely you can stay here."

"No, I …" She wasn't going to like this, and I couldn't blame her. "The hotel where I've been staying, Mam. Since Saturday."

Her face fell. "You've been here since *Saturday*?"

I suggested we sit down. The extension was divided into three defined spaces: kitchen, dining, an area with a TV and couches. I followed my mother to the dining table. She sat at one end of it, I sat beside her. There was a little pile of ceramic coasters sitting in the middle of it that I remembered her buying at a crafts market in Delft, and a half-drunk cup of tea.

"Where's Dad?" I asked. "Is he here?"

"Your father is somewhere between here and Killarney." She stood up again so she could get her phone out of her pocket. "I'll call him. He only left a couple of hours ago and I think they were stopping for breakfast so—"

"Mam," I said, reaching to take the phone off her, "don't. There's no need."

"Do you think he's going to want to play a round of golf when he sees your face on the front of all the papers? He's coming back anyway. We might as well save him the petrol."

I rolled my eyes. "Can you just sit down?"

Now *she* rolled her eyes, but did what I'd asked.

"Look," I said, "this isn't a big deal. There's no need to freak out. But ..." I gave her the highlights reel: Malone and Shaw knocking on my door, the new murders, and me going to talk to Will.

"Jesus," she said when I'd finished.

"Mam, listen. This is all private, okay? You can't repeat any of it to anyone."

"Jackie says it's all over the papers."

"That doesn't mean you have to go around offering confirmations. There were reporters at the hotel this morning. And more photographers. If they find out I'm here ..." I sighed. "Look, if anyone knocks on the door or rings your phone or puts a note through the letterbox, just ignore it, okay? Just ignore it."

"I'm not an idiot, Alison."

"But you think you have to be polite. You don't."

"Well, I can't not answer the door, now, can I?"

I looked at her incredulously.

"What?" she said.

"Mam, that's *exactly* my point."

"But what if it's one of the neighbors?"

"You shouldn't be talking to them either."

"Alison"—another eye-roll—"in all fairness—"

"I mean about this. Don't talk to anyone about it. Anyone at all. And since I know what you're like, that means not talking to anyone, full stop. They'll all get on fine not knowing what color knickers I've on for the next few days."

My mother pulled at her shirt's collar, admonished. Then she said, "I didn't tell that man anything."

There was a flicker of panic before I realized she was talking about back then. After Will had been arrested but before he'd been formally charged, a reporter had door-stepped my mother at the house in Cork. The property was on a lonely country road just outside the city and at first this reporter, a man, had pretended to be lost and looking for directions. Somehow he steered the conversation onto "that awful business up in Dublin" and my mother inadvertently revealed—or rather confirmed—that she was a bit-player in it. By the time he left, she'd told him that she and I were very close, that Will was a lovely boy, and that she was convinced this "silly business" was a misunderstanding that would all be sorted out very soon.

WE STAND BY THE CANAL KILLER, they went with on that one.

Remember how, back in the playground, some bullish girl would come up to you and say, "Angela *knows* you hate her," and you'd instantly get that sick feeling, the sudden descent of a cold, hard stone of dread into the pit of your stomach that would sit there until the lies, misunderstanding, rumor—whatever it was—could be corrected, until you'd found Angela and made it clear that that's not something you'd have ever, ever said? Well, times that by the readership of an Irish national newspaper. People you *can't* contact to clarify. And add your mother, the person responsible, dismissing your hot shame, telling you that you're being silly, that it doesn't matter, it'll all be forgotten in a few days and, anyway, who cares what people think?

"You haven't talked to anyone already," I said. "Have you?"

"Like who?"

"Like your friend Jackie. How much does she know?"

My mother muttered something under her breath.

I asked her to repeat it.

"I said she knows a lot more than I do."

A pounding was starting at the front of my head.

"You don't talk to us," my mother went on. "About this. You never have."

Here it came then, approaching like a freight train while I lay, helpless, tied to the tracks. The Conversation. The one that had been hanging over our heads for the last ten years. Their visits to the Netherlands, our holidays abroad: they came with an unspoken agreement that there'd be a reprieve from the threat of this, and plenty of conversation topics—the sights, the food, how sullen that waiter was—to help us honor it.

But there could be no reprieve here. Sitting at my mother's kitchen table in Dublin, I knew I was facing it head-on.

And I *couldn't* face it.

Just the mere threat of it felt like walking through a hammering shower of sharp glass shards.

"I don't want to talk about it, Mam."

"But you'll go see that boy in prison and have a grand old chat with him, will you?"

"I was in there for all of ten minutes."

"You came back for those ten minutes. You've said no anytime we asked you to come back for us."

"The Gardaí *made* me."

"Oh, come off it, Alison. How could they make you? Surely that'd be illegal."

I rolled my eyes; my nineteen-year-old self, a muscle memory waking up. "You *know* what I mean, Mam."

"Alison," she said, leaning her elbows on the table, "for the love of God. Something awful happened to you, yes. Awful things happen all the time. People deal with them. People deal with a lot worse. They recover. They put it behind them. They move on. But you just ran off, ran away. And I understood that, at the time. You were only nineteen. When you're that age, you've no perspective on things. You can't be expected to, you haven't been around long enough. So I'm sure it did feel like the end of the world to you. We let you go for that reason, because we understood that. But I thought that a few months down the line, or maybe after you'd finished your degree, you'd realize that what happened didn't quite warrant your reaction to it."

I blinked at her.

When I spoke again, it took some effort to keep my voice even.

"Will murdered five girls, Mam. One of whom was

my best friend—and you're accusing me now of being *melodramatic*?"

"That's not what I'm saying at all. You're taking me up wrong."

"You're making it easy to."

"You're making sure you do." My mother clasped her hands in front of her, set them on the table. "Look, love, I understood back then. I did. But not now, ten years later. What are you holding on to all this for? We only do what works for us. What are you getting out of this?"

We only do what works for us.

She hadn't come up with that one by herself, that was for sure. That was her daytime-TV-talk-show habit rearing its ugly head.

"I'm not holding on to anything," I said. "I'm fine."

"But you don't come home."

"*Breda* is my home."

"And then you come back for him."

"Not *for* him, Mam. That's not what happened."

"And I don't hear anything about boyfriends or, you know, maybe getting married one of these d—"

"Jesus Christ." I stood up and started making a loop around the table, just because I couldn't stay still anymore. "Are you serious? Your big concern here is that I don't have a *boyfriend*? Not everyone wants the same things, Mam. And guess what? It's not the fucking fifties."

"Language, Alison, please." My mother stood up too, to take her cup of tea into the kitchen and wash it out in the sink. "My only concern, always, is you. I don't know whether or not you have what you want because I don't know what you want. I don't know how you are or what you're thinking or what kind of pain you might be in. I don't know anything at all because you *don't tell me*. You tell me about what happened at work and what you did last weekend and how much the carpet cleaning cost you, but you never ever tell me how you *feel*."

Tears sprung to my eyes and I hated my body for betraying me. I swallowed them back.

"Oh, come *on*," I said. "When did we *ever* talk about how I felt? I didn't even *like* Liz half the time, did you know that?"

"Did *you*?"

"What's that supposed to mean?"

"Alison, if you think I didn't see what that girl was really like, how she treated you—"

"I guess I must have blanked out all our cozy mother–daughter fireside chats about it."

My mother swung around to face me. "The problem with you, Alison, is that you had your teenage years too late. You were no trouble to us at all until you went off to college. You decided to have all your adolescent angst then. But then … Then Will happened and you got stuck there. You've never moved past this thing that happened then, so you don't let yourself get past that age. You've never given yourself a proper chance to." She paused. "And I don't just mean with me, love. I mean in your life in general. In all things. And there's just no need for it. No one blames you for anything. No one even remembers it, at this stage."

"I'm on the front page of a *newspaper* today, Mam."

"Yes, well. If you had talked to me or your father before deciding to do this, to see that … To see him, we may have been able to help you make a better decision."

"A better …? You *just* said …" I pointed at her. "That's blaming me. Right there. *You're* doing it, right now."

"Oh, Alison, that's not what—"

"Look, I don't want to talk about this, okay?" I moved toward the door that led to the hall. "That's not why I came here. I'm looking for my photo albums. Where are they? Are they here?"

My mother said nothing for a long moment. I didn't like the look on her face, the hurt in it. I couldn't look at it.

I looked away, out toward the back garden, instead.

"Everything of yours is upstairs," she said then. "The back bedroom."

I went to leave the room.

"I'm done with this, Alison," she said. "Just so you know." I stopped, but didn't turn around. "I'm done with pretending this didn't happen. With not talking about it. With not talking about anything that means something. I'm not going to let you do it anymore. We all need to change. I've already let this go on for way too long. And yes, it'll be hard and it'll hurt and you won't like it, but you're just going to have to suck it up and push through to the other side." She paused, took a breath, exhaled slowly. "Now—are you hungry? I was going to have my lunch out but I can go pick us up something. Any requests?"

I shook my head. "Whatever you're having."

"Right so."

"Thanks."

"It's all right."

I left the kitchen and went into the hall, climbed the stairs to the first-floor landing. The door at the top of it looked to lead into a small, narrow bedroom that faced the back of the house.

I made it inside and managed to close the door behind me—just—before I burst into tears.

alison, then

Until I went to college, I'd never had a boyfriend. Liz and I were on the same page there, although for different reasons. She seemed wholly unimpressed with the boys our age, rolling her eyes at what she saw as their pathetic attempts to impress us, and the desperate fumbling that ensued if they managed to. Meanwhile, I didn't know how to actually go about getting a boyfriend, or how anyone did. The meet-cutes of Hollywood movies, Ross and Rachel, the *Sex and the City* box set I'd snuck past my mother—what relevance did they have to a not-very-confident all-girls secondary school student growing up in Cork? Even glossy magazines produced closer to home had features like "101 Date Moves Guaranteed to Get His Attention," but no disclaimer that, actually, this life may not apply to you. Ever, or maybe just not yet. For now, you were seventeen and still lived with your parents, and so even though it felt like everything was running behind, it was actually all going to arrive right on schedule. Until then, I was left to worry about how I never found myself talking to nice guys in queues, or felt a spark as I brushed hands with someone else reaching for the last pair of gloves, or met some tall, dark, handsome stranger's eyes across a crowded room. But then, drunk and in a club, someone drunker tried to untie my top and someone slightly less drunk came to my rescue.

And just like that, Will and I had met.

He was in St. John's too, studying law but not sure he really wanted to. He was also living in Halls. His parents lived in Dublin but out on the coast, in a place he made sound very far away. That first night, we'd walked back to campus via Leeson Street, then down along the canal.

When he kissed me goodnight in the shadow of Block A, it wasn't at all what I was expecting. He looked into my eyes, caressed my cheek with his hand and then kissed me once, gently, slowly, deliberately, on the lips.

And I thought, *So that's what all the fuss is about.*

All the songs, they weren't about the desperate fumbles. They were about moments like this.

He left me there, walking away into the night with a hand raised in a wave, and when I woke up the next morning with his name on my lips, I wasn't entirely sure I hadn't just dreamed the whole thing.

It would be five days before I ran into him again, in a café in the village of Ranelagh, where I was hiding out. Liz, Claire, and I had had more than a fair share of fun during Freshers' Week, but my energy stores for other people were depleted to a critical level, and I knew I needed some alone time before a second weekend's activities kicked off. I'd snuck out early and just kept walking—past Baggot Street, through leafy suburban streets, trying to keep the canal on my right and my expanding virtual map in my head so that I wouldn't get completely lost. I'd happened upon a stretch of trendy cafés and restaurants with a village feel, and picked the one that had cushy armchairs visible through the front window.

I was sitting there, curled up with a book I had a class on in the coming days, not draining the end of my coffee because I didn't want to leave and I really couldn't afford to buy another one, when I heard my name and I looked up and he was there.

"Well, this is weird," I said.

He smiled. "And hello to you too."

I closed my book. "You live in the block next to me, but I see you in here?"

"I saw you come in," he admitted. "In a non-stalker way. I was across the street." He pointed to his head. "Haircut."

Now that he'd said it, it did look a bit less unruly than it had on Sunday night.

"Nice," I said. "There isn't a place closer to campus?"

"That put vouchers in the student union welcome packs for 50 percent off? No."

"Ah."

"What are *you* doing this far from home?"

"Hiding," I admitted. "It's been a long week."

"You just needed some time off campus?"

"And away from everybody, yeah."

"Oh, okay then." He turned to go.

"No …" I rolled my eyes. "You know what I mean."

A grin. "So I don't have to go?"

"You don't have to go," I said. "No."

"Here's an idea," he said. "Why don't we *both* go?"

*****

Will had a car with him and, as I sat into it, it occurred to me that this was exactly the kind of thing my mother had warned me not to do. No one knew where I was, no one knew who I was with. Even *I* didn't really know who I was with. I felt an undercurrent of nerves, and not just because I'd been daydreaming about him for the last five days straight, building a "him" out of the scant information I had, and now to be faced with the reality was both thrilling and terrifying.

"Where are we going?"

He shrugged. "I was thinking the beach?"

"Is there one near?"

"Sandymount."

"Where's that?"

"Close. You can actually walk there from St. John's."

I hadn't realized. All my Dublin fantasies took me from campus in the other direction, into town. But here was a massive stretch of sand, extending so far out that the water's edge looked like it could be a mirage, an end of a rainbow you could start toward but might never reach. Two enormous chimney stacks extended into the sky on a peninsula on the north end, while off in the distance, on the southern tip of the bay, a cluster of buildings dominated by a church spire suggested a seaside town.

Poolbeg and Dun Laoghaire, he told me.

"I think I came to look at a place near here," I said.

"I didn't even realize it was near a beach."

Will looked at me. "You didn't want to be in Halls?"

"I somehow ended up on their waiting list."

We walked down onto the sand and then southward, parallel to the shore.

"You have to be careful here," Will said, "the tide comes in really fast. People are always getting stranded."

"It's lovely, though," I said.

"Everywhere is lovely when the sun shines."

We'd covered all the basics on our walk back to campus in the early hours of Monday morning: siblings, aspirations, likes/dislikes. Now as we walked the beach, we talked about how we'd ended up in St. John's, why we'd chosen the courses we had, and what we planned on doing with our degrees once we had them.

While he talked, I studied him, logging details in my mind for later daydreams. The fine hairs on his forearms, bleached white by the sun. How the knot of hair in the depression at the base of his neck was much darker. Blue-gray eyes. The wind picked up and he turned against it, letting it blow the thin cotton of his loose T-shirt against his skin, revealing sharp shoulder blades, a narrow waist.

I longed to step forward and wrap my arms around him and, as if reading my thoughts, he reached out his hand and took mine, and then pulled me into him for a long, deep kiss.

Right in the middle of the beach, where we had an audience of dog-walkers and Yummy Mummies jogging in pairs.

How can this be my life? I wondered.

So much had changed in the space of a week. It

seemed like I'd been waiting for years and years for something to happen and now everything was, changes coming as fast as falling dominos, one after the other, with not enough time in between to make an individual sound. I was breathless and scared and exhilarated and certain, all at the same time.

And then Will and I were rudely interrupted by a gust of wind that blew every strand of hair I had into the space between us.

"God," I said, pulling away.

"Sorry. That's my fault. I thought beaches were supposed to be romantic."

"Is that why you brought me here?"

"No, I just love the feel of sand in my shoes." He smiled and dipped his head to kiss me again.

We started back toward the car soon afterward. On the way, I felt a buzz in my pocket: a text message from Liz.

Where the hell are you?!

*****

Claire and Liz were waiting for me outside our block. I said I'd walked as far as Ranelagh and left it at that. "I just needed to get off campus for a couple of hours." Liz said she would've come with me.

"I woke up really early," I said. "I didn't want to wake you."

"Jesus." Liz rolled her eyes. "Do you think I spend half the day in bed or something?"

I realized I'd used the exact same excuse when I'd gone for coffee with Claire.

We all had a library tour at four o'clock. The library was stuffy and hot, and the librarian taking us around spoke in a dreary monotone. After half an hour, Liz and I bailed. Claire said she'd stick it out, so we were down to two again.

It hadn't been that way much this past week, and I wondered if that was partly why I felt so exhausted. It'd been all new people, all of the time. But Liz and I, alone together, was familiar and easy.

Most of the time.

"I feel like I've barely talked to you all week," she said to me.

"I know."

"It's been so busy."

"Yeah."

"And we're way behind on *Lost*."

I smiled. "Priorities."

"We could've skipped the library tour."

"That would've been one episode, maybe one and a half."

"What time is it?" Liz checked her watch. "We could squeeze one in now, maybe?"

Liz suggested we go to her apartment, because her weird roommate was always out during the day. I wondered if this was really because she didn't want Claire coming back and joining us. And I wondered how she was going to react when I told her about Will.

I did it just before we hit the PLAY button.

"Liz," I said, "I've something to tell you."

"It better be about the guy you met on Sunday night."

"What? You ... you *know*?"

"Of course I know. Do you think you were wearing your invisibility cloak that night in the club? I saw you and him. He looked cute, actually. I've been waiting all week for you to tell me about him. So"—she put her hand under her chin in a theatrical show of intense interest—"who is he? What happened? Does he have any equally good-looking single friends?"

I rolled my eyes. "All right, all right. Calm down."

"Tell me everything, Ali. Come on."

So I did.

And Liz wasn't bothered at all. She was delighted. She lapped up every detail. She made all the appropriate sounds.

She was so enthusiastic, I felt bad that I'd thought badly of her.

I shouldn't have.

alison, now

A minute, I gave myself. I let the tears flow, sank into my sadness, let it all in. Then I pulled some tissues from the box on the windowsill, wiped them away and said, *Okay, that's enough. That's it.*

The back bedroom turned out to be, essentially, a nicely decorated storage room. There was a single daybed pushed against one wall, facing a row of white, built-in wardrobes with sliding doors. As I pushed them back, rows of opaque plastic boxes were revealed, neatly placed on the shelves inside and all labeled in my mother's handwriting. They were all filled with stuff of mine. The last compartment had no shelves, just a rail. A number of garments hung from those kind of quaint, stuffed hangers that have little bows on them and smell of floral things. After a second, I realized all the clothes were mine as well.

A fall of black with a splash of diamante, encased now in a dust cover: the dress I'd worn to the Freshers' Ball. Thick, gray cable-knit: the sweater I'd practically lived in during Sixth Year, because it was baggy and warm and comforting, and perfect for studying late at night in. Silvery silk shirt with a delicate floral print, the wraparound silk belt carefully detached, smoothed out and tied neatly around the hanger: what I'd been wearing the night I'd first met Will.

It had been Liz's, originally.

I'd loved that shirt so much, loved how I'd looked it in. It had probably been the first item of clothing I'd owned that wasn't from some disposable-fashion store, that needed to be treated delicately, that won compliments whenever I put it on. I fingered the silk, trying to remember being the girl who'd worn such a beautiful thing, who'd *wanted* people to turn and look at her, who felt good when they did.

What would she be doing now, if things had been different?

Who would she be?

I took the gray sweater off the hanger, pulled it on over my pajama top. It smelled faintly of lavender, which I guessed was the hanger's fault. It wasn't quite as billowing on me as it had once been, but it still felt like a security blanket.

Bracing myself, I turned to the boxes.

I had no idea what I was about to find. When Will had been arrested my parents had come to collect me from Halls and take me back home with them to Cork. Two days later I was on a flight to the Netherlands with only the bag I'd packed in a rush two days before. It was in the weeks after that my mother had gone back to St. John's and cleared out all the stuff I'd left behind. I think she thought I'd be back soon, that I might even pick up college somewhere else in Ireland come September.

I already knew: I was never coming back.

Let's start with something easy.

I pulled out the box marked BOOKS and sat it on the floor. The contents comprised entirely of the texts on the English Lit first-year reading list. *The Riverside Chaucer. Shakespeare: The Complete Works. Literary Theory: An Introduction.* All hefty, expensive tomes. Their smooth, unblemished spines and the clean gloss of their covers were a reminder that I'd been a terrible student, distracted by all the shiny bits of the college experience that had nothing to do with being educated. The heady rush of being away from home for the first time. The endless adventure that living in a city like Dublin offered. Will and his eyes and his arms and his touch.

I replaced the lid and pushed the box to one side.

Next up, DESK.

Did this mean the stuff that I'd kept in my desk in Halls? Lifting the lid, I saw a clear plastic wallet with my proof of college registration and college ID inside it, so yes. This was the contents of my three junk drawers, which my mother had evidently organized and neatly stored. There was a lilac envelope thick with ticket stubs that, as far as I remembered, had been tacked to a noticeboard in my room. I saw her in my mind's eye, carefully unpinning each one. Two grubby, yellowing refill pads were held together with an elastic band; I had a flashback of bringing them into lectures and then only doodling nonsense across their pages while the lecturer droned on. I worked my way through various folders, a St. John's prospectus, little trinkets and mementos I'd collected along the way, and got to the bottom of the box without finding a single thing connected to Will.

No cards, no pictures, no CD, or borrowed notes. Had I thrown them away or had she? I hadn't had time to. I scanned the remaining boxes but nothing was marked as obviously as WILL.

My mother hadn't been merely organizing my stuff. She'd been editing it too.

I pulled down a box marked PHOTO ALBUMS.

I took a deep breath before I removed the lid—and then laughed at what was sitting on top of the stack of albums inside, as if waiting for me all this time.

The Brick.

It wasn't even fifteen years old but the world had such a ferocious appetite for new tech—and the tech companies were in such a rush to satisfy it—that the camera looked now like a relic from a bygone era, a prop from a Space Age show that envisioned a future of jet packs and teleporting, a future that had never transpired. It was about the size of a half-dozen egg carton, and just as clunky. Sharp corners, thick buttons, sliding switches (switches!) and a match-box sized screen. Its dull gray case was heavily scratched and the strap was missing. I pressed the ON button but nothing happened, the batteries inside long dead.

I smiled at the idea that I'd once thought I was the height of sophistication with that thing, lugging my little brick around, carrying it in my bag on nights out. In my defense, our phones were just about taking blurry pics back then and we couldn't do much with them except send them to each other.

I set the camera carefully on the floor and started on the photo albums. I couldn't put them off anymore.

The first album was nearly all shots of campus in the snow. I'd got the camera at Christmas and when we'd returned to St. John's in January, there'd been one day, just for a few hours very early in the morning, when the entire place was blanketed in white, fluffy snow.

Most of the shots were of me and Will. Liz must have taken them.

I imagined her, holding the camera in front of her face, looking at the little screen.

I wondered what she'd been thinking at the time.

Thinking about her now, I felt a stab of pain.

I tried not to linger, but I didn't go quite quickly enough to stop myself from falling into some of those memories, marveling at this nineteen-year-old version of me who seemingly knew how to have more of a life than this twenty-nine-year-old one. I was smiling in every picture, my eyes sparkling. In many of them a hand or a fall of hair would be blurred, because I'd been moving, unable to stay still even for one moment.

I looked so *alive*.

I didn't like getting my photo taken now. I didn't like the dark possibility of where the images might one day end up.

I stopped at a picture of Liz and me, stood in evening dresses the night of the Traffic Light Ball. They were our Debs dresses; we'd just swapped them over for the occasion so we'd each have something new to wear. Liz's floor-length, fishtail black strapless dress looked different on me than it had on her, the material stretched across the small swell of my stomach, the corset part of it pinching the skin under my arms. She'd told me I'd looked beautiful in it.

I looked at Liz, her wide smile, thought about what was coming toward her, hurtling toward her, and none of us knew it—

The picture blurred.

I turned the page.

Overleaf was one of Will, sitting on my bed with his phone in one hand—a Motorola RAZR, all the rage back then—and looking into the lens with a question on his face, as if I'd just called his name and caught him by surprise. He was wearing a navy sweatshirt I remembered well, whose material I could feel now, well-worn and thick, soft against my face.

I could almost remember the smell of it. Of him.

In the picture, there was a half-smile on his lips, as if whatever I could want from him, whatever request I had of him, he'd be willing to give.

Because he was kind. Because he was a good person. Because when I pressed my hand to his chest to feel his heart beating, he'd look down at me and say, "That's all for you," and it didn't feel cheesy or fake, but real and incredible, and I wanted to feel it again, just for one second.

I didn't believe I would ever feel it again, couldn't with anyone else.

I'd give back the whole of my first year in St. John's, those nine months with him, just for one more moment with him now because I missed him, I missed that, I missed *us*.

I loved him and I missed me, the old me. I wanted to be with him and I wanted to be her again.

But he'd killed the girl on the previous page.

And, in other ways, he'd killed the girl I was supposed to become.

I was crying again, salty tears dropping down my cheeks, the taste of them on my lips.

The truth was I'd never stopped loving Will. I'd just accepted that the Will I'd known and loved was dead. Ten years later, I was still trying to come to terms with the fact that he'd never really existed in the first place.

I looked at the caption on the photo: January 28, 2007. If Will was guilty, then the boy in this photo— the kind, good boy who'd loved me—had, at that very moment, already ended a life and had successfully— *totally*—hidden all traces of his dark secret from me.

And was planning his next.

Was that even possible?

Yes, okay, it was possible. Psychopaths were skilled in such deceptions, because entire personalities could be performances, a costume of humanity easily put on or taken off. I'd watched enough TV to know that.

But was it *likely*?

I thought back to him in that buttery yellow room, pleading with me, pleading his case. Wishing he could show me what was in his head so that he could prove to me that he was telling the truth.

Just as an experiment, I tried it on: the idea that Will was innocent.

It took some effort. Will would have to have been incredibly susceptible to coercion, if that confession was false, *and* caught the eye of the country's most prolific serial killer just at the moment he was looking for someone to frame. And then Will would have had to lack the sufficient motivation to do anything about it for nearly ten years.

But I imagined it anyway.

Just for a second, because that was all I could stand.

Because it instantly brought everything crashing down. What I'd done then. What I hadn't done since then. The promise that was Will and me, broken for no reason at all.

Liz, killed by a stranger. Even more terrifying than what I'd imagined in the dark corners of my mind these past ten years.

If Will really was innocent it felt like I might lose everything, like the ground would shift and tilt and everything I had would slide away and fall off.

So he couldn't be.

Anyway, he wasn't innocent. There was too much evidence against him. Evidence I couldn't ignore. Behavior I couldn't get past. Coincidences too improbable.

I swiped at my eyes before hurrying through the rest of the album. Pulled out the next one; flipped quickly through that. More Will, me, and Liz, and a sea of smiling faces I'd long forgotten. Closed it; on to the next one. An album filled almost entirely with crowded group shots, candid snaps, taken during nights out. People changed by having been caught in action, bodies turned away, dim lighting or a plume of cigarette smoke or spots of rain on the lens changing faces, hiding characters, obscuring identities.

I went through each one, sliding my finger across the photos, as if I was following words on a page.

At some point, I heard the garden gate creak from

outside. My mother was back. My stomach started to growl at the anticipation of food.

I found it in the third-last spread from the end.

There was a photo of us standing in a row: Will, Liz, me, and two girls who I think might have been in my Early Theatre class. One peroxide blonde, one jet-black hair. A picture taken on a dance floor of some nightclub, the harsh light of the flash illuminating our sweaty faces, our dilated pupils, the shabby decor of the club beyond. All hidden from us by the dark, on the night.

The first thing I noticed was that Liz wasn't looking at the camera. I was standing in between her and Will, and her head was turned, looking in my direction but past me, at him. She wasn't smiling but it was hard to read the expression on her face.

The second thing I noticed was who was standing behind Liz, with one arm slung casually around her waist.

The man from the CCTV images. Red Baseball Cap.

Out with us, in a club. Back then.

With his arm around *Liz*, one of the Canal Killer's victims.

Downstairs, keys rattled in the front door. Footsteps in the hall, followed by the murmur of voices.

I pulled the photo from the album and brought it close to my face, studying every detail. Who was this guy? Liz hadn't dated anyone while we were at St. John's that I could remember. Was it just some random connection at the club? Just a pose for this photograph?

How could this possibly be a coincidence?

It couldn't be.

I had to tell Malone. I took my phone from my jeans pocket, found his number and pressed CALL.

Somewhere in the house, a phone started ringing.

My mother's voice, calling up from the hall. "Alison? Alison, are you up there? There's some people here to see you."

Malone picked up after one ring.

"We're here," he said. "Shaw and me. Downstairs."

alison, now

They were in the kitchen.

Shaw was pulling out a chair at the dining table while my mother fussed around him, producing a milk jug and matching sugar bowl, and asking him what strength he liked his tea.

Malone was standing just inside the door, waiting for me.

"Are you all right?" he asked. I nodded. He touched my arm. "You sure?"

I remembered then: I'd been crying. I was probably all red and splotchy, puffy-eyed.

"Yes, fine," I said. "My mother and I, we were talking. I got upset … It wasn't about before."

"What happened before, exactly?"

"Just like I said in the text I sent you. Reporters and photographers outside the hotel. I couldn't go back there."

"But why were you outside?"

"I wanted some fresh air."

Malone sighed. "Well, next time, let me know."

"I did."

"*Before* you leave. And then wait for me to get there so I can take you."

"Don't worry," I said. "I don't plan on going outside ever again." I looked over at Shaw. "What's happening?"

Malone motioned toward the table. "Let's sit down."

"As long as it's hot," Shaw was saying to my mother amidst the clinks of crockery and cutlery. "That's all I require. Don't be going to any trouble now, Mrs. Smith."

"Oh, it's no trouble." My mother turned and saw me. "Alison, I got you some lunch—"

"I'll have it later," I said. "Thanks, Mam."

Shaw was sitting on the far side of the table. Malone took the seat next to him. I wondered if they were contractually obliged to always sit side by side.

"We've met before, I think," my mother said to Shaw. "Haven't we?"

"Just the once, Mrs. Smith. I came down to Cork."

The electric kettle clicked off.

"Tea?" my mother said to Malone.

"Mam," I said, "can you, ah, go into the other room?"

"But, Alison, I … Well"—she looked to Shaw—"shouldn't I stay?"

"Please." I smiled tightly at her. "Thanks."

"Don't worry," Shaw said to her. "It's nothing serious. We'll only be a few minutes."

"Well then, why can't I stay?" she asked him.

"Because I'm thirty years old," I said. "Mam, please."

"Twenty-nine," she corrected. Then she hovered, looking uncertainly at her tea-making accoutrements.

"Really won't be long," Shaw said with a smiley face that didn't suit him. "Just a quick chat, that's all we'll be having."

"I'll make the tea," I said. "It's fine."

"There's biscuits in the—"

"Mam, *please*."

"All right, all right." She held up her arms. "I'm going, I'm going." After throwing me a look that said I'd proved her point—I *was* acting like a teenager—she finally, reluctantly, left the room.

I poured two cups of tea and brought them to the dining table, pushing one across the tabletop to Shaw and another to Malone before realizing I hadn't asked him if he'd wanted any.

The radio was off now, I noticed, which meant it'd be easier for my mother to eavesdrop on our conversation from the other side of the door. But then Shaw said, "Do you think the lady of the house would mind if I had a smoke out the back there?" He nodded toward the patio doors, giving me the opportunity to suggest that we all move out into the garden.

The chairs out there were missing their cushions, but Shaw sat on one anyway. Malone perched on the low wall that separated the patio from the higher, green level of the garden. I remained standing, facing the house, looking at my own reflection in the extension's windows.

"I hear you've had quite the morning," Shaw said. He lit his cigarette and the smoke immediately began to drift in my direction. He waved a hand at it. "Sorry about that."

"Can I have one?"

He raised his eyebrows in surprise. "You don't smoke."

"I don't."

He snorted. "Nah, neither do I."

Shaw held the packet out to me and I took one, lit it with his lighter. He watched me with a smirk on his face, that infuriating look some men who smoke give women they've just discovered do—or do sometimes—as they wait to see if we know how, if we'll actually inhale.

He offered the box to Malone next, who shook his head.

I made a point of taking a long first drag. Bitter tobacco taste filled my mouth. I'd smoked for a couple of years when I'd first moved to the Netherlands, on and off, eventually giving up one particular freezing January when, buoyed by New Year motivation, I couldn't face standing outside and I refused to stink out my house. Every time I'd smoked since it was the idea of it, the anticipation of that first drag, that was the only bit I enjoyed. But I'd bloody smoke this whole sour thing now, though, just to show Shaw.

"Yeah," I said. "I thought the press wasn't going to find out I was here."

"We did our best, love. Unfortunately their job is to find out the things we don't want them to know."

I took another drag. Each one tasted worse than before. If I took long pauses between them, at least most of the cigarette would burn down by itself.

"They called it a date," I said.

"They want to sell papers."

Shaw took a long, deep drag of his cigarette and looked to Malone, signaling for him to talk.

"We want to bring Will in for a formal interview," he said.

I asked why.

Malone opened his mouth to answer but Shaw cut in before he could.

"We just do," he said flatly. "And he's refused."

"Can he do that?"

"Will's already serving five life sentences," Malone said. "Threats of further punishment are like water off a duck's back."

"Look," Shaw said, "yeah, we could arrest him, haul him in, threaten him with charges, and he could sit there and tell us "No comment" every thirty seconds for the rest of the day. But we'd prefer it if he *wanted* to talk to us." He paused to inhale, then he pointed the lit end of the cigarette at me. "I think if you put your mind to it, you could convince him to do it."

"You want me to see him again?"

Both men nodded.

I didn't want to, but I wondered if maybe Will would know the man in the photograph.

"I have something for you." I pulled the print from my back jeans pocket and explained where it'd come from. "That's the man from the CCTV pictures, isn't it? Who was wearing the red baseball cap? And that's me, Will, and Liz on a night out somewhere in Dublin." I handed it to Malone. "Will, Liz, me—we've all met him."

"Jesus Christ," Shaw breathed. "And Mickey here said you saw this guy outside your hotel as well?"

"Maybe," I said. "He was too far away to know for sure."

"Who is he?" Malone asked me.

I shook my head. "That I don't know. Sorry. But

you must have ways of finding out, right? That's a much better picture, and maybe you could find one of those other girls and they'd remember. Or maybe Will would—he hasn't seen this yet. And it tells you this guy was in or around St. John's back then. That's good, right? I mean, why would he be copying the original crimes if he didn't have some connection to the first lot?"

Shaw was making a face like he'd swallowed a fly. "He could still be at St. John's, that's the problem. One of those guys who stay there getting degree after degree, postponing the real world. That would explain his midnight canal walks. He could just be going to and from campus. He could have nothing to do with this." Shaw handed the photo to Malone. "Get this to the incident room."

"He might be one of the names," Malone said.

"What names?" I asked.

"The phones have been hopping since we released the CCTV images. We collate all the names supplied and make a list of the ones that come up again and again. We can't check everyone so that's how we narrow it down."

"*Malone*," Shaw said warningly.

Malone turned and went inside. I watched through the glass as he walked through the kitchen and out into the hall. I didn't know if he was leaving but I was afraid that he might be.

When I turned back to Shaw, he was stubbing out his cigarette and watching me watch Malone.

"He's very chatty altogether," Shaw said, "isn't he?"

I knew by "chatty" he meant overly generous with details of Garda investigations.

I feigned ignorance. "Is he?"

"Do you believe him?" He took the cigarette pack out of his pocket and started to light another. "Hurley and his little innocence spiel?"

My cigarette was finally done. I flicked the butt into one of my mother's plant pots and sat down on the spot of the wall Malone had vacated, feeling a little lightheaded from the smoke.

"I don't have to believe him," I said. "It's not up to me. I'm not the one handing down judgments."

Shaw snorted. "You're saying if Hurley was innocent but still stuck inside, it wouldn't bother you because you're not the one *handing down judgments*?"

"*Is* he?"

"What?"

"Innocent."

"No."

Shaw met my eye and we stared at each other for an uncomfortably long moment. I felt like he was waiting for me to break, for tears to come, for some other truth to burst out.

But I held my nerve.

"He is guilty," Shaw said, hoisting himself out of the chair. "And he should be in a prison, but nah, we have him in the CPH because he's"—Shaw made air quotes—"*depressed*. So they put him with a therapist three times a week, and give him some coloring pencils or whatever it is they do. At least the holiday's over soon. Off to Clover Hill he goes. You know what's ironic? If you consider the turnover of staff in the CPH and the sheer number of them Will encounters there on a day-to-day basis, he's had more contact with people who live in the outside world than he would've had with his fellow prisoners if he'd been in Clover Hill all this time."

"What does that have to—"

"Back in 2007, we found this girl, right?" Shaw started pacing around the patio, waving his cigarette around as he talked. "Heather Buckley. She'd been mugged walking home early one Sunday morning after a night on the town during Freshers' Week. *Attempted* mugging, I should say, because two guys out for a dawn cycle came upon the scene while the incident was in progress, and the guy ran off. They didn't get a good look at him, but nothing in the description they *did* give would rule Will Hurley out. And this happened by the canal. And Heather was in St. John's." He was standing in front of me now and he stopped there to tell me the next part. "I think that was his first attempt, thwarted by the two Lycra Lads. Here's what's interesting, though. Heather said that the guy who ran off wasn't her attacker. He was actually a Good Samaritan who'd stopped to see if she was all right, prompting her *actual* attacker to run off. But when the cyclists came on the scene, the Samaritan *runs off himself.* What does that tell you?"

"I'm sorry," I said, "I'm not following."

"There's Boy A and Boy B, right? Boy A attacks the girl. Boy B comes along and scares Boy A off, thereby leaving Boy B alone with the girl. She thinks he's a nice guy, stopped to help a girl out. Her knight in shining armor. Then maybe he offers to walk her home, maybe he offers her his couch while they wait for the guards to arrive. Or this is 2007, so maybe he says you can use my landline. Landlines, eh? Remember those? My point is, he's got her, this Boy B. She trusts him. And if Boy A and Boy B are buddies, well …"

Shaw looked at me pointedly.

"You think they were working together," I said, "and that the cyclists ruined their plan, and that one of them was Will and the other was the guy who's out there, the new cases."

"Clever girl." Shaw took a deep drag, even though his cigarette was already down to the filter and I could see the paper glowing dangerously red against his fingers. "Have you ever considered a career in An Garda Síochána?"

"That's ridiculous."

"I know. The hours are terrible and the pay is shite."

"I meant your theory."

He coughed loudly, a wet, phlegmy sound. "I even had a code name at the ready. 'Operation Gentleman.' What do you think?"

"I think you should probably stop smoking."

"It would explain a lot, wouldn't it? Like how he manages to incapacitate these girls and get them into the water five feet from a busy road, in the dead of night when a splash would be a loud noise. And then walk away, soaked to the bone." Shaw paused to cough again. "I think it's quite clever, actually. Tag-teaming. One attacks, the other saves—but the one who saves is the real attacker."

"And then what?"

"Who knows? Maybe they both come back to do the deed, or maybe they take turns being the Good Guy." More coughing. Shaw was going a little red in the face and his eyes were watering. "Now, maybe I'm wrong. That girl had been through something, and she was upset. Maybe the guy ran away because one of the Lycra Lads was his dad or his older brother and it was five o'clock on a Sunday morning and his eyes were like bloody saucers. It's just a theory. But because our Willie Boy has got a case of the sads and is in the CPH, he's easier to get to than he would be in prison. If you needed to, you know, *plan something*. Do you see what I'm getting at, love?"

"You think he might have got to Will in there. The new killer."

"Exactly. We've checked all visitation applications. No joy. But I know the first thing I'll be doing with that photo is checking it against their employee records. This morning I got them to search Will's room. I've got guys going through all the correspondence he saved, just in case."

"Have you talked to that Heather girl?"

"She was never able to provide us with a detailed description."

"You could show her the photo now," I suggested.

"We will."

"So when do I go?"

"Home?"

"To the CPH."

Shaw looked at me sideways while stubbing out his cigarette. "You're saying you'll go?"

I stood up, pausing to check the lightheaded feeling had passed. "I want to know who the guy in the photo is too."

"One more thing," Shaw said. "I've been in this job a long time. I can't tell you how many times I knew a guy wasn't telling me the truth but I didn't have the evidence to prove it. You can't just go in and tell the judge, 'I know he's lying.' Unfortunately. Now with Hurley, we did have the evidence. We had forensics and his little stalker manual, which, helpfully, he was keeping in his own locker. But even before that, I knew we had our guy. Because from the *moment* he came into that interview room, I knew he was lying to us." He stepped closer. "There's no case where everything fits together perfectly, love, okay? You never get all the dots to join. That's just the nature of the beast. Hurley, he might say things to you that make you think, *Hang on a second, there could be something here*, but trust me, that's not what *we* think when we hear them. We think, *Oh, okay, this is just like any other case, then.* You're always going to have discrepancies."

"Like what?"

"Well, I'm sure Will's already provided you with a highlights reel. Let me guess. We forced him to confess, the blood was planted, he'd never seen that folder before in his life?"

"Pretty much," I said, "yeah."

"It's all bullshit, love." Shaw's expression had softened, and his tone was more gentle now. "I'm just trying to help you, you know. Get you back to Holland in one piece."

"You said you knew Will was lying when he came in for the interview, *before* you found the stuff in his locker and the blood?"

"Yeah."

"What made you bring Will in in the first place, then?"

Shaw hesitated a moment. Then he said, "He was on our list."

"What list?"

"*The* list. Of suspects."

"But why?"

Shaw looked away, into the kitchen. "Well, he knew Liz Whelan."

"So did a lot of people."

"Yeah, well. A lot of people had alibis."

"For when? For the night of Liz's murder?"

"For all of the nights. All of the murders."

"And Will didn't?"

Shaw looked back at me. "Why do you ask?"

Now *I* hesitated.

"I don't really remember the order of events," I said then. "It's all a bit of a blur to me."

"I can understand that. By the way—thank you." Shaw said this with an uncharacteristic sincerity. "For doing this. For coming here. You did the right thing."

"Well … That's okay."

"Now if you could just get Will to have a little chat with us, I'd really appreciate it, Alison. Really."

"When you knocked on my door, you didn't think he actually had any information, did you? You thought it was a waste of time."

"I most certainly did."

"Then why bother asking me to come here at all?"

"It was for him." Shaw nodded toward the house. "Mickey Boy. He was beating himself up over Louise Farrington. He wanted to exhaust every possible avenue. I was just letting him."

"And now?"

Shaw frowned. "What?"

"You haven't sent me home yet."

"Well, now that you're here, love, we may as well make use of you, eh?" Shaw grinned.

"Yeah." I smiled back. "You know something?"

"What?"

"*You're* pretty chatty too."

I turned on my heel and went inside.

Malone was coming through the kitchen. Any relief I felt at his still being here instantly dissipated when he said, "We need to go. We have a female St. John's first-year missing since last night."

The pressure in his skull is so bad he fantasizes about the bone cracking open, fissures starting at the crown and spreading out in all directions, releasing it. Releasing him. He punches two chalky tablets out of a blister pack and swallows them with a mouthful of cloudy water from the kitchen sink, wincing at the bitter taste when one of them begins to dissolve on his tongue. Sweat collects at his hairline and under his arms. He wipes at his forehead with a sheet of cheap paper towels and puts on his blazer to hide the damp patches on his shirt. He rests his palms on the kitchen counter, leans his weight against it, closes his eyes. Tries to convince himself the blackness brings at least a slight relief.

When he opens them again he sees the garden shed, thirty feet away at the end of the garden. The window over the sink frames it perfectly. The shed sits at an angle, its front directed a few degrees away from the back of the house, and from this vantage point he notices something he didn't before: it has a large window set into its left side.

The doorbell rings. They're early.

The man on the stoop is friendly, all smiles. The woman next to him is straining her neck to see into the hall, a sour expression on her face, as if the house is a muddy field she's going to have to navigate in nice shoes.

As he checks their names against his appointment book and welcomes them to the house, he feels the woman's eyes wander onto his forehead, to the beads of sweat he knows must be glistening there. This only makes him sweat more. When he turns to lead them down the hall into the kitchen, he feels a warm stream of it sneak down his spine and pool in the small of his back.

The pain in his head throbs in time with his pulse. It hurts to think. Although his spiel is well practiced, he's not sure he can deliver it just now. He needs the pills to kick in, to sand down the sharp edges of the pain. So he hands over one of his glossy brochures and suggests they go explore the house by themselves. He says he'll meet them after, here, in the kitchen, to answer any questions they may have.

He suggests they start upstairs and work their way down. He tells them to take their time.

As soon as they've left the room, he drops into one of the chairs at the dining table and puts his head in his hands, willing the pulsating in his brain to slow or stop. It's been developing for the past hour, threatening since the middle of last night. He should've taken something for it hours ago.

He hears the woman's voice in the hall mutter, "Fucking shit tip."

"You have to use your imagination, Em."

"And that guy looks like he has Ebola."

"Ssshhh …"

He can barely think through the pain. He knows the pills will start to dull it soon, but what until then? The kitchen starts to feel like its spinning. He pulls one of the brochures toward him and tries to focus on the text, a steady center in all the movement.

> *R&P Estate Agents are proud to present this superb three-bedroom semi-detached home in this ever popular, mature, and sought-after location. The property is close to all amenities and offers easy access to the M50, public transport links, and all main arteries through the city and beyond. Accommodation is over two floors, the centerpiece being an open-plan kitchen/living space, which offers flexible options to suit any style of living, thus enabling the purchaser to tailor their new home to their family's needs and put their own stamp on the property. It benefits from a south-facing garden, ample off-street parking and built-in storage in all three bedrooms. The main bathroom requires some modernization but it is a sizeable space with great potential. The previous owners began the conversion of the attic space into a fourth bedroom, a project which, when complete, will offer panoramic views over South Dublin. Welcome home.*

He wrote it himself, so he knows what it really means. R&P Estate Agents will pretend to be proud to present anything you pay us to, including this musty, neglected, bog-standard three-bedroom semi. The housing market being the way it is, we could park a septic tank in the shell of a burnt-out house anywhere between the sea and the motorway and get more than the asking price from one of the hundreds who'd queue up to view it. Easy access to the M50? Sure. But only before eight in the morning and after seven at night, because there's about fifteen sets of traffic lights to get through before you get to the on-ramp. Since you're going to have to gut the place entirely, you might as well make it look the way you like. You can start with removing the storage upstairs, which comes in the form of unsightly 1970s-era built-ins that dominate every room to the point of oppression. They actually finished the attic conversion but never secured planning permission for it, so we can't say they did. Bonus: the ceiling up there is so dramatically sloped that the Velux window is at chest height, so if you bend down a bit you'll get a view of a sea of slate roofs and, beyond them, the monstrous eyesore that is the new incinerator at Poolbeg.

The "welcome home" bit was the boss' idea. All the agents add it with an eye-roll to the end of every property description R&P put out.

He hears footsteps directly above his head, dull thumps on the bare floorboards in the master bedroom. He folds his arms on the tabletop and rests his head on them. He wishes he could sleep. He will when they leave. He'll take a nap. There's an old blanket in the boot of his car. He can put it on one of the cold, damp beds upstairs and lie down on top.

He slides into the bliss of that idea. That's all he

needs: to sleep for a while. He'd been up all night. A couple of hours of it and he'll be able to think clearly. Then he can sort everything out.

He just needs to sleep …

Footsteps, on the decking outside.

He wakes up with a jolt, nearly knocking over the chair he was sitting on in his rush to get to the kitchen window. The couple are outside, in the back garden. They must have gone out through the double-doors in the living room. *He* must have dozed off.

The man is walking toward the shed.

The pills are working hard to dull the pain, making him groggy. He struggles to turn the lock in the double-doors here, in the kitchen, and half-stumbles out onto the deck.

The woman is out there, flipping through the brochure.

"So no garage?" she says to him. "I didn't see one …"

He answers automatically. "There's certainly space for it."

The man is at the shed now.

The padlock on the door glints in the sunshine. But it's not the door that worries him.

It's that side window.

"I think they're taking that with them," he calls out as he starts down the garden, trying not to look like he's hurrying.

The man turns, frowns at him. "The shed? Really? Do people do that?"

"Sometimes, yes. Have you seen the side entrance?"

"Yeah, on our way in."

"Your wife was asking about a garage."

"Wife," the man repeats. He smiles. "She'll love that."

"Oh, is she not …?"

"We're not married, no."

The woman is standing on the decking, shielding her eyes from the sun, looking at them.

"Why don't we go back inside?" he suggests. "You two can take a closer look at the kitchen."

The man hesitates. He looks at the shed again. "Yeah …"

"Filled with junk, that thing is." He points at it. "Right to the door. They'll have a hell of a time clearing it out before they move it. I don't envy them."

The man nods. "Probably a good thing they're taking it with them. I'd do exactly the same thing." He laughs and starts back up the garden, back toward the house.

Away from the shed.

Finally.

On the deck the woman is looking bored and impatient. She starts walking toward the man.

"They're taking the shed," he tells her, raising his voice to cover the distance between them.

She makes a face. "Do people do that?"

When both halves of the couple are within feet of the deck again, he goes to the shed's door and tugs on the padlock, double-checking. Locked. Then he goes to the window, which is grimy and partially blocked by a stack of shelves inside, but still offers a narrow view of the interior of the shed.

The wheeled plastic garbage bin is still standing there.

PROPERTY OF ST JOHN'S COLLEGE, it says on the side.

At the sight of it, the pain in his head throbs harder. It's all gone wrong and he's not sure how to make it right. He turns and heads back to the house.

alison, now

When Malone said *we*, of course, he meant he and Shaw needed to leave.

"What about Will?" I asked. "Am I still going to see him?"

"Maybe one of the local lads could bring her?" Shaw suggested to Malone.

"Yeah, maybe." He turned to me. "Leave it with us."

"When do you think …?"

"It'll be a few hours, at least."

"You're taking the picture," I said. "I won't be able to show it to him."

"I don't want you showing him," Shaw said. "We"—he indicated him and Malone—"need to see Will's reaction for ourselves, and we need to record it. I want a formal interview. That's what you can do: get him to talk to us."

"I'll call you," Malone said to me.

After they left, my mother made lunch for both of us, peppering me with questions about what the detectives and I had talked about between bites. I dutifully filled her in, sticking to the bullet points.

"A girl is missing," I said then. "A first-year from St. John's."

"Oh, no." My mother shook her head. "God, that's awful. Her poor parents. Imagine what they must be thinking." She started clearing the plates. "I'll put on the news. They might have something on about it."

I had no interest if they did.

"Can I take a shower, Mam?"

"A shower?" She smiled. "I have something *much* better than that, love."

Turns out my mother's newfound love for interior design extended to indulging in luxury bathroom features as well. She led me upstairs, to the en suite off the master bedroom and then motioned for me to go in so I'd discover it for myself: a giant, freestanding bathtub that almost came up to my hip. There was a wire shelf set across it, providing a resting place for various bottles of bubble bath and maybe a book.

"I situate your father downstairs," she said, "and I come up here, put in my bubbles, pour a nice glass of wine and then I have the Kindle but do you know what I do with it? I put in a ziplock bag! Isn't that a good idea? You can have that one for free."

I couldn't help but laugh. "Mam, what *is* all this? The house, the bath, the garden. Did you guys win the Lotto or something and decide not to tell me?"

"No, I just … You know." She gave a little shrug. "What else would I be doing? I have to occupy my time somehow." She smiled, denoting it a joke, but the translation I heard was, *My only child refuses to come visit, and grandkids? What are those?*

I was beginning to see that I wasn't the only one who'd lost a part of herself to the past.

My mother left me with soft towels and an array of smelly things, and only after I'd told her three times no, no, really, I wouldn't have any wine. The tub took forever to fill but the wait was worth it. Sinking my shoulders beneath the hot, rose-scented water was a moment of pure, unadulterated bliss.

I closed my eyes.

I thought of Will.

My phone began to ring.

I'd left it on a facecloth on the wire shelf. I pulled myself up out of the water again to check the screen.

Sal.

Before I could think too much about what would happen next, I picked up the phone and answered it.

"Ali? Sorry, I didn't expect you to answer … I was just going to leave a message. Are you okay? What's going on? Can you talk?"

"Sal." It was so nice to hear her voice. It felt like an age since I'd spoke to her last and, for us, it really was. "Sal, listen. There's something I need to tell you."

"What's wrong?" Her words were sharp with concern.

"I'm fine. Physically fine, anyway. Everyone is. The reason I'm here … I came here because …" I didn't know where to start. "It's a really long story."

"I have time."

"I should've told you it long ago."

"That's okay," she said, although she sounded a little uncertain. "You're telling me now."

"It's about something that happened before I came to the Netherlands. It's why I came to the Netherlands, actually."

"Ali, whatever this is—do you *want* to tell me it? Don't feel you have to."

"No, no. I do. I want to." I bit my lip; tears were threatening. "I *need* to, Sal."

"Well … I'm listening."

It would be better, I decided, to do this quickly. All in one go. Rip off the Band-Aid.

I took a deep breath.

"I went to college in Ireland," I said. "For one year. Before I went in Den Hague. A place called St. John's, here in Dublin. And while I was there, there was a series of … of murders. Five girls. There's this canal that runs through the city, right by the campus, and each of them—they'd been walking home late at night and someone had attacked them, pushed them in."

"I think I remember that," Sal said. "I remember seeing something about it on Sky News. They got the guy, though, right? The one who was doing it. Wasn't he a student there too or something?"

"Yes," I said and that was the last word I got out before the tears came. The sounds of my crying traveled down the line. "Yes, he was."

"Ali? Ali, what's wrong? Did … did you know one of them? One of the girls?"

"Since primary school. Her name was Liz."

"Oh, no. Oh, God. I'm so sorry. That must have been awful." She paused. "But why am I only hearing this now? Why wouldn't you tell me that?"

"Because …"

Just say it. Just tell her. Just do it.

"Because I knew *him*, too."

There was a moment of silence. By the time Sal asked, "How?" I was beginning to panic, beginning to fear that what came next was judgment, disgust, and disbelief, but it was too late to turn back now.

"We were, um ..." I wiped at my eyes with the back of my free hand. "We were together, Sal. I ... I loved him."

In a rush, I blurted out the newest chapter in the story. A copycat killer, the Gardaí asking me to talk to Will, me coming to Dublin and discovering that maybe what I thought had happened back then wasn't the real story, or at least not all of it. Me wondering if Will really was who *they* said he was, or who I'd thought he was back then.

"Best-case scenario," I said, "he had an accomplice, which means I'm an even bigger idiot than I thought I was, because I didn't see anything, ever, that pointed to that. So not only was this killer right under my nose, in my *bed*, but this whole—this whole other clandestine operation was going on around me as well. And I've stepped back into all this for nothing *and* he's fooled me yet again, because I've been second-guessing everything, thinking that he's ..." I took a breath, exhaled. "And that's the worst-case scenario, Sal. That's he's innocent. That he didn't do these things. That I thought he could've ... That he had hurt Liz. And I ran away, I abandoned him, and he's been in there all this time rotting, losing the best years of his life, and I"—my voice cracked—"I can't even deal with the *prospect* of that."

I don't know what I expected Sal to say to this, but

it certainly wasn't, "I'm getting on a plane. I'm coming to you."

"What?" I could hear noises, like her moving stuff around a desk. It was Monday afternoon; she'd be at work. "Sal, no—"

"Is there an evening flight from Schiphol? Or maybe Eindhoven. I could get Dirk to drive me there."

"Sal, wait. No. Seriously. There's no need."

"Are you *kidding*?"

"Sal," I said, "really. I love you and you're amazing—that's amazing, that you would do that—but you don't need to come here. I'd never ask you to—"

"You didn't ask."

"But I'm coming back tomorrow. So there's no point. Really. I mean it."

"Are you sure? I could just go for the night and then come back with you. Are you flying back into Schiphol? If I came to you now then you wouldn't have to come down on the train by yourself when you get back. We don't even have to train it. We could get Dirk to collect us."

"You're really hell-bent on getting Dirk to drive somewhere, aren't you?" Sal laughed. "Look, I'm sure. There's no need. Thank you, though."

"Okay, well, phew," Sal said. "I didn't see *Line of Duty* last night and I was really looking forward to watching it after work. I'd have resented you for delaying it. For a long time. And so would Dirk, because I told him if he watches it without me that's, like, automatic divorce."

I smiled and felt the warmth of it spread across my chest. I should've called Sal long before now. She was a welcome breeze of normality wafting through all this stuff. She was *my* normality, reminding me that this wasn't my life but a mere detour from it, and as soon I returned to Breda everything would be all right again.

So long as this time, I got myself some closure first.

"I don't know what to do." Careful not to drop the phone, I leaned back against the cool ceramic of the bath. "Tell me what I should do. Please."

"What are the options?"

"I'm not even sure."

"Well, talk to me. Can you just leave? Come home now?"

"No, I have to go see him again. Later. They want me to convince him to be formally interviewed."

"'They'?"

"The Gardaí."

"Do you really *have* to, though?"

"I don't know, to be honest. No? But I want to."

"Why?"

I thought of the photograph. "There's something I want to ask him."

"Were you still dealing with this when I first met you?"

"Well, yeah. It had just happened at the start of that summer."

"Shit, Ali. I'm so sorry."

"It's not your fault."

"I wish you'd told me. We could've talked about it."

"I should've. But I was mortified, Sal."

"About what?"

"About not knowing. I mean, how stupid do you have to be to be in love with a person who *murders* other people and not know about it? Murder, Sal. What kind of person do you have to be to do that? And he did it five times."

"Well," Sal said, and I just knew by her tone a joke was coming, "I will have to stop accusing you of being too picky."

I rolled my eyes, but I was smiling. "I can't believe you just said that."

"Humor's how I deal, okay? Deal with it."

"But seriously."

"Seriously? Ali, he murdered five girls. That's at least four murders the police didn't solve right away, four times they failed to catch him. And they're the *police*. There's hundreds of them. You were just one teenage girl. How in God's name *could* you have known?"

I didn't have an answer for this. Only that no matter which way I looked at things, I still felt like I should have.

"Did you say he confessed?" Sal asked then.

"Yes."

"I'm just asking the question here, but doesn't that make his guilt pretty cut and dry?"

"That's what I used to think."

A beat passed. "*Used* to?"

"Apparently the confession was coerced. It's false. Or it could be. That's what he says, anyway. And there's this detective here, Malone, who seems to think there might be something to it, that Will might be innocent, and that the quote unquote *real killer* is the one out there now, doing it again."

"Why does he think that?"

"In Ireland if you plead guilty, there's no trial.

Malone says because of that, the evidence against Will wasn't … *interrogated* is the word he used. There wasn't a lawyer in a court room somewhere defending Will, saying, 'Yeah, okay, but what about *this*?'"

"That's his name? Will?"

It was strange to hear his name spoken in Sal's voice. It had always been this gulf between us, this dark void—and Sal hadn't even known it was there. At least, no matter what happened now, I had closed that up and let her in. I'd finally told her everything.

Almost.

"Yeah," I said. "Will."

"How long were you together?" Sal asked.

"All of first year. Well, up until he was arrested. That happened at the start of May. So about nine months."

"What was he like?"

No one had ever asked me that without hoping I'd unconsciously reveal some trait that absolutely pointed to him being a serial killer. Sal, I knew, just genuinely wanted to know.

"He was … He was great. Kind and smart and funny and caring. And gorgeous, I thought. I'd say I spent our entire time together just totally … *distracted* by him. I couldn't concentrate on anything else. He was my first proper boyfriend, so there was that, too, but still. I'd never met anyone like him before. I haven't since. He was just … He was perfect. I mean, nobody's perfect but for me—to me—he was." I paused. "I think this is where one of us uses the phrase 'too good to be true.'"

"Okay, so look," Sal said. "The police. They're trying to catch this new guy, right?"

"Right."

"And if they do and if the new guy admits he killed the girls ten years ago, that will prove Will's innocence?"

"If and if, then yes."

"But otherwise, Will is guilty? I mean, it's not like *you* can prove his guilt or innocence, right? Not by yourself."

"No …"

"Are you trying to?"

"No," I said again, although I wasn't sure. I'd gone looking through my photographs, hadn't I? I'd told myself it was because I wanted to know where I knew the CCTV guy from.

But was that the real reason?

"Ali, you say you don't know what to do, but really, you shouldn't be doing anything at all. You don't have to. All you need to think about is how you're going to react to however this turns out. I mean, do you *want* your life to change? Do you want to ditch your job, move back to Ireland and live with Will, happily ever after?"

"God, no." The idea was preposterous. I couldn't even picture it, let alone examine whether or not I wanted it. "No. Not at all. That's not what this is about."

"Then what is it about?"

"Doing the right thing."

"For who?"

I exhaled. "In general."

"So you flew to Dublin on Morals Air, is what you're saying?"

"I owe him this."

"*Owe* him? You owe him nothing!"

"That's not strictly true."

Sal sighed. "Explain."

I shifted my weight. The water was going cold around me.

"I did something," I said. "Back then. I made … I made a mistake."

A beat of silence. "Go on."

"The reason they arrested him—" I swallowed, trying to hold back the tears that were trying to break through once again. "I think they arrested him because of *me*."

alison, now

I borrowed a freshly laundered T-shirt of my mother's to slip on under my gray sweater, took the time to blow-dry my hair straight, and applied a little of the expensive makeup I found in the bathroom cabinet. There was a nearly empty bottle of some floral perfume in there as well and, after a second's hesitation, I spritzed some of it on. But now, seeing the look on the face of the uniformed Garda who'd been tasked with driving me to the CPH, I wondered if maybe I should've just changed my T-shirt and left it at that.

She'd flashed her badge and ID at me: Garda Emily Cusack. Half a foot taller than me, Cusack had large blue eyes and that kind of fresh-faced, natural-beauty look that I knew I'd never achieve without a makeup bag.

"Alison Smith?" she'd said after I'd opened my mother's front door to her. "I need you to come with me, please. I'm to escort you to the Central Psych Hospital for a patient visit."

There was a squad car parked outside the garden

gate with its engine running and another uniformed
Garda behind the wheel. Cusack motioned for me to get
in the back on the passenger side, then sat in the seat in
front of me. The central locking clicked and we drove
off, tires squealing.

I'd never been in a proper Garda car before, not one
of the liveried ones. A clunky-looking laptop computer
was mounted to the dashboard, angled toward the driver,
and there was some sort of radio or walkie-talkie thing
charging on the dash. I would've thought there'd be a kind
of grate or Perspex partition between the front and back
seats, but there was none. I must watch too much TV.

The two Gardaí spoke in low tones to each other
up front, but not at all to me. I was grateful they took
the M50 to Dundrum, reducing the awkwardness to a
twenty-minute drive.

At the CPH, neither Shaw nor Malone was
anywhere to be seen, but I'd been expecting that. Malone
had called to say they were tied up with the missing girl
and he'd check in with me later. In the meantime, I was
to meet Will as planned and try to convince him to talk
to them as soon as they had a chance to talk to *him*.

Everything was different this time around. I had
to produce ID, have my photo taken, pass through a
metal detector, and submit to a pat-down by a security
guard. My bag and phone were placed in a locker, but I
was—inexplicably—given the option of keeping small
change on me. I was brought to a waiting room where
I was surprised to find a man standing with a dog on
a leash until the dog started circling my legs and I
realized he was working.

I felt bewildered by all this, and confused as to why

this was my third visit but my first time experiencing any of it.

A few minutes later, the door to the waiting room opened and a familiar face walked in.

"Alek," I said, relieved.

"Welcome back." He shook my hand. "You get the full visitor experience this time."

"Yeah, I noticed," I said. "But why?"

"Well, it's been in the papers, hasn't it? There's no point in special measures anymore. We're going to put you in the visitors' room this time. You're entering the main area of the hospital and you'll be in a space where other patients will be after you leave, so we've had to process you like we would any other visitor. The director has granted an exception for you to visit outside of regular hours, but other than that"—Alek winked— "you're not a VIP anymore. Sorry."

Using his staff keycard to open various locked doors along the way, Alek led me through the building and into a glass corridor, which formed a connection between the main building and another smaller, newer one behind it. A security guard there checked my name against a list on his tablet computer and, judging by the way he peered at me, matched me to the photograph they'd taken back at reception as well. Then, into the visitors' room: a huge, open space that reminded me of the PE hall at school or a local community center. Breezeblock walls painted magnolia, overly bright fluorescent lights, navy and blue checkered carpet tiles. A number of tables paired with four chairs each— eight, I counted—were spread around the room and away from each other, all unoccupied. There were two vending machines in a far corner and, set into the back wall, some kind of hatch or service counter with its shutters rolled down. A security camera was mounted in each corner of the ceiling and a heavyset security guard stood against the opposite wall. She had her arms folded and was staring right at me, coldly.

"Anywhere you like," Alek said. "But visitors must sit facing the door. During the visit, physical contact must be kept to a minimum. A hug hello and goodbye is okay, but keep it to that. Normally we'd have teas and coffees available but as this is outside regular hours, you're stuck with the vending machines. If you use them, you can get something for Will but he must remain seated. The patient can't move around the room. Do not attempt to pass the patient any other items. If you have any, you must declare them to security and submit them for screening. They will then determine their suitability and, if approved, give them to the patient. Any questions?"

It sounded like Alek had, at some point in this speech, slipped into reciting a spiel he knew off by heart.

"Are you staying?" I asked.

"I'm going to go get him now but yeah, I will. Have a seat."

I picked the closest table, the one furthest from the guard, and hung my jacket over the back of the chair. My mouth felt bone dry; I wished I'd brought in some water. There were probably bottles of it in the vending machines, but I didn't want to draw the guard's ire by getting up again so soon. I ran my tongue around the front of my teeth, licked my lips to moisten them. The dryness was spreading to my throat, tickling the back of it.

About three minutes later, Alek returned with Will in tow.

He wasn't restrained in any way; I was beginning to understand that it was the building itself that was tasked with that. I hadn't noticed on previous visits, and maybe it was just because now I was watching him walk across a room to me, but he was in normal clothes, jeans and a dark blue T-shirt with some kind of print splashed across its middle. I wondered where his clothes came from. Could he buy things in here? If so, where did he get the money from? I'd asked him practically nothing about what his life was like; all I knew about it had been volunteered by him.

He was smiling at me, pleased to see me, and clearly a lot more alert and upbeat than he'd been when I'd last met him.

That's what I was thinking when, instead of stopping at a seat on his side of the table, he kept coming, around to mine, arms lifting away from his sides and, on auto-pilot, I pushed back my chair, stood up, turned to him—

Will wrapped his arms around me, dipping his head, turning his face into my neck so I could feel his breath on my skin and the heat of him through the thin material of his T-shirt.

For a moment I froze with the shock of it.

In the next, I forgot myself. I put my arms around his waist. I turned my head to press my right cheek against his chest. I closed my eyes, breathing him in. I heard him breathing *me* in, a long, deep breath in through his nose.

I longed to let go, to let the edges of us blur and merge.

To lift my face to his.

It wasn't about him. It was about having someone, being with someone, and he was all I really had to remember of that.

The security guard coughed pointedly and I pulled away, embarrassed.

"You okay?" Will said in a whisper reserved for when you're only inches from the person you want to hear you. The intimacy of it was disorientating.

I nodded. "Yeah."

"Take your seats," the guard commanded.

Alek had taken up a position directly opposite the guard, against the other wall. So we had one of them on either side, but we were much closer to Alek and still a few feet from both.

"I recognize that jumper," Will said, sitting down across from me. "That can't be the same one, though, surely?"

"It is, actually." I looked down at it. "It was at my parents' house, packed away. I didn't bring enough clothes with me so I threw it on."

"Did you find the photos?"

"Um—yeah. Yeah, I found one."

"With the CCTV guy in it? Really?"

"Yeah. I think so."

"Can I see it?"

"The Gardaí have it," I said.

"So who is he, then?"

"I don't know. I found him in a photo of us on a night out, in a club, with Liz and two girls whose names I don't remember, and that guy—that guy had his arm around Liz."

Will frowned. "Like they were together?"

"I don't remember her seeing anyone at St. John's."

"But one of us must have known him if we were out with him, right?"

"Well, one of us in the picture," I said. "He could be a friend of one of the other girls."

Will asked me to describe the guy as he appeared in the photo, and then the two girls as well. When I was done, he shook his head. "I've no idea who any of those people are. When can I see the photo?"

"The Gardaí want to be the ones to show you. They want to talk to you, Will. Formally. An interview. And they'd like it if when they ask you questions, you answer them."

"Nope," he said flatly. "Not happening."

"Why not?"

"Because I'm guessing Detective Sergeant Jerry Shaw is involved."

"He's a sergeant now?" I didn't know.

"He made a point of telling me when they came to see me last week."

"And you don't want to talk to him."

"He's the reason I'm in here. He's the one who bullied that confession out of me." Will folded his arms. "They searched my room this morning, confiscated half my stuff. I bet that's his doing as well?"

"They're just trying to catch this guy, Will."

"I bet."

I glanced at our audience, gauging how well they could hear from their positions. Then at a volume I judged low enough not to be overheard but not so low as to make it obvious that I was aiming for that, I said, "There's been another one. A St. John's first-year is missing."

His eyes widened. "Since when?"

"I don't know any more details than that. All I know is Shaw and Malone found that out at lunchtime today."

"Jesus Christ," Will spat. "What are they *doing* out there?" He exhaled. "I don't get it. That's three now. Why didn't they stake out the canal? Or impose a curfew. Didn't they do that with us?"

"As far as I remember we all kicked off about the curfew," I said, "and I don't know if this girl's disappearance even involves the canal."

Will shook his head. "It's ridiculous. Do they have *anything*?"

"I don't know."

"What's in the news?"

"I haven't seen any."

A shadow crossed Will's face. "Didn't you look up that website?"

"What website?"

"The one I asked you to. The one that John told me about."

I'd clear forgotten about it. "Sorry, I haven't had a chance to yet. I was only here last night."

"What about the letter?"

"What was I supposed to do about that?"

Will sighed, frustrated. "Find out about it."

"How?"

"I don't know. Why don't you ask one of your little Garda friends?"

A beat passed.

"Sorry," Will said then. "Sorry. It's just … I'm just

frustrated. I can't do anything. I'm powerless in here."

"It's not all plain sailing for me out there," I said. "The press found out about us meeting. They're calling it a date. And there's at least one newspaper this morning with my picture splashed all over the front page."

Will's face fell. "Shit."

"Yeah, it is."

"This is my fault. I asked you to come here."

"It's not all you. I could've said no."

"Why didn't you?"

I shifted in my seat. Glanced at Alek, at the guard. "Because I felt guilty."

"Ali, look, I get it. I understand. I couldn't at the time but looking back now, I see why you did it. Our lives imploded, the press was everywhere … If the roles were reversed, I might have run away too."

My heart was pounding, thumping. My ears filled with the sound, as if the audio of someone else's heartbeat was being piped into the room.

I hadn't been planning on telling him. I hadn't been planning on telling anyone, ever. I didn't even like reminding *myself* of what I'd done.

But just like on the phone to Sal earlier, I could feel it coming, feel the truth rushing to the surface, determined to break through.

I couldn't stop it.

I wouldn't try.

"Will," I said, "there's something I have to tell you."

alison, now

"I did something." My voice was a whisper. "Back then."
I couldn't look him in the eye. I focused on his hands,
resting palms down on the table. I wondered how quickly Alek could get to the table. I didn't know how Will
would react to this. "At the time, I thought I was doing
the right thing. To be honest, I didn't even realize I was
doing a *thing* at all."

Will frowned. "What are you talking about?"

The room felt so still that I bet if the dust particles in
the air became visible, they'd all be hanging in suspended
animation, unmoving, frozen in place.

"I never thought for one second …" I bit my lip.
"I just didn't want to get in trouble. Or for you to. I
thought I was helping."

"Alison, what did you do?"

"They talked to us all," I said. "The Gardaí. Back
then. Do you remember? After Liz died? They came to
the campus, set up that room at Halls. We all went in
one by one. They were just taking statements. You went

in before me. I was standing outside the door. I could …
I could hear everything, Will. I heard what you told
them. About the night Liz died. You said you were with
me all night, but you … You weren't. Not technically."

Will's face had hardened into an expressionless
mask.

"I left your room," I went on. "Do you remember?
I left yours and came back to mine because I had a
meeting with my tutor early the next morning."

Will folded his arms. "No, I don't, really. It was ten
years ago."

"Well, it's true."

"So? I might've been asleep when you left."

"You were, I think."

He threw up his hands. "Then why did it matter?"

"Because that's not what you told them. The Gardaí.
And because that was …" I swallowed. "Because that's
not what I told them either. I went in afterward and
said the same thing. I thought that's what had happened.
I was confused, because they kept asking about our
phones, about why I didn't hear them ringing, but
everything was so crazy then, so mixed up … I wasn't
thinking straight. But then later, when I was back in
my room, I saw the calendar I'd up on the wall and I
saw that I'd that meeting with my tutor, and I realized I
hadn't stayed the whole night. I'd left to go back to mine
at some stage. Around one, one thirty, I thought. I'd got
my nights mixed up."

"Wait a second, wait a second." Will tapped a finger
on the table. "Are you saying …? Did you think I went
somewhere after you left, that I could've—"

"I was 100 percent sure you hadn't." *At the time.*

"I thought you'd just made an innocent mistake. Got mixed up like I had. But then they had that service at the chapel, and the chaplain gave that speech about us knowing more than we might realize, about how no matter how small the piece of information, no matter how irrelevant we thought it was might be, even if we were *sure* it had nothing to do with it … He said we should tell them." Will was glaring at me. "I didn't want to get you in trouble, and *I* didn't want to get in trouble for telling them something that was wrong—"

"What did you do, Ali?"

I looked down into my lap. "I had Shaw's business card. I called him and corrected what I'd said."

Will exhaled loudly.

"I thought I was doing the right thing," I went on. "It … it wasn't even about you, Will. It was about me. I'd made a mistake. I was fixing it. I didn't think for one second it would matter in the scheme of things—"

"Let me get this straight," Will cut in. "You overheard me tell the Gardaí I was with you all night the night Liz died, but you remembered waking up at some point to go back to your own room, leaving me alone, sleeping, and instead of coming to me and saying, "Hey, I think you might have got your nights mixed up," you went back to the Gardaí and told them I'd *lied about my whereabouts* the night Liz died?"

I shook my head. "That's not what happened. Not at all. I thought I'd stayed there all night so I said that I had, but then I realized I hadn't, so I went back and made a correction. That's all."

"While you were doing that, did you happen to mention to them that I was *definitely* with you, all night, every *other* night one of those girls was murdered? Did you tell them that?"

"I honestly didn't remember if you—"

"Well, I *was*," he spat at me. "And if you *did* leave me that night, you left me fast asleep. What about the next morning? Where did we meet again?"

I bit my lip. "In your room."

"In my room? Oh, really?" His tone was mocking. "And what was I doing in my room, when you got there?"

"Sleeping," I said quietly.

"I was sleeping! So if I hadn't woken up during the night, how would I have known that you'd even left? Wouldn't I think you'd been there the whole time?"

"Try to understand," I said. "My best friend had just died." Will rolled his eyes at this and I hated him for it. "I was only nineteen, for God's sake."

"So was I, Ali," Will spat. "*So was I.*"

"I'm sorry."

"No, it's fine." He waved his hand, faux-dismissive. "I get it now. You never thought I was guilty; you just needed me to be. So you wouldn't have to spend the rest of your life feeling bad that you'd taken away mine."

"Will, what did I do? *You told them you did it.* That's what happened next. It's not all my fault."

"I told you, they forced that out of me. I didn't kill those girls. They *made* me say those things. And"—he started to shake his head, disbelieving—"now it turns out I mightn't have been in that room at all if it wasn't for the person I cared most about in the world, the girl I loved, the one who I thought loved me."

"I just told them I was w—"

"You took away my alibi. You *made* me a suspect."

"It can't have just been that, Will. There was ev—"

"You fucking bitch."

I recoiled as if I'd been slapped.

I'd never heard Will say anything like that, let alone to me. Each word had been dripping with white-hot anger.

"You know what's funny?" He laughed now, a soulless, mechanical sound. "All this time, I'm sitting here thinking that *I* hurt *you*, and it turns out that *you* fucking did this to *me*." His face crumpled. "You did this to me. I loved you and you're the one who did this to me …"

They were there then, bodies, standing on either side of us, casting shadows onto the tabletop: Alek and the security guard.

A hand on my arm, keeping me in my seat.

A hand on Will's arm, pulling him up out of his.

Alek led Will out of the visitors' room while I sat at the table, silent and dazed. A few minutes later Alek came back for me, and I wordlessly followed him back along the glass corridor, through locked doors and into reception where someone helped me open my locker and handed me my bag and phone.

It took me a second to realize it was Malone.

He asked me if I was okay. I lifted my head to look at him but I couldn't think what to say.

"The press have converged on your parents' house," he said. "You can't go back there. Not right now, anyway. We're going to bring you into the station for a couple of hours, to wait it out. Okay?"

The station. More Gardaí, more people, more

fluorescent lights. I couldn't deal with it. I wanted to go somewhere where there were no other people. Somewhere I could close my eyes, curl up, and hide away.

"Is there anywhere else?" I asked. "I just …" I started shaking my head. "I can't …"

Malone thought for a second. "Okay. There is. Come on."

alison, then

It was a relief when classes finally began. I'd been craving routine and neither my wallet nor my liver could've taken another day's worth of Freshers' Week. I was also anxious to start my course, to see what it was like, to see what *going to college* was like. I'd been waiting long enough for it.

Secondary school and I hadn't got on. I'd hated pretty much everything about it. The fact that most of the day was taken up with instruction in subjects I detested; that everything was taught by the same small group of teachers so if you had been lazy or stupid in another subject in a previous year, the teacher would make that judgment of you whenever you met again; the itchy, scratchy uniforms; the long days; the hours and hours of homework that ruined what little of our lives were left over afterward. I felt uncomfortable every single day, like my own skin didn't quite fit, and counted down the weeks—six years' worth of them—until it was over. College was to be my reward.

So I threw myself into it wholeheartedly, armed with
a collection of smooth, unblemished notebooks and
three tote bags from the campus bookshop, stretched
to capacity. (The three things my parents were happy
to cover the cost of without complaint: shelter, food,
and books.) I came to class with the book read cover-to-
cover, having highlighted sections and made notes in the
margins as I went. I gave myself hand-cramps furiously
scribbling down every last thing the lecturer said, then
going straight to the library afterward to type my notes
up on my laptop while the lecture was still fresh in my
mind. I had a filing system for these in a series of color-
coded folders. The teaching staff were all passionate
about whatever their specialist subject was and I couldn't
help but catch it from them.

I was in a constant state of exhilaration and panic at
the thought of all the books I was going to read, all the
books I could read, and how little time there was, really,
to read books.

This lasted a week, maybe two.

After that I downshifted into more of a trying-as-
hard-as-I-can mode. I read what I knew I'd be questioned
on in class, or at least enough of it to form answers
that implied I'd read the whole thing. I stopped typing
up lecture notes. Then I stopped, by and large, *taking*
lecture notes. If I hadn't finished a book by the time the
class on it came and went, I wouldn't bother going back
to finish it, even though the word *exam* loomed on the
horizon.

Sometime in mid-November I started going to
classes wholly unprepared, and soon figured out a way to
hide this. I'd choose a seat out of the teaching assistant's

eyeline. I'd scribble notes furiously. I'd *ask* questions, rather than answer them. The lecturers were all teaching their specialist subjects; it didn't take much to set them off talking about them. Some of the books I'd bought the first week of term stayed in the bag I'd carried them back to Halls in.

I missed a class here and there, waited for some repercussion, but none ever came. There was no penalty for not going, it seemed.

By the time December dawned, I was skipping lectures, going to only some classes and was lucky to find a tattered notebook and a single working pen in my bag when I got there. I'd nudge the person next to me just as the TA came in and say, "Which text was for this week?"

Because I was distracted.

By *him*.

Will and I had become a couple slowly but steadily, although I was too scared to say anything to him that would invite confirmation or denial of this fact. We saw each other every other day, then every day, then we were living out of each other's pockets.

It wasn't so much that my life opened up a space for him and he moved in, it was more like our lives dramatically and suddenly melded together. He was just always there now.

I wondered what I'd done with my time, my feelings, my need to be touched, before him. Had I even had such a need?

He was like a new friend, in the beginning. Now he'd become something else. Something more. If I wasn't with Will, I always wanted to go see him. When he was there, I didn't want to leave.

I'd never felt that way about any other person. It was like the world had been dim and flat and now suddenly it was in Technicolor 3-D.

Whenever Liz was with us, other people were too. I didn't know if we'd engineered this, he and I, or if she had. But Will and I were always either alone together or in a group. A little one formed by me, him, Liz, Claire, Claire's boyfriend Tom, and Lauren, who we didn't see all the time but most weekends, or the bigger one we made whenever we went to the campus bar or out in town at night, collecting or joining other little groups comprised of our classmates or St. John's Halls neighbors.

I think that's probably why I didn't notice it for so long.

*****

We'd all been looking forward to the Traffic Light Ball for ages. It was to be held on the Friday before the mid-term break, the last day of classes for a whole week. The morning of it, most of us had some form of assignment or essay due, the first ones since we'd started at St. John's. The Traffic Light Ball would not only be a chance to dress up and a fun night out that we had a whole week to recover from, but it would also be our reward for getting those damn assignments in.

It was being held at the Burlington Hotel, not far from campus. We decided it'd be fun to walk there in our finery, holding our floor-length skirts and dresses off the pavement, navigating uneven paving slabs in our towering heels, shivering because we'd refused to taint our outfits with outerwear appropriate to the temperature.

Liz and I both wore our Debs dresses, but swapped over. Her mother had had a business meeting in Dublin the week before and had brought them up for us, taking us out to lunch afterward so we could update her on how we were getting on.

"Don't say anything about Will," I'd whispered to Liz at the very last moment, as we turned off Dawson Street and into the restaurant where her mother had made us a reservation. "I don't want it getting back to Mam."

Liz made a face. "You haven't told her?"

"Why would I?"

"I don't think she'd mind."

I shook my head. "I don't want to find out for sure. And I don't want the FBI-style interrogation that'll come with it if she gets wind of this." I shivered at the thought. "It's just easier this way. Trust me."

She'd winked at me. "Your secret's safe with me."

True to her word, she'd mentioned nothing about him at lunch.

Will wore a tux to the ball, and I couldn't stop looking at him. He'd worn it to his Grads ball, which I hadn't asked too many questions about but which I'd inferred had been a week or two before he'd met me. I felt a tug of something at the idea that he'd been to a black-tie affair with some other girl on his arm, but I tried to swallow it down.

He didn't know me then. It didn't matter now. Being jealous was horrifically pointless. We were together, at this, now, tonight.

"You look beautiful," he whispered in my ear as we entered the ballroom.

I didn't think I did normally, but that night—

although I'd never have admitted it to anyone—I believed him.

We picked up our stickers on the way in: red for in a relationship, green for single, orange for somewhere in between. Some of the guys took "wrong" colors for the laugh, and some of the girls refused to wear any at all. (Maybe they'd had their first Gender Studies module. Maybe the colors clashed with their gowns.) I took a red one and folded it somewhat discreetly around one of the straps of my dress.

The venue was a huge ballroom with a stage dominating one end; the band played from there. The bar was just outside it. A few tables had been installed on either side, but the majority of the few hundred students took to the dance floor and stayed there. We set up shop at a table near the stage, so we could dump bags and the boys' jackets and have somewhere to leave our drinks, which weren't permitted on the floor. But this also meant quite the trek from our table to the bar and back again.

Will had hopped up anytime my glass was nearing emptiness, so much so that I started to feel bad and offered to go get the next round. I checked with Liz and she convinced me that we should both get cocktails. I was waiting at the bar for more than fifteen minutes for them to be made.

When I got back to the table, Liz was sitting on Will's lap.

She was sitting on his lap, angled to the side, with her arms wrapped around his neck. She was talking to a guy I didn't know who was sitting next to Will, in the seat Liz had been occupying when I'd left. Will was looking toward this guy too. He had reddish hair and freckles, and a thin, angular face, and if you were going off first, fleeting impressions and you were being unkind, you might have labeled him with terms like *dweeb* or *nerd* before it was cool. He was smiling widely but I could tell by the look on Liz's face that she wasn't enjoying listening to him as much as he was clearly enjoying talking to her.

And then, as I watched, she leaned her head to one side, turned and kissed Will slowly and deliberately on the side of his face, an inch from his mouth.

It looked so intimate, my stomach dropped.

It had been a job to carry two cocktails and Will's bottle of beer back across the dance floor and I was lucky they didn't slip from my hands now. But I also felt like I absolutely could not, *would* not, react in any way.

What was going on here?

Liz and Will didn't even *hug*. I had never seen her touch him. It wasn't something I ever thought I'd have to see. But now she was sitting on his lap, something I had never done, something I wouldn't do—such public displays of affection were embarrassing to me and, I would've thought, to him too—and doing it in front of everyone, in front of everyone we knew and this guy with the red hair that I didn't know, and I'd just watched her *kiss* Will too?

I reached the table then and Will looked up and saw me. He flashed a look that, although the length of a blink, communicated enough for my chest to open up again and permit me to breathe.

He didn't know what was going on either and he wasn't happy about it. Whatever this was, *Liz* had done it.

"Here you go," I said loudly, putting Liz's drink down in front of her with a touch too much force. The pink liquid inside it sloshed and slipped over the lip of the glass.

She didn't hop up in surprise or turn to me blushing with guilt. She just smiled and said, "Thanks." Picked up the drink, took a sip.

Like nothing was weird.

Like she wasn't sitting on my boyfriend's lap and had just kissed him on the cheek.

"You were gone ages," she said. "Was there a big queue?"

I noticed that Will's hands were resting on the sides of his chair. He wasn't touching Liz anywhere except for the places where she was touching him.

"No," I said, "there were two cocktails to make." I met her eyes. "What did I miss?"

"Oh, this is …?" She turned to the thin, red-haired boy. He was wearing a green sticker. I saw that since I'd gone to get the drinks, Liz had taken hers off.

"Dan," he supplied.

"Dan," Liz repeated.

I smiled at him briefly. "Hi, Dan."

There was an awkward moment then when none of us said anything at all.

"Excuse me," Will said, shifting in his seat. "I'm going to need a bathroom break before I drink that beer."

Liz stood up to let him do the same. She sat back down again in his vacated seat.

Will came straight to me, still standing by the side of the table, and slipped an arm right around my waist, pulling me toward him.

"I don't know what the hell that was," he whispered in my ear. "She just jumped in my lap." He kissed my cheek. "Don't go anywhere, okay?"

After he walked off, I resumed my seat: the one next to Liz.

"We're all really good friends," she was saying to Dan. She turned to me, put a hand on my thigh. "I think I need a bathroom break too. Come with me?" When I looked up at her face, she was staring at me with a similar look to the one Will had had on his face a few moments before, like she was trying to tell me something, reassure me.

I didn't know *what* was going on.

"I can watch your stuff," the red-haired guy offered.

I let Liz pull me up and off toward the bathrooms. She started swearing under her breath before we'd even cleared the dance floor.

"That *guy*," she spat. "Dan. He's been following me around all night. He is *such* a weirdo."

I'd never seen him before I'd seen him at our table.

"I'm sorry about Will," Liz said in a gentler voice. "I just thought that was the best thing to do when he came over. So Dan would think I had a boyfriend. You don't mind, do you?"

Ah. Now it all made sense.

I could feel warm relief flooding my veins, loosening my stomach muscles, restoring order to the world.

"No," I said. "No, of course not."

"He might leave me alone now," Liz said, pushing open the door the ladies' bathrooms. "Let's hope."

*****

Sometime the following afternoon I woke up in Will's bed. In a matter of weeks I'd gone from being paranoid that I was the only eighteen-year-old on earth who hadn't had sex yet (and also feeling abject terror at the thought of changing that) to sleeping with Will almost every night. It wasn't a big deal. It felt perfectly normal. It reminded me of something I'd read in a magazine a few years ago that I didn't quite understand at the time. *Sex is like air. It's only important if you aren't getting any.*

We'd stumbled home after the sun had come up, having stayed out for so long that we'd come back practically sober, and fallen into bed, happily exhausted. I didn't have a headache but my stomach was sore and unsettled, which I put down to the bottle of Cava that had appeared toward the end of the ball. I wanted a shower, something greasy for breakfast, and a day spent watching movies on my laptop. With Will, in bed.

Not this bed, though. The room was stale and smelled of beer. We should go do it at mine. When Will woke up, I told him this.

"That was weird last night," he said as I lay in his arms. "With Liz. Wasn't it?"

I hadn't had a chance to tell him why Liz had done it: to get rid of that weird guy by convincing him she had a boyfriend. I did now.

"Hmm," was all Will said.

"What?"

"It's just that … I don't know. It happened *before* that guy Dan ever appeared. Liz had been sitting in my lap for, like, more than five minutes when he came over."

I sensed there was something Will wasn't telling me.

I rolled over onto my stomach, rested my chin on his chest. "*And?*"

"And what?"

"What aren't you telling me?"

"She'd had a few too many. And she's your friend. I'm sure it wasn't … It probably wasn't anything."

"*What* wasn't?"

Will touched my hair. "You were gone to the bar. Just. She started going on about how we'd make a great couple. Her and I. And then she was all, "'I'll prove it,'" and that's when she got up and sat on my lap."

I turned and lay on my back again, stared at the ceiling.

"Are you mad?" Will asked.

"No."

He smiled. "Liar."

"She just had a few drinks. A few too many. Like you said."

"I meant at me."

"At *you*? You didn't do anything."

"I tried to let her know I was really uncomfortable."

I wanted to ask how he had done that. I wanted a second-by-second debrief on exactly what had occurred. I wanted reassurance, several times over, that he hadn't for *one moment* enjoyed the feeling of Liz being so close to him, that he hadn't imagined for as much as a second what it might be like if he was with her instead of me.

But more than all that, I didn't want Will to think I was crazy.

"It's not a big deal," I said. "Don't worry about it."

We lay there in silence for a minute. Then Will leaned over and kissed me, pulled me closer.

"Can I ask you something?" he said.

"Mmm."

"You and Liz … Do you even like her?"

I scoffed. "Of *course* I do. She's my best friend."

But Will's question was a tug on the thread. Soon, there would be an unraveling.

alison, now

Malone drove me to his place.

We took the motorway. Outside of the city, grassy hills rose up into the sky ahead of us. The Wicklow Mountains, I presumed. This was an unusual sight for me: the Netherlands was as flat as a pancake, with uninterrupted horizons on offer as far as the eye could see.

After a half hour or so, he took an exit named for a place I'd never heard of, leaving the mountains behind us. We passed a massive retail park and then, a stretch of nothingness later, turned into a complex of newly built apartment blocks, the only blip on an otherwise flat and featureless landscape. The block closest to the entrance had a number of commercial units on its ground floor, each one sitting vacant with a PRIME RETAIL SPACE OPPORTUNITY sign hanging amidst the grime and dust on the storefront. The windows on the first floor were dark and bare. Someone or something had punched a jagged hole in one of the panes of glass.

Malone turned the car onto a road to the left, the tires crunching on loose gravel.

"Ghost estate," he explained to me. "Ran out of money before they could finish it." I could see a large green area on our right, tall with grass and thick with weeds. Beyond it, access to a row of small, boxy houses, sans windows, was blocked by a chain-link fence. "It's bleak, I know. They say they're picking construction back up in the next couple of months, though, now that the country's getting back on track a bit."

Those were the first words either of us had spoken since we'd left the CPH. After we'd got into his car, Malone had told me that this is where we could go. I'd nodded silently, then turned to stare out the window.

I could only think about my meeting with Will, the pain etched on his face, the sick feeling in my stomach. I'd feared, all this time, that the Gardaí picking him up back then had had something to do with me correcting my statement. I'd always told myself that there had to have been more to it than that.

But was there?

"It's fine," Malone was saying, "so long as you don't look out the windows too often. And we got it for a song. I just keep telling myself that."

The *we* brought me back. Was there going to be someone else here? I couldn't face a stranger right now. Malone wore no ring, but that wasn't to say he wasn't living with someone.

"I spoke to your mother," he went on. "That was when I thought we were going to Pearse Street station, though, but she knows you're with us. I said you'd be back to Bray tonight once the press pack outside give up for the day, but I think she'd appreciate a call from you. She said to tell you your dad's back. Oh, and your suitcase is in the boot. Garda Cusack collected it for you from the hotel. We checked you out of there."

"What about the girl?" I said. "The missing one."

"We're looking for her."

"Do you think she's …?"

Malone kept his eyes straight ahead. "We don't know yet. The Sub-Aqua team is at the canal."

"Who is she?"

"Her name's Amy Boylan. One of her roommates raised the alarm this morning. Under normal circumstances we wouldn't move on this so quick, but with circumstances being what they are …"

"Where was she last seen?"

"That's the thing: in Halls. Someone saw her go into her apartment around nine last night. But she's not there now and she hasn't been heard from since. Plus there's some … Well, let's just say there's a couple of reasons to be concerned for her safety, based on what we found in her room."

"Her *room*? Do you think he was in there?"

"We don't know. We don't know anything yet."

"What about the guy in my photo?"

Malone had pulled up in front of an apartment block to the rear of the complex. He cut the engine, turned to me. "We've made some progress. The photo was posted by several online news outlets an hour or so ago, and I hear we already have several actionable leads. And I have a list of St. John's Hall residents for the year you were there. You can have a read of it. You might spot his name. Remember it when you see it."

"So you don't know who he is yet?"

"I think we will soon. Especially because his face is going to be all over the papers in the morning. With a headline about another girl missing, so people will have to take notice. We've also got officers canvasing the public along the canal, from Grand Canal Dock all the way to Portobello."

His apartment was on the second floor of a four-story block, overlooking the wild, weed-filled green and facing the fenced-off, unfinished houses. I parked my suitcase in the hallway, next to the cardboard archive box Malone had carried up with him from the car. I paused to listen, but elsewhere in the apartment there seemed to be only silence. I was relieved we were alone.

I walked into an open space that seemed to be the kitchen, dining room, study, and living room all rolled into one. It was spacious and full of natural light, but also felt bare and cold. The fading light coming in the double balcony doors had an odd quality to it, as if this was a film set and the bulbs playing the part of the sun had been hung in the wrong place. Furnishings-wise, there was only an oversized black leather couch, an IKEA coffee table with a coffee ring in one corner and a large, flat-screen TV on an eighties-era chrome stand. A silver laptop was thrown on the couch. There was nothing on the walls and few personal effects.

"I know," Malone said. "It doesn't get much better inside, does it?" He started a circuit of the room, turning on the three floor lamps—more instantly recognizable IKEA bargains—as he went. "My ex was the decorator and she took it all with her." He pointed to the wall above the couch where, now that I looked, I could see a number of bare picture hooks and, close to the window, the faint outline of something that might have once hung there. "I've been embracing the minimalist look. Maybe now that we've a few hours to kill you can help me buy some cushions online or something. I don't have a clue. Your place was really nice. Really homely."

He turned and smiled at me.

I burst into tears.

It was as if I couldn't hold back the pain, the stress, the shock of all this another moment longer; I'd spent everything I had doing it this long. I didn't have any strength left to be embarrassed about it. I just let myself break open.

And then Malone was there, putting his arms around me, holding me, which only made things worse, even *more* embarrassing.

His skin against mine.

Like Will's had been.

I pulled away.

"I'm sorry," I said, wiping my eyes, regretting that today of all days was the one I'd elected to wear a coat of my mother's mascara. "I'm sorry, I just … That meeting with Will was—" I stopped. I couldn't say it.

"What happened?"

"I told him something." I sat down on the couch, pushed my hair out of my face, trying to pull myself together. "He didn't react well."

Malone sat down beside me. "What did you tell him?"

I explained about overhearing what Will had told the Gardaí when they'd come to talk to us on campus, and initially telling them the same thing. But then realizing, after I saw the tutor appointment on my calendar, that I'd mixed my days up and, actually, I hadn't stayed in Will's room the whole night.

"I didn't really think it was a big deal," I said. "I didn't want to get in trouble, that's all. I didn't want him to get in trouble either. I didn't think he would—he'd been asleep, how was he to know?"

A shadow of something crossed Malone's face, but all he said was, "Hmm."

"But I think now that's why Will was brought in for questioning. Shaw said the others on the list had alibis, so when I took Will's away, effectively … And if the confession *was* coerced … This could all be my fault."

"Alison, you can't think like that. Really. You don't know what would've happened. You can't blame yourself."

"Easier said than done." I shook my head. "This is *such* a mess."

"Everything might be different tomorrow." Malone sighed. "Are you hungry? I could order some food. Or make some, but that would just delay the ordering because, trust me, we'd end up doing that anyway."

I managed a smile. "Okay."

"Pizza all right?"

"Pizza's great."

Malone took his phone out of his pocket and pulled up a delivery app. "Any dietary requirements?"

"Just calories."

I waited until he'd placed an order. Then I asked him, "Do you still think he's innocent?"

Malone frowned. "I never said I did. I said I thought there was a chance he was. I wasn't sure."

"Because the evidence doesn't match up?"

"Because I'm not sure it would've survived in a courtroom."

"Shaw said it's always like that. Not everything adds up."

"That's true," Malone said, nodding. "That's very true. But I think this goes a bit further than that."

"In what way?"

A beat passed.

"Look, Alison. Shaw pulled me up this morning for telling you too much, and he was right to. I've tried to stick to the closed case, to Will's case, and I would argue I haven't told you anything that you couldn't have read online somewhere. You didn't, though, did you? Read stuff about the case? Before we came to see you in Breda?"

I shook my head. "Until you knocked on my door, I'd avoided knowing anything about it."

"So you're hearing all this for the first time."

"Yes. But now I *want* to know. I want to know the truth. I want to know what actually happened. I don't want to go back home and spend the next ten years wondering if I spent the *last* ten being right or wrong."

I met Malone's eyes.

"In that case"—he got up to pick a remote off the TV stand—"I have something to show you."

"What?"

Malone collected his laptop from the floor and came and sat next to me.

"Will's confession," he said, opening the computer's lid. "Video of it."

alison, now

"Back in September," Malone explained, opening an internet browser, "a two-part documentary aired here on TV3. The theme was personal safety in the digital age, but they did a segment on the Canal Killer case. They opened with it, actually. Their thesis seemed to be that people around the country—especially in Dublin—changed their behavior because of it. Women avoided walking home alone, they regularly changed their daily routines, they didn't share personal information in public arenas. But now, ten years on, the lessons of it have been forgotten, things are worse than ever, we need to be more mindful of how we use social media—that kind of thing."

What a luxury it must be, I thought, to be *able* to forget.

"They featured a few cases," Malone continued, "from here and abroad, where online information—Facebook posts, geo-tagging data in photos, video blogs—inadvertently provided what was essentially a digital map to the victims' doors. They also brought in some security experts who combed through the digital footprints of some willing participants to show them just how much information could be mined about their whereabouts, habits—things like that. The segment on Will featured footage from his confession. Now the whole tape is, like, ten hours long or something, so what they showed is a snippet. And I should say, Shaw is both a great detective and a seasoned interrogator. He's actually delivered interrogation training to some of us, myself included. But I watched this when it aired and, well ..." Malone picked up the TV remote and pressed the power button. "See for yourself."

His internet browser was on a catch-up TV player. He navigated to a list of video clips, selected one and then clicked the icon that would make it play on the TV screen.

"Have you ever seen any of this?" he asked me. I shook my head, *no*. "If you want me to turn it off at any point, just say so."

"Is there ...?" I swallowed. "Does he ... does he give details?"

"There's nothing graphic in these clips, no."

Malone skipped the video through the opening titles and shots of a man with gray hair walking along Grafton Street, speaking directly into the camera, faces in the crowds of shoppers behind him turning to look.

"I'll just show you the interrogation bits," he said as a shot of a nineteen-year-old Will being led into a Garda car in handcuffs flashed up on screen.

My palms were suddenly clammy. I rubbed them against my jeans.

Then there it was: the interrogation, playing on screen.

The footage was of low quality, fuzzy like a well-worn VHS tape, despite only being ten years old. It showed a small corner of a gray room, in which a table had been pushed up against a wall. A flat black box was sitting on it: the recording equipment, I supposed. The camera was mounted on the ceiling.

On one side of the table, with his back to the camera, was a man in a blue shirt with patches of gray hair only partially obscuring the sheen of a bald head: Detective Shaw.

Sitting across from him, hunched over: Will.

My Will. I even recognized the T-shirt he was wearing. I'd slept in it, once upon a time.

Another man was sitting beside Shaw, but only his legs were visible in the shot.

"Who's that?" I asked, pointing.

"That'll be Detective Inspector Gerald Moynihan. He sat in, but it's Shaw who conducted the interrogation."

"There's no solicitor?"

"Before 2014, solicitors weren't in Garda interviews under Irish law. As far as I know Will came in voluntarily at first, anyway. A casual chat. After a few hours the tone changed and he asked for a solicitor. But he and the solicitor would have met privately. The solicitor could advise Will about the interview, but when the interview itself began, the solicitor would've had to leave the room."

"Even though he was only nineteen?"

Malone nodded. "Nineteen is still an adult."

Large figures appeared floating in the middle of the screen: *11:23.*

"They show a series of clips," Malone explained, "in chronological order, and they've time-stamped each one. I think their point is, look at this nice guy, you'd think butter wouldn't melt in his mouth, you'd have no qualms about him if you met him on the street, but watch as he eventually breaks down and confesses to his horrible crimes. This is right at the beginning."

The audio was mumbled, barely coherent in places, but captions accompanied it at the bottom of the screen.

Shaw: Where did you meet your girlfriend?

Hurley: She's in St. John's too, but the first time we had a conversation was in a club.

Shaw: What did you do, buy her a drink?

Hurley: This creepy guy was annoying her. I went over and pretended to be her boyfriend to make him go away.

Shaw: That was very gentlemanly of you.

On screen, Will laughed easily, smiled.

Hurley: That's what she thought, too.

Malone glanced at me and I could feel my cheeks start to color.

"I didn't realize the entire nation had been treated to that story," I said. "How wonderful."

"Don't worry. They bleeped out your name."

I didn't bother pointing out that any half-arsed Google-user could find it pretty quick.

The presenter reappeared, this time walking across the front lawn of St. John's, and Malone quickly skipped ahead to the next interview shot.

Will looked to have slouched a bit more in his chair but other than that, his demeanor hadn't changed.

13:25

Shaw: You live on campus. You must be coming and going by the canal all the time. You and your girlfriend. She lives on campus too, right? *****?

Hurley: Yes.

Shaw: You ever see anything unusual around there, Will? Anything that might assist this investigation?

Hurley: No.

Shaw: What about on the nights of the murders?

Hurley: I don't know when they were.

Shaw: You don't watch the news?

Hurley: I mean, I don't remember those nights specifically. I couldn't tell you where I was. But ***** and I have only spent a handful of nights apart since October. More than likely I was with her.

Shaw: But you must remember the night Liz died.

Hurley: Of course, yeah. I knew her. She was *****'s best friend. I meant the others.

Shaw: So you know where you were?

Hurley: With *****. We went to a bar, then she stayed over in my room.

"He starts off with Liz," Malone said, speeding forward again, "because Will knew her. So Shaw is thinking, that's the one where it'll be the most difficult for Will to keep himself detached from what he did. For Will to be able to lie about it. The others, they were practically strangers to him, but with Liz—his girlfriend's best friend, his friend—there might be a way in there. A crack in the armor Shaw can try to pry open."

14:05

Shaw: ***** spent the whole night with you? When you woke up, she was there?

Hurley: Yes.

Shaw: On the night Liz died?

Hurley: Yes.

Shaw: What time did you guys wake up?

Hurley: I don't know.

Shaw: Was it bright outside?

Hurley: Yes.

Shaw: Could you estimate a time?

Hurley: I don't know. Maybe eight o'clock? That would be a guess, though.

Shaw: Did you set an alarm?

Hurley: No. I don't think so.

Shaw: What time did you go to sleep?

Hurley: We didn't bother going onto the club so around eleven maybe?

Shaw: If we asked ***** where she was that night, what would she say?

Hurley: The same. That's where she was.

Shaw: You know I'm not sure she would.

Hurley: I don't understand.

Shaw: According to campus security, she accessed the door of her apartment at St. John's Halls at 1:35 a.m. She met a friend of hers in the stairwell as she was leaving around eight the next morning. So she didn't spend the night with you, did she? She went back to her own room at 1:35 a.m.

On the screen Will frowned, confused.

Shaw: What do you have to say to that?

Hurley: I don't know. I was sure she did.
When I woke up, she was there.

Shaw: In the bed with you?

Hurley: No, she was already dressed.

Shaw: Let's move on to Lauren Murphy. You
knew her too, right?

Hurley: Sort of. Not very well.

Shaw: But you'd been out with her a few
times?

Hurley: As part of a group, yeah. I'm not sure
I ever really talked to her, though.

Shaw: Did you ever follow her home, Will?

Hurley: What? No. Of course not.

Shaw: Maybe follow is the wrong term. Did
you ever walk her home? Or walk
behind her to check she got there
safely without her knowing?

Hurley: No.

Shaw: You sure about that?

Hurley: One hundred per cent.

Shaw: So if we asked her friends, they

wouldn't tell us that they frequently saw you following Lauren across campus, watching her from across the classroom, somehow always ending up in the same bar, the same club, the same spot?

Hurley: If they did they'd be lying. They're insane if they're saying that. Are they saying that? They must be mixing me up with someone else.

"*Were* her friends saying that?" I asked.

Malone shook his head. "Listen to how Shaw phrased it. "So if we asked her friends …" He hasn't asked them. He's just trying to convince Will that he has, that he already knows what's gone on. Shaw's whole thing is, 'I already know the truth. All I've to do is sit here until you confirm it for me.'"

"Can he do that?"

Malone started speeding ahead again. "That's the whole aim of the game, Alison. We can't go into interrogations with the attitude that the subject is innocent and we just want to double-check. We're there to get what we need. And notice that this doesn't even occur to Will. After all, it's not supposed to. His reaction is to explain away the fact that the friends have said that. Will asked for a solicitor after this. They talked for an hour before the interview resumed. You can see how he's changed. He's realized this isn't a friendly chat. He knows he's in trouble."

Indeed, in the next section of video, Will was very

different. He wasn't as animated and he wasn't answering Shaw's questions as quickly. He looked tired to me.

17:05

Shaw: We know what happened that night. We already know. We know everything. We know all the details, the exact sequence of events, who was where, who did what, when. All we need is for you to confirm for us. We're just trying to help you out here, Will. You help us, we help you. You want to see your parents, right? You asked for your dad? We can bring them in. But first we need to hear some truth from you.

Hurley: I'm not the Canal Killer. This is crazy.

Shaw: How did you get them in the water, Will? How did you get them in without them making any noise? That's the bit I can't figure out. Just tell us the truth and we can get you out of this room, Will. Come on, now. You'll feel better. Look, I'll tell you what. I'll say what I think happened, and you just confirm yay or nay, okay? That might be easier for you. I know this is hard.

Hurley: I didn't do anything.

Shaw: Will, we know what happened. I've told
        you this. Just tell us what happened.
        Let's work backward. Let's start with
        Liz.

"This kind of thing went on for hours," Malone said,
fast-forwarding. "Look at the time stamp on the next clip."

21:15

Shaw: You can't get out of this, do you
        understand me? We've collected
        evidence against you. We know
        exactly what happened. We just need
        to hear it from you. Look, Will, we
        all make mistakes. Things happen in
        the heat of the moment. Nobody's
        perfect. Maybe you didn't mean to
        hurt those girls. But if you don't tell
        us what happened, we can't help you
        here. Cooperation is key, Will. Come
        on now. Help us help you.

The figures on screen morphed into slightly different
positions: some footage had been skipped over, edited
out. Now, Will seemed to have caved in on himself,
shoulders hunched forward, head dropping.

Hurley: [inaudible]

Shaw: Okay what?

Hurley: [inaudible]

Shaw: Say again?

Hurley: I did it.

Shaw: What?

Hurley: Liz.

Will wiped at his face with the back of his hand. He'd started to cry.

Shaw: I need more than that, Will. I'm going to need specifics. You're doing so well. Can we go a little bit further? Can you give me specifics? Let's work backward. Most recent first. What can you tell us? What about Liz?

Hurley: She fell in the water.

Shaw: Fell? I don't think she fell, Will.

Hurley: [inaudible]

Shaw: It wasn't an accident. You put her there.

Hurley: I'm so sorry. I didn't mean it.

Shaw: What happened before she went in?

Hurley: I don't remember.

Shaw: Come on, Will. We both know that's not true.

Hurley: [inaudible]

Shaw: You had an argument, okay. And then
      what?

Hurley: I pushed her in.

Shaw: What happened before that?

Hurley: Before the argument?

Shaw: After the argument but before she went
      into the water.

Hurley: I don't know.

Shaw: You don't know? Come on now, Will.
      We're making progress. Don't go
      backward on me.

Hurley: I hit her.

Shaw: You hit her.

Hurley: I don't remember with what.

Shaw: That's okay. We'll come back to it. For
      now, though, I want to move onto
      Lauren.

"Turn it off," I said. "I can't … Just turn it off."

Malone pointed the remote at the screen and it
went black. "That's practically all of it, anyway. Of what
they included in the show, at least."

"I thought I was going to be convinced after this." I
flopped back against the sofa cushions, deflated. "There's
no smoking gun here. Yeah, okay, they bullied him a bit.

They kept at him for hours. But I think that's probably okay when five teenage girls have been dragged dead out of the canal."

"No," Malone said, "there's no smoking gun." He tapped the laptop's keys. "But there is this. Listen."

From his computer's speakers came the audio of the last few seconds of the clip. Without the benefit of reading the captions, I had to concentrate purely on what was said.

And this time, when Will said, "I hit her," I heard something slightly different: a question instead of a statement.

I hit her?

"He's guessing," Malone said. "Will's guessing what Shaw wants him to say, because he wants out. And here's the thing: how the girls got their head injuries was kept out of the press. We knew it was from an impact with concrete but we held that back for verification purposes. The Canal Killer was knocking them unconscious by knocking them down to the ground. But Will couldn't have known this. All he knew was that they had head injuries, so he assumed—like, I think, most people would—that those injuries were inflicted with a weapon of some kind. And Shaw, sensing that Will was going to contradict this, quickly redirected him."

Malone played the audio once more.

"I hit her?

"You hit her.

"I don't remember with what.

"That's okay. We'll come back to it. For now, though, I want to move onto Lauren.

"But why?" I said, throwing up my hands. "Why,

why, *why* would anyone ever confess to a murder they hadn't committed? I just don't get that."

Malone shrugged. "It happens all the time. The subjects are tired, stressed, *young* usually, and they have someone trained in interrogation telling them they know what happened, they know they committed this murder—"

The doorbell went. The pizza had arrived.

"I might just wash my hands," I said as Malone stood up to answer the front door. While he was paying the pizza guy, I collected my suitcase and took it with me into the bathroom down the hall.

It occurred to me that someone—Garda Cusack?—would've had to pack for me. When I'd left the hotel that morning I'd thought I was just going out for coffee and had left stuff strewn about the room. A quick check confirmed that everything was present and accounted for, although an eyeshadow pallet had broken and dusted glittery specks everywhere.

I pulled out some makeup wipes and did my best to clean up the mess on my face made by my latest mortifying crying episode. I sprayed some deodorant and washed my hands. I took off my heavy sweater and folded it away inside the case and it was then, when I was zipping it back up, that I saw it: the small pocket at the front of the case, on the outside of the lid, was open.

I never used it, because I thought it was the quickest way to get something stolen from you. Anyone could reach a hand in there while you were trailing your case behind you and grab a passport or a phone. But now the zip was gaping open, and I knew I hadn't done it, so I reached my hand in and swept it back and forth inside the pocket, thinking Cusack had chucked something in there.

I felt a sting and jerked my hand out, seeing a thin slice in the skin on the tip of my index finger: a paper cut. Sucking on it, I pulled out what had caused the injury with my other hand.

A fresh sheet of A4 printer paper, folded in half.

I unfolded it, rotated it.

Stared at it, confused.

It was a photocopy of a short typewritten letter. There was no date in the letter itself, but a stamp in the top right-hand corner said it had been received at some unnamed place on April 17, 2007.

Sir—

Congratulations on your article of 14 April last, "Privacy is the Best Protection." I'm glad to see that someone understands what this is all about. They're looking FOR me instead of AT them. If they'd been more careful, I wouldn't have had to get involved at all. Keep up the good work.

CK

The letter Will had mentioned that that other patient had told him about. The one the killer had supposedly sent to the *St. John's News,* the college's student newspaper. This must be it.

But why was it in my suitcase?

My first thought was that Cusack had put it there, because she'd packed up my stuff. But that made no sense.

My second thought was my open hotel-room door.

I'd convinced myself that it was a side effect of a dead lock battery, and the fact that nothing had been disturbed backed me up. But what if it nothing looked disturbed only because nothing had been taken? What if someone had come inside to *leave something* there instead?

My third thought was of the man on the bench outside the hotel, the one I thought was the same guy in the red baseball cap captured on CCTV cameras in and around the canal of late, who was *definitely* also the unidentified guy I'd gone to a club with at least once back when all this had began.

Had the killer been in my hotel room?

Did he leave this for me?

This is his first dead body.

He stands in the shed with his arms folded across his chest, regarding the garbage bin like a foe. He knows better than to use the internet to search for help with something like this. He read a couple of books a few years back on the subject, but he can't recall any hard facts from them now and he doesn't want to leave her here, alone, while he drives home and gets them.

He's just going to have to figure this one out.

He's glad he slept; his headache had dissipated. Another benefit is that the afternoon and early evening have passed and darkness has fallen. He can leave the shed door cracked open while he works. He needs to because something—a rodent, maybe?—has crawled into some nook or cranny and died there, judging by the smell. A sweet, putrid smell with a sting in it that reaches right to the back of your throat.

Amy doesn't smell. Not yet. There is a whiff of

household rubbish when he opens the bin, but that's not from her.

When he upends it, she slides out onto the floor like one giant lump of limb, holding her shape: legs bent, knees pulled up to her chest, arms tucked in front of her, head at an angle. He's taken aback to see that she's already stiff with death. He didn't think that would happen for hours yet. Lying on the floor, her pose is wholly unnatural, and it unnerves him. He finds himself looking around her rather than at her. Her eyes are wide open and have turned cloudy and faintly blue and the blood on her face and neck has dried and flaked, and started to turn brown.

He feels sorry for her, in a way.

But for himself, too, just as much.

He's failed to truly appreciate the waters of the canal until now. They do all the work. Absorb the body. Block the airways. Wash away the evidence. If no one notices the girl lying on the riverbed, the waters will even wait patiently for her insides to fill with gas and deliver her back to the surface, where it's unlikely she'll be missed a second time.

He and Amy never made it to the canal.

Nothing about last night went to plan.

She wasn't supposed to come home after work, that was the first thing. He had let himself in to find something of hers, something he could take. Something that she would see and know without doubt was hers, wonder what it was doing in a strange place, this proof that her private space had been infiltrated.

It was his way of warning them: one last chance to save yourself. Realize something is badly wrong and do something about it. Tell someone. Don't walk home alone like you may have planned. Call an authority.

They never did. He'd yet to work out whether this was because they didn't get the significance of seeing their possession somewhere it shouldn't be, or because they were too embarrassed to do any of the things he hoped they would.

So he'd been in Amy's apartment at St. John's. He'd chosen his item: a rainbow-colored dream catcher that Amy had hung off the end of her curtain rail. Half the time, he bet, it was obscured by the curtain itself, but that was perfect. It was the kind of thing she might not miss for a few days, but would instantly recognize as her own when she saw it somewhere else, somewhere wrong.

He was just reaching for it when he heard the lock turn in the apartment's main door.

Amy was supposed to be at work, going straight out afterward. Her roommate was supposed to be out already. He'd spent a terrified, panicked second standing in the middle of Amy's bedroom, paralyzed with indecision. What should he do?

Make a run for it. He couldn't, she'd see him.

Get in the wardrobe. Too small and what would he do if she pulled open the door?

Get under the bed. It was his only option. Maybe she was just picking something up that she'd forgotten and would leave again soon.

She was supposed to go straight out after work. He'd even seen her take a tote bag with a change of clothes in it. The club had a drinks promotion on that night in an attempt to lure students out on a Sunday, the dregs of the weekend, when all their money was already spent and their livers were struggling to cope. The club had set up a Facebook event advertising it, and Amy had registered as attending. He was going to tail her for the evening and hope he'd get the chance to walk her home.

Amy never walked home alone, but that didn't mean she didn't make other bad decisions. She'd demonstrated that, time and time again. Her life was all over the internet and he'd followed her nearly ten times now without her ever noticing—and in broad daylight. Clearly, she still needed his help and he needed hers. She would make a good example, serve her time as a cautionary tale.

Like Louise had.

Like Jennifer was currently doing.

Reminders that not everyone was as nice a guy as him.

Amy may not walk home *alone*, but she'd chat to the nice man who'd bought her a drink at the bar just at last call, tolerate his company when they both turned out to be walking home in the same direction, fail to notice as their pace slowed, as he maneuvered himself around her until he was on her right side, the dark waters of the canal of her left, watching for a gap in foot traffic, a break from passing cars.

He was counting on it.

But then, instead of going out, she'd clattered around the kitchen for a bit, showered and, inexplicably, got into bed.

For a while he'd simply laid there, silently seething. His whole night, all his careful plans, had been ruined. But then, slowly, he'd realized something: Amy was doing what he wanted more than anything. In abruptly changing her routine, she was protecting herself.

A slow pride smile had spread across his face.

But then she'd woken up and saw him as he was trying to leave.

Saw his face. He couldn't have that.

He did it there in the room, grabbing her by the shoulders as she jumped up from the bed and ramming her as hard as he could, face-first, into her wardrobe door, right where the sharp ridge of the steel handle was sticking out.

He heard a sickening *crack*. Blood spurted from what was left of her nose. She went limp, the echo of her aborted scream hanging in the air.

There was blood everywhere.

That's when he realized he hadn't thought it through.

Blood on the wardrobe door, brushstrokes in it from her hair as she'd slid down. Blood dripping from her nose and, he saw now, the wound in her head as well. The skin on her scalp had split dramatically and one ragged edge of it was hanging loose, flapping open, like wallpaper that had come unstuck. The blood was dropping onto the carpet, onto his clothes, onto her clothes. As he picked her up under the arms, he felt more blood falling onto *his* arms, spilling down over them, collecting in sticky pools in the cuffs of his shirt.

Swallowing down panic, he forced himself to think methodically. He pulled a blanket from her bed, rolled her up in it and carried her into the bathroom, setting her down in the shower tray. She slumped, lifeless, against the tiled wall, but holding a finger directly under the mess of fragmented bone and blood that had been her nose, he detected a faint breath. He took off his shoes and placed them in the shower tray with her. Then he found a packet of antibacterial wipes on the floor under the toilet and retraced his steps with them, down the hall as far as the bedroom door, checking for drops of blood.

He found none. The blanket had caught them all.

On into the kitchen. There was a small bin by the fridge filled with pizza crusts, empty cans, and used teabags.

And a plastic carrier bag.

Back down the hall into the bathroom. He checked his watch. Still plenty of time. So long as the roommate didn't change her plans, too. He put a hand on the back of Amy's head, trying not to transfer more blood, and gently pulled her toward him.

Then he fit the plastic bag over her head, pulled it down as far as it would go and tightly knotted the handles of it under her chin.

Slid the shower door closed.

Went back into the bedroom. Started the cleanup.

He wasn't worried about making the blood go away; he knew it was impossible now, really, to do that. He just didn't want anyone to notice what had happened in there for a while. Give himself a day, maybe two. So he wiped down the wardrobe door. Blotted the carpet stain, moved some of the clothing debris pile over it, carefully arranging it so it appeared to be just as haphazard as the rest. All the used wipes went into a bin liner he'd pulled from the wastebasket in the bathroom.

While he worked, he heard a faint knocking noise coming through the wall. Movement in the shower, it sounded like. He ignored it.

A few minutes later, it stopped.

In the moments after he smashed Amy's skull into the wardrobe, he had no clue how he was going to extract her body from the apartment—from the apartment *block*, one of several, right in the middle of a well-lit college campus. But he trusted himself to think of something in due course and, by the time he had finished cleaning up, an idea had come to him.

It was the bin in the kitchen that made him think of it.

There were garbage bins, kept in a small enclosure outside, round the back. If he could get one of them up here without being challenged, he could get Amy out in it again. He'd use the fire exit at lobby level to avoid meeting other students coming and going through the front doors; he knew the warning sign about the fire exit being alarmed was just for show.

So that's what he did. Found an almost empty bin, brought it upstairs in the elevator, stuffed Amy into it. Wheeled her out again. Lifted the bin into the back seat of his car, lying it lengthways. He was worried about the weight of it, but he found that by lining it up with the door and then tipping the end of it up, he was able to slide it in without too much effort. Then he drove to the three-bed semi in Ranelagh, let himself in the side gate and wheeled Amy into the shed.

It was nearing midnight by then. He didn't have time to go home and shower, so he fetched his uniform from the boot of his car and changed into it before heading back to St. John's to start his shift.

Kevin was on, reading a lads' magazine in the security booth. Lazy, incompetent Kevin who would be easy to blame if anyone came looking for footage later and found it wasn't there.

"Hey," he said to him. "Time to clock off."

Kevin stood up, stretched. "Not a moment too soon, let me tell you. Not a moment too soon."

"Anything strange or startling?"

"Nah." Kevin yawned. "Sunday night, isn't it? You on again tomorrow?"

"I'm only part time. Not back again until Friday."

"Lucky you." He collected his things. "Well, have a good night."

"Thanks," he said. "You too."

He waited until he saw Kevin's car drive past the camera mounted at the staff car park's gates before he went into the security camera system and started searching for tonight's recordings, deleting where necessary as he went. There'd been plenty of times over the last few months when'd regretted taking this job— three days a week he had to stay here, awake, all night and then go into R&P and pretend to be awake for eight hours more—but that night, he was glad of it.

That still left Amy's body, the one lying at his feet now in the shed. This was his listing; no one else from the agency would have reason to visit. The owner, however, might. He wasn't sure how close by they lived. But if they happened to visit, they might see the shiny new padlock on the shed's door and wonder why it was there. They might look inside.

He's inside now, poking around the shelves, lifting lids off boxes, picking through the tools hanging off nails on the back wall.

Looking for something.

Something sharp.

alison, now

When I opened my eyes the next morning the first thing I saw was another pair: large white ovals with little black dots floating in the middle, glowing in the near-darkness, staring at me.

What the—

Cartoon eyes. They were cartoon eyes, painted on a round little ball of blue that, now that my eyes were adjusting, I could see was supposed to be an owl. A plastic owl, with a little slot cut into his head. A pair of sunglasses were resting in the slot, their lenses at an angle over the eyes.

It was a glasses holder, shaped like an owl. *Malone's* owl-shaped glasses holder, to be specific. Sitting on his bedside table.

And me, asleep in his bed.

Well, not quite asleep. I'd spent most of the night lying awake, staring at the ceiling and thinking of all that had transpired yesterday: discovering the photo of CCTV Man among the photos from St. John's, telling

Will I'd corrected my statement about the night Liz had died, watching the videotape of his confession. And, of course, finding a copy of the letter a killer sent, potentially left in my hotel room by another one.

Or maybe the same one.

It was getting hard to keep everything straight.

I didn't know what to think anymore. The only thing I was sure of was that I'd welcome a holiday from thinking altogether.

When my phone beeped with the alarm I'd set for seven, I quickly silenced it and strained to listen for any other sounds. There was only silence. Malone must still be asleep on the couch.

Thanks to a lack of sleep, every limb felt weighted down, my head foggy, my stomach hollow and unsettled. After discovering the letter last night, I'd sat mostly in stunned silence while Malone tried to take my mind off things with some humorless comedy film and what was cold, greasy pizza by the time we got around to opening the box.

He'd never seen the letter before.

"I'd heard about it," he'd told me, "but there's no copy of it in Garda files. The original was lost, I thought."

"Then where did this come from?"

"I'd say the source is someone who worked on the paper back then. They could've made copies. They more than likely did. But as to who put this in your suitcase, and how *they* got it, that I don't know. I can have it checked for prints, but prints are no use unless you have a set to check them against, so …"

"Why give this letter to me?"

Malone had shrugged his shoulders. "Your guess

is as good as mine. Because you've been seeing Will? Because you'll tell him about it?"

"He's the one who first mentioned it to me."

Malone raised an eyebrow. "How did he know about it?"

"He said some other patient told him. He'd read about it online."

I'd pretended to watch the film then and mechanically chewed a few bites of pizza without actually tasting it. By the time the credits rolled, my eyelids were heavy with a longing for sleep and the thought of going back outside, into the dark and the cold, and driving all the way to Bray only made me feel even more exhausted. I didn't argue when Malone suggested I stay in his place for the night, or give my mother a chance to argue with me when I told her that's what I was doing. I sent her a text saying I was staying somewhere in town, that it was too late to drive out to Bray and that I'd call her in the morning. But then, having crawled gratefully into the warm softness of Malone's bed five minutes later, sleep suddenly proved elusive.

After I dressed, I sat on the bed and listened again for signs of life. I didn't want to wake Malone, which I'd probably do the second I opened the bedroom door. The couch was right outside it. I'd let him get up first, even though I so desperately wanted a cup of coffee I could almost smell it, like some kind of olfactory mirage in the middle of a decaffeinated desert.

Except …

Was I *actually* smelling it?

I heard it then: the tiniest little tinkle of steel against ceramic. A teaspoon in a cup. While I'd been sitting here waiting to hear Malone up and about so I wouldn't disturb him, he'd been up and about as quietly as he could be so as not to disturb *me*.

I found him in the kitchen setting two large mugs of steaming coffee on the breakfast bar, the kitchen's only border with the living room. A half-empty cafetière was sitting on the countertop, an inch of coffee left in it, sodden black grounds packed tight at its base.

"Morning." He pushed one of the mugs toward me. "I was just about to knock on the door. Did you sleep?"

"No," I said, "not really."

"But you were so tired."

"Yeah, well. My brain didn't care."

As I mixed sugar and milk into my cup, I noticed that Malone was wearing a dark shirt that seemed to be specked with raindrops. "Were you outside already?"

He lifted a brown paper bag off the countertop. "Foraging for croissants."

"You didn't have to do that." I hoped my stomach wouldn't rumble a contradiction. After only a couple of bites of that pizza yesterday evening, I was starving.

"No, I really did," Malone said. "Otherwise your breakfast options would've been a jar of slicked gherkins or a tube of tomato purée. Or a combination of those two things. As for that"—he pointed at the cafetière—"I had to YouTube how to use it. Normally, I just chuck a spoon of Nescafé in the general direction of boiling water and hope for the best."

"Well, I appreciate it. The coffee, especially."

"Come on, then," Malone said. "Bring your cup."

He crossed the living room to the sliding doors that led out onto the balcony, nudging them open with an elbow. I followed. The balcony was small, only big enough for a café-style set of a chrome table and two chairs, and the room to walk sideways, crab-like, around them. Directly above it hung the underside of the balcony of the apartment on the floor above. But this also meant it was sheltered from the weather; the table and chairs were dry even though the railing was splattered with raindrops.

We set our cups on the table and sat down.

I looked through the gaps in the railing at the overgrown green, glistening with dew, then lifted my eyes to take in the fenced-off row of half-finished houses, then—

"Oh, wow."

Beyond the houses, in the far distance, was a mountain range. Green hills rolled unevenly across the horizon: rounded peaks, wide valleys. In places, stark, bare rock poked through. Off-white clouds, heavy with rain, hung low in the sky above them, casting enormous shadows that moved as I watched.

"Nice, isn't it?" Malone said. "I bring my Nescafé water out here every morning. If you sit just right, you have a great view."

"Yeah," I said. "It's wonderful."

There was no noise at all. No other people, no traffic, not even birdsong. The air was fresh and cool and although the weather was gray and wet, there was something fantastically impressive about the view from Malone's balcony. It was a reminder that even with all that was going on, even the mess that lay around us, life was bigger than this mess. *I* was. The view soothed me. I sank down into my chair, letting my muscles relax. Breathed in the smell of my coffee, took a sip and savored the buzzy caffeine hit. Told myself it was a normal morning.

Just a normal Tuesday morning. Nothing out of the ordinary. Nothing to see here.

The doorbell rang.

It wasn't even eight. Malone was already getting up out of his seat. He didn't seem at all surprised that someone had called around this early in the morning.

He'd been expecting this, I realized.

"We should go in," he said.

"Who is it?"

All I got in answer was the rattle of keys against the front door. By the time I'd picked up my coffee, stepped back inside, and slid the balcony door closed behind me, Garda Emily Cusack was standing in the living room.

And she was glaring coldly at me.

"Here it is," Malone said, handing her the plastic wallet he'd put the letter in. "I talked to Shaw last night so he's expecting it. Alison handled it so we might need her to come in and provide prints." He looked at me.

"That's fine," I said.

"You found this in your suitcase?" Cusack asked me.

I nodded. "Yeah."

Malone asked Cusack if she remembered whether or not the outside pocket had been open when she'd picked it up from the hotel.

"All I did was throw the stuff in and zip up the main compartment." She held up the plastic wallet. "And this could be nothing. It could've just been from some crank. That's what they thought at the time. It might not even be that letter. Somebody could've made this on their computer."

Then she turned and looked at me.

Accusingly, I thought.

"Want some coffee?" Malone said to Cusack. I got the distinct impression he was trying to distract her. "I made the proper stuff."

"I highly doubt that," Cusack muttered. But she went into the kitchen, opened a cupboard and took down a mug. "Did you hear? About the CCTV appeal?"

Malone glanced at me.

"I have to call work," I said. "I'll do it from the bedroom."

I dialed Suncamp's number and left a message confirming I wouldn't be in today either, and that tomorrow was looking bad. After I hung up, I listened: low mumblings were coming through the wall. Malone and Cusack clearly needed a few minutes to discuss in private whatever had happened with the CCTV appeal, so I took the opportunity to call Sal.

Voicemail. I checked the time. Breda was an hour ahead. She'd already be at work. I left a message saying I was fine and I'd try to call her later.

I waited in the bedroom for another three minutes, perched on the edge of the bed, looking out the window. Then I went back outside. Just as I opened the bedroom door, I heard Malone say, "... watched the confession."

Cusack was rolling her eyes. "You and your conspiracy theories. You'll need a tinfoil hat soon."

Malone saw me. "Everything all right?"

I nodded. "Yeah. All good."

All three of us stood there in awkward silence then.

"Right," Cusack said, "I'm off." She took one last swig of her coffee and set the cup down on the countertop. To Malone, "Can we, ah, talk for a second?" She jerked her chin toward the hall.

The two of them left the room, him following her.

A moment later, furious whispers started in the hall.

This time, I didn't think they were talking about the case. I was guessing Cusack was the one with all of Malone's decorative accessories. She had keys to this apartment and knew her way around his kitchen.

Still, I couldn't see it, couldn't imagine them as a couple. Although wasn't the point that they weren't together anymore? *That* was easier to see.

My eyes fell on the cardboard box Malone had brought in from the car last night. Someone had scribbled in marker on its side: SJ ACCOMMODATION APPS *2006/07*. Application forms for on-campus accommodation in St. John's, I was guessing. A single A4 sheet that we'd had to submit by post. Thanks to the idiocies of the Irish college application system, you only found out if and when you'd got a place a few weeks before term began, making late summer a mad, desperate dash for student digs in every college town in Ireland. St. John's guaranteed a room on campus for all incoming freshmen, but only for those who'd won their places in the first round. Liz, for instance, had only got in on the second one, and so had to go on the waitlist. I'd managed to accidentally end up on the waitlist after failing to properly confirm acceptance of my first-round place.

Hadn't Malone said something about getting me to look at a list of residents to see if I recognized CCTV Man's name? We'd never got around to it, overtaken by confession videos and letter discoveries.

I looked toward the hall. The whispering was still going strong.

I hoisted the box up onto the coffee table and lifted off the lid.

There were three ring-binders inside: application forms for the academic year 2006/2007, arranged alphabetically by surname. I sat down on the couch and transferred the first one into my lap. The first page in it was completed in barely legible handwriting, dated August 2006. The binder was several inches thick with more.

I took another sip of my coffee and started working my way through.

The forms were well thumbed, some folded down at corners, many curled and yellowing. A handful were in plastic wallets because their punched holes had ripped through to the edge and would no longer stay on the binder's rings. Some had handwritten notes scribbled on them; others had been branded with a date stamp. In the bottom right-hand corner of each was a large blank box marked ALLOCATION, and these had been filled with a code that corresponded to single rooms in Halls: A4, B18, C20. Each letter was a floor, each number a room on it. Each form was signed and dated by a member of St. John's staff.

I scanned only the student's name on each form. I recognized some as my former classmates, but none seemed possible candidates for the man in the photo.

The majority of forms were on white paper, but some had been printed on blue. I was halfway through before I realized why that was: all the blue ones had a box marked "W" ticked at the top and a submission date in September.

"W" stood for waitlist.

Waitlist. The word snagged on something in my subconscious.

It started rising, tugging an idea to the surface.

Quickly, I flipped through the inch-thick sheaf of paper in each binder and pulled out all the blue pages, all the waitlist forms. I ended up with a stack of thirty or so. Every form had a room allocation written on it, so these were, clearly, only the forms of people on the waitlist who had subsequently secured a room.

I licked a finger and thumbed through the blue stack.

Lauren Murphy. *Check.*

Caroline Brady. *Check.*

Rachel Folen. *Check.*

Elizabeth Whelan. *Check.*

Ciara O'Shea. *Check.*

They were all there, all five victims from before. All five of them had been on the St. John's Halls waitlist.

And someone else was in there too: Heather Buckley. Also an incoming freshmen in the autumn of 2006, also on the waitlist for accommodation in Halls. That had to be the same Heather Buckley who Shaw had said was a victim of a thwarted attack, the one saved by a Good Samaritan who'd then inexplicably run off.

When Malone came back into the room a couple of minutes later, I was tapping keys on his laptop.

"Sorry," I said, "but I think I found something." I turned the machine's screen toward him. Heather hadn't changed her name and, better yet, she hadn't left Dublin. She hadn't even left *St. John's.* According to the university website, she was working there as a research assistant, based in the college library.

"Who's that?" Malone asked, squinting at the screen.

"Someone who can help us, I think."

"Help us do what?"

"Find the Canal Killer." I looked up at him. "Can you drive me to St. John's?"

alison, now

"We never really had to consider that," Malone said as we crawled through the South Dublin suburbs in heavy morning traffic. "How he was choosing them, I mean. Will did it, he was a student, he lived in Halls. So did all the victims. That was the connection. Case closed."

"But if it *wasn't* him," I said, "then how he chooses them becomes important, right?"

"To say the least."

"And if we figured it out, it could help find the guy now."

"Possibly, yes."

The car inched forward.

"The letter said the focus should be on the victims," I said, "not the killer. If that's real, it sounds like he's saying there's a connection between them *other* than him. Right?" I felt Malone's eyes on me and I turned to him. "What?"

"Are you saying …?" He looked at me questioningly.

"I just want to know the truth," I said. "I'm not saying anything yet."

We were stopped at red lights that had just turned green, and Malone hit the horn to alert the driver in front of us to this fact.

"What does them all being on the waitlist tell us?" he asked.

"Maybe nothing," I said. "But I can't believe that. You saw how many accommodation forms there are. Halls must be able to take hundreds if not thousands of students. But only thirty or so of the freshmen in that binder—the freshmen who ended up living in Halls—came from the waitlist. And all five victims, plus Heather Buckley, who Shaw thinks might have been the Canal Killer's practice run or failed first attempt or whatever, were on it too. It has to be the connection. They must have all done something or met someone or been somewhere that only people who are on the waitlist do or meet or go."

Before we'd left his apartment, Malone had printed out the best shot of CCTV Man from the images the Gardaí had collected, and a copy of the photo I'd found of him in my old album from a scan of it Malone had stored on his phone. They were sitting in my lap.

"I think this is a bad idea," he said as he took a right turn onto a street that ran parallel to the canal. "You walking around that campus."

"That's where Heather is."

"Maybe I should come in with you."

"No. That makes it too serious, too scary. I just want her and me to be able to have a chat."

The canal was a hive of activity. I counted several uniformed Gardaí, two satellite trucks, and dozens of nosy onlookers, collected by the GARDA SCENE: DO NOT

CROSS tape that had been strung between the trunks of
the trees on the canal bank.

"Did they find something?" I asked.

"No," Malone said. "Not yet."

He parked across from the main entrance to the
campus on Haddington Road.

"You sure about this?" he said, turning to me.

"I won't be long. I don't plan on hanging around."

"I'm going to follow you, but I'll keep a distance
behind. Where's her office?"

"In the basement of the library."

"Okay, well, when you go in there, I'll wait outside.
Afterward, we meet back here. If you see any press or
anyone starts bothering you, call my phone. Okay?"

"Okay."

I got out of the car and crossed the street.

The first thing I saw was the lettering above the
entrance: ST JOHN'S COLLEGE, DUBLIN. A different font
to what I remembered; they must have rebranded since.

Everything else looked exactly the same.

I bit back the urge to turn around and run. *It's just
a place. Buildings made of brick and glass, surrounded
by strangers*. Nothing bad had happened here, if
you discounted my meeting Will—which actually,
technically, *hadn't* happened here. We'd met in a bar in
town.

It wasn't a bad place, it just held bad memories. Or
good memories gone bad since.

St. John's campus had always seemed to me to be a
metaphor of sorts for what being a St. John's student was
like. The entrance on Haddington Road was a narrow
archway between two imposing limestone buildings, the

classical architecture reminding you that St. John's had been around for a couple of hundred years and your brief enrollment there would be but a blink in its history, so don't go getting any notions. The campus had been built on the site of an old army barracks but Haddington Hall, as it was known, was the only original building the college had kept. It was what everyone thought of when they thought of St. John's: history, tradition, money. It even formed the logo.

But walk through the arch, and you'd soon see what St. John's looked like to its mildly disappointed student body: a sprawl of eighties-era structures, haphazard and mismatched, almost every one of them an eyesore. The science block with its innards on the outside, aiming for the Pompidou Center but landing much closer to a sewage treatment plant. Postgraduate accommodation clad with white panels that had looked sleek and clean for about five minutes, and then only dirty and streaked with deep brown rust stains after that. A library built to look like a giant concrete block with long, narrow windows buried deep in folds of gray brick. One summer, it had been used as a filming location for some bleak dystopian Hollywood movie. It had served as a prison in it.

People sent their children here because they figured it'd been around for so long, it must be something special. But students soon discovered that the sheen of reputation, much like the cobblestones, didn't extend much beyond the archway. Inside, it was just like any other college.

It was still early Tuesday morning; the campus was busy, but not thronged with people yet. I headed straight for the library, walking fast, eyes down. I had no plan, really, other than to find Heather's office, knock on her door, and tell her who I was.

I hadn't anticipated the turnstiles, or what to do to get around them. When I'd been a student here, we'd just walked straight in. I pushed against the horizontal steel rod at my hips, but it didn't budge. A small black device with a glowing red light was mounted on the side, sliced through the middle: you needed a keycard to get in. Your student ID, probably.

While I stood there trying to decide what to do, a young girl with headphones on approached the next turnstile over. I watched as she whipped her ID card through the device. The light turned green and there was a little electronic *beep*. When she pushed against the steel rod, it gave.

After shooting me a look, she sauntered on through.

"Are you all right there?"

I turned. There was a counter off to the left, and a woman wearing a campus security T-shirt was standing behind it, looking at me questioningly.

She narrowed her eyes now and said, "Library's just for students."

I didn't want to say that I was here to see someone, because that would no doubt necessitate providing a name and Heather being warned in advance of my arrival. So I said, "I forgot my ID." That probably sounded a bit weird considering I was making no effort to search for it in any pocket or in my bag, so I added, "I just realized."

She raised an eyebrow. "What course?"

"English. First year."

The other brow shot up. "You're a *freshman*?"

I smiled. "Yes. A mature one."

We stood there for a second longer than was comfortable, with her staring at me and me smiling inanely at her. God, what did she think I was going to do in there: steal a load of literary theory texts because I found them just so damn *riveting*?

Another student approached the desk then, putting Security Lady under pressure. She threw me one last suspicious look before pressing some unseen button, turning the light on my turnstile green.

"You won't be able to borrow anything," she warned.

"I'm just checking something." I pushed through. "Thanks."

I walked past a long counter manned by library staff, through a seating area, around some sort of gallery exhibition showing photos of the campus throughout the years, and on to the elevators. I didn't see any stairs so I got in the first available car and pressed B for basement.

When the doors opened a floor below, I found myself in a labyrinth of gray-carpeted corridors, each one the same as the one before. Little signs hung beside every office door but the numbers seemed, at best, to be following some sort of hidden code, rather than any logical sequence.

"Can I help you?"

A short, gray-haired man was suddenly standing in front of me, clutching a sheaf of papers with one hand and pushing his thick-framed glasses back up his nose with the other. He managed, somehow, to look both suspicious and friendly at the same time.

"Ah, yes," I said. "Well, maybe. I'm a bit lost. I'm looking for Heather Buckley's office?"

The man looked me up and down. "Are you here for the interviews?" He turned and pointed down the hall. "Go right, then left. You'll see a waiting area. Have a seat there and she'll come out and get you." He winked at me. "Best of luck, now. Don't be nervous. Heather's lovely."

I thanked him and started down the hall. I soon found the seating area, but no one was waiting there. I sat down.

Moments later, the door to the nearest office swung open, throwing golden light out into the dim hall. A young girl of maybe twenty came out first, smiling and laughing, turning to say something to the older woman who was following behind.

Heather.

It had to be.

Her unnaturally white-blonde hair was chopped up short into a style that aimed for ease rather than flattery although it flattered her all the same, and she was tall and thin, but not gaunt-looking. She was dressed head to toe in black: black boots, black tights, black skirt, black shirt. She wore no make-up that I could see but still managed to look luminous, somehow.

Maybe *because* she didn't wear any.

"Thanks so much for coming in," she was saying to the young girl. "And sorry again for making you wait. It's been a bit of a morning around here. We'll hopefully be in touch in the next couple—" Her eyes landed on me. She frowned, then took a step closer. "*Alison?*"

"Hi," I said, surprised that she'd recognized me. But

then I remembered that my face had been on front pages yesterday, and someone who'd potentially had a brush with the Canal Killer might be interested in keeping up with the facts of the case. "I was, ah, hoping we could talk? If you have a minute?" When a look of horror crossed Heather's face I added, "I'll be really quick."

The younger girl was looking from one of us to the other and then back again, unsure of whether she should stay or go.

"Thank you," Heather said to her pointedly, and the girl turned and went. Then, to me, "I'm going to bloody kill him."

"Sorry?"

"The Gardaí have only just left. Please don't tell me he's been bothering you too?"

I was completely lost. "Sorry—who?"

"Daniel," Heather said with an eye-roll. "He's why you're here, isn't he? What *else* has he bloody gone and done?"

alison, now

Heather's office was small, the width of the window that ran floor to ceiling at its far end. One wall was taken up with rickety bookshelves, thin MDF slats affixed to unsightly brackets, each one bending and bowing under the weight of books, papers, and stacks of magazines. A desk was pushed up against the other one, with only a computer, a bottle of water and a neat stack of manila folders sitting on it.

Heather slid in behind the desk, motioning for me to take the hard plastic office chair on the other side. I noticed a thin silver band on her wedding finger but there were no personal photographs anywhere in the room. I wondered who she was married to, if it was someone she'd met in St. John's. I wonder if maybe I knew him.

"You don't remember me, do you?" she said, once we'd both sat down. "You were in a few of my classes."

"Oh." I didn't. "No, sorry."

"Did you really not know?"

"It's all so long ago," I said. "And I try *not* to remember—"

"I meant about him."

"I ..." I felt my cheeks coloring. "I—"

"Sorry," Heather said. "That was rude of me. Forget I asked." She folded her arms. "Should you really be here? I saw the newspapers. Yesterday *and* today. Isn't this like ground zero? Aren't you making it easy for them to find you? And if they do, they'll get a shot of you on campus. I don't think that's good for you *or* the university. Do you?"

I didn't know if it was my lack of sleep or Heather herself, but I was finding it hard to navigate this conversation.

And who was *Daniel*?

"I came to ask you for your help." I took my phone out and brought the nightclub picture up on screen. I passed it to her. "Do you know who—"

"Yeah," she said. "That's him. And it's him in those CCTV pictures too. I *told* the guards all this already."

"You told ... I'm sorry, I'm not quite following."

"That's Daniel," Heather said. "Daniel O'Dowd. And no, I don't know where he is if he's not at home." She looked at the picture again. "Where did you get this? Is that you?"

"It's mine; I had it in an album. So was Daniel at St. John's too or ...?"

There was a blur of movement in my peripheral vision. I turned to my left and saw that someone had arrived at the seats outside the office and was looking around. Another young girl. She hesitated for a moment, then sat down. Heather's next interviewee, probably. When I turned back, Heather had begun tapping something out on her keyboard. I thought for a second she was trying to get rid of me until she twisted the monitor around to show me what was onscreen.

A website. The header photo was a moody black-and-white shot of water with a hand-sketched map of what looked to be Dublin layered over it. Superimposed on that, cartoonish red lettering dripping with droplets of blood: BENEATH THE SURFACE.

"That's Daniel," Heather said. "That's his"—she rolled her eyes again—"*blog*."

I could only see the title of the most recent blog post. *Breaking News: Garda Water Unit Searching for SJC Student in the Grand Canal.* He must have posted that this morning.

"He's obsessed," Heather said. "Started off with this, must be, I don't know, six or seven years ago? Added a podcast a couple of years back when that other true crime one got really big. That American one. I think he's convinced he's headed for the big time too but as far as I can tell, it's only a handful of people listening." Another eye-roll. "That was before the new girls, though."

I peered at the screen. "Daniel blogs about *crime*?"

Heather frowned. "Don't you ever Google yourself? Daniel doesn't blog about crime. He blogs about *one crime*. He's the internet's foremost nutter when it comes to the Canal Killer case."

I tried to get this information straight in my head. Daniel O'Dowd was the man captured on CCTV and the man in my photo from back then. He was probably the man who'd been sitting outside my hotel, on the bank of the canal, too. And his main occupation was blogging about all things to do with the Canal Killer?

I was tempted to pause and text Malone his name right now, but Heather seemed all over the place and I didn't know how she'd react.

"He has credibility because"—Heather put on a dramatic, movie-trailer voice—"*he was there*. In first year, although it was his second year on campus because he changed course. And in the beginning, yeah, okay, it wasn't *that* weird. We were all obsessed with it, in our own ways. I mean, any student who was here at the time is lying if they say they didn't trot out that fact whenever the subject came up. I bet hundreds of graduates are *still* feeding off the anecdotes at cocktail parties, first dates, whatever."

I thought of Stephen, Sal's newest ex-pat find, leaving a dramatic pause during introductions back at the Patrick's Day dinner party.

Then I thought, *God, had that just been four days ago?*

It seemed like another lifetime now, felt like another planet.

"But Daniel was different," Heather said. "He was serious. He got stuff from the investigation: photos, reports, that kind of thing. God knows how. And then he declared he was going to prove what really happened, whatever *that* meant, and started badgering me to sit down for an interview about the night I was attacked." She sighed. "Look, I like the guy. He's an innocent. And he had some trouble a few years ago. All this blog and investigation stuff, it helped him get back on track. Gave him focus. And it was harmless when it was all back in the past. But since these new girls started showing up in the canal, he's wandered *right* off the reservation.

Especially these last few days. Especially when he found out you were in town. He'll *freak* when he finds out you were in my office."

My mind was racing, desperately trying to sift through all this, looking for the pieces that, when fit together, would make some kind of sense.

"So you're friends with him?" I asked.

"Duty bound." Heather sighed. "I'm married to his sister."

"Oh."

"Yeah. Guess you didn't remember *that*, either."

"Heather, look, it's not just you. I really don't remember a lot from back then. I try not—"

"I feel sorry for him," she said, cutting me off. She turned to look out the window now. "He had a thing for Liz. A secret thing. So when she died, he was grieving too, but he couldn't show it. He was afraid people would think he was just trying to elbow his way to the front of the mourners' queue, after the fact. And they *would've* thought that because people are assholes, aren't they?"

I was furiously flipping through my memories of back then, looking for something—anything—of Daniel. I couldn't remember the night that the photo had been taken. But what was that thing that had happened at the Traffic Light Ball? The weird guy she'd said had been bothering her? Could that have been Daniel?

"Do you know if he tried to contact me?" I asked. "These last few days?"

"He did say he was going to try to call you at your hotel."

"I think maybe he did. I had a hang-up."

Heather shrugged. "Maybe he chickened out."

"How did he know where I was staying?"

"Wasn't it in the papers?"

"Maybe …" Only *after* Daniel had paid me a visit, so he must have found out by other means. "I think maybe he broke into my room, too."

Heather blinked rapidly, theatrically. "Um, *no*. No, he didn't. He wouldn't do something like that. He's a crazy, yeah, but not breaking-the-law crazy. Which is what I told the Gardaí."

I decided to switch gears. "Did *you* know Daniel back then, back in college?"

Heather nodded. "We were in the debating society together. He's how I met Deirdre."

"So there's no possibility that Daniel could be one of the men who attacked you? You would've recognized him, right?"

Yet another eye-roll. "Oh, come *on*."

"I'm just trying to figure this all out, Heather."

"How nice for you. But keep Daniel out of it. He's done nothing wrong." She turned her computer monitor back to face her. Then she looked back to me. "Wait. 'One of'?"

"What?"

"You said 'one of the men' that attacked me. There was only one."

"I just meant, like, one of the men there. The attacker or the guy who came and helped afterward— but then ran off?"

Heather looked at me for a long moment. Then she said: "Neither of them was Daniel."

"Was either of them Will?"

She shook her head, *no*.

"You're sure?"

"I knew Will. Well, to see. I would have recognized him."

I let a beat pass.

"Detective Shaw," I said. "You might have spoken to him about this? He has a theory about what happened to you that night. Well, two theories. The first is that it was, like, a practice run. That it was the Canal Killer—"

"Will," Heather said.

"—warming up. Wait—I thought you said it *wasn't* Will?"

"I don't think Will was the man who attacked me that night. But I also don't think what happened to me had anything to do with the canal murders."

"What makes you say that?"

She turned up her palms. "Because I'm not dead." I thought it was more because Heather didn't want to think that she'd only just escaped the clutches of a serial murderer by the skin of her teeth, but I didn't say this out loud. "What's this detective's other theory?"

"That the guy who came to your aid—the one who ran off—was actually part of it. That he was the attacker's partner in crime, literally and figuratively. He swoops in, knight in shining armor, wins your trust. Then, well … You know. Why else would he have run off when those cyclists came?"

Heather drummed her fingers on the table. "Is this conversation just between us?"

I nodded, because saying yes without actually saying it felt like less of a lie.

"Look, I knew the other guy, okay?" Heather said. "He was a friend. We'd been out together that night and he—being the *complete* idiot that he is—made a move on me. I didn't want it; he didn't want me not to want it; I decided to go home. He was following me. I mean, not like stalker following me. Just a friend following me, making sure I actually got back to Halls. So he sees someone cross the street to walk behind me, he sees something happen, sees me disappear from the path, he comes running. I'm in the damn *reeds* when he gets there, almost in the water."

"When was this?"

"The Thursday night of Freshers' Week."

Within a college term, someone would have started murdering girls by attacking them on their walk home to campus and pushing them into the canal to drown. How could she possibly think her attack wasn't connected?

"He starts shouting," she continued, "kicking the guy who's, like, on top of me by now, and that guy runs off. Maybe ten seconds later, the two cyclists rock up and the first thing one of them says is, 'I've called the Gardaí.' Well, that sent my friend bolting. Because he hadn't *just* been drinking. Neither had I, as a matter of fact. When the Gardaí came, I didn't want to tell them about him, because I knew they'd go pick him up and find out that he was off his face, and he'd get in trouble just for trying to get me *out* of some. So I said I didn't know him either, or why he'd run off."

"But you really *didn't* know the first guy, the attacker?"

"No."

"Did you get a good look at him?"

"No."

"But he wasn't Will or Daniel?"

"No."

"How can you be—"

"He was taller. Wider. And he just seemed … I don't know. *Older*."

If Daniel was obsessed with the Canal Killer case, that would explain his frequenting the canal late at night. That would eliminate the CCTV images of him as being anything other than his bad luck. There was also, potentially, not quite an *innocent* explanation for me seeing him outside my hotel, but an explanation nonetheless.

But who had attacked Heather? Was there a third suspect, someone totally unknown, someone never captured on CCTV, who was, in fact, the real Canal Killer? Someone who was able to go about his business while the Gardaí thought they had got their guy way back when and were now searching the city for a guy doing research for his *blog*?

"I never even saw the guy," Heather said. "Neither did my friend—I checked. He came up behind me. I never saw his face." She shifted in her seat. "I have an appointment now. I think she's waiting outside."

"Right. Sorry." I stood up. "Just one other thing, Heather. All the victims back then—and you—were on the waitlist for a room in Halls. Can you think of anyone you might've met on campus or some place you would've gone—something you did—that first-years who *weren't* on the waitlist didn't need to do?"

"Well, yeah. I went looking for somewhere to live."

Searching for alternative accommodation.

It was so obvious, now that I thought about it. Students who were assured of their room at Halls all along wouldn't have to bother. Those who may or may get a room needed a Plan B.

"This girl I knew from home," Heather went on, "she and I were going to be roommates if Halls didn't work out, and honestly, we really thought we were going to be like Monica and Rachel until we actually started going to see the kind of places we could afford. Jesus, they were grim." She shook her head at the memory. "There was this one house, I'll never forget it. Harold's Cross. Student Shit-tips R Us. The garden was all overgrown. The front door was rotting. All the doors inside were just, like—what's that really cheap, flimsy stuff? Chipboard? MDF? Anyway, *not* door material. And the dirt, I'd never seen anything like it. The room itself was like a cupboard with a toilet in it. You could actually flush the toilet from the bed. But the worst bit was that when we were leaving, this guy who was living downstairs came out of his room, and not only was he in his underwear in the middle of the day and in it in the *hall*, but he also had what looked like a serious case of pink eye, which—correct me if I'm wrong—I think you get from scratching your arse and then poking your eye?" Heather made a face. "It was truly disgusting. And miles from campus, anyway. And get this—*too expensive for us*." She laughed. "We were lucky we got into Halls."

"Yeah," I said absently. "Listen—how did you go about that? Did you go to an agency or something?"

"No," Heather said. "We just looked places up online."

"How many did you go see?"

"Six, maybe? Seven?"

It was a bit too random to be the connection. Five

girls on the waitlist, each one searching for properties on the internet, each one ending up going to different ones ...

But this would've been near St. John's, only days before college began, and in Dublin City during the height of the boom.

"Heather," I said, "can I take your phone number?"

alison, then

Christmas break was going to be a month long.

As much as I loved Christmas, it was just one day. Two, if you included Christmas Eve. That left nearly four weeks of being stuck at home, with Liz and without Will. He was going away to some ski resort in the French Alps for a fortnight. He left at lunchtime on the last day of term. Liz and I were taking the train down to Cork together the following morning, so I had a night on campus without him. Claire had already left, so I had the whole apartment to myself. I was looking forward to hunkering down for the evening, with a movie or a good book, drinking endless cups of tea, and just basking in a night of alone time. If I couldn't spend the evening with Will, it was the next best thing.

But Liz wanted to do something.

"*I* know," she said, sitting across from me in the student cafeteria. "We should have a Christmas night. Go look at the Christmas shop in Brown Thomas. Get some hot chocolate at a fancy hotel. The Westbury, maybe. Or the Shelbourne. I bet their decorations are *amazing*. That's what we should do. Have ourselves a little Dublin Christmas before we go down to Cork."

Liz's eyes were bright with excitement and I couldn't help but think that, actually, that *would* be a nice thing to do. I'd never been in Dublin at Christmastime and the last couple of weeks had been the shock of exams suddenly looming over us and then a mad scramble to shove enough information into our heads to fill the answer booklet before they got here. I hadn't really had a chance to go walk around the shops. I was only ever off-campus at night, and then huddled in a corner with Will in a pub or out at a club with everybody, drinking.

I was guessing the fact that Will couldn't join us was also contributing to Liz's enthusiasm. She wouldn't run the risk of being a third wheel. I felt bad that a night with just the two of us was now a rare occasion. I actually couldn't remember the last time we'd had one that didn't involve studying or pulling an essay-writing all-nighter.

So I said yes, let's do it.

Liz knocked on my door at seven that evening wearing a Santa hat.

I laughed. "What the …?"

"No need to be jealous, Ali," she said, producing a second one from behind her back, "because I brought one for you too."

It started off as a really nice evening. Grafton Street was strung with twinkling lights and the buskers there had switched to Christmas playlists. Brown Thomas' famous windows had displays of seasonal party finery, arranged in wintry scenes. (I'd heard grumblings on the radio that this year's window scheme wasn't kid-friendly and that next year they should at least try to include a few toys.) Every single shop we went into was copiously decorated, with Christmas music playing. There was only a week to go until the big day and plenty of shoppers were taking advantage of the extended opening hours this Friday night.

I bought a few small presents for my parents—a book for my mother, some whiskey for Dad, chocolates in the shape of reindeers for both of them—and Liz and I got mulled wine and mince pies from a food truck parked up under the intricate curl of a Georgian streetlamp on Stephen's Green. We sat on the icy stone steps of one the square's townhouses and admired the decorations hanging from other facades around us.

"They should put lights in the trees," Liz suggested, nodding at the black shadows beyond the wrought-iron railing of Stephen's Green across the street.

"Hmm," I said through a mouthful of mince pie.

The park closed at dusk every day; adding anything that only served its purpose in the dark would be pointless.

I didn't say this aloud, though. Liz didn't like being contradicted.

A horse-drawn carriage trotted past, carrying two people—tourists, surely—huddled under a furry sheepskin blanket while taxis screeched by. They were followed a moment later by the pungent smell of what one of the horses was steadily depositing on the street as it sauntered along.

Liz started coughing. "Oh, my God."

"Let's go." The smell was already at the back of my throat.

Feeling warm and loose from the wine and slightly sick from the smell, we decided to skip the hot chocolate and start back toward St. John's.

We'd just reached the canal when Liz said, apropos of nothing, "Did Will find that ski jacket he was looking for?"

"What?"

I hadn't heard anything about any jacket. All I knew about Will and skiing was that he wasn't very good at it and loathed having to go do it for the next fortnight with his parents and siblings in tow.

"Yeah," Liz said. "He was looking for it out in Dundrum."

"You mean in the shopping center? When was this?"

"Oh …" She shrugged her shoulders. "Thursday, maybe?"

I tried to keep my tone casual. "You saw him out there?"

"We had lunch." She looked at me. "He didn't tell you?" He hadn't and that fact was all over my face, I could feel it. Liz was looking worried now. "You know what? He had a little bag with him. Like from a jeweler's or something. I bet he was out there buying your Christmas present. Maybe he didn't want to ruin the surprise."

It made sense.

I *wanted* it to make sense.

So I smiled half-heartedly and said, "And now he's busted."

"God, I'm so sorry. Pretend I didn't say anything, okay?"

Later that night, when I was back in my room

alone, Will rang from France. I asked him how it was over there.

He sighed. "Cold and dark."

I laughed. "Sounds fabulous."

"I already want to kill them all. My brother's come up with this "season of good Will" joke that he thinks is hilarious and original. He's wrong on both counts."

"Well," I said, "season of good Will: I miss you."

"I know it's not cool, it's only been like six hours, but I miss you too."

"You're worried about being cool? Because I'm sorry to have to tell you this, but …"

"I happen to think I'm very cool."

"Hey," I said as casually as I could. "Were you in Dundrum on Thursday?"

A pause. "Why?"

"Liz let it slip that she saw you."

"What else did she say?"

That seemed like a strange follow-up question, and Will's tone was disconcertingly cautious.

"That you two had lunch," I said.

"*What?*" Will cursed. "We didn't have *lunch*!"

"No?"

"I thought you were going to say that she told you what I got you for Christmas. No, I just ran into her. In the middle of the shopping center. She was with that Lauren girl. They were going to Penneys to look for Santa jumpers or something. I had your present in a bag and … Well, it was obvious what it was from the bag. But I asked her not to tell you. I didn't want her ruining the surprise. But *lunch*? Bloody hell. I talked to her for maybe a minute and then I went on my way. I was trying to get back to meet you after your Victorian Lit class." And he had—he'd been waiting for me outside my last class. It was off campus, in rooms in a converted Georgian house that was mostly used for postgraduate study. He didn't like me walking back after it by myself in the dark. "Are you sure that's what she said?"

"Were you looking for a ski jacket?"

"Yeah, but they didn't have my size in stock."

"Oh."

"It's crazy that she would say that." He swore again. "Us having lunch. As if. I mean, what the …?"

"Yeah," I said lamely.

I didn't know what else to say, but I knew who I believed.

So what the hell was Liz up to?

*****

The next morning, Liz and I took the train down to Cork together but didn't speak much. She dozed and I read. We were used to sitting together in cars, buses, and trains in companionable silence, so I doubted she sensed that there was any motivation behind mine.

Everything had changed so much in the last three months, my head was spinning. I thought back to when we'd traveled up to Dublin back in September, the palpable excitement, that first night in St. John's. And I thought of what lay ahead of me: nearly a month without Will. The idea set me adrift—which was so strange when, twelve weeks ago, I hadn't even known he'd existed.

I hung around the house my first couple of days

back, deeply appreciating the ease with which things could happen. There was always food in the fridge. There was never anyone in my way in the kitchen. My dirty clothes magically disappeared from the laundry basket in my room and I didn't have to worry about having clean towels or toilet paper or toothpaste. Mam was on hand to make endless cups of tea. She even brought them when I didn't ask for them. Everything was already there, supplied. I basked in this, took advantage of it, lazing around reading novels belonging to my mother that had absolutely nothing to do with the St. John's curriculum, and tucking into the boxes of chocolates she'd stocked up on for Christmas.

On my third day at home, I stepped out of the shower to hear voices in the kitchen. I paused at the top of the stairs, listening, but I couldn't identify who my mother was talking to.

Then I heard the high pitch of Liz's laugh.

I hurried down, worried that she might have already said something that would reveal Will's existence to my mother. I wasn't ready for that. I wasn't sure *my mother* was ready for that. She seemed to think Dublin was a den of iniquity where only the mortal sins await. A boyfriend, to her, would be proof of that. She'd say I was there for a degree, not an unplanned pregnancy. I knew that'd be her first thought, and my cheeks burned hot at the idea of discussing that with her. *No*. Not yet. She needed to be primed for it. I had a plan: come January, I'd start dropping his name into conversation. Telling my mother about Will was on my Things to Worry About in the New Year list, not today's.

"Hello, stranger," Liz said when I entered the

kitchen. "I'm heading into town for a walk around. You want to come?"

"Of course she does," my mother said. "Be careful, though, because the oxygen might go to her head. She hasn't left the house in two days."

I rolled my eyes. "I could just go back to Dublin if it's bothering you."

"Off with you then, love. You'll have to wait for me to dry those four loads of clothes first, though. You can't pack them wet."

Liz looked away, biting back laughter.

I made her wait upstairs with me while I got changed and dried my hair, just to be on the safe side. She had her mother's car with her. We parked in Merchants Quay and started down Patrick Street, pushing against a tide of Christmas shoppers. Liz's mother had given her a list of things to pick up. Compared to Dublin, Cork seemed impossibly tiny now, especially when we started bumping into people we knew.

I had never, in all the time I'd lived in Dublin, bumped into anyone I knew accidentally, except for Will in that café in Ranelagh—and he'd admitted that wasn't entirely accidental. Here, you couldn't move for people you knew popping up at random. Worse than that, though, was being seen by people who knew you but who you *didn't* know, like friends of your parents. It meant you could never get away with anything.

We were browsing the racks in River Island when a familiar voice said hello. When we turned around, two girls we'd gone to school with were standing there. One of them was Sharon who'd had the CAO offers party that I hadn't gone to because I thought Liz was in a sulk.

The other one was a girl called Amanda who had been in another class, who I only knew from seeing around.

We chatted for a few minutes about how college was going, for them and for us, and how Dublin was compared to Galway, where Sharon was.

Then Sharon turned to me and said, "And I heard you have a *boyfriend*? Louise is in Trinity and she knows his friend Matt, she said? Does he have a friend called Matt?" I said he'd mentioned that name a couple of times. A school friend, I thought. "Well, I only heard good things. Lou said he's hot." She looked to Liz. "Is he hot? There's no point asking her because we know what she's going to say."

Liz hesitated. "Well, he's not *my* type, but …"

Sharon laughed and said to me, "I supposed that's just as well, isn't it?"

I forced a smile.

I was thinking, *He's not your type? What's that supposed to mean?*

"He's *skiing*," Liz said pointedly, loading the word with meaning. None of us had ever been, or knew anyone who had.

"Doesn't everyone in St. John's do that?" Amanda said slyly. "You two will have to start."

St. John's had a reputation for educating the kids of the upper classes, the ones decked out in designer threads, kept in Volkswagen Golfs and taken skiing every winter. It deserved this—those kids were there—but they were just one part of the student body. It was an image St. John's couldn't possibly shake, though, being situated in the most expensive postcode in the country: Dublin 4.

Will came from a family like that, from what I

could gather, but you'd never know. He never acted like he was any different to the rest of us.

"What about you, Liz?" Sharon asked.

"Me?" Liz raised her eyebrows. "*Skiing?*"

"No—boyfriends."

"Eh, I don't *think* so." Liz made a face like she'd just sucked on a lemon. "Being stuck in someone else's pockets, like, *all the time*? Never going anywhere without them? Never *wanting* to go anywhere without them?" She sighed dramatically. "God, no. That'd drive me insane. No, thanks."

My face was rapidly coloring.

"Jeez," Sharon said. "Tell us how you really feel."

She and Amanda exchanged a glance.

We said our goodbyes and made vague promises to arrange something for Stephen's night. As Liz and I walked out of the store and back onto the street, I was overwhelmed with a sad, dense anger.

Liz was chatting away, oblivious, about some top she'd seen and how it'd be perfect to wear on New Year's Eve, as if she hadn't just cruelly and casually insulted me, and I just couldn't stand it a second longer.

"I'm going home," I announced abruptly. "I don't feel well."

Liz swung around to face me. "What?"

"I have a headache. It's been building up all morning but now it's making me feel a bit sick. I think I'm getting my period. I just want to go home to bed."

"Oh, shit. Well, that's okay. Let's head back toward the car."

"No, no," I said quickly. "You have to get that stuff for your mother, don't you? I'll just take the bus."

"Don't be silly, we'll just—"

"*No.*"

Liz blinked at me.

"No," I said again, more evenly this time. "It's fine, really. I'll just get the bus. It stops practically outside my door. Honestly, it's fine. I'll call you later."

"Okay …" Liz sounded uncertain.

I gave her a limp hug and then turned off Patrick Street, heading for the bus stops on the South Mall.

With steam coming out of my ears, I was sure.

I was just so tired of this, of Liz's little mood swings. When she was happy, she was such fun to be around. We were best friends, really. I felt better after seeing her.

But if Liz wasn't happy, if she was in one of her inexplicable moods, I either felt like I had to walk on eggshells around her or that I was the prime target on her warpath. Or sometimes, both.

And it was one thing when she working her little digs into our private conversations, but to so blatantly insult me in front of other people?

That was it. Limit reached. Line crossed.

I'd just missed a bus. I found some cold stone steps leading to a closed bank branch and sat on them to wait for the next one.

A few minutes later I heard, "Alison? Well, hello again."

Sharon and Amanda. Done with their shopping and headed home too. They asked me where Liz had disappeared to and I explained that I wasn't feeling well and had elected to go home.

"Headache," I said, rubbing my temple for effect.

Amanda fished in her bag and handed me two

Ibuprofen in a blister pack. Sharon had a few mouthfuls left in a bottle of water. I couldn't very well refuse so I took them and thanked them. I'd nearly convinced myself that I *was* getting a headache, anyway.

"So what's he like, then?" Sharon said. "Will, isn't it? I heard he's a really nice guy."

I said he was. I told them how we met.

"Listen," Amanda said, leaning closer, "don't worry about her, okay? She's always been a bit of jellyfish." Sharon threw Amanda a sharp look. "What? It's not like she doesn't know it. She can't not. She just got stung herself. We were there."

It took me a second to figure out what she was talking about. "You mean *Liz*?"

"Look," Sharon said, digging Amanda lightly in the ribs, "ignore us. She's *your* best friend."

I looked to Amanda. "What's a jellyfish?"

The two girls exchanged another glance.

"It's when you have a friend," Amanda said, "who is really nice, like, most of the time, but then they'll suddenly say something mean or rude, like a little jab, a little sting, and then they just carry on as if nothing has happened and you're left there thinking, *Did* something just happen or am I imagining it? Didn't you ever see *Bridget Jones*?"

"I like Liz," Sharon said. "She's a laugh. But she *does* do that."

"A lot," Amanda added.

Their bus came then. Mine was still another ten minutes away. I thanked them for the painkillers and said I might see them around over the break.

*****

But I didn't see them or anyone else over the break.

On Christmas Eve I woke up with a stuffed nose and by the morning of Stephen's Day I was knocked out by full-blown flu. I realized pretty quickly that all the other times I'd thought I'd had the flu, I had, at worst, a heavy cold. This was something else entirely. Headaches, chills, sweats, a heavy pressure on my chest. After two really bad days of it Mam rang our GP, who said yes, it was flu, and there was really nothing to do except take something with paracetamol in it to keep my temperature down, *lie* down, and wait for it to be over.

The only saving grace was that I got it at home, where I was waited on hand and foot. I don't know how I would've coped at college. I commandeered the couch where I lay cocooned in a sea of pillows and blankets, presiding over a kingdom of pots of Vicks Vapour Rub, crumpled tissues and half-drunk cups of tea. I read or napped during the day and watched episodes of *The West Wing* with my parents at night. Mam had bought Dad the DVD box set for Christmas and after a couple of episodes, we were all hooked. Mam would slip upstairs at some point to plug in the electric blanket for me. In the morning, she'd wake me with breakfast in bed and change the sheets while I showered.

If it wasn't for constantly feeling like I'd been run over by a truck, I would've enjoyed it.

I didn't see Liz at all, but we talked on the phone. Will called a couple of times, but on both occasions I was in the living room and it was difficult to talk to him normally when my parents were within earshot without giving something away. We constantly texted each other too.

One day, while I was asleep, Liz called over and left a stack of glossy magazines with my mother. They were wrapped up like a present and had a gift tag that said, "Get Well Soon."

It was my mother who eventually opened them and started leafing through the top one from the pile.

My plan had been to go back to Dublin a few days early, on the Monday before classes began. Will and I were going to have our Christmas then. We planned to go on a bit of a road trip down the coast, toward Wicklow, and maybe stay in a B&B here and there. I'd been looking forward to it for weeks. But after being a plague-ridden burden for most of my stay at home I felt guilty, and elected to stay on there instead. Will understood and we arranged to just have a weekend away instead. I booked a train for that Friday.

But that was all forgotten, though, when, on the Thursday morning, my mother knocked on my bedroom door to wake me up, poked her head in once I'd sleepily responded and said to come downstairs.

There'd been a girl found in the canal near St. John's. They were saying on the news that she was a student. Liz was waiting on the phone.

"It's Lauren," she said when I got on the line. "Claire's friend? She came out with us a few times?"

I wasn't even awake yet. "What's Lauren?" I asked through a yawn.

"It's *her*, Ali," Liz said. "On the news. She's the girl who's been murdered."

alison, now

"Mam," I said as soon as she answered her phone, "listen to me. Places we went to see in Dublin. Where were they?"

"Hmm?" My mother was distracted by something, I could tell by her voice. "What? Alison, what's going on? I thought you'd ring me last night. Your dad's been waiting to talk to you. Where are you?"

I was running across the lawns outside the library, heading for Haddington Hall. I didn't think to look for Malone in the faces of the students milling about, or about how I was only drawing attention to myself by running across the grass, shouting into my phone.

There was no time for that.

"Mam, *listen*. We went to look at places. Student accommodation. Apartments. Remember? With Liz. Because we didn't know if either of us was going to get a place at Halls." I was hurrying under the arch now and could see Malone's car parked across the road. "Where did we go, Mam? Do you remember? There was a place in Rathmines. A tiny room in this really awful, dirty house. I think there was also an apartment, maybe? It was really expensive, though. And a house. There was a house with a tiny room up in the attic and a young guy showed us around, his father owned it." A horn blared as I darted between passing cars to get across the street. "Is any of this ringing any bells? Where were those places?"

"Alison, what in the name of God is going on? You sound like you're being chased. I'm going to get your dad, hang on—"

"No, don't. Mam, *listen*." Malone wasn't in the car and pulling on the passenger door handle told me it was locked. "I need you to think about this, Mam. Try to remember. It's important."

"Why?"

"I don't have time to explain. Just do it." That sounded a bit harsh so I added a, "Please." There was an electronic *beep-beep*. Malone was coming toward me, pointing his keys at the car. I pulled the door open and got in. "Mam, are you there?"

"I'm thinking, Alison, I'm thinking."

The driver door opened and Malone sat in too. I mouthed *pen* at him and made a scribbling motion with my free hand. He pulled one from his pocket. I pulled the picture of CCTV Man—Daniel—out of mine, turned it over to the blank side and took the cap off the pen with my teeth.

"Mam?"

"What's going on?" Malone whispered.

I held up a finger to indicate that I'd tell him in a second.

"Okay," my mother said, "well, the expensive apartment, I know where that was. Sandymount. We only went to see it because the man who owned it was a friend of your father's. Liam Keane. The bank owns it now." My mother sounded inordinately pleased about that. "It was never going to be a realistic option, that place. Between you and me, I just wanted a nose around inside."

"Do you remember where in Sandymount?"

"In the village," she said. "It overlooked the little green there."

"Was it a new build?"

"Well, new-*ish*."

"Great." I rolled my eyes. "Any other details?"

"There might have been trees? Right outside it."

I wrote these details down on the paper.

Sandymount. New (ish). Trees?

"What about the other two we went to see?" I said. "Do you remember those?"

"Well, I don't know the name of the road in Rathmines, but it was a long line of red-brick terraced houses, sort of curved at one end. That was the place with the awful bedsit. Where you could flush the toilet and make your dinner at the same time. And what they were charging for it!"

"Near the canal or no?"

"Ah … Near it. But not close enough to see it."

"So a street back from it?"

"At least."

"Anything else?"

"It could've done with being demolished. It was like something you'd see on *Hoarders*."

Rathmines. Red-brick terraced. Curved street. Near canal. Hoarders.

"Okay, good. What about the other house, Mam? There was one with the room in the attic, I think?"

"That was … Out past Rathmines." A pause. "Dartry, maybe?"

Dartry.

"Do you have a street name, or an estate?"

"No," my mother said. "What is all this about?"

"What about the place itself? Do you remember anything about it that might help us find it now?"

"What do you want to find it for?"

"I'll explain everything later."

"Is this to do with the murders?"

"Mam, please. There isn't time." I took a deep breath to keep myself from swearing, which would only set her off on a reprimand about that. "I really just need you to answer the question. Do you remember anything else about the place in Dartry?"

"What about *you?*" she said. "What do you remember? Your mind was considerably younger than mine was back then."

"But I didn't know Dublin at all. You did."

"That's hardly going to help me with remembering what a house looked like from the outside, now, is it?"

I closed my eyes and tried to conjure up an image of the Dartry property, but all I could see was the house in Rathmines and a modern apartment block built by my imagination, overlooking a patch of grass in Sandymount village.

"There was a secret garden," my mother said then.

"What?"

"A secret garden. Like the one in that film. The one with … Oh, what's her name? You know your one.

With the teeth. I remember it because I'd never seen one before. Not here, I mean. London, yes. Dublin, no. Oh—what was the name of that film?"

"Mam," I said, "forget about the film. Tell me about the garden."

Malone tapped me on the shoulder and whispered, "Speakerphone."

I'd forgotten he was there. I pulled the device from my ear and pressed the speakerphone icon.

"One of those ones in the middle of all the houses," my mother's voice said, booming now inside the car and accompanied by white noise that wasn't there when she'd just been in my ear. "With a big fence around it. You could only go in if you lived there. And it was just like in the film too because there was all trees and bushes right up against the fence so you couldn't even see in. Oh, God, what was the name of it? I can see it, you know. I just can't think—"

"*Notting Hill*," Malone said.

"That's it!" my mother shrieked. "Wait, who's that?"

"Detective Garda Malone," he said, leaning closer to me and so to the phone. "We met yesterday, Mrs. Smith. You said the garden was in the middle of the houses. Does that mean the houses were arranged in a square, all around it?"

"I don't think there were houses facing the main road," my mother said. "That was where you drove in. So maybe a U-shape. Or three sides of a square?"

I added *garden* and *U-shape/3 sides* to my list.

"Okay, great," Malone said. "So arranged around a fenced garden, but only on three sides. Were all the houses the same or were they different?"

My mother made a *hmm* noise. "I'm not sure …"

"If you had to make a guess, which one would you pick?"

"I'd say they were probably the same. It was a small estate."

"Old or new?"

"Am I guessing again?"

"Yes," Malone said.

"Old, then."

Same. Small. Old.

"Do you remember anything else, Mrs. Smith?"

"No. Sorry. What's this about?"

"I'll call you later," I said, "and explain everything, okay?"

"Why can't you explain it now? Where are you? And your father wants to talk to you."

"Gotta go, Mam. I'll call later, I promise. Bye."

I pressed the END button on the phone and turned to Malone.

"I have some questions too," he said with a half smile.

"Hang on." I pulled out the business card Heather had given me and started tapping her office number into my phone. The call rang once, twice. I wondered if she'd pick it up when that girl who'd been waiting outside was probably sitting across from her right now. It rang a third time.

"Heather Buckley," a voice said then.

"Hey, it's me. Alison."

"Well, that was quick."

"Here's what I have. You ready?"

"Go."

"A new apartment in Sandymount."

"Sandymount?" Heather laughed. "I was a student, not a stockbroker."

"Okay, next one. Red-brick terrace in Rathmines. On a … a curved street? Near the canal. Could that be the one you were talking about?"

"No, that was at the opposite end."

"Last one, then." The rush of thinking I was onto something was fading fast. "Houses arranged in a sort of U-shape around a fenced garden that only residents had access to, somewhere in Dartry. Possibly the houses were—"

"Yes."

"—all the same. Wait, did you say yes?"

"Yes, I went to see a place like that. I don't remember the name of it, but it was near Trinity Hall. Which is in Dartry, right? And I remember the garden, because I thought it reminded me of the one in—"

"*Notting Hill*," I finished.

"Yeah." A pause. "What does this mean?"

"I don't exactly know yet, but when I find out, I'll let you know. Thank you." I hung up and turned to Malone. "Okay. The man in the CCTV images is Daniel O'Dowd. Heather knows him. He's her brother-in-law, in fact. He was in St. John's too, back then, and nowadays he writes a blog all about the Canal Killer case. She's already had a visit from the Gardaí today so the appeal must have worked. That's what Cusack told you this morning, isn't it? She said something about the news on the CCTV?"

Malone nodded. "Yeah. She told me they had a short list. His name was on it. They haven't picked him up yet, I don't think. He wasn't at home."

"I don't think it's him. He's not the Canal Killer. He's just obsessed with the case—and with proving the killer isn't Will. I think he called me in my hotel room and sat outside my hotel and put that letter in my suitcase. But I *don't* think he killed those girls."

Malone's facial expression was neutral, giving nothing away about whether or not he believed this.

"Okay," he said. "So, what's all this about the houses?"

"Heather Buckley was attacked that September by the canal, by a man she says wasn't Will *or* Daniel. Right? Then there were five victims, including Liz. All six of those girls had something in common: they were all waitlisted for a room in Halls. With only a small number of students overall ending up on the waitlist and then getting a room after all, that's a big coincidence not to be some kind of connection. So what do they do that other students don't? *They look for somewhere else to live*, just in case. Liz and I, we went looking, because I was on the waitlist too. We were going to share if we didn't both get allocated a room."

"But—" Malone started.

"I know, I know. It's too random, because we're all going to look at different places and we all use different methods to find them. There're ads in the newspaper, ads online, going into agencies, just hearing about places from other people … There's loads of ways. That's what I thought, too—at first. But then I started thinking: there's actually *not* loads of properties. You want a place close to college, right? You want a place that's cheap. You can only look at places that are still available in the week or two before college begins, which alone dramatically narrows things down. Now and back then. So what if all six went to see the same place, and *that's* the connection? What if they met the killer there?"

"Louise Farrington," Malone said. "She was waitlisted for a room at Halls. I remember seeing the blue form in her file ... I don't know about the other two, but ... Jesus." He was staring out the windscreen, looking a bit shell-shocked. "And with the Dublin rental market the way it is at the moment, this guy could be asking them to do anything, even just for a viewing. Fill out forms, submit photo ID, provide bank statements ..."

"And the way it is now is similar to the way it was then. We went to St. John's at the height of the boom, and now things are getting back on track here, right?"

Malone nodded. "Yeah. There's a queue of fifty people to see every half-decent bedsit."

"And here's the kicker," I said. "He's not their landlord. They don't see him again after the viewing, because they don't actually move in. They move into Halls instead. So it doesn't even look like a link. And now we know that Heather and Liz went to view the same place around the same time: the secret-garden house in Dartry. I was there. I went with her. So if *he* was there ... I might recognize him. We just need to find the house and hope he still owns it. Or, failing that, that whoever's there now can give us his name or something."

Malone had turned around in his seat to face me. "This is good, Alison. This is really good." He reached over me to open the glove box, retrieved a tablet computer from inside. "We need to find some Wi-Fi."

"What about Will?" I asked. "Where does he fit in to all this?"

I asked because I was thinking, *I'm not sure he does anymore.*

"One thing at a time," Malone said, starting the engine. "One thing at a time."

alison, now

There happened to be a parking space by the café, a quaint little storefront with a vintage bicycle parked outside and a white picket fence separating the outdoor tables and chairs from the street. It looked familiar.

"I think I used to come here," I murmured.

Malone killed the engine and booted up the tablet computer.

I frowned at him. "Aren't we going in?" "Let's check if we can pick up the Wi-Fi first. We may not have to."

"I think they call that stealing, Garda Malone."

He grinned. "We'll come back and buy something later, if it makes you feel better."

I checked my phone for messages. Sal had sent me one, looking for an update on yesterday's meeting with Will.

My chest burned at the memory of that conversation, of how upset he'd been. If he'd really had nothing to do with this, then I really *was* responsible for him being in that place, for him being convicted of five murders, for him losing the last ten years of his life …

I pulled myself back from there, told myself we weren't sure of anything yet.

"Should you tell someone what Heather said?" I asked him. "About Daniel? Like Shaw, I mean?"

"What did she say?"

"That he's an innocent. Harmless. Although I don't know about that. I mean, he *did* break into my hotel room to leave that letter … If that was him. But who else would it be? And it's weird, isn't it? A normal person would've just slipped it under the door."

"Didn't you say the Gardaí already spoke to her?"

"Yeah."

"Then let's assume she told them too. I bet she did." Malone was powering up the tablet. "And somehow I don't think her saying Daniel is 'harmless' will have Shaw calling off the search for him. Do you? Besides, there's another way of looking at it. Daniel is obsessed with the Canal Killer. He has a blog, a podcast, whatever, and he wants more people to notice it. So he uses his extensive knowledge of the original crimes to attempt to recreate them, thus bringing fresh attention to the case, thus bringing new readers to his blog."

This hadn't occurred to me. "Do you think that's what happening?"

"My feeling is no," Malone said. "But you never know."

"And she said her attacker definitely *wasn't* Will, so that torpedoes Shaw's theory that Will was part of a duo."

"Well, I make a point of not telling Shaw he's wrong, so …"

"Where does he think you are right now?"

"Asleep in bed. I'm not in until later so I can work tonight. I'm on canal duty."

"Can we find out if Jennifer Madden and the one who's missing—Amy Boylan, isn't it? Can we find out if they were on the waitlist for Halls? And maybe get a list of places they viewed if they were?"

"I'll call Emily, get her to do it. Right"—he was swiping at the tablet's screen—"let's do this. I'm going to start by Googling 'Dartry secret garden estate.'"

I raised my eyebrows at him.

"What?" he said. "Maybe it'll be that easy."

It wasn't.

"No luck," he said. "It seems to think I'm actually looking for a dirty little secret *in* a garden and all the results are tabloid stories about neighbors from hell."

"Great. Well, Heather said it was near Trinity Hall, the Trinity College accommodation complex. Maybe try that and 'secret garden'?"

More tapping.

"Nope," Malone said then, swiping at the screen. "Now it's all just stuff about Trinity Hall. What if we just look for it? Visually, I mean. On Google Maps. A garden with houses around it on three sides, near Trinity Hall. Can't be that hard to find, surely? How many estates in Dublin have fenced-in gardens in the middle of them?" He leaned closer to me so I could see the screen better, and opened the Google Maps app. It automatically loaded at our current location. He started swiping, moving the map southwest. The green areas stood out starkly against white streaks of streets and the dull gray background.

Immediately, I saw a problem.

"The only green areas are really big ones," I said. "Parks and golf courses. A little communal garden in the middle of a housing estate isn't going to show up on this." I shook my head. "Shit."

"Hang on." Malone tapped the screen. "Let's try Satellite View."

The screen changed to an intimidatingly detailed overhead shot filled with what must be hundreds of tiny houses. It looked a bit like a close-up of the circuits on a computer chip.

My heart sank. "We'll never find it in all this."

"Let's start at Trinity Hall and work out." Malone zoomed in until we could make out the complex's accommodation blocks and then started systematically searching the area around it. I looked too, but I couldn't make out anything that might be the estate we were looking for.

Then: "There," Malone said, pointing. "Could that be it?"

On the map, to the east of Trinity Hall, was an approximately square patch of green filled with what looked like huge trees. A road encircled it, and facing that road were ...

Eight houses? No, sixteen. They were semi-detached.

"Maybe," I said. "Can you do Street View?"

Malone tapped. The screen changed to an image of a street alongside a fenced-in green area. The houses were across from it, on the left. Malone tapped the screen again, angling the view toward the green. A thick hedge pressed up against the chest-high wrought-iron railings while, beyond it, a dense network of tree branches and their leaves obscured all but a few patches of blue sky beyond. The screen moved again, shifting to the left. The view now was of a large gate in the fence with a keypad mounted by the lock.

"That's it!" I said. "I remember it."

"'Doolyn Gardens,'" Malone read. "Are you sure?"

"As sure I can be. Unless by some crazy coincidence there's a similar estate nearby?"

We spent a few minutes scanning the map, but that was the only one of its kind we could find. All the others had open green areas with neatly mowed grass and no trees.

We went back to Doolyn Gardens. It looked to be about three streets from Trinity Hall. A five-minute walk, at most.

"Don't suppose you'd know which house?" Malone said.

"They all look the same. I doubt it. But let's do a loop with Street View, just in case."

But they didn't all look the same.

Most of them did, yes. Red-brick, semi-detached, a bay window on the ground floor and a dormer window in the highest. A small, mature garden behind a low wall, more large trees dotted in almost every one. Shiny new front doors. Polished brass knockers. Proud homeowners inside, presumably.

But one of them wasn't like all the others.

One of them had a front door whose paint was peeling. What looked to be original windows, left to rot and grow a thick, grimy film. A massive, overgrown tree in the front garden that completely blocked the bay window that must be hiding behind it. Plastic bins outside the front door with "23" written on them in white paint, black refuse sacks poking out from beneath the lid. No garden gate at all and, in the gap left by its absence, a view of uneven paving slabs, being forced up from below and kept company by the weeds growing in the cracks.

"Well," Malone said, "we are looking for *student* accommodation. Let's see what happens when we Google the address."

The top result was a listing for a rental property, an attic studio, at 23 Doolyn Gardens, Dartry, Dublin 6. There was a collage of four photos at the top of the screen. A view of a red-brick semi-D with bay windows. A picture of a large double-bed with a brightly patterned two-seater couch backed up against it. A small but clean bathroom suite the color of avocado. A tiny kitchenette with a dining table just big enough for two, pressed up against a window offering a view of the garden outside. The top of the tree in the house's own garden was brushing against the very bottom of the window pane.

"That's it," I said. "A shoebox, right up in the attic. That's it!"

Online, it looked lovely. No wonder we'd gone to see it. There was no Google Street View back then to warn us off. These days, I presumed it was the demand/supply imbalance that still sent people to it. On the flight on the way here I'd overheard the passengers seated in front of me talking about how affordable rental properties were so scarce in Dublin, people on shift-work were time-sharing bedsits.

The listing was marked as "TO LET" at 850 euro a month.

"That's not a bad price for that," Malone said.

"That'll get people to come look. And it's a private letting, no agency involved." He scrolled down the screen with the tip of an index finger. "There isn't even a first name on this. Or a phone number. You can only contact the owner by messaging them through this site." He looked up at me. "That alone is a bit suspicious."

"So what now?"

Malone considered the question. "Let's go there. Do a quick drive-by." His phone beeped with a new text then. "Shit," he said, reading it.

"What?"

"Daniel."

"What about him?"

"They've found him at a house in Stillorgan." He sighed. "They're going in to arrest him right now."

He's called in sick to work. Last night, he swallowed a sleeping pill before he went to bed and didn't set an alarm. Made sure the blackout curtains met each other and closed the bedroom door so no light would leak in from the landing. He let his body tell him how many hours of rest it needed, let sleep stay until all the hours of it he'd missed the night before had been replaced.

It was nearly noon when he finally woke.

He's made some breakfast and taken it into his study, sitting the plate of hot, buttery toast and cup of sweet tea down next to his laptop on his desk. Messy stacks of printed papers, pages torn from magazines, and stories cut from newspapers take up the rest of the space. He boots up the computer and gets to what he likes to think of as his morning rounds, leaving sticky fingerprints on the keyboard as he works.

He starts on the *Beneath the Surface* website, checking for new comments, mostly. He likes to know what people are saying about the case. Sometimes he even responds to what they say, although always anonymously and only with thoughts that wouldn't draw any unwanted attention to himself. The latest post is, of course, about Amy. A commenter calling himself Derek0294 thinks it's too soon for the Gardaí to be dragging the canal, considering that Amy is so different to the other girls, what with her being last seen at St. John's Halls.

He wants to leave a comment commending Derek0294 on this insight, but he doesn't think that would be a good idea.

He moves on to news. Puts Amy's name into Google and scans the results for the latest stories. He reads them quickly, scrolling constantly down the screen, as most of them contain the same details only wrapped up or arranged differently. A theme, he notices, is emerging already. They're saying she *vanished off the face of the earth*.

It's the last known sighting of her entering her own apartment that has them all shocked and confused. Apparently another student passed her in the hall on the way in. They also have the electronic lock record, which shows she used her key seconds later to gain entry to her place. He hopes they don't notice the lack of activity immediately after that, or that if they do, they'll mistake it for Amy turning in for the night.

Not him systematically deleting all entries he made with his own key, surreptitiously programmed in the security office during his very first shift. If St. John's have noticed deletions from the security cameras, they haven't let the press find out yet.

He wonders for a moment if this is actually more

effective than doing it along the canal. He has, from time to time, read subtext in the reporting of those ones like *this is what happens to you when you walk home in the middle of the night, girls, drunk and alone.* But Amy was at home, and at home because she elected *not* to go out drinking. She couldn't be any more blameless if she tried. He'll have to keep this in mind, although he doesn't want to deviate too much from the original blueprints.

Still, little adjustments can be made if they serve the cause.

Like the one he's going to make for Alison Smith.

He didn't recognize her at first, her pinched face turned away from him on the front page of a Sunday paper. It was the headline that got him. Poring over the story at home, he put the pieces together: she had been that idiot guy's girlfriend. And it had been *her* friend who got herself added to the victim list. She was only a teenager at the time, this Alison; not even he could blame her for being so stupid. But she was a woman of, what, thirty now? And visiting this guy in prison, ten years after the fact?

He couldn't allow that.

He eyes his black leather notebook, within reach on the desk. Should he start a chapter on her? A quick internet search leads him to believe he'd have very little to add to it: he can find no social media accounts for her. And really, he only wants to talk to her. He doesn't need to demonstrate that her decisions may have terrible consequences when she's already quite effectively demonstrated that herself. He only needs to *remind* her of it.

The doorbell rings: a three-note electronic call that

sounds foreign inside this house, followed by a sharp knock.

He hurries downstairs to see who it is, still thinking of Alison, and maybe that's why he opens the door without looking through the peephole first, and when he sees who's on the doorstep, his heart leaps into his mouth and he thinks, *I should've looked. I should've checked. I shouldn't have answered.*

But it's too late now.

alison, now

Outside my window, shopfronts were rushing by. We were on a kind of main street, packed with restaurants and boutiques. It had a village feel and, judging by the cool, expensive clothing I was seeing fly by on mannequins in windows and the number of artisan coffee shops with pithy sayings on chalkboards set outside, everyone in the village had a lot of disposable income.

Malone brought the car to a stop at an intersection, flicking on his right indicator. When I looked I saw that, across the street, on the other side of a lane of traffic going in the opposite direction, was a neat U-shaped row of red-brick houses. A blue street sign had been set into the perimeter wall by the entrance. It said DOOLYN GARDENS beside a box with a "6" in it—the postal code.

There was a space just a house down from 23. Malone pulled into it, cut the engine.

I turned to look at the house. It was exactly as it looked on Street View. The only thing missing was the bins.

"That's it," I said. "It looks exactly the same as it did online." I started unbuckling my seatbelt.

"Whoa," Malone said. "What are you doing?"

I looked to him. "What?"

"We're staying in the car."

"Why?"

"Because this could be the home of the serial murderer at the center of this investigation. We can't just go knock on the door. You, especially, cannot have anything to do with this. You're not only a civilian, but a potential witness. You could jeopardize the entire case, if he does have something to do with it. We *stay in the car.*"

I rolled my eyes, frustrated. I wanted to get out, to do more, to be closer. "Then why did we come here?"

"To verify it still looks like it did online," Malone said. "To check that there isn't a kid's bike in the garden and new windows in. To see if he still owns it."

"How do we know that from sitting here?"

"Let's just watch for a few minutes."

I lasted no more than ten seconds of sitting in silence.

"Can't we go talk to the neighbors or something?" I said then.

Malone shook his head. "No."

"You let me talk to Heather."

"I gave you a lift to St. John's so you could talk to an old college classmate. That's different."

"I could pretend to be a prospective renter or something."

"Alison, no." Malone looked at me. "What's with you?"

Momentum was what was with me. Figuring out

the waitlist connection, talking to Heather, putting everything together—it felt like a rush, a flood of adrenalin that was still pulsing through my veins, urging me not to sit still, but to keep going, to keep moving.

I didn't want to stop now.

And somewhere below that, there was an undercurrent of anger. Of frustration. Of rage, even. Because a girl was missing. Because she was the eighth one. Because it was becoming increasingly clear that what I'd thought for the last ten years didn't match the truth and I couldn't take a moment more of just *waiting* for the real story to emerge.

And if the real story was different to the one I knew, then Will was somewhere he shouldn't be.

And I was someone I shouldn't be.

I wanted it to end.

I said, "I'm sorry."

I don't know what Malone thought I was apologizing for but he started to smile and say, "That's okay. I get impatient t—" But by then I'd depressed the handle on the passenger-side door, pushed it open and was getting out.

"Alison. *Alison!*"

I closed the door. The window was down a crack and through it I said, "I'm just going to go knock on the neighbor's door. I can't just sit here. It'll be fine. I won't give my name."

Malone was hurriedly unbuckling his seatbelt. "Alison, get back in the car."

"It'll be fine."

"*Alison.*"

I turned and started toward number 24.

A few steps later I heard a car door open and close and footsteps rushing to catch up with me.

"Alison," Malone said when he was alongside me, "for God's s—"

"It'll be fine."

He shook his head. I didn't know him well enough to be able to tell if he was mad but I thought I could take an educated guess.

He was furious with me.

But it was too late: we were on No. 24's garden path now. Bundling me back into his car would draw more attention.

Through the house's bay window I could see a sliver of the living room: a large TV screen fixed to the chimney breast and a leather chair sitting to one side of it, its back to a built-in bookcase. The front door was painted a glossy emerald green and had a "2" and a "4" affixed to it in polished brass, below a frosted windowpane. I pressed the doorbell and a short musical note sounded in the house.

"We shouldn't be doing this," Malone said. "You shouldn't. I should've stopped you."

I could see movement through the frosted glass, a dark blurry shape, growing bigger.

"You don't have to do anything," I said. "Let me do the talking."

"What are you going to say?"

We could hear footsteps on a hard surface, coming closer.

"It'll be fine," I whispered. "It's just a neighbor."

The door opened and a man I would've guessed to be in his mid to late thirties appeared. The hallway behind him was dark. A small gut was pushing against the material of his T-shirt, making a bid for freedom over the waistband of his jeans. He appeared sleepy, his hair sticking out at odd angles. He was looking at us both questioningly for a moment, then stared at me.

"We're sorry to bother you," I said. "This is a bit awkward but we're trying to track down one of your neighbors. Your next-door neighbor, actually. He owns the house next to us and his tenants are driving us crazy. Parties all night, rubbish in the garden. It's … Honestly, it's been a nightmare." I nodded toward the tree in 23's garden. "I think you might know what I'm talking about?" The man glanced toward the house next door but said nothing. I could feel Malone's eyes on me. "The thing is, we can't get him on the phone. You wouldn't happen to have a number for him, would you?"

The man's mouth was hanging open. He turned to Malone, looked him up and down, looked back to me. Blinked rapidly.

"Yeah," he said then. "I probably have a phone number somewhere." He rolled his eyes. "For that useless fecker."

"You know him, then?"

"To see. To wave at. Not well."

"What's he doing with that tree?" I jerked my head toward the monstrously overgrown one in the garden of 23.

"Don't get me started," the man said. "The roots are actually coming in here now, under the wall." He pointed out the damage: a crack of daylight in the middle of the low brick divider between the two gardens. "It singlehandedly brings down the average house price in this estate. But there's just no talking to him."

"No need to tell me that," I said, making a face to go with it. "How long has he had the place here? We're not too bad, he only just bought the one next to us a few months ago."

"Ten, eleven years, maybe?" the man said. I had to consciously not react to this. "His father had it before him, but he used to look after it. Nice man, his father was."

"So he owns the whole house?"

"Yeah."

"I thought he might just have one of the units in there."

The man frowned. "Units?"

I looked toward number 23. "It isn't divided up?"

"No," the man said. "Not that I know of." He turned to go back inside. "Let me get you that number. Hang on a second."

Malone and I exchanged a glance. He shook his head, just once, to indicate that we shouldn't talk. Moments later, the man returned with a mobile phone number scribbled on a piece of paper.

"Here you go." He passed it to me. His fingers brushed mine as I took it from him. His hand was warm.

"Thanks so much for this," I said, taking a step back. "We really appreciate it."

"What's your name?" the man asked me.

I was thrown by this and hesitated, and then I realized how suspicious that was and since it was the first girl's name that wasn't my own, inappropriate as it may be, I blurted out, "Amy."

I could feel Malone tense up beside me.

"Amy," the man repeated slowly. "I'd never have guessed. You don't look like an Amy."

"Don't I?" I smiled tightly. "What does an Amy look like?"

"Is he around here much?" Malone said. "We don't see him round our place very often."

The man frowned. "What do you mean? He's here all the time." He pointed next door, at number 23. "He lives there."

alison, now

It made perfect sense, when you thought about it. A rental property he never actually rented out. He wasn't the landlord there, but the *resident*. Living there and also showing it to accommodation-seeking students as if he wasn't, as if no one was. Malone had turned a paler shade at the thought that the guy—the killer?—was inside that house at this very moment, potentially seeing him and I outside, and I had, in turn, felt a hot stone of guilt settle in my stomach for not obeying Malone's instructions to just stay in the bloody car.

But then No. 24 said No. 23 was likely to be at work. He didn't know what his neighbor did for a living, but he seemed to work weekdays and wore a suit.

We thanked him and hurried back to car.

"I shouldn't have used Amy," I said. "It was just the first name that popped into my head."

All Malone would say is, "Let's just get out of here."

Once back in the driver's seat, he tapped his phone's screen and put it to his ear. He started the engine, threw the car in gear. "Em, it's me. Listen …"

While he filled her in, my thoughts strayed to Will. I wondered what he was doing right now. I imagined going to see him again, telling him that we'd found the Canal Killer. The *real* one.

But had we?

A wave of nausea came over me. I turned toward the window and closed my eyes, waiting for it to pass. The ground felt unsteady, everything did, like plates were shifting fast beneath my feet and everything on them— my whole life—was threatening to move and change.

This guy could just be a copycat. But why copy a killer who'd been caught? And why now, after all this time? Why not just go and do your own evil thing?

Unless Will and him were working together. But how would that work? They started as a tag-team, now this guy was going solo. Why? And again, why *now*? What had he been doing all the years in between?

And was Daniel really just wrong place, wrong time, or was he involved in the murders in some way? If he was, how did he and No. 23 fit together? And how did they tie in with Will?

I groaned inwardly. There were no answers, only more questions.

I was literally sick of asking them.

"Okay, yeah," Malone was saying. "I will … I *will* … All right. Bye." He ended the call and twisted the steering wheel, pulling the car out of its parking space. He drove the rest of the way around the U-shape of Doolyn Gardens and turned into the city-bound traffic on the main road.

"What's happening?" I asked.

"They have Daniel O'Dowd in custody. Shaw is looking for me. He and I are going to do the interview." With one hand he tapped his phone again, put it to his ear. Waited through what sounded like a voice message. "Sarge, it's me. Cusack passed on your message. I'll be at the station within the hour and I'm on this number in the meantime." He tapped the screen; the phone locked with a *click*.

"What did Cusack say about number twenty-three?'

"She's checking property records. She also thinks I'm actively trying to lose my job."

Malone's phone rang. He glanced at the screen.

"It's Shaw," he said to me. Into the phone, "Malone."

I could hear Shaw's voice but not the individual words. At first Malone was nodding and saying, "Yeah," periodically. Then, "I have Alison Smith with me. Did Cusack tell you …? Yeah … Yeah, I know. That's what I thought too … Okay … Okay, yeah. Right. Will do." He ended the call, turned to me. "He's going to call me when the warrant comes in."

"So what now?"

"We wait. Maybe Em will come up with something on number twenty-three before the interview with Daniel starts." He drummed his fingers on the steering wheel. "What about you? I could drive you out to Bray?"

I thought of Malone's balcony, the peaceful view from it.

"Could I just wait at yours? It's closer, and it doesn't have my mother in it."

I was relieved to see him grin at this.

"I like your mother," he said. "But sure."

"Sorry about back there."

"It's okay," Malone said after a beat. "No harm done."

We drove back to his place each lost in our private silence.

Just as we arrived, Shaw called again to tell Malone to come in for three; it was just past noon by then. We'd picked up fast food drive-thru for lunch and sat in front of Malone's TV with it, staring vacantly at the screen. Neither of us could have recalled any detail of what we were watching, not even if our lives depended on it.

At some point, I fell asleep.

I dreamed of us all. Will and I. Liz. Heather. Daniel. We were all in the water and something was pulling on our ankles, dragging us down. The water ran up my nose and down my throat and reached into my lungs and squeezed and I couldn't breathe—*I can't breathe*—and someone was screaming—

I opened my eyes.

Malone was shaking me and, after a moment of sheer terror when I didn't know where I was or whose arms were around me, I realized that they weren't constricting me but supporting me, and we were sitting so close, and I could only look at him, not quite at his face but down at his chest, and a heat bloomed between us, and his arms closed around me, pulling me in, and it felt like melting, like disappearing, or everything else disappearing, and I breathed in deep, pulling him in, and he pulled me closer—

And then his phone rang, breaking the spell, and reality came rushing back like a slap.

I was so mortified, I couldn't think. Every blood cell in my body was making a beeline for my face.

Meanwhile, Malone just answered his phone, like a normal person.

It was Cusack. I was sitting close enough to hear every word.

"Bad news, bad news," she said.

"Oh, great." Malone rubbed at his eyes. He looked like he might have dozed off too. "Go on."

"The property at twenty-three Doolyn Gardens is registered to a Mr. and Mrs. Thomas and Margaret O'Rourke with an address in Ennis. They actually own number twenty-four as well. Landlords. Landlords currently not answering their phone. I can only go back fifteen years before I have to go looking for physical records, but it's been in their name all that time. So whoever lives there isn't an owner-occupier, but he could be related to Mr. and Mrs. O'Rourke, I suppose. Or he could just rent off them. I ran the address through PULSE but nothing came up. The utility bills would tell us more, but I'd need a warrant for them. And trust me when I say nothing is happening here that isn't related to Daniel O'Dowd right now, so you're shit out of luck on that front."

"Great." Malone shook his head. "What's the other bad news?"

"The telephone number his neighbor gave you is a dud. It belongs to a researcher on a radio show in Limerick city. The radio station pays for the phone and were happy to email me a scan of their most recent bill. It all checks out."

Malone looked at me.

I whispered, "Double-check?"

The note was in Malone's pocket. He unfolded it

now and called out the number again. Cusack had taken it down correctly.

I held out my hand and he passed the note to me. The digits were clear. This wasn't a handwriting error. The guy must have given his neighbor the wrong phone number on purpose.

"Okay," Malone said. "Well, thanks for all that, Em."

"I'm not done with the bad news."

He sighed. "Go on."

"The address wasn't in PULSE," she said, "but I did find it somewhere else. Shaw was getting me to cross-reference all the names that came into us during the original investigation with the ones we've been getting in now, in response to the CCTV appeal. He sent me an Excel spreadsheet prepared by one of the analysts. And get this: the address was on that. Someone put together this waitlist/property search connection back in 2007 and compiled a list of properties each of the girls had viewed. But it stopped there. I think they got Will Hurley then and the property connection wasn't explored any further."

Malone looked at me and I looked away.

If this was the same guy, they had him back in 2007—or were about to get him, until I corrected my statement and pulled them off the trail.

I felt sick.

I put a hand to my mouth, worried that I would be.

Then I felt Malone's hand on my other hand. I let him turn it over, lock his fingers into mine, squeeze it once, tight.

I dared look at him.

His face was full of sympathy. He'd tell me it wasn't

my fault, I knew, but that's exactly whose fault all this was.

"What'll I do with all this?" I heard Cusack's tinny voice say.

"I'm going to bring it to Shaw," Malone said. "When I come in. See what he has to say. I mean, we have to interview Daniel either way. Even if he's not the guy, he's spent hours surveying the canal. He's bound to have something useful for us. Any update on Amy Boylan?"

"Nothing yet, no. Shouldn't you be on your way in already? It's nearly half-two."

Malone raised his eyebrows at me.

I mouthed *go*.

He squeezed my hand again and told Cusack he was on his way.

alison, then

Lauren's death felt both strange and personal.

On the one hand, we'd known her. Not very well, but we had. We felt grief, not really the *I miss her* kind, but the *this is so tragic* kind. We were all sad, but poor Claire was bereft. She and Lauren had grown close over the term.

But on the other hand, *she'd been murdered*.

That was the bit we couldn't process, the thing we couldn't understand. That felt outside of us, other, made up, even. How could someone *we know* have been *murdered*? That kind of thing only happened on TV.

For days we just wandered around aimlessly, listlessly, asking each other that question. Everything else stopped. Classes passed in a blur. I didn't go to half of them. We didn't go out. Liz, Will, and I hung out in either my or Liz's apartment, or sometimes in the subdued student bar, and traded information we'd gleaned from the news or from another student or from a friend of a friend whose uncle was a guard. The college arranged buses for anyone wanting to attend Lauren's funeral in Galway City. We went. There were free counseling sessions at the student center for anyone who had been affected by Lauren's death. We didn't go to those.

The Gardaí had interviewed Claire, but no one else we knew. The rest of us hadn't been back in St. John's yet. Lauren had only returned the morning of her murder, coming back a few days early because she'd been able to get a lift off a friend of hers who was driving to Dublin.

Information was scant, but it seemed like she'd been walking home alone, alongside the canal, and someone had pushed her in.

Over the course of the next two weeks, Lauren went from the top-of-the-hour headline to halfway through the news, to an update about the investigation, maybe, in the Sunday papers. The noise levels in the student bar gradually returned to normal, with boisterous laughter and loud music filling the space again. We started going out again, hitting the clubs on Harcourt Street, crossing the Luas tracks to go back toward the canal, to come back home. Lauren stayed in the past and her death took on an implausibility. After a while we wondered: Had she ever really been here at all?

Then they found Rachel Folen.

She'd been missing for two days. I'd never met her, didn't recognize her when I saw her face on the front page. Even though she'd lived in Halls, it was a big complex, and she'd studied a science subject that was taught on the far side of campus to where all my classes were.

The Gardaí quickly downplayed any connection between her and Lauren, but we all thought that was just not to start a panic. We all thought, *Someone is out there doing this.*

And we were right. Less than two weeks later, the body of Caroline Brady was pulled out of the canal.

That made three. Three in three months.

All hell broke loose then.

*****

"I don't believe this," I said. "Look how busy this place is."

We were in the 1-A, the biggest lecture theater on campus. It could hold upwards of five hundred students but right now, there wasn't a seat to be had. After I pointed this out, Liz, Will, and I shuffled along behind the top row of chairs, weaving around the throng already gathered there, and sat down in the last remaining space on the far steps. There was no noise in the hall other than student voices but that alone was a soundtrack playing at a deafening level. The melody suggested fear, but pulsing underneath—although no one would ever admit it—was a beat of excitement.

Meetings like these were being held across campus. *Information meetings*, they were calling them, innocuously, but we all knew what they were about. I even knew the running order. A briefing from a couple of Gardaí on personal safety. An assurance from them that they'd flooded the campus with officers in plain clothes. A plea not to panic. An appeal for information. A presentation from the Student Union's welfare officer on a new service the SU was providing: free shuttle buses from Stephen's Green at midnight every night.

Finally, the college president would get up on stage

and deliver the bad news: they were instigating a curfew. If you lived in Halls, you had to back in them by 1:00 a.m. Nothing would be said about what might happen if you weren't, but of course one thing in particular was implied: you could die.

The meeting would end with some information about a candlelight vigil that was going to be held on Front Lawn and a reminder that if we needed to talk to somebody, there were resources available to us.

I wasn't scared. I was sad for the girls and their families, yes, but I wasn't *scared*. They had all been walking home alone, by the canal, in the early hours of the morning, and I wasn't going to do that. I assumed they all had some kind of connection to whatever psycho was doing this; I was sure I didn't have any. I knew some girls who had cut or dyed their hair because all the girls who'd died had lots of it and were blonde, but if they thought that was how the killer was picking his victims, he had about two-thirds of the student female body to choose from.

If there was a threat, if there was going to be more, then it felt distant to me. Separate.

But Liz was starting to freak out.

I'd thought it was melodrama at first. She wouldn't have been the first person on campus to relish being so close to the action. She wouldn't even have been the thousandth. She'd taken to sleeping in my bed when I stayed at Will's, because she didn't trust her weird roommate to keep their front door locked. If I didn't stay with Will, Liz slept on our couch.

She was sitting next to me now, perched on the edge of a carpeted step, knees drawn up to her chin and arms wrapped tightly around her legs. Will was on my other side; I was leaning against him. The meeting unfolded exactly as I'd heard it would. Afterward the two uniformed Gardaí remained onstage with the president, talking, and a number of students headed toward them instead of the lecture theater's doors.

We'd stood up and started toward the doors when Liz gripped my arm.

"I think I should go up there," she said, nodding at the stage. "I think maybe I should talk to them."

"To who?" I asked. "The *Gardaí*?"

"Yeah."

"About what?"

Liz's hand was still on my arm, squeezing. "I think I might know something."

This was the first I was hearing of this.

Will had moved in behind her. He rolled his eyes at me.

"There's this guy," Liz went on. "I keep seeing him everywhere. I think he's following me. Maybe. You've met him, actually. He was in Essence a while back. We were talking to him. I think he was even in a picture with us? And he was at the Traffic Light Ball. The red-haired guy. Didn't he say his name was Dave or something? Derek maybe? It was something with D."

I didn't remember his name. I could barely picture him. There was another memory of that night that was so vivid, I didn't have room left for storing anything else.

"Liz," I said, "hang on a second. You can't just go around accusing people of things like—"

"I'm not *accusing* him of anything," she hissed. "I just think he's weird. And they said *all* information, even if we think it's trivial. Even if we think it's not related. They want everything we have."

"Liz, I—" I stopped, not knowing what to say to her, and looked to Will for help.

"What did this guy do?" he asked Liz. "Exactly?"

"I think he's following me," she said.

Will raised an eyebrow. "Why?"

"Because I always see him around."

"Where?"

"Around *here*."

"On campus?"

She nodded. "Yeah."

"Liz," Will said, exasperated, "of course you do. He probably *goes here*."

"No, no," she said. "It's not like that." She let go of me and took a step down the stairs. "I'll tell them. They'll understand."

*****

Will was supposed to have a class afterward but skipped it, and he and I went back to his room.

"This is awful," I said. We were lying on his bed. The rooms at Halls were so small, there was really nowhere else two people in it could be. "Do you think there'll be more?"

"I hope not," Will said. "But, yeah, probably. Unless they catch him."

"What about what Liz said?"

A beat passed. "She's your friend."

"Meaning?"

"Meaning I don't want to say bad things about her."

I made the sign of the cross with my hand. "I grant you a pass."

"Well …" Will sighed. His hand was on my back and he slipped it now, up under my T-shirt, and started gently, absent-mindedly, rubbing the small of the back. "Look, I think some people are getting off on this. They're excited by it. They love that there's this major news story going on right on their doorstep and they think it's thrilling to have, you know, the Gardaí around, and all that. And I actually think that's probably not that unusual a reaction. I mean, that's why cars slow down when they're passing a traffic accident, right? Or why people watch true-crime documentaries, or read books about Ted Bundy. This stuff is, in a weird way, exciting. Right?"

"You think that's what Liz is?" I said. "Excited?"

"I think she wants more drama. She wants to think she has more of a direct connection to this. That guy? That night at the ball? He was a slip of a thing. A strong breeze would've blown him over. He's not out there killing anyone. His worst crime is—*maybe*—having a bit of a crush on Liz. She's just completely overreacting." He sighed again, then leaned over to kiss me on the forehead. "You and her are so different. I really don't see how you guys are friends."

"You don't like her, do you?"

"No," Will said after a while.

*****

Later, when I went back to my apartment, Claire was in the kitchen. In whispered tones, she told me that Liz had knocked on the door, crying, and was now curled up in my bed.

"What was wrong with her?"

Claire shrugged. "She wouldn't tell me. All she'd say was that she had to talk to you."

I assumed that her talk with the Gardaí hadn't gone well. I thought maybe they'd dismissed her out of hand, or maybe even admonished her for wasting their time. I wondered what Claire, having a lost a friend to this faceless killer, thought of Liz and her dramatics.

When I went into the room and sat on the edge of the bed, she turned over and said, "Why do you *always* choose him over me?"

Her eyes were puffy and red and in the silence after her question, she sniffed.

I didn't know where this was going. "What's that supposed to mean?"

She lay back down and pulled a cushion into her chest. Sulkily, she said, "You *know* what it means."

"He's my boyfriend, Liz. I want to spend time with him."

"I'm not talking about time."

"Then what are you talking about?"

"You *believe* him over me."

Now I was confused. I waited for her to enlighten me.

"He says that guy isn't following me, so you agree."

"Liz, I thought that before he said it."

"Oh, yeah, *right*."

I sighed. "What's going on?" She didn't answer. She started crying again. "Liz, come on. Talk to me."

Muffled, because she said it into the cushion: "There's no point."

"Why not?"

"Because you don't get it."

"Get what?"

"You don't see what's going on."

"Tell me, then."

"I shouldn't have to. You should know. You should *realize*."

I rolled my eyes.

I was tired. Physically tired, because to be on campus now was emotionally draining. Emotionally tired, because it had been a long few months with Liz. And I was also tired of taking the bait. I was tired of playing her game. I was tired of acting like her crazy moods, her toddler tantrums, were normal behavior.

I had had it.

I was done.

"Look, Liz," I said, standing up, "I don't have time for this fucking juvenile shit, okay? If you want to talk to me, talk to me. Otherwise, please, just *fuck off*."

I walked out of the room without waiting to hear any response, slamming the door behind me, shaking from the anger of my own words.

And surprised by them.

alison, now

I went back to sleep for a while. By the time I woke up for a second time, the light coming in through the balcony doors had changed.

Immediately, I reached for my phone. There was no update from Malone, but there was a text message I'd missed earlier from my mother, asking where I was staying tonight and what my plans for the rest of the week were. *Your father wants to see you! Come and stay here? The paparazzi are gone now.* (Paparazzi?!) I replied saying I'd think about it. I couldn't make any decisions until I knew how all this was going to pan out.

Something fluttered in my stomach at the idea that I might stay here again tonight.

I tried watching some TV, but couldn't focus. I found myself reliving that feeling that had passed between Malone and I, basking in it, replaying it over and over in my mind as if, on repeated viewings, I might find something new in that two, three seconds. Thinking that I might just get through all this if I had someone who, every so often, made me feel a moment like that.

And then wondering if he had felt anything at all, other than a friendly consolation.

And then feeling guilty that I was thinking this while Will's life, or at least how he'd spend the rest of it, hung in the balance.

While Amy was out there somewhere, waiting to be found.

While Daniel was in a room being accused of something he probably didn't do.

I walked around the apartment, opening doors, peering into cupboards and wardrobes. I discovered a washer/dryer hidden in a closet next to the bathroom and decided to wash the few items of clothes I had with me. I rinsed out the cafetière and mugs we'd used this morning, and found the bag of croissants Malone had gone out and got still sitting on the counter, untouched. I had one with a fresh cup of coffee.

By then it was approaching seven o'clock and the sun was slipping down behind the mountains. I wrapped up in my scarf and jacket and took a second cup of coffee out onto the balcony, and sat there watching the sky until full darkness came.

In the distance, the mountain range was no longer visible; it had merged with the black sky. The only clues that it was there at all was the absence of stars in its silhouette, and a single red, flashing light that flickered atop one of its peaks. There must be a mobile phone mast or something up there. After a while I realized why it felt so dark out, even though it wasn't that late in the day: no streetlights. They were there, I noticed, but they weren't turned on.

Only a few yellow windows burned elsewhere in the estate. While I was on the balcony, two cars pulled into the spaces down below, half an hour apart—and that was it. A few minutes later the shrill of Malone's buzzer cut through the air, making me jump. This was followed by quieter versions of it, a cascade of them, as if whoever was trying to get in had pressed each buzzer downstairs, indiscriminately, in turn. Then they stopped abruptly; someone let them in. There was no one around—no one walking a dog or getting a run in. Probably because it was simply too dark to be safe. Across the way, the empty windows of the unfinished houses gaped like toothless mouths.

I started to shiver. The temperature was dropping fast. I put my hands in my jacket pockets and felt something crumpled up in one of them: the note the neighbor had given us with the phone number on it.

It was a plain piece of white paper, perfectly square, like a sheet from a memo block. Angling it to catch the light spilling out onto the balcony from the living room, I studied the writing to see if a mistake had been made anywhere, if the neighbor had just taken down the number wrong. There was none that I could see.

I did, however, see something else: an impression in the paper.

I went back inside and examined it under the ceiling light. Numbers were carved into the paper, like someone had pressed down hard while handwriting them on the sheet that had been on top of the one I held in my hand. If it was from a memo-block, that would make sense.

Out of curiosity, I rifled through Malone's kitchen drawers until I found a pencil, and then ran the lead of it back and forth over the impression in broad strokes. Slowly but surely, the numbers appeared. Oddly, it was the same number the neighbor had given us—except for the last number. Here, the number ended in a nine instead of a one.

I stood in the middle of the living room, holding the piece of paper, frowning at it.

On one hand, this was No. 23's *neighbor*. It didn't matter what phone number he had last scribbled down. On the other, wasn't it strange that the last number he'd scribbled down had been so similar to the one No. 23 had given *him*?

Maybe someone else had asked him for it recently, and this was proof he'd given us the wrong number, off by one digit.

I picked up my phone and unlocked the screen, but then I thought better of dialing the number from it. They'd be able to see mine then. I looked around the apartment, but it didn't look as if Malone had a landline. I even considered calling Harcourt Terrace station for a second, asking for Garda Cusack and telling her that I'd found the *actual* phone number for the tenant at No. 23.

But was that what this was? It could be a waste of time. She wasn't my biggest fan. No need to confirm for her that she was right the first time.

Ultimately, I decided to just wait until I could tell Malone about it in person.

I locked the balcony doors, then double-checked that the front door to the apartment was secure too. I'd seen a stack of old paperbacks in Malone's bedroom, including a couple of tech-thrillers I thought might keep me mildly entertained. I figured I'd take a shower, climb into bed, and read until I could fall asleep.

It was while I was in the shower, in the en suite, that I first heard the noise: a muffled bang, like a cupboard door closing.

I hit the button reflexively, stopping the flow of water. Held my breath. Listened.

I couldn't hear anything except the beating of my own heart, which suddenly sounded thunderous. There was only silence and, somewhere beyond that, the very, very faint vibration of the washing machine. So nothing at all, really, but then, because I was straining so hard to hear *something*, the low-frequency thrum of the absence of sound.

Something had probably just fallen over. Or it could be coming from next door. *Or, you know, you might have just imagined the whole thing, because you've spent the weekend trying to find a serial killer and it's left you a little bit jumpy.*

I turned the water back on, but my ability to relax had vanished. I just kept listening out for another sound. In the end I gave up and got out. I'd been in there five minutes, maximum.

Malone hadn't been expecting guests and although the towel hanging over the shower door was dry, I wasn't 100 percent certain it was clean. I didn't want to go snooping, so I lightly dried myself with it and quickly put on what served as my pajamas: a ripped pair of yoga pants and an old T-shirt. Put back on my glasses. My hair was sopping wet at the ends, steadily dripping onto my shoulders. I put the towel back where it'd been and went to check on my clothes in the machine. Another five minutes to go before the cycle would be complete.

The note with the phone number was still on the kitchen counter.

It was killing me not to try the one I'd revealed, but I didn't want to call it from my phone.

I drummed my fingers on the countertop, thinking. What could you do with a phone number, other than call it?

I went back down the hall and into Malone's bedroom, picking up my phone off the bed. I pulled up the internet browser and copied the phone number into the search box.

The top result was for a profile for someone called Brian Conway, BSc (Hons) Prop Mgt & Val, HDip Mgt & Mkt, at R&P Estate Agents in Ballsbridge. I clicked on the link and the page loaded with a professional headshot of him, suited and smiling, next to a short bio, the phone number I'd just searched for and an email address, hosted on the R&P website.

What didn't make any sense was the man in the accompanying photo.

It was the neighbor we'd spoken to earlier at Doolyn Gardens.

The man in the photo was the man who lived at No. 24.

I blinked at the screen for a five full seconds while the jigsaw pieces moved and slid and rotated—

The number pressed into the memo pad was Brian Conway's number. Brian Conway was the man who lived at No. 24. So when we'd asked him for the man at No. 23's phone number, he'd given us his own, but with one digit wrong. The last one.

The O'Rourkes in Co. Clare owned both houses, No. 23 and No. 24, but Conway complained about his neighbor driving down property prices. Why would he care, when he must rent?

Amy? You don't look like an Amy.

And then suddenly—horrifically—everything clicked into place.

And then I heard the noise again.

A dull thud, coming from the kitchen. Before I could dismiss it, rationalize it, minimize it, I heard something else.

Footsteps.

Tentative, on a hardwood floor.

Someone creeping. Trying to be quiet.

I held my breath, listening.

And knew for absolute certain that elsewhere in this apartment, someone else was doing exactly the same thing.

We'd driven from Doolyn Gardens straight here, stopping only to buy drive-thru fast-food for lunch. We'd sat in Malone's car outside the house for a couple of minutes before we'd driven away. We'd given Conway plenty of time to get into his own car and follow us here.

The fear was immediate and all-encompassing and overpowering, and for one interminable moment I thought it was going to totally overwhelm me and that I might just give in and pass out and die—

You will *die if you don't move.*

I felt rooted to the spot. Fear had glued me there.

The bedroom was wide open.

Locked doors.

I had to put as many locked doors between me and

him as I could. The bedroom and the bathroom were all I had.

Footsteps in the kitchen.

Coming this way.

Clutching my phone, I tiptoed to the open bedroom door—looking at the handle as I approached it, seeing *yes! A lock!*—and closed it as quickly and as quietly as I could and then *shit, fumbling* with the lock, my hands shaking, unable to turn it, the mechanism stiff or maybe even stuck.

And here was the fear, pushing itself up again, coming now, and I heard myself make a noise, a kind of "ah" sound, the kind you might make it you'd just burned your hand off something hot.

The footsteps, louder now, crossing the living room, almost here.

Not caring about being quiet anymore.

Underneath my fingers, the lock finally turned.

I rushed into the bathroom, closing the door behind me. I didn't know why I was trying to be quiet, it wasn't rational; he knew I was here.

I was shaking now, every limb trembling uncontrollably, afraid to breathe, my chest burning with the strain.

I looked at the lock on the bathroom door. One of those locks where you turn a tiny switch in the middle of the handle. Flimsy and easy to override. A kick would break it.

I turned it anyway.

"Alison?"

The voice was muffled, his mouth right against the bedroom door and me hearing it through two of them, but it was so calm and normal, it sent the fear climbing up my throat and a trickle of warmth running down my leg.

I bit down on my lip, hard, tasting blood, in order to stop myself from screaming out.

"It's just us," he said. His tone was pleasant, friendly, upbeat. "Why don't you come out of there so we can talk?"

I unlocked my phone. The page for Brian Conway on R&P's website was still onscreen. Fingers shaking violently, I screenshot it and sent it to Malone with my third attempt at typing a word underneath it: *hELp.*

I couldn't get out of this. Not out of the apartment. We were a floor up. I could maybe get out of the bedroom window but I couldn't think now what it looked like and I didn't have enough time to waste some of it trying to figure out how to open it, or which bit of it I had the best chance of getting through.

A sudden, loud *bang* against the bedroom door.

Quickly followed by another bang, and the sound of splintering wood.

No no no no no oh God no please.

A crash, something heavy and large clattering onto the floor. Footsteps now, striding across the bedroom floor. He was in.

A ferocious bang against the bathroom door. I watched it shake, shudder everywhere except the point where the lock mechanism touched the frame.

I began to feel strangely detached. Resigned. Another bang of body against the door and the lock would give way.

I was trapped, I was alone, he was going to come in here and kill me.

And there was nothing I could do about it.

I thought, *Maybe this is what I deserve after sending away an innocent man.*

My heart thundered in my chest.

And then I thought, *Fuck that.*

I scanned the bathroom. I was facing the door; directly behind me was the sink with a mirrored medicine cabinet mounted above it. Could I break the mirror? Use a shard as a knife? To my right was the toilet. Would the top of the cistern come off? That would be heavy. I could try to knock him out. To my left was the bath, the electric shower mounted above it. The shower curtain was fixed to what looked like a plastered-in plastic rail. Useless.

A *bang* as the whole door shook.

I knew, the next time—

This is it this is it this is it.

I threw myself behind the door just as he slammed into it again and *crack* the door swung open, fast and hard, and in the mirror on the bathroom cabinet I saw the blur of him entering the space and as the door started to slam back on me I put both hands up and pushed it back on him as hard as I could with everything I had—*how dare you do this to me to Will to us*—and just as he was turning around to look behind him the door smacked into the side of his face and recoiled and I pushed it again I pushed and I kicked and now the skin just below his hairline was separating a trickle of blood was filling the slice of dark space between the two pieces and he put a hand to it, stunned, and he started to fall, and before his body touched the ground I was already moving, pulling back the bathroom door, and then I ran, I ran, I ran, out of the bathroom and out of the bedroom.

To the front door.

Get out get out get out.

Neighbors. I'd seen lights on in other windows. There had to be some of them around here. I'd find someone. But the door to the apartment was locked, dead-bolted from the inside, and as I fiddled with it, my fingers shaking, not obeying the instructions I was screaming at them from inside my head, I heard him, coming out of the bathroom, and footsteps approaching, running.

Open the door open the door please please no.

And then CRACK—

Everything faded to black.

He doesn't have to be quiet, doesn't have to worry about being seen. There is no one here but him and her. A few lights shine in other blocks, yes, but he's spent the last few hours sitting outside, watching this one, making sure they're alone. There were no lights on anywhere except the guard's apartment, the one with the balcony on which Alison had sat, but just to make sure he pressed each of the block's six buzzers in turn. No response, not even from her. He was about to look for another way in when a man pushing a bicycle appeared in the lobby and opened the door from the other side.

"Is there a McCarthy here, by any chance?" he asked. "I think I might be in the wrong place."

The cyclist shook his head. "There's only two of us in this one, and the other guy's name is Malone."

"Oh." He made a show of taking his phone out of his pocket. "I better call them. I knew I'd get lost out here." He held the door open for the cyclist, making sure not to close it all the way again.

He was in.

He'd never had it so easy. Isolated location, no internal cameras, not even street lights outside. Even the door to the Garda's apartment posed no problem, because he'd thought to bring his bunch of master keys from work. Different developers used different ones, but for developments like this, most made a choice from the same small collection. He practiced on a door down the hall first, an empty apartment where keys turning in locks wouldn't alert anyone.

It was the third key he tried.

Silently, he let himself into the guard's apartment. He had no idea what waited for him on the other side, but just by opening the door a crack he could see there was a hallway. That made it easier to slip in. Closing the door behind him, he heard the hiss of a shower running and smiled to himself.

This was going to be even easier than he'd thought.

He just wanted to talk to her. He thought it was time they had a chat. But of course, she didn't want to listen.

He wanted to tell her he wasn't like those other guys, that she didn't need to be afraid of him, that he was a *nice* guy. But she didn't even give him the chance to. She just assumed he *was* like the others.

And that made him very, very mad.

Now she's lying on the floor at his feet, unconscious, while a thin line of dark blood slides from her hairline and trickles down the side of her face.

Onto the Garda's wooden floor.

He looks down at her, shaking his head, annoyed at himself.

Annoyed at her.

She doesn't understand, that's the problem. Young girls today, they're so careless. They don't realize what kind of creeps are out there, what those monsters might do with all this information they're volunteering, posting out there in the world. He'd tried telling them, taking them aside and explaining it to them, but then they just mistook *him* for being one of *those*.

So he decided to show them instead.

Back then. Now, again.

Because after he saw that documentary a few months back, he realized that his lessons from ten years ago had long been forgotten. Things were worse than ever. These girls, they were practically sending these creeps illustrated maps to their own homes nowadays.

So he had to show them what the consequences could be.

And no one would pay attention unless those consequences were the worst imaginable.

A few sacrifices to the cause would be worth it, in the end. They'd thank him for it. He'd have saved them from the creeps, from the guys who might do a lot worse than him.

His intentions were good. That's what they didn't understand.

What *he* didn't understand was Alison going to prison to visit a convicted killer. And she isn't a young girl anymore, but a grown woman. She should know better now. He had to point that out.

It didn't matter that her boyfriend hadn't done the things she thought he had. What mattered was that she thought he had, and she still went to see him in spite of it.

He wonders if he should wait for her to wake up. They could talk then. He could explain that he didn't mean to hurt her, that he was only doing it so she wouldn't run away.

But then he hears a phone ringing. He leaves her to find the source.

The device is on the floor of the en suite bathroom. Its screen is cracked, but he can still read what's on it. MALONE. That's the name of the guard, isn't it? He lets it ring, waits it out, watches until the call gets kicked to voicemail.

And then sees his own face appear on screen.

What the …?

He picks the phone up to look closer, but the screen goes dim in his hand. When he presses a button, a keypad appears, demanding a passcode.

He throws the phone so hard across the room that it cracks the mirror above the sink clean in two.

She knows who he is.

He should've been more careful earlier, when they showed up at his door. But he was nervous and excited and confused, and he wasn't thinking straight. Now look what he's done, the mess he's made.

Another one.

She probably told the guard. That's why he was ringing just now.

He can't stay here.

They can't.

If he can't talk to her, he'll have to teach her a lesson another way.

And he knows now the stupid mistake he made with Amy. It all got too messy, too complex. The water is the only thing for it.

He knows what he has to do.

Decision made, he starts to feel calmer. There was a part of him that always knew the final sacrifice would be himself.

But if he can't wake Alison up, she'll have to come with him.

That's the only way this is going to work.

alison, now

When I opened my eyes, I saw only an inky blackness. Panic rose in my throat as I thought for a second that the blow to my head had cost me my vision. I touched my face; my eyes were open.

Then why was there no light? Why was there no difference?

My head and neck throbbed, and something wet was around my neck. Sticky and thick. Blood? Was I bleeding?

I saw a tiny pinprick of light, a single dot, far off in the distance. While I watched, it turned red.

And then I realized: it wasn't off in the distance at all. It was right there. It was a tail light.

He'd put me in the trunk of his car.

I was lying on my left side, curled up, with my left arm underneath my body. I tried to lift myself off it, to pull it out, but I couldn't move it. Was it broken? I could feel it, burning with pins and needles, but I couldn't move it. Why not? I tried my legs. They were fine. I wiggled my toes. All okay. With my free hand I reached out and felt the furry, hard inside of the car boot. Touched the surface around me. Above me. Nothing.

There was nothing else in here with me, and I could find no handle or button to press.

I'd no idea how long I'd been out. How far had we driven? Where were we? I couldn't hear any noise beyond the roar of the engine.

The pain in my head was moving, growing, like something sharp unfolding itself, spreading its wings, in the middle of my brain.

White spots danced in my vision.

My eyelids were growing heavy. It was exhausting to feel this much pain. And it was dark, and the surface my cheek was pressed against was furry. It felt nice.

Maybe I should just close my eyes and go to sleep. It might be better that way.

Minutes passed. Or maybe hours.

Then the car slowed. The noise of the engine dimmed, then fell away to a low hum. From the first time, I could hear sounds from outside. Muffled voices. I rolled forward, wincing as a current of pain streaked up from my tailbone. Nausea gripped me and I tasted bile in my throat.

But I was closer to the red of the tail light now. I pressed an ear against the trunk there, strained to listen.

The car had stopped but the engine was running.

A woman's voice, then: "Where are you heading tonight, sir?"

His voice answered her, but I couldn't make out the words.

"I'm afraid there's no access to the canal this evening, sir, not past this point. It's due to a Garda operation. We have detours in place …"

She was a guard, I realized.

And I knew what I had to do.

I opened my mouth and screamed as loud as I possibly could, louder than I ever had in my life, screaming and screaming until I felt like I'd swallowed liquid fire and my lungs were threatening to burst. For good measure I started kicking and hitting the underside of the lid of the trunk too.

The engine roared to life and the car took off, at such speed that I was pushed forward, face-first, into the hard side of the boot.

A new wave of pain broke in my head.

Then people were shouting.

The car kept going. Swerving from left to right. Accelerating.

There was a hard turn to the left—

A sudden *bang*, a screech of metal.

Silence.

I felt my body lift, rise, heard a woman scream, and I *knew*. I knew what was happening.

The Gardaí had him. They knew his name. They knew where he lived. They knew how he did it. And I was pretty sure he had just broken through one of their cordons at the canal, with me screaming in his boot.

It was all over for him.

That was good. He was going away now.

But it was over for me too, because he was taking me with him.

Impact.

There was a thud, a splash and then a rush of water against the car, engulfing it, sucking it down.

The thoughts came calmly.

I'm going to die now.

This is how. Now is when.

I should've stayed in Cork and I should've stayed away from Will and I should never have made that phone call and I shouldn't have answered the door in Breda and I should never have come back here.

But it was too late to make good decisions now.

A stream of water was trickling into the trunk by my feet.

Which way was up, even? I didn't know anymore.

I'm going to die now.

After everything that had happened, it almost felt like a relief.

I was so tired. So very tired.

I closed my eyes.

*****

Water.

Water is splashing on me, running over me, tickling my face.

But I can breathe.

I open my eyes, bring my free hand to my face. I can feel it.

It's not underwater. I'm not underwater yet.

*****

Banging.

A banging noise. More than one. Someone is banging on the trunk of the car. Shouting. At me? More voices.

I want to go back to sleep.

The water is cold.

*****

I close my eyes. I can't keep them open.

*****

A burst of light. It hurts my eyes, I shut them. Water, going into my mouth. I cough. Hands. Around my arms and legs.

It's freezing. I start to shiver violently.

It's too bright.

*****

Something hard and cold. I'm lying on it and it hurts my back. Cement. They've put me on the ground. Lots of voices now. Someone is touching my hands, my wrist, opening my mouth.

I feel like I'm going to be sick so I turn my head and cough, and I can feel water coming up. I can hear it.

I open my eyes.

Bright discs of white light. What are those?

"She's breathing!"

"What about him?" someone says.

*****

I turn my head the other way. See water. Futuristic glass buildings. The river. No, the *basin*. I recognize it now. Grand Canal Dock. Where the canal meets the river.

I'm just a few feet from the edge of the quay, I think. Everything is blurry beyond two or three feet; I've lost my glasses. They've laid me out on one of those flat marble blocks that serve as benches. The black water is choppy, but I can't see anything in it. Blurry figures are standing at the edge, leaning over to look in. Some glance back at me. Someone is pulling off his soaking-wet clothes while another shrugs out of his jacket to give to him. Another pats the wet man on the back and says, "Fair play to ya. Fair play."

*****

"What about him?"

I turn my head the other way and there he is. Lying on the ground a few feet away. Arms by his sides, palms up. His shoes are missing. Not moving. Blood on the side of his head, from where I hit him with the door. His skin is wet and very white, almost waxy looking.

Did I hit him with a door? That seems unlikely.

Did I?

A man stands near his feet.

No, not a man. A boy. A teenager. His face is pinched in concern. But …

Not for Conway. For the woman leaning over him.

Knelt on the ground by his side, pressing on his chest, dipping her head periodically to put an ear near his nose and mouth.

"Mum?" the boy says. "Is he …?"

She looks up at him and shakes her head solemnly, *no*.

In the distance, sirens.

alison, then

We hadn't been planning to go out that Sunday night. Will and I had gone to the cinema at Dundrum Town Center early that afternoon and only when we'd emerged, blinking, back into the sunlight, did Will see the text from his roommate. A bunch of them were at a pub in Portobello, the one by the canal. Claire and her boyfriend were there too. We could hop on the Luas, be there in fifteen, twenty minutes. He sent a text back, saying we were on our way.

"The curfew," I reminded him.

Will said we wouldn't stay long. "We'll just go for a couple."

But when we got to the pub, we discovered that a gang from St. John's had practically taken over this pub's beer garden. Everyone was there. It was also an unusually sunny spring evening, and two pints of cider in I was warm and woozy and not at all in the mood for going home. There was an atmosphere, and I liked it. Something between defiance and giddiness.

We'd been there for maybe two or three hours when I felt the stab of a finger in the flesh of my back and looked up to find Liz staring down at me. I opened my mouth to say hi but she was already moving on, searching for an empty seat around the table. She found one diagonally across from me, next to Claire. I watched as Claire greeted her, and then as Liz leaned in and whispered something in the girl's ear.

Claire's head lifted and she looked around and her eyes found mine.

And narrowed.

Will returned then. After he'd set two pints down in front of us, he turned and saw my face.

"What's going on?"

"Liz is here," I said.

He looked across the table and saw her. She was looking away now, deep in intense conversation with Claire. "Have you guys talked?"

"Not since …" I shook my head. "No."

"Well, this is awkward."

"Tell me about it."

"Do you want to go?"

"Yes."

He nodded at the drinks. "Can we drink these first?"

"Can we drink them inside?"

We stood up, collected ourselves and turned to make our way through the throng back into the interior of the bar.

Before we could, I felt the pinch of a hand on my arm and Liz's voice, sharp and cold, behind me: "Where are you going?"

I stopped to turn to her and in that moment

someone pushed between Will and me, so I couldn't reach out and alert him to the fact that I was caught. He carried on, oblivious, carrying the drinks into the bar.

I turned around.

"We were just going inside," I said lightly. "What's up?"

"I need to talk to you," Liz said.

"About what?"

A pause. "About Will."

"What about him?"

"Well"—Liz looked around—"this isn't really the place for this conversation."

Under normal circumstances I might have said something like, "Let's go to the bathrooms then," or, "Come outside, to the front. We'll find a quiet spot." But I was so sick of Liz's amateur dramatics and hurt by her antics—and, no doubt, emboldened by alcohol—that instead I said, "Why bring it up, then?"

She blinked in surprise. "What?"

"Why even bring it up if this"—I made air quotes; I was on a roll, now—"*isn't really the place* to talk about it? But then, wait. Do we even need to talk about it? Or can I guess what it is now? Let me see. I'm spending too much time with him, is that it? Or he's not your type, you don't like him, so you don't want to spend time with me if he's around? Or is this something to do with you running to the Gardaí to tell them your completely and utterly irrelevant information about that poor guy who made the mistake of—gasp!—trying to *talk to you* at the Traffic Light Ball, God forbid, leaving you so bloody traumatized that you had to sit in my boyfriend's lap and fucking kiss him?" I shook my head. "You just think I'm going to take it all, don't you? That you can behave however the fuck you want, however badly you want, however like a bloody toddler you want, and I'll just stick around. I'll take all your little digs and insults. Your shit-stirring. Oh, you had lunch with Will in Dundrum, did you?"

Liz bit her lip. "I didn't say we had *lunch*—"

"That's exactly what you said. Quote unquote."

"Well, I didn't mean—"

"You think I'll just sit there and smile while you make a face and say to friends of mine that my boyfriend isn't your type. What the hell was that supposed to mean?" I held up a hand. "You know what? Don't bother. I don't care. I really don't. Not anymore. This isn't friendship, Liz. Newsflash. I don't know *what* this is. I don't honestly know what could be going through your head when you, like …" I had to take a breath. "When you say those things. Honestly. Why would you insult someone who's supposed to be your friend?" My anger had fizzed out, but I wasn't done. "Seriously, Liz. What's going through your mind when you act that way? I'm actually asking. Because I don't get it. Why do you want to hurt me? I'm supposed to be your *best friend*. And I thought you were mine."

"Hey." Will had appeared by my side. " He looked from me to Liz to me again. "Everything okay here?"

Liz looked away. Her lip was quivering.

"It's nothing," I said to him. "Did you get us a table?'

He nodded. "Yeah. Just by the doors."

"I'll meet you there."

He turned to go and I started after him, but Liz grabbed my arm and pulled me back.

"It's because I'm jealous, okay?" she whispered in my ear. "Are you happy now? It's because I'm jealous. Because I ... Because *I like him too*."

I stopped dead, turned around to her slowly.

"I'm really sorry," she rushed on. "It's not like I wanted this to happen. I just ... I don't know. I have feelings for him. More than ... more than just a crush. I'm sorry, Ali. But you must be able to understand that, of all people. Only imagine you can't be with him. Imagine someone else is. And you always have to see them, right in front of your eyes, all the—"

"Are you for *real*?"

Liz blanched.

I didn't think for a second she was being serious. This was just more bullshit. *Liz* liking *Will*? Since when? How? *Why*? She'd never been alone with him. I wasn't sure they'd ever had a conversation I wasn't a part of. And she'd said it herself: he wasn't her type.

No, no. This was more of it. More drama. More theatrics.

She didn't like Will; she just didn't like me having someone like him.

"I'm telling the truth," she said. "And I'm sorry."

I put my hands on my hips to steady myself. I was definitely more drunk than tipsy now.

"Let's say that's true," I said. "Pretend I believe you. Let's say, okay, that's why you've been such a temperamental bitch since I got together with him." I leaned in close until my breath was on her face. "What was your excuse for all the years before that?"

Liz didn't respond. She dropped her eyes to the floor.

"I'm leaving," I said.

Before she had a chance to respond to that, I did.

*****

The next morning, I felt the regret before I even felt awake.

In the cold light of day, I could see that I'd completely overreacted. Even if Liz was, for some reason, just out to cause drama by saying that she liked Will, there'd really been no need for me to say the things I had. Not all of them, anyway. And especially not the last thing I'd said.

Now that I thought about it, I wasn't sure Liz had committed any worse crimes in our fifteen years of friendship prior to St. John's that couldn't be classified as a bad mood. We all got into them. No one was sunshine and light all the time. And as for the last few months …

Well, maybe she was telling the truth about Will, in which case she must have been really hurting.

We should've waited until we were sober, then had a proper talk. We could've worked everything out.

I groaned aloud. *Damn you, cider.*

While still in bed, I fumbled for my phone and typed out a text to her, saying we needed to talk. No response. I checked for one incessantly as I crossed campus to the Arts building and kept my phone on vibrate during the meeting with my tutor, hoping I'd feel a buzzing against my thigh. None came. When she hadn't texted me back by the time I'd started back toward Will's apartment, I tried calling her. No answer.

It was late afternoon when the whispers started.

Another girl, they said. In the canal.

Then, at the end of the day, I came out of my last lecture and saw Will waiting for me. Saw the look on his face.

In that split second I thought she'd called *him* and told him everything.

"What's wrong?" I said when I reached him. "Did you talk to Liz?"

He shook his head. He couldn't look at me.

Then his arm was around my shoulders and he was steering me, gently, down the hall. There was a little breakout area there, two sofas, set at right angles to each other. I noticed that there were two men there too, in suits, and a Garda in a bright yellow flak jacket. I wondered what they were doing there. The men in suits didn't look like faculty, and they certainly weren't students. The Garda I connected vaguely with the curfew, increased campus security, although I'd never seen one of them inside.

Will sat me down on one of the couches, sat down himself too, and took both of my hands in his.

"I'm really sorry," he started.

His voice sounded like he was being strangled.

I had no idea what was happening.

"It's Liz," he said. "I'm so sorry, Ali."

"What about her? Did you guys talk?"

Will shook his head and when he looked up at me, I realized with a shock that he was crying now, streaks of wet tears running down his face. And I started to cry too, even though I didn't yet know what was happening. I was just crying over the fact that *he* was. An instinctual response, a reflex.

"What is it?" I squeezed his hands. "What's wrong?"

"It's Liz," he said again, and that time I got it.

All the pieces fell into place. And I thought of what she'd said, about that creepy guy following her, and how I'd dismissed her—

And then I thought of the pub the night before, what I'd said to her, the horrible, *horrible* things, the unforgivable things now, because there was no one to forgive me, no one to listen while I tried to take the words back, and I felt like I was suffocating, choking, the guilt was a solid block pressing down on my chest—

I made a sound like I was in physical pain.

I fell forward, into Will's arms.

I don't really remember much of what happened after that.

*****

Liz died on Sunday night, or technically in the early hours of Monday morning. I got the news on Monday evening. My parents arrived on Tuesday, checking into a hotel nearby. I didn't want to go home with them, didn't want to leave Will—who they'd met now, suddenly and unceremoniously—and I'd been asked by the Gardaí not to leave campus permanently until they had interviewed me.

The funeral was to be in Cork at the end of the week. I was, obviously, going home for it.

What I didn't know at the time was that I wouldn't be coming back.

I felt broken. Exhausted. Empty. Numb, but also not numb enough. I couldn't sleep but I didn't want to be awake. Mostly I just sat curled up on the couch in my apartment, wrapped in a blanket or in Will's arms or nestled against my mother, or in a merciful, drug-induced sleep in my bed. Faceless figures moved around me. They offered me things: food, sympathy, advice.

I paid them no attention.

I couldn't even talk to Will. I'd never said anything to him about what Liz had said to me in the pub, and now there was no way I could. All I wanted was to bury my face in his chest and stay there until the rest of the world went away.

Liz's parents arrived on campus soon after mine. I'd never seen such pain on a person's face. They looked like they'd aged ten years overnight. It struck me then: whatever she was to me, she'd been a daughter to them. A sister to her brother, Ben, somewhere in the skies between here and Sydney. A granddaughter. A niece. A cousin. I'd only ever really thought of Liz in relation to me, as the person she was around me, *to* me. I couldn't face any of her relatives now.

Not just because of what I'd said to Liz, but because this feeling now—this pain—wasn't pure grief. It was shame, too. Regret. Guilt. Embarrassment. It was *about me*. My pain was egocentric. Thinking about myself first and foremost, even now.

Which only made me feel *more* of those things.

At some point during that awful week, Will and I—and some other freshmen we knew—had to go to the Provost's office to be interviewed by the Garda detectives in charge of the Canal Killer case, as the tabloids were now calling it. My mother had forced me to shower but I hadn't bothered to dry my hair, and I was dressed in loose, gray things. A sweatshirt, leggings. I didn't care what I looked like. I just wanted to take one of the magic pills and go back to sleep as soon as I possibly could.

Will went in first. I waited outside on a hard plastic chair with my mother by my side. It was in the evening; no staff were around. The hallway and the other offices off it were completely quiet.

Because of that, I could hear everything that was being said inside.

"You saw Liz on Sunday night, I believe?"

"Me? Very briefly. At O'Shea's on Harcourt Street. But Alison talked to her for a bit. I only said hi, I think."

"But then not again?"

"No."

"Do you know what they talked about?"

"No. But …"

"What?"

"I think one or both of them might have been upset about something."

"You don't know what?"

"I don't know the details, no."

"You and Alison returned to Halls?"

"Yes. We were back by eleven, eleven thirty, I think."

"Liz called you, though, at one point?"

"I didn't realize she had, until one of … Um, Garda Collins, I think it was? He asked me to check my phone. It showed a call from Liz at around three in the morning— but I didn't talk to her. I was asleep."

"But the call was answered. It is possible Alison talked to her?"

"I mean, it's possible, but she would've said, surely."

"How do you explain it, then?"

"I think I probably just reached out to switch it off, to stop the ringing, so it wouldn't wake up Alison, and I must have pressed accept instead."

"Alison was there all night?"

"Yeah, she stayed over."

After about ten minutes of this, it was my turn.

There were two men in suits—detectives—and a female Garda in uniform waiting for me in the room. When they saw me, their faces softened. A student welfare officer was sitting in the corner, managing to look both fascinated and concerned.

I dropped into the chair they pointed to and fixed my eyes on a spot on the floor.

"We'll keep this brief," one of the detectives—Shaw—said. "I'm sorry for your loss, Alison, but we're doing everything we can to get who did this. I know this is hard, but if you could just confirm a few things for us …"

They didn't so much ask me questions as they asked me to confirm everything Will had said. Had I seen Liz on Sunday night, early on, at that pub? *Yes.* Had I talked to her? *Yes.* Did she seem upset? *I don't know.* Other people said she looked upset. Do you know what about? *She said someone was following her. She said she'd talked to you guys about it.* You didn't see her again? *No.* You stayed with Will that night? *Yes.* Do you remember his phone ringing? *No.* Well, if you think of anything … *Okay.*

I went straight back to my room, back into bed. Will got into it with me, held me. Neither of us spoke, each lost in our thoughts.

I swallowed another pill and waited for the darkness to descend.

When I woke up the next morning, the room was filled with bright sunlight; the curtains in Halls were a joke, practically transparent. Will wasn't there and the space in the bed beside me was cold. My head felt like it was filled with a fog, the aftermath of the sleeping pill, of three or four consecutive nights of taking it.

I rolled over, squinted in the sun—and my eyes landed on the calendar tacked to the wall above my desk.

I saw my handwriting, lopsidedly written in to last Monday morning: *tutor @ 9:00 a.m.*

And I remembered: getting up in the dark, pulling on the clothes I'd been wearing earlier, heading out into the dark night.

That night.

alison, now

I opened my eyes.

Speckled ceiling tiles. A strip of fluorescent light, powered off. A pouch of clear liquid hanging above my head, the tube attached to it going into the back of my right hand. A thick, heavy cast on my left, from fingers to elbow. My skin itched inside it. A throbbing in my head, and something scratchy across my forehead—a bandage? A thin blue curtain, daylight showing through from what must be windows on the other side.

"Welcome back."

I turned and saw Malone, sitting on a chair by the side of my hospital bed.

My mouth was so dry my tongue felt thick and swollen in it. I managed to croak some approximation of the word *water*, and Malone produced a Styrofoam cup with a straw in it. He held it to my lips.

"What's the damage?" I said once I'd gulped back as much as I could.

"A broken arm, a concussion, and I think fifteen

stitches in your head." Malone moved to go. "I'll go get the doctor."

"Don't. Tell me what happened first."

"We can do that later. You should get some rest now. Your parents are in the cafeteria. They'll be back up soon."

"Get some rest?" I tried to smile. "I *just* woke up."

"They told me not to tell you anything. And I was supposed to tell someone if you woke up, so …"

"Look at me. I've earned this."

"Fine," Malone sighed. "What do you want to know?"

"Is he dead?"

"Yes."

"He drove us into the water?"

"At Grand Canal Dock. He was stopped at a checkpoint on Mespil Road, and the guard there heard screams coming from the trunk of the car. She asked him to step out, and that's when he took off. A show was about to start at the theater down there, so the place was busy. Lots of people around. Luckily no pedestrians were injured. But it meant that, immediately, you had help. People jumping into the water. Apparently the car was sinking front-first—and you know you can't open the doors until the whole thing is gone beneath the surface—so someone had the bright idea to open the trunk and see if they could get in through there. When they did that, they found you."

"Was it him, then? Conway was the Canal Killer?"

"It seems that way, yes."

"Was he back then, too?"

Malone nodded. "Yeah. Twenty-three Doolyn

Gardens is a treasure trove of physical evidence. We've found files on the victims—both 2007 and 2017—and even items of clothing belonging to them, some other possessions, too. It seems you were right. He was using that attic apartment to gather information on St. John's students. We found stacks of forms with personal details like phone numbers, addresses. Photocopied IDs. Even some bank statements. Oh, and the O'Rourkes in Ennis? They're his grandparents. He was paying them rent—or some rent, at least—for both houses. And he wasn't just an estate agent, Alison. He also worked three shifts a week as a security guard at St. John's Halls, where he made himself his own set of keys and had been regularly deleting footage from the security cameras." He paused. "Without being detected, so I think it's safe to say St. John's will have a civil suit on their hands soon enough."

"Did he have that job in St. John's back then, too?"

"No. In 2007 he was a graduate student, living there himself."

"God." I shook my head. "It just seems so ... So ordinary, or something? That's not the right word, but ... I don't know. I just thought—"

"There'd be more to it? Like he'd have special powers or something?"

"I couldn't understand how he was doing this, how he was getting away with it."

"All he had was *access*. Access and something very, very wrong with his moral code."

I asked if Will had known him.

"We're still trying to ascertain that but it doesn't seem like it, no."

"So you don't think … that he was involved in some way?" "It doesn't look like it, no. Remember how I said there were other prints on the folder they found in Will's locker? Preliminary testing suggests they were Conway's."

"But they could've been working together."

"Really, Alison, there's absolutely no evidence to support that. I think they'll be dropping all charges against him. He didn't have anything to do with this."

"The blood under the desk …?"

"Conway was living in Halls himself at the time. It's not beyond the realm of possibility that he could've planted that there. Or," Malone shifted his weight, "that someone else might have, someone who wanted to make sure they had enough to convince the DPP to accept Will's guilty plea, and close the case. But, ah, that's just a theory, and not one you heard from me."

"How did this happen?" Tears were stinging my eyes. "How did this happen to Will?"

"I think Conway probably felt the net was closing in, saw that Will had been brought in, and spied an opportunity. He went about making sure then that the investigation stopped at him."

"What does Shaw say about the confession?"

"What can he say?" Malone shrugged. "I feel a bit sorry for him, to be honest. We've just caught a man who murdered eight young women, but all the press are going to be interested in is how he made a mistake the first time around."

"Why did he do it?" I asked. "Conway, I mean."

"He seemed to think he was helping women avoid the clutches of men who would do them harm. They found a half-finished manuscript on his computer, a kind of personal safety guide for women."

"You're joking."

"No. Look, I'm sure it made perfect sense to him."

"And then, what? He went home to twiddle his thumbs for ten years until suddenly he felt the urge to do it all over again?"

"The documentary I showed you? With the tapes of Will's confession? He had that recorded on his Sky box. It'd been viewed."

I raised my eyebrows. "You think that set him off?"

"I think maybe he thought it was time for more cautionary tales. The theme of it *was* that everyone had forgotten about the Canal Killer case, after all."

"Was he the man that attacked Heather Buckley, then?"

"We don't know." Malone shrugged. "All she really remembers is his height, which fits. We might find something on her at Doolyn Gardens yet but unless we do, we can't know for sure."

"What about Daniel?"

"As you suspected, all he was doing was collecting information for his blog. And continuing his crusade to free Will. He did admit leaving a copy of the letter in your hotel room. He said he was going to slip it under the door but that when he got there, the door was open, so he slipped it into your case instead. For safe-keeping, he said."

"How did he know I was there?"

"He had a source on the inside. A friend of his from college now works as a civilian administrator in the Phoenix Park. She got wind of your trip to Dublin and passed the information on. She's been let go, needless to say."

"What made Daniel think Will was innocent?"

"The same thing that made me think it, I guess. Not all the pieces fit."

"Where did he get the letter?"

"He tracked down someone who'd worked on the staff of the newspaper when it came in, an old college friend of his. They had a scan of it stored on an old computer."

"And Conway really sent that?"

"We don't know, but we think so." Malone turned to look over his shoulder. "I think maybe that's enough questions for now. I really should go get the doc—"

"What about Amy? Did they find her?"

Malone nodded. But I could tell by his face the news wasn't good.

I asked where.

"In a house R&P Estate Agents were selling," he said. "In the shed."

"Shit."

"How did you figure it out?" Malone asked. "That the guy we spoke to was Conway?"

I explained about the phone number impression, Googling it.

He smiled. "You'd make a good detective, you know that?"

"Hardly." I yawned. "I only realized it when he was already in the next room."

Malone reached over and took my good hand in his, squeezed it. "I'm sorry for leaving you there," he said. "Once it got dark, it occurred to me that you were out in the middle of nowhere, all alone, so I sent a uniform to sit outside. But by then it was too late. When I saw your text—"

"What happens now?" I didn't want to talk about that. "Does Will get out?"

"It'll take some time for the machinery of the courts to do their business but, yeah, ultimately he will. And then he'll probably seek some kind of compensation deal. I know I would." Malone frowned at me. "I think I'm going to leave you to go back to sleep."

"Yeah," I said. My lids were getting heavy. "Okay."

"Oh, and your friend Sal? She called me. Got my number off your mother, apparently."

"*Sal* called you?"

"She's on her way here. Her flight gets in at five."

I smiled. Good old Sal. "Have you talked to Will?"

"I haven't," Malone said, "but I think someone has."

"So he knows?"

"They told him this morning."

I thought of Will's last ten years, how awful they must have been for him. How hopeless he must have felt.

And Liz. Poor Liz.

When, in the dark shadows of my imagination, it had been Will who'd taken her life, I saw her confused, maybe realizing too late, maybe not getting a chance to realize at all. But with a stranger …

She must have been terrified.

All these years, when I'd thought of Liz, it was always like there was something between my memories of her and my grief that she was gone. A wall. A pane of glass. Because, yes, we'd been friends all those years, but by the time we arrived in St. John's I wasn't even sure I *liked* her anymore. The last things I'd said to her … They didn't bear thinking about. Stupid, teenage, immature things—forever frozen in time because of what had happened next. But worse than that, I was the reason she was dead. Because if I'd never met Will, he'd never have met her, and she wouldn't have—I stopped, pulled myself back from that particular edge. It was too much to feel, to much to let in. Grieving for Liz would come with a guilt that would, I'd always feared, overwhelm me.

But now I knew it wasn't Will who'd killed her, but Brian Conway. I didn't remember him from all those years ago, from the day we'd viewed the flat in Doolyn Gardens, but in my mind's eye I inserted his face from yesterday, from last night, into the vague scenes I could recall from that September day all those years ago.

And my heart broke open.

For Liz. For all the life she'd missed out on. For the nineteen-year-old girl she'd always be.

I started to cry.

"It's over," Malone said. "It's over."

He was still holding my hand. He leaned over the bed now, brought it up to his lips and kissed it gently.

alison, now

"Are you *sure* about this?"

My mother and I were sitting at her kitchen table, having breakfast, and she was asking me that question for the umpteenth time. The entire space was filled with glorious early morning spring sun and she'd laid on such a spread that I felt like I was in a hotel. Freshly cut fruit, pastries, poached eggs on toast. I was on my second cup of coffee, the same kind I enjoyed while I was at home— because, while I'd been in hospital, Mam had made polite enquiries of Sal, our current houseguest and her new best friend, and had *gone out and bought the same machine*. This was on top of the gorgeous guest room I'd been installed in, with some carefully chosen—read: innocuous—things from the boxes in the back bedroom put on the shelves to make it feel like mine, and the little wardrobe of clothes and bag of toiletries she'd gone out and bought me as well.

Sal had been put up in the room next door. I'd convinced my father to take her to Powerscourt Estate today just so she could say she'd seen something of Ireland while she was here, and because it meant there'd be two fewer concerned faces staring at me all day.

Mam had refused to go in case I experienced an only-one-good-hand emergency while in the house by myself.

"Yes," I said. "Still sure. No change since you asked me three minutes ago."

"But can't you wait? You're only out of hospital a few days, and he's only just—"

"I want to get it over with it, Mam. Okay?"

"But why do you have to do it at all?"

"Because I didn't the last time. I just ran off—and look where that got me. No, this time, I want to see him. I have to apologize—"

"You don't have anything to apologize *for*."

"I *need* to."

My mother turned her coffee cup with the tips of fingers. "They showed it on the news last night."

"What?"

"The house." She shook her head. "You should've seen what was coming out of it, Alison. Bags and bags and bags. He must have been a right hoarder. But we didn't see anything like that when we were there, did we? I don't remember seeing anything in the halls."

"He probably just kept the hallway, the stairs—and the attic apartment—clear. It's a good thing, though, Mam. That he kept everything. Malone said that that will help."

"Ah, yes." My mother grinned. "*Malone*."

"What?"

"Can't you call him Michael?"

I rolled my eyes.

The doorbell rang.

"That'll be him," I said, getting up. "I'll see you later."

"Is he not coming in?"

"No, we have to get going."

"Will you bring him in later?"

"Later?"

"When he drops you back."

"What for?"

"So I can say hi."

"Absolutely not."

I got up to go, then turned back to my mother. I reached down and hugged her from behind, kissing her cheek. It was soft and delicate and smelled of soap.

"Thanks, Mam," I said. "For everything. And I'm sorry about … About everything else."

She reached up and squeezed my good arm.

"You better go." Her voice was tight. "Don't keep him waiting out there. That fella out there in the Jeep will only be snapping more pictures." She touched her hair, checking it. "I'm going to have to get my roots done if those photographers don't feck off soon."

When I went outside, Malone had got back into his car.

I sat into the passenger seat and turned to him. "Good morning."

"Morning," he said, returning my smile. "How are you feeling?"

"Okay. Tired."

"You don't have to do this. We could put it off. He won't be going anywhere for a couple of weeks at least."

"No, no. I want to get it over with."

"Well"—Malone reached into the back seat and grabbed a large, manila envelope with my name handwritten on it, handed it to me—"have a look at this. I think it might make things easier for you."

"What is it?"

"Shaw's under a lot of pressure to explain exactly what pointed to Will back then, so this was dug up. It's the reason they made Will a suspect in the first place. Alison, it wasn't because of you at all."

alison, now

The car slowed, then turned left into the now familiar driveway, sloping uphill. There were the two concrete pillars, there were the metal gates. The spiky razor wire curling across the top of them glinted in the sun as they shuddered, then retracted, slowly opening up to let us in.

"I never want to see this place again," I said.

Malone glanced at me. "You won't, after this."

He parked right outside the two-story concrete block that acted as a gateway to where Will was housed, even closer than we had the other times. He told me to stay where I was, then hurried around to open my door for me and help me out.

"It's just my arm," I protested.

But I let him help me in.

Alek was in the lobby. He turned toward us with a smile on his face that promptly slid off when he saw mine. "Alison!"

"I'm fine," I said. I felt his eyes crawl over the

bandage on the side of my head. They'd had to shave a small square of hair in order to put the stitches in, and strands of the hair they'd left behind had since got itself caught in the sticky parts of the bandage, and I couldn't wash it because I couldn't get it wet and— well, let's just say I wasn't going to be winning any beauty pageants anytime soon. "Really. It's worse than it looks. How's Will?"

Alek made a *tut-tut* noise. "It's difficult. Two extremes, you know? He's so relieved and happy that he's getting out but ..." He sighed. "Ten years is a long time. Especially these ten years, when he was so young."

"Yeah," I said. "So, do I have to go through the whole visitors screening extravaganza again?"

"No, we're going to put you in the family room."

"And we're going to take the easy way there," Malone said.

It turned out to be an elevator.

"I can actually walk," I said to him as we waited for the car to arrive. "My legs are fine."

"You need to take it easy."

The elevator doors opened and we stepped inside. As soon as the doors slid closed, he put an arm around my waist and I leaned in against him, resting. We moved apart just as the doors slid open again.

Down a short hallway, the family room was a smaller version of the visitors' room I'd been in the last time. As we walked down the corridor to it, it was on our left, and we could see in through a bank of windows. The room was clearly intended to make children feel comfortable. There was a play mat, a box of toys and children's books, and colorful paint on the wall.

Children coming in here, to this place, was the most depressing thing I could think of.

Will was sitting inside, hands resting on the table in front of him, but he didn't react to our passing the window.

One-way glass, I thought.

Malone stopped me a few feet from the room's only door and turned to me.

"Okay, well." He squeezed my good arm. "Good luck, then. I'll be right out here."

I nodded at him and went inside. Alek was right behind us and the same security guard from last time was already there. They took up positions on opposite walls.

Will bolted upright in his chair when he saw me. "Ali? Jesus. Are you okay?"

I waved a hand. "It's not as bad as it looks. Really." I took the seat opposite him, wincing as I sat down. My muscles and ribs and back were only feeling worse as each day passed.

"I heard what happened," he said.

"It's all right."

"I'm sorry it happened to you."

"It wasn't your fault."

We both fell silent for a long moment.

"Honestly," I said then, "I don't even know what to say to you."

"What can you say, Ali? What can anyone?"

"I just feel so …" I swallowed hard. "I feel like I could've done so much more. I should've."

Will started shaking his head. "Don't. You couldn't have. Who were you? Who was I? We were just kids, Ali.

We didn't even understand what was happening to us. I know I didn't. And what you went through, losing Liz and then seeing me ... seeing me charged. I can't even imagine it."

"Will, please. Don't make this even worse than it already is by worrying about what *I* went through. You've been in here ten years."

"But I'm getting out."

"You should never have been in here in the first place."

"Look," Will said, reaching across the table to take one of my hands. I let him. "Here's the way I'm looking at it. It doesn't matter what we do or what we say. We can't change the past, not a thing about it. But we can decide what we do now, what we do tomorrow. So I say, let's wipe the slate clean. Start again. That's what I'm going to do." He smiled. "Well, maybe not *tomorrow*, but whenever I do get out of here."

"That's easier said than done, Will."

"But it's worth doing, isn't it? I mean, what's the other option? Dwell in the past for the rest of our lives? Let what ruined us then ruin us for ever?"

I let go of his hand. "What happens now?"

"My solicitor is working on it. He says a couple of weeks."

"You have a solicitor now?"

"I always did."

"He didn't want to help you before?"

"He had nothing to help me *with*. We needed new evidence."

Silence bloomed again.

Then I said, "Have you seen him?"

Will nodded. "They showed me the picture from the estate agency website."

"Did you recognize him?"

"No, can't say that I did. But they said he was on campus back then, as a postgrad? It's possible my path crossed with his somewhere. They think he knew they were closing in on him, he saw me talking to the Gardaí, he realized I knew Liz, and he got to work. Planting the folder in my locker. Planting the blood in my room— maybe. I mean, he would've have access, right? He lived there at the time. And that Daniel guy, from the Canal Killer website—I heard they'd arrested him?"

"They did. He was the guy on the CCTV images— and in that photo I found of all of us on a night out. But it was just wrong place, wrong time. He had a thing for Liz. But he had nothing to do with ... With the recent cases. He's just obsessed with the Canal Killer. Or *was*. I'm guessing he's had his fill now."

"Do you think ...? Liz used to say some weird guy was following her, didn't she? Do you think that was Daniel?"

"I don't know. Maybe. Maybe she saw him once and the other times it was Brian Conway, and she just assumed it was all Daniel. I don't know." I paused. "What's your plan, then? For when you get out?"

"Besides getting some really good food and having a proper shower that doesn't smell of disinfectant—oh, and sleeping in a room where it goes completely dark at night—I don't know, really. I did hear *The Late Late* want me, though."

"To do an *interview*?"

"Yeah."

I exhaled. "Wow."

"I know. It's crazy, isn't it?"

"Are you going to do it?"

"I think so, yeah." He paused. "They, ah, they might want you, too …?"

"*What?*" I laughed. "No. God, no. I'm outta here. Back home to the Netherlands. Back to where nobody knows me. There'll be no prime-time national TV for me, thanks very much."

"Are you sure?"

"Positive."

We smiled at each other.

"I *am* sorry," I said.

"It's not your fault."

"Still."

"Thank you. I wonder—" Will stopped, hesitated. "Do you ever wonder what would've happened to us, if this hadn't?"

The truthful answer was no. Up until a few days ago, I didn't want to imagine such a hypothetical, because I never thought of the boy I'd loved who turned out to be a serial killer.

Now that I knew he wasn't, that he had always been that same boy I'd loved, I couldn't bear to.

"It was a long time ago, Will. We were so young—"

"We still are. Can we be friends, at least?"

"We can stay in touch, yeah." I wasn't sure that was the truth, but it couldn't hurt to be kind in this moment. "There's something I need to know first, though."

Will raised his eyebrows. "What?"

"I need to know exactly what happened the night Liz died," I said. "Because I know you talked to her. I know you lied."

alison, now

Ten seconds passed during which Will stayed completely silent. His eyes were down. He barely moved.

"The Gardaí," I said. "Back then. They didn't bring you in because I corrected my statement. They brought you in because they knew you'd talked to Liz that night, even though you initially told them you didn't. I've seen Claire Collins' phone records."

He looked up, surprised. "Who?"

I told him what Malone had told me. There'd been a call from Liz's phone to Will's phone at 3:55 a.m. on the night she died that lasted for forty-three seconds. Will maintained that he'd been asleep when the phone had started to ring, and he'd reached out intending to silence it but had accidentally hit the ACCEPT button. On the other end, he suggested, Liz must have accidentally dialed his number. Otherwise, why stay on the line for forty-three seconds when no voice came down the line?

At first, the Gardaí had been inclined to believe him. But then a witness, Claire—my roommate in St.

John's Halls—had come forward to say that Liz had come up to her on Harcourt Street and asked to borrow her phone. Liz said the battery on hers had just died. When the Gardaí checked Claire's mobile phone activity, they found that Liz had used it to call Will a second time.

At 4:02 a.m.

This time, the call lasted ten seconds.

"One accidental answer they could believe," I said now, "but two is stretching it."

Will hung his head.

"What happened?" I asked. "What did you guys talk about? You must have been the last person to speak to her, before … Before him."

"That's why I didn't want to say anything." His words were muffled, the sound buried in his chest. "Because I didn't help her."

"Help her do what?"

Will looked up. "She was still in town," he said, "and couldn't get a taxi. She thought she'd seen the guy she said had been following her. Or maybe it was some other weird guy. I'm not sure. She was rambling, not making much sense. She sounded … At the time I thought she was drunk, but now, looking back on it … I think maybe she was just scared."

I concentrated on breathing to steady myself.

In. Out. In.

The world was threatening to tilt crazily and slide again.

"She wanted me to come meet her," he said. "She didn't want to walk home alone, didn't want to have to deal with campus security—because she'd be coming back in after the curfew. And I …" He shook his head, as if disgusted with himself. "I said no. I couldn't be bothered, to be honest. I hung up on her and went back to sleep. A few minutes later she rang again from Claire's phone. Claire wasn't coming back to Halls, she was going somewhere else. I said just go wherever Claire was going. Walk home when it's bright. That wasn't far away. An hour, maybe an hour and a half. She didn't want to do that and I ... I didn't want to do anything except go back to sleep, so I did." He swallowed. "And now I'll have to live with that for the rest of my life."

"She didn't call me," I said.

Will shook his head. "She didn't think you'd answer."

I let this sink in.

Then I said, "So you *knew* I wasn't there all night, all along?"

"Yes and no. You weren't in the bed when I woke up, but the light was on in the bathroom, and I was still half asleep ... And then when I woke up in the morning, you were there. You were already dressed, but I assumed you'd brought those clothes in a bag or something. I just thought you'd stayed the whole night. But to be honest, Ali, I didn't think too much about it. I was more worried about whether or not you knew Liz had called, and whether or not you'd be mad at me for not going to get her. You didn't mention it, so I said nothing. And then ... Well, then we got the news."

A beat of thick, heavy silence.

"I should've gone," Will said, "I know. If I had—"

"You don't know that."

"I think I do."

"Well, if you failed her," I said, "so did I."

"You were only nineteen."

"Yeah," I said, looking at him. "Exactly."

More silence.

"You told the Gardaí all that?" I asked then.

"Yeah," Will said, "but not right away. That was the problem. My mistake. Well, my second one. I should've just been honest with them from the start. I didn't …" He smiled sadly. "I actually didn't want to tell them because I was so embarrassed about it, so ashamed. I thought they'd think I was the worst person in the world. Can you believe that? I was worried about what kind of person they thought I was when I should've been worried about the fact that they suspected me of five murders."

"You probably couldn't even imagine it, let alone anticipate it."

"Yeah, well. It was hours in when I finally came clean, and then—of course—they thought I was lying, because I'd spent so long telling them I *hadn't* talked to Liz at all. That was, like … I don't know, fuel for them or something. Proof that I was a liar. I was so tired by then, I couldn't even think straight. But they were, like, stronger than ever. They had me now. That's what it felt like. It was all downhill from there. I couldn't … I didn't know how to get things back to normal. Everything … It had gone too far."

"God." I rubbed at my face. "Don't you wish we could just go back and do it all over again, but right this time?"

"All the time. But the past is behind us now. And we can't change it."

"No."

Our eyes met.

"I better go," I said.

"Okay."

"I hope you … I hope you like it out there."

Will looked surprised. "You won't be back again?"

"No."

"Oh." His shoulders slumped. "Okay."

I stood up.

"Ali?"

"Yeah."

Slowly, Will got up too and came around to my side of the table. He looked at me, as if for permission, and then pulled me into a hug.

"Thank you," he said into my hair. "I mean that. Really. If it wasn't for you, I'd be staying in here. I know … I know it's probably not appropriate, and you don't have to respond—in fact, please don't—but I just want to say to you, just one more time: I love you."

I couldn't say it back, but I wanted to give him something.

So I said, "I loved you."

"That's enough," he said, after a beat. "That's enough."

*****

Malone was waiting outside. He took my hand and we started down the corridor.

My lips were trembling, tears threatening. I'd been fine in the room but now the shock of it, the truth of it, the *enormity* of it, was hitting home.

It was over.

Will was getting out.

Yet in other ways, it was only just beginning. The *After* I thought I'd made it ten years into had just been swept clean away. The pain was once again fresh.

I had to start all over again.

Malone squeezed my hand. I nodded in response because I couldn't speak. Tears were spilling out now, down my cheeks.

He stopped and pulled me into his arms.

"So, I have a question for you," he said. "Is now a good time to go cushion shopping?"

will, one week ago

The words floated up out of the background noise, slow-ly rearranging the molecules of Will's attention, pulling on it, demanding it, until all trace of sleep had been banished and he was sitting up in bed, awake and alert.

"*Gardaí are appealing for witnesses after the body of St. John's College student Jennifer Madden, nineteen, was re-covered from the Grand Canal early yesterday morning—*"

It was coming from a radio. Tuned to a local station, it sounded like; a national one would probably have reminded listeners that the Grand Canal was in Dublin. The rest of the news bulletin had been drowned out by the shrill ring of a telephone.

As per the rules, the door to Will's room was propped open. He leaned forward now until he could see through the doorway and out into the corridor. The nurses' station was directly opposite. Alek was standing there, holding his laminated ID to his chest with one hand as he reached across the counter to pick up the phone with the other.

In the moment between the silencing of the phone's ring and Alek's voice saying, "Unit Three," Will caught another snippet—"*head injury*"—and by then he was up, standing, trying to decide what to do.

Wondering if there was anything he *could* do. Unsure whether he should do anything at all.

He might just make things worse.

He looked around—at his small, bare room; the grate on the window; the yellowing sheets on the narrow bed—and rolled his eyes for thinking things could get any worse.

But actually, they could.

He could be moved to Clover Hill. A proper prison. There'd been talk of it for a while now. He'd done his best to convince Dr. Carter that he should remain in the CPH, which was probably a resort hotel compared to Clover Hill, but he wasn't sure it'd worked.

Time was running out to get out of here.

Until now, his plan was to potentially come clean. One of the other patients had mentioned a recent case to him where the charge was downgraded from murder to manslaughter, a case that actually involved a drowning. Both charges came with a maximum penalty of life imprisonment, but manslaughter usually got ten to fifteen years, and there was every chance that if Will's charge was changed, his sentence would be too. He might even get out straightaway on time already served.

That had been his plan, but it was fraught with problems. Getting someone to listen to him. Getting someone—anyone—to believe that he was telling the truth now but had been convinced to lie back then. Even if it worked, there was no knowing what the outcome would be. He might end up in Clover Hill anyway, and he might have to stay there for the rest of his natural life, having played his only remaining card.

But now there was a girl in the canal. A new girl.

What if *he* had put her there?

Will had always been convinced that the man who had done it would kill again. That kind of thing, it wasn't an isolated killing spree. That guy wasn't out there now being normal. He'd have had to do it again.

He hated to say such a thing, but Will hoped he would.

Because it would be a lot easier for him if the Gardaí finally got the right guy, the *actual* Canal Killer, than it would be for Will to try to convince them that he wasn't him.

He was just the scapegoat, the guy the Canal Killer had framed.

*****

He should never have answered the phone that night. Every minute of every day after, he would wish he hadn't. Liz had sounded hysterical, upset, crying down the phone. At first, she was talking about Ali and something they were fighting about, but then her tone changed and she said, "Oh, God. Will, I know this is awful to ask but can you come meet me, by any chance? There's, like, no taxis and I don't want to walk home alone." She lowered her voice to a whisper. "That weird guy, the red-haired guy, he's *here*. He's across the street from me, staring. I bet he'll follow me back."

Still half-asleep, Will had said, "Where are you?"

"Harcourt Street. By the Luas stop. But hang on—"
Muffled sounds, like Liz was talking to someone there
while holding the phone to her chest. Then, "But these
guys, they're heading for Trinity so I could go with them
as far as Stephen's Green? Would that be better?"

Lying in bed, Will rolled his eyes. Stephen's Green
was still ten, fifteen minutes' walk away. And fifteen
minutes' walk back.

And it was four in the morning.

And he'd been asleep.

But …

What if something happened to Liz? What if he
said no, I can't be arsed, and then something happened
to her on the way home? He'd be to blame.

Going to meet her was doing the right thing.

"Okay," he said, throwing back the sheets, sitting
up. He noticed that Ali wasn't there, that the sheets were
cold. He had a vague recollection of hearing her get
up. The bathroom light was on, but there was no noise
coming from beyond its door. Had she gone home? "I'll
meet you there. Wait—where in Stephen's Green? Top
of Leeson Street?" No response. "Liz?"

He pulled his phone away from his ear and heard
the *beep-beep-beep* of a disconnection.

Now he was confused. Had they agreed to meet?
Did Liz hang up because she thought he was already on
his way to Stephen's Green?

He got dressed.

The phone rang again. He didn't recognize the
number, but it was Liz on the line again.

"Sorry," she said. "My phone's died. The ATM at
the top of Leeson Street. Is that okay?"

"Give me fifteen minutes," Will said. "Well, ten."

He grabbed his keys, left the room. As soon as the apartment door locked behind him he realized he'd forgotten his phone, but was there any point going back for it? Liz's phone was dead and he'd be coming straight back here.

He decided not to bother.

No one knew exactly what would happen if you tried to get on or off campus after the infamous curfew, but Will discovered now that the answer was not very much. There was a security guard at the exit onto Haddington Road, but all he did was nod at him. Maybe it'd be harder to get back in, but from the look of things, he doubted it.

Will followed the canal up to Leeson Street bridge and turned from there onto Leeson Street Lower. He jogged most of the route, both trying to get there quicker and trying to wake himself up.

It was deathly quiet out. The place was practically deserted. He passed one, maybe two other people on his walk, and he suspected one of them was a plain-clothes Garda going by the suspicious look the man gave him.

It'd be light within the hour.

Liz gave him a big wave when she saw him, then started hurrying toward him. Her eye makeup was smudged and her pupils were enlarged, but he'd known she was drunk before he'd got close enough to see that. She was wobbling slightly, teetering on her heels.

She grabbed his right arm and linked her left through it.

"Thanks *so* much for this," she said. "I owe you big time."

"No problem," he murmured.

He wondered what Ali would think about it when he told her tomorrow morning.

At first everything was fine. They just chatted easily about Liz's night. But when they reached the bridge, she said something about a stone in her shoe and led Will a few feet off the path, down to the water's edge, to one of the benches overlooking the dark canal.

"Sit down," she said to him, when he didn't.

"We should get going, Liz."

"I want to talk to you about something."

"Now?"

He looked up and down the canal. There was no one around, and the air was cold and sharp. They were equidistant between two streetlights; the thick trees that separated the canal bank from the main road made the shadows darker still.

He wished he was in bed, that he could be magically teleported back there.

"It won't take long," Liz said.

He moved to go. "Let's do it on the way back."

"Ali and I, we had a fight. Did she tell you about it?"

"No …" He was not going to talk to Liz about Ali when Ali wasn't there—especially when he didn't even know what they'd talked about earlier. "Let's go, Liz. Come on."

Liz wasn't looking at him now, but at the water in front of her. She was hunched over on the bench, her elbows on her knees.

"I told her," she said, "that I like you." She looked up at him. "I *like you*, Will. The same way *she* likes you."

He didn't know what was happening, but he knew he needed to stop it.

"Liz," he said, "let's go. Now. Come on."

"Didn't you hear what I said?"

"I think you've been drinking—"

"Tonight, yes. I have. That's true. But I've felt this way for months."

In his mind's eye, Will was seeing himself having to relay this conversation to Ali. He groaned inwardly at the thought. Especially because, knowing Liz, she'd twist it all around, make it sound like something else had happened here.

Like that time she'd told Ali they'd had lunch together when the truth was they'd spoken for a couple of minutes in the main drag of a shopping center.

He tried one more time. "Let's go back, Liz. Please."

"Can't we talk about this first?"

"I don't know what you want me to say."

"Say what you think."

"I think I'm with Ali."

"So you don't have feelings for me?" She stood up, came to stand next to him. Close to him. Reached out a hand, pressed it against his chest. "That night, at the ball, I thought I felt—"

"Liz, no." He pushed her hand away. He laughed, trying to diffuse the situation. "This is ridiculous."

"Why?"

"Because I'm with Ali."

"Is that the only reason?"

"Isn't that reason enough?"

He meant, *Ali is your best friend and I'm her boyfriend so why are we even having this conservation?*

But Liz didn't hear that. Liz heard, *Yes, that's the only reason.* Liz heard, *Yes, because I have feelings for you too.*

That could be the only explanation.

Because then there was a blur of movement as she stepped closer and then he felt her lips on his—

"*Liz!*" He moved back, catching his foot on the uneven surface, the muddy grass here at the edge of the canal, feet from the thick buffer of tall reeds that separated them from the glassy black water.

How had doing a good deed turned into this shit?

When he'd righted himself again, he said, "Look, I'm going back now. Follow me or don't."

He went to leave but she stepped in front of him, blocking his way.

"You're just going to leave me out here, alone? What would Ali say about that, Will?"

"What would she say about what *you've* been saying to me?"

"I don't know." Liz folded her arms. "But I can't imagine she's going to be very happy about the fact that we kissed. She seemed pretty upset about it when I just sat on your lap, so …"

Will felt the brush of a cold dread.

"We did *not* kiss," he said, slowly, pronouncing each word distinctly, so there could be no mistake.

Liz glared at him. "We did whatever I say we did."

"Right," he said. "That's it. Make your own way home." He turned his back to her and started back toward the path.

"Will, wait—"

It happened then.

She caught his left hand. To stop him, he'd think later, when he was replaying every single moment of this through his mind for the millionth time. Angry now, frustrated, annoyed, he swung around and pulled his hand from hers at the same time—he's pretty sure it went like this—and the force of that, the unexpectedness of it, the momentum, pulled Liz toward him, toward where he'd been standing, and if he'd stayed there, if he'd just stood still she would've been fine, *he'd* have been fine, *everything* would've been fine, but he moved, so then Liz was moving toward empty space, and then she kept coming, falling forward, falling over, and he saw that she had her other hand in her pocket so she'd only the one to try to break her fall and it didn't quite work, she needed them both, and she hit the ground face-down, hard, and then—

Silence.

For a second he didn't move, didn't breathe, didn't think.

What the …?

Then, all at once: full panic mode. Every single cell in his body suddenly flooded with adrenalin, bubbling white hot with it, sending his heart rate soaring, his pulse thundering in his ears—

Act.

He dropped to his knees and rolled Liz over. She was alive, she was breathing. But unconscious. A horrible gash streaked across her forehead. It was bleeding freely and had bits of leaves and dirt stuck to it. He looked where her head had been and saw the remnants of a broken beer bottle caught in the tangles of a root, pushing up out of the muddy grass.

Help.

He should get help. But his phone was back in his room and he knew that wherever Liz's was, it was dead. And it's that, this delay, that gave him a moment to—

Think.

He thought about what this looked like. About what people would think of him. About how he was nineteen years, six months and three weeks old and it took just *one second* after all that to do this bad thing, to change everything.

It was an accident. Truly, honestly, genuinely an accident.

But is that what Liz will say it had been?

It all flashed through his head in an instant. Liz saying he attacked her. Him being charged with it. Getting kicked out of college. What his parents would think of that. A criminal record. Prison, maybe. He'd never get a job, mightn't even be able to travel.

And he'd never, *ever* get to practice law now. He wasn't even sure he wanted to, but he knew that's what his father had planned for him.

His whole life, destroyed, over this *one second*.

And Ali. Losing her.

Maybe even her believing this.

Over just one second?

And that's when the panic turned to cold calculation. He would remember it later as a distinct moment, like downshifting gears in a car.

The first part, yes, that was an accident.

But what came next was not.

*****

Will felt like he'd been in the room at the Garda station for hours. Days, maybe. He'd lost all track of time. And he was tired. So, so tired. He was having trouble speaking coherent words. He didn't have the energy left to string sentences together. He just wanted to sleep. He wanted to go home. Not back to Halls but back to his parents' house. He wanted to talk to his parents. He needed to get out.

He knew now he'd made a huge mistake.

"We know what happened," Detective Shaw was saying. "We already know. We know everything. We know all the details, the exact sequence of events, who was where, who did what, when. All we need is for you to confirm it for us. We're just trying to help you out here, Will. You help us, we help you. You want to see your parents, right? You asked for your dad? We can bring them in. But first we need to hear some truth from you."

"I'm not the Canal Killer," Will said. His voice was weak, every word scratchy against the dry walls of his throat. "This is crazy."

"How did you get them in the water, Will? How did you get them in without them making any noise? That's the bit I can't figure out. Just tell us the truth and we can get you out of this room, Will. Come on, now. You'll feel better. Look, I'll tell you what. I'll say what I think happened, and you just confirm yay or nay, okay? That might be easier for you. I know this is hard."

Will shook his head. "I didn't do anything."

"Will, we *know* what happened that night," Shaw said, looking right in his eyes. "I know you're lying. Do you know how I know? Because when you first came in, you said you didn't talk to Liz that night. You promised me. You swore. Over and over again, for hours. Even though I told you I knew the truth. Then, lo and behold, the second I bring in Claire Collins' mobile phone records, you say, 'Okay, okay, actually I did talk to her.' So you know what that tells me, Will? That tells me you're a liar. A good one. But it's time for the truth now." Shaw paused here. "Just tell us what happened, Will. Tell us what happened with Liz."

There'd been hours of this. Hours and hours. He didn't know anymore if it was day or night. They let him take breaks but they wouldn't let him sleep. He hadn't slept much the night before either. Ali had been so upset and whenever he closed his eyes, he saw himself by the canal, being the reason …

They couldn't know, though. How could they? If they *did* know what had really happened, they wouldn't be accusing him of the other ones too, would they?

He must be safe.

He just needed to stay alert. To stay awake.

To get through this until he got out of it.

Back at the canal, he'd pushed Liz into the water, knowing she was unconscious, knowing she would drown in there, imagining—hoping—that, when they discovered her, the Canal Killer would get the blame. It was the only answer at the time, the only way to prevent that *one second* from destroying the decades of his life he had left.

Now, he didn't understand what was happening, why they thought he was the Canal Killer.

And he was so tired he couldn't think straight.

"You can't get out of this," Shaw said, "do you understand me? We've collected evidence against you. We know exactly what happened. We just need to hear it from you. Look, Will, we all make mistakes.

Things happen in the heat of the moment. Nobody's perfect. Maybe you didn't mean to hurt those girls. But if you don't tell us what happened, we can't help you here. Cooperation is key, Will. Come on now. Help us help you."

We all make mistakes.

In the heat of the moment.

Help us help you.

"I'm not the Canal Killer," Will said again.

But he was *a* killer. He'd taken someone's life. If he'd just called an ambulance, if he'd had his phone …

It didn't matter what she was going to say about him. She didn't deserve what he'd done. No one did.

The guilt, the remorse, it was like a physical substance, bubbling up in his chest, pushing its way up his throat and out into—

"Okay," he said.

Shaw leaned forward, suddenly alert. "Okay what?"

"I did it."

"What?"

Will started to cry. "Liz."

"I need more than that, Will."

He explained as best he could what had happened. The relief of finally telling the truth filled his ears like the sound of rushing water. He didn't even hear half of what Shaw said to him.

Until he said something about *the other girls.*

"What?" Through the fog of his thoughts, the rush of relief, Will heard a distant alarm bell. "No, no. There were no other girls. I don't know anything about them. It was just Liz. And that was an accident. I swear."

"Yeah," Shaw said. "Look, Will, I'm going to pop

out now for a bit so you can lie down on that couch there and have a nap. Then we'll resume for another hour or so, and then you can bed down for the night. But listen to me: don't waste our time. I want you to think about this. Don't waste my time, or yours, when I come back in. You've just spent the whole day telling me you didn't do anything, and now you say you killed Liz. So you were lying to me, like I knew you were, since the moment you came into this room. Now we can go through what we just did over and over, one time for each girl, and get to the truth. Or, you can save us all the bother, quit the shit, cut the crap, and admit to them all when I come back in. Okay? You think about that."

"No … I didn't …"

Shaw stood up. "I'll see you in a bit."

"No, please—"

"Get some rest now."

"But I'm telling the truth."

"Yeah, finally. That's good. Good for you and good for me. Now, we can get somewhere, maybe. I want more of it when I come back, okay?"

"But—"

Shaw was gone.

The door had closed again and Will was left alone in the room.

He wasn't even sure what had just happened, but he knew if he'd been in some trouble before, he was in a hell of a lot more of it now.

And he didn't know what to do.

He put his head down on the table and started to cry.

*****

When Will saw Shaw again, he was being formally charged. They'd found "evidence." A notebook or something in his locker. A spot of blood in his room.

He didn't know what was happening. It was only later, in the weeks and months to come, that he'd begin to consider that the real killer had got wind of his arrest and had seen an easy way out.

No one was interested in the truth, it seemed to him.

After a while, not even he was.

He'd killed a girl. Taken a life. No, he hadn't put his hands around her neck and strangled her, but he may as well as have. He'd put her in the water, knowing she wouldn't—couldn't—get out, and let the water do the dirty work for him.

He deserved to be in here.

He *was* a killer.

But as time went on, the dark cloud that had numbed him those first few months, those early years, began to lift. Yes, he'd done something awful, something horrific, something truly bad—but it had been a second's action when he was only nineteen. It was not something he'd ever do again. Sometimes he couldn't even believe he'd done it that time. Was his whole life a suitable punishment? Or was ten years just about enough?

And now, the news bulletin.

"*Gardaí are appealing for witnesses after the body of St. John's College student Jennifer Madden, nineteen, was recovered from the Grand Canal early yesterday morning—*

"*… head injury …*"

What if he was at it again, out there? The real guy? Could this be Will's way out? He'd have to be careful, to think everything through, and he'd have to find someone who might actually believe him.

Who was left?

He could only think of one person, the one person he'd never even got to profess his innocence too.

But how could he get her to come and see him?

He decided to speak to Alek. They were friends, or at least what qualified as friends in here. Friend*ly*. Will waited until the nurse had finished on the phone before he crossed the corridor.

acknowledgments

Before the thanks, an apology. Dublin City, I've messed with you a bit. I've demolished the National Print Museum at Beggar's Bush and put a fictional university in there instead. I've also renamed the Central Mental Hospital in Dundrum and modernized its facilities. So apologies to Dublin, a city I love, and apologies to any reader who goes down Haddington Road looking for the entrance to St John's. You won't find it. If it's any consolation, you will find the café with the white picket fence and, inside it, excellent coffee.

First and foremost, huge thanks to this book's midwives: my editors Sara O'Keeffe and Stephanie Glencross, who patiently and expertly helped me get this story out of my brain and onto the page. Thanks to my fabulous agent, Jane Gregory, and everyone at Gregory and Company, Corvus Books, Blackstone Publishing, and Gill Hess. Thanks to Hazel Gaynor and Sheena Lambert for the gin, the wings, the infinite email threads, and everything else in between. Thanks to all the lovely women writers in my life who are so hugely supportive, incredibly generous, and throw epic launch parties. (Carmel Harrington, I'm looking at you for that last one!) A huge thank you to all the writers, booksellers, reviewers, bloggers, and readers who supported *Distress Signals*, with special mentions for Liz Nugent, Mark Edwards, Margaret Madden, and everyone I've come to know on the crime scene. Thanks to Iain Harris for being Instagram-ready at the Irish Book Awards (even if your idea of hangover food is juice made from the leaves of things. Um, no ...) and to Andrea Summers, Eva Heppel, and Michelle Oliver for traveling long distances to be at my book wedding—I mean, ahem, book launch. Thanks to Sheelagh Kelly for always believing and thanks to the most enthusiastic and occasionally mortifying publicity team an author can have: Mum, Dad, John, and Claire.

Last but certainly not least, thank you for reading.